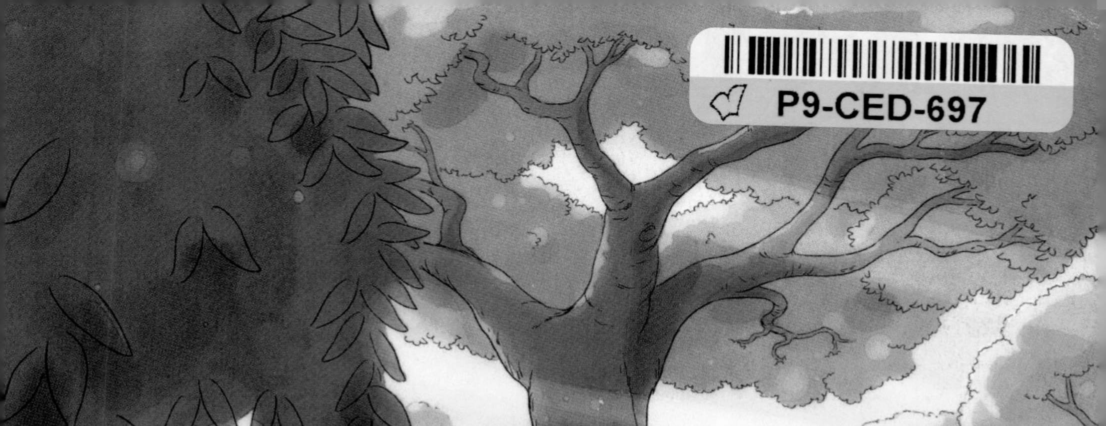
Wait for me, Iris!
Hurry up, Sam, we're almost at the lake!

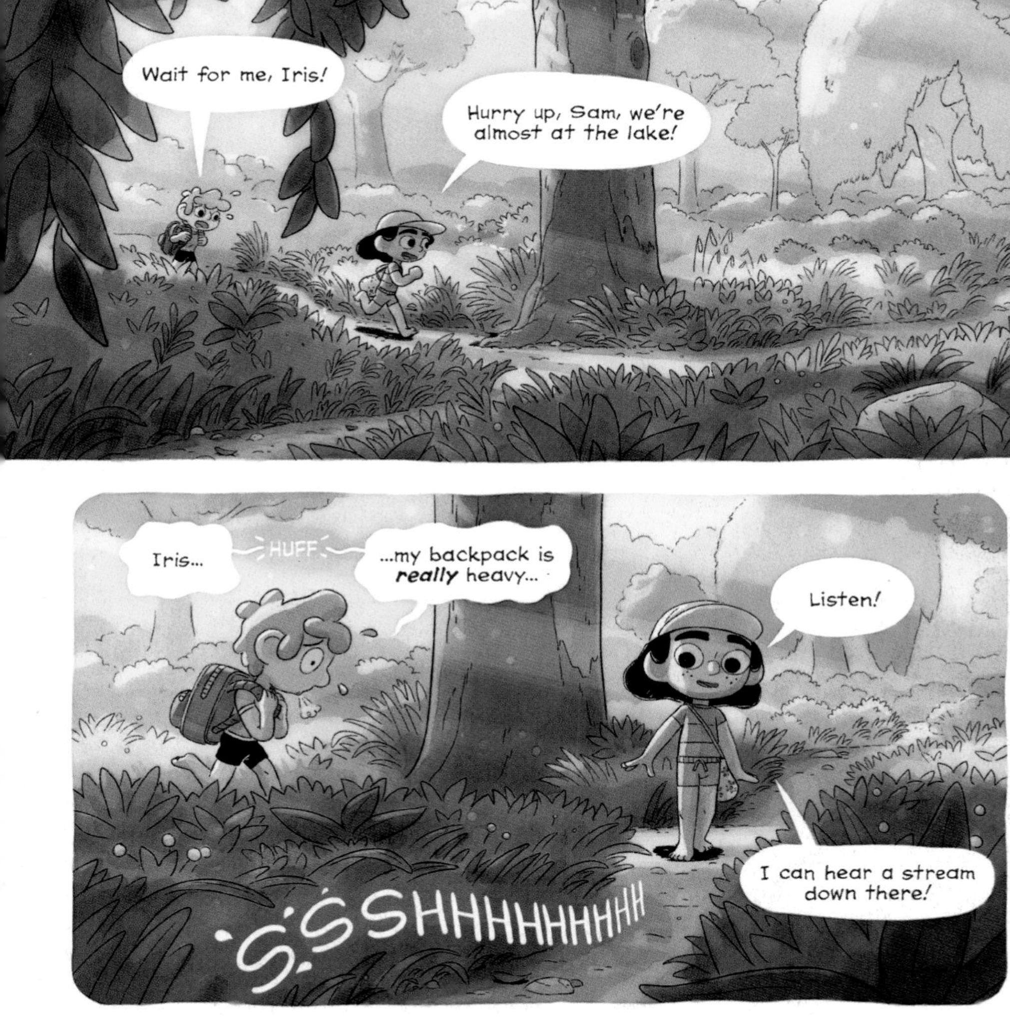
Iris...
HUFF
...my backpack is ***really*** heavy...
Listen!
I can hear a stream down there!
SSSHHHHHHHHHH

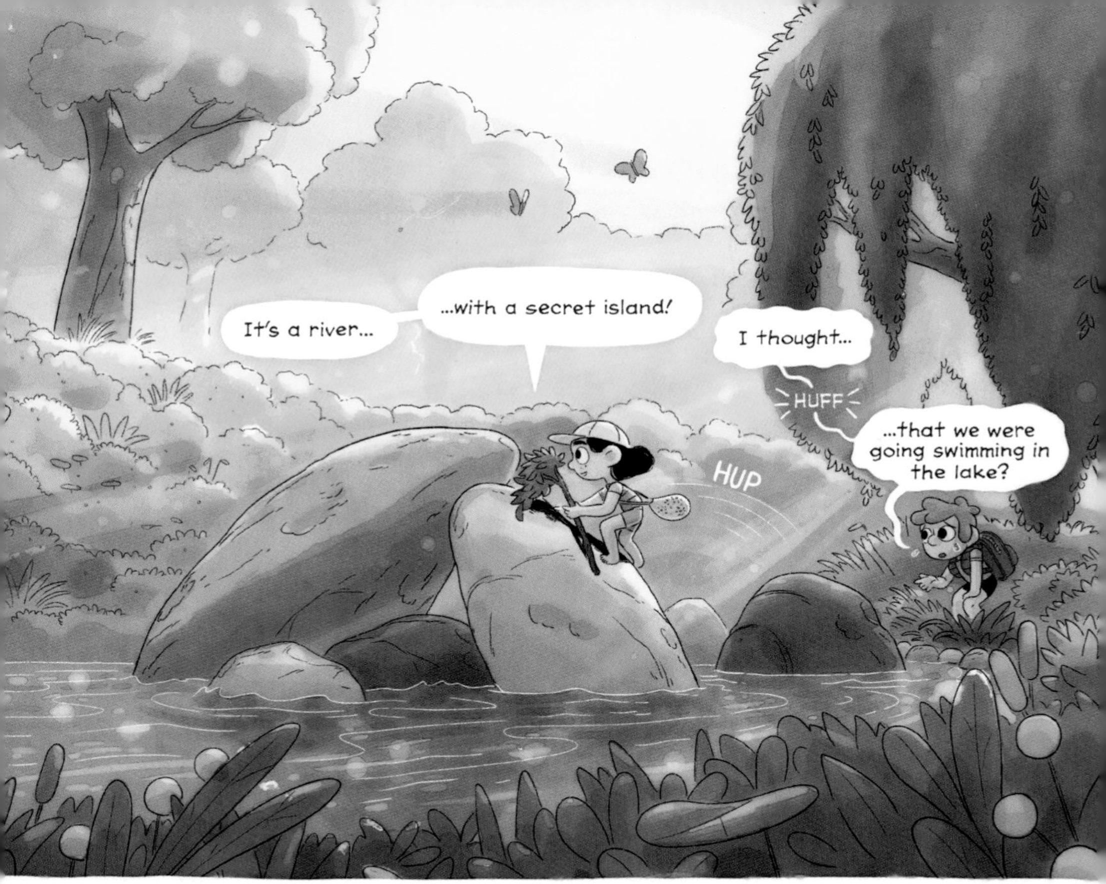
It's a river...
...with a secret island!
I thought...
HUFF
...that we were going swimming in the lake?
HUP

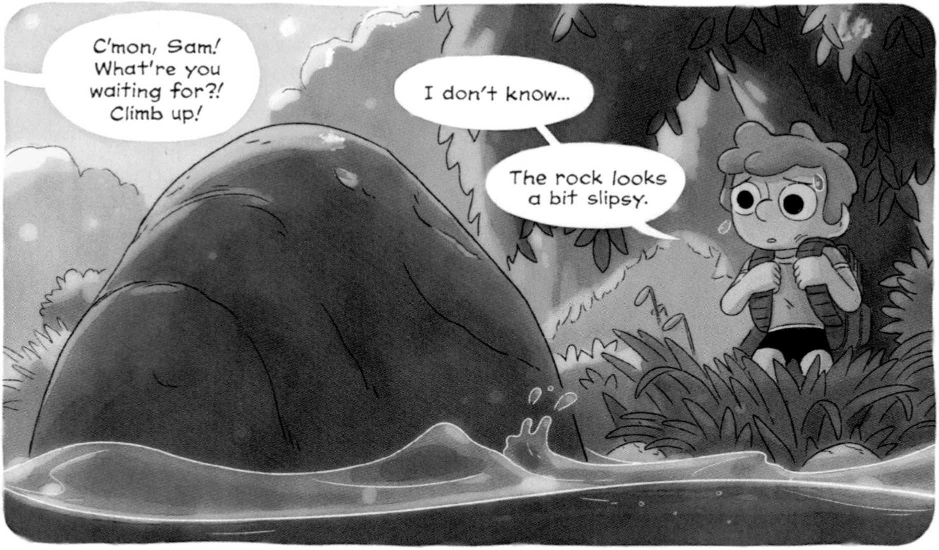
C'mon, Sam! What're you waiting for?! Climb up!
I don't know...
The rock looks a bit slipsy.

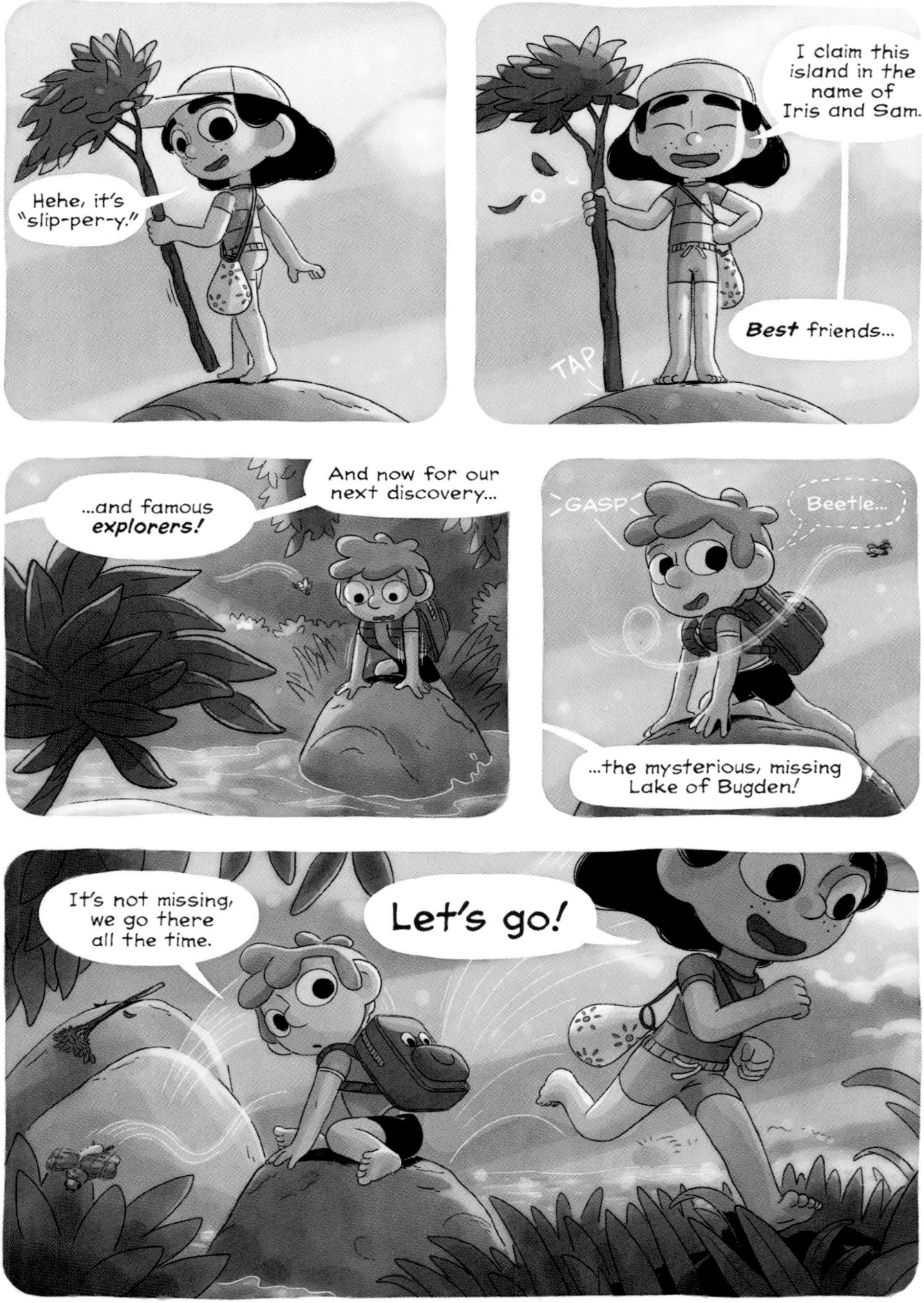
Hehe, it's "slip-per-y."
I claim this island in the name of Iris and Sam.
Best friends...
TAP
...and famous explorers!
And now for our next discovery...
GASP
Beetle...
...the mysterious, missing Lake of Bugden!
It's not missing, we go there all the time.
Let's go!

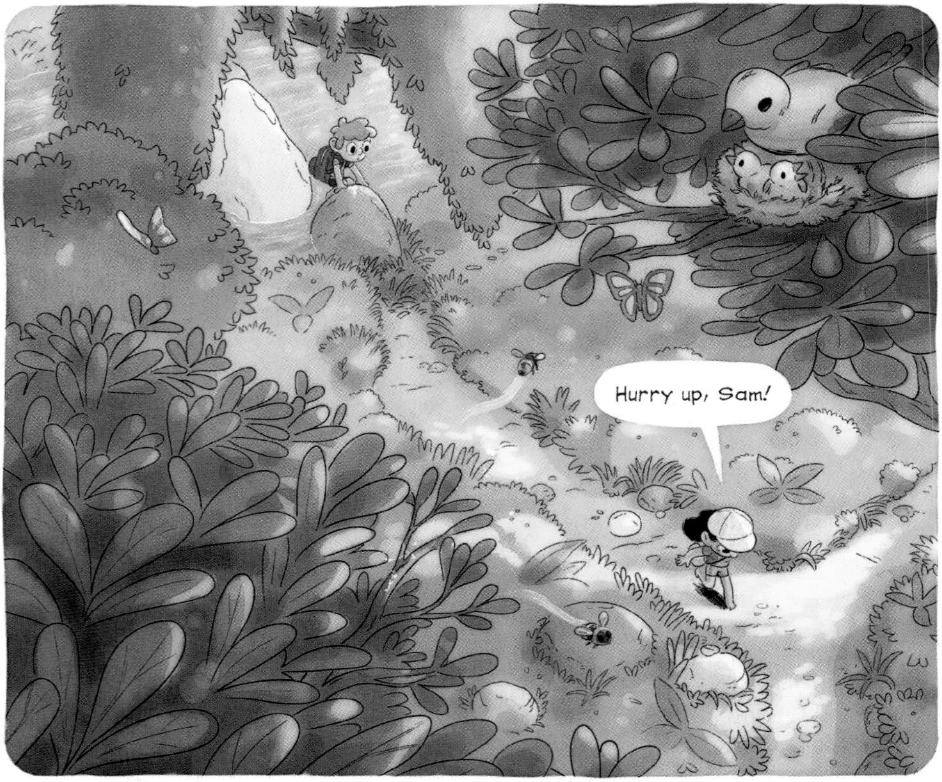
Hurry up, Sam!

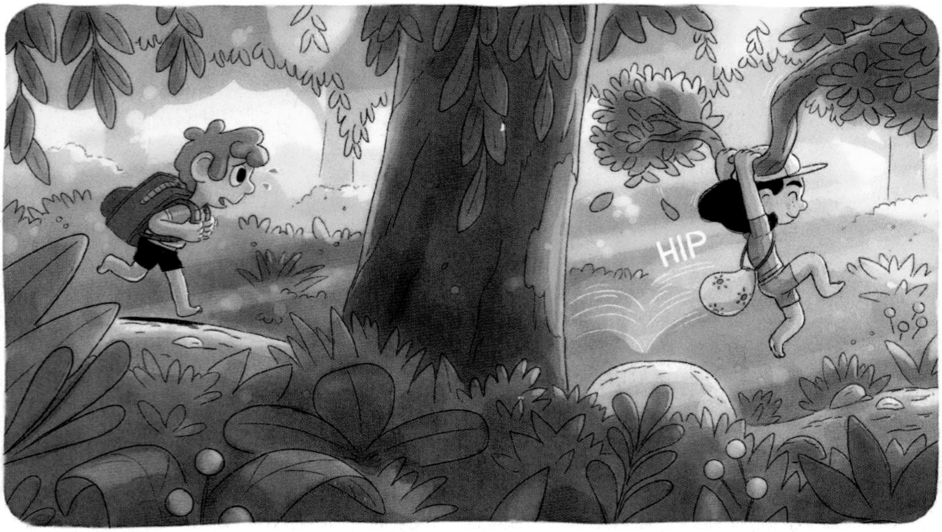
HIP

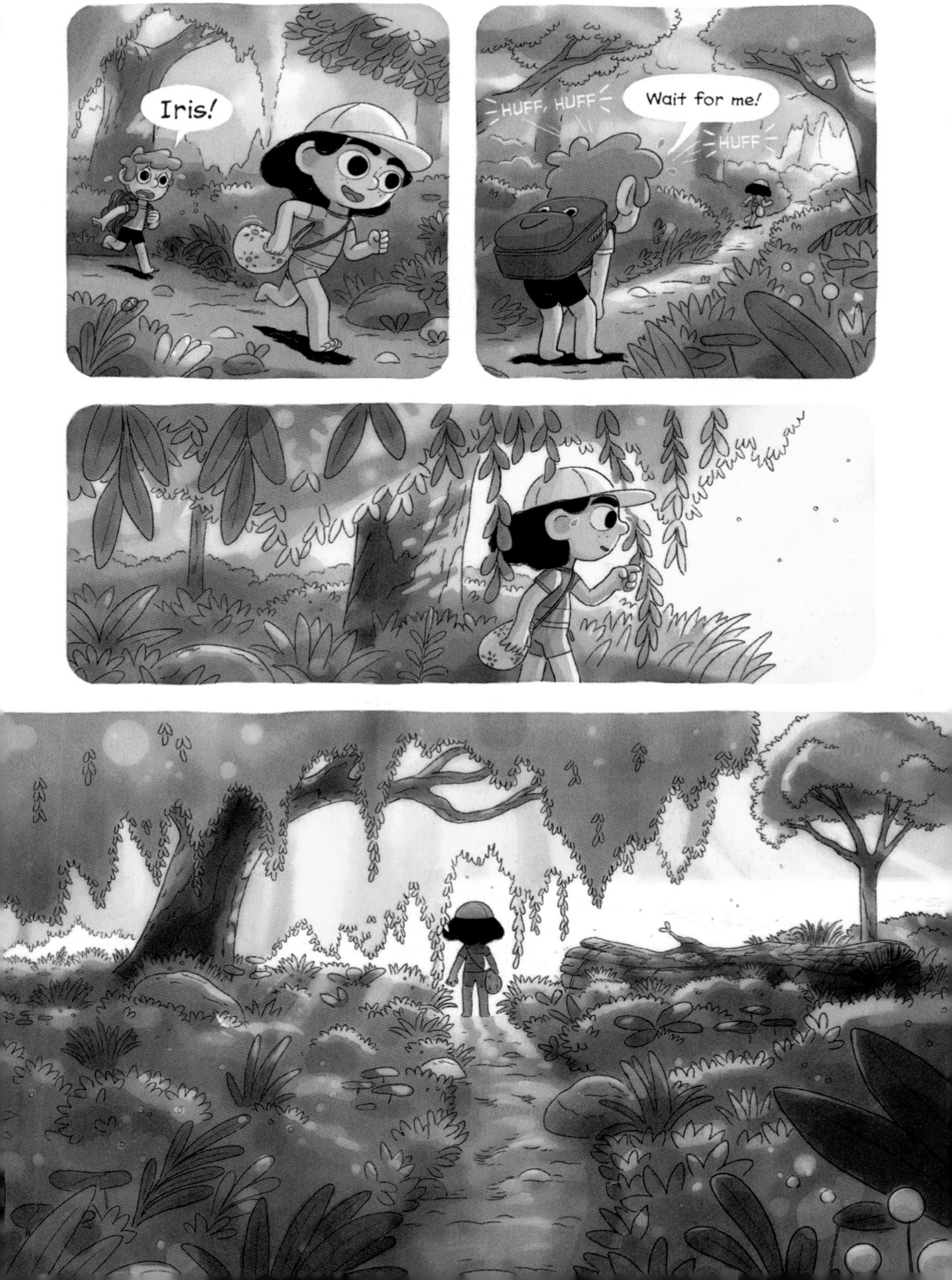
Iris!
HUFF, HUFF
Wait for me!
HUFF

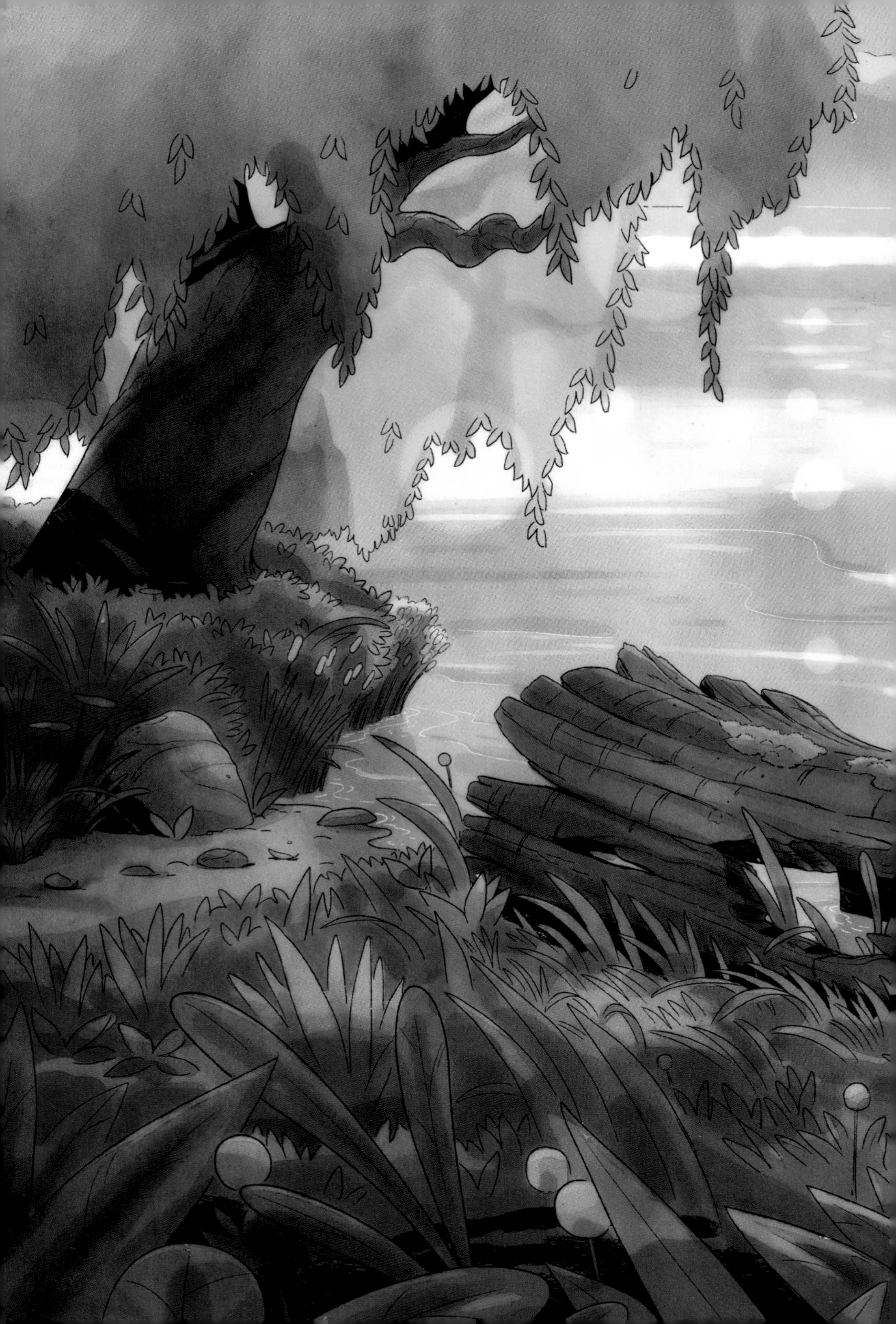

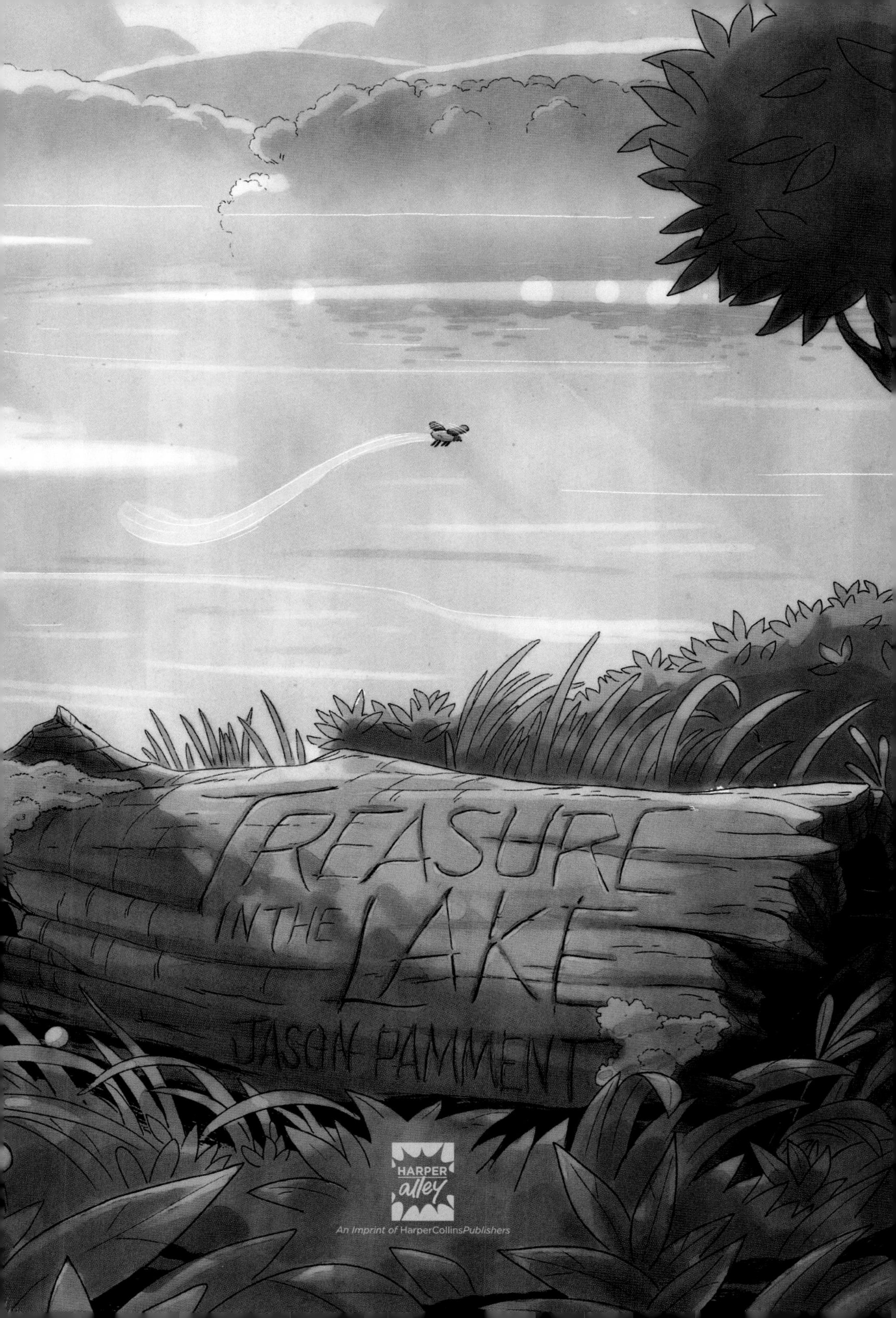
TREASURE
IN THE LAKE
JASON PAMMENT
HARPER alley
An Imprint of HarperCollinsPublishers

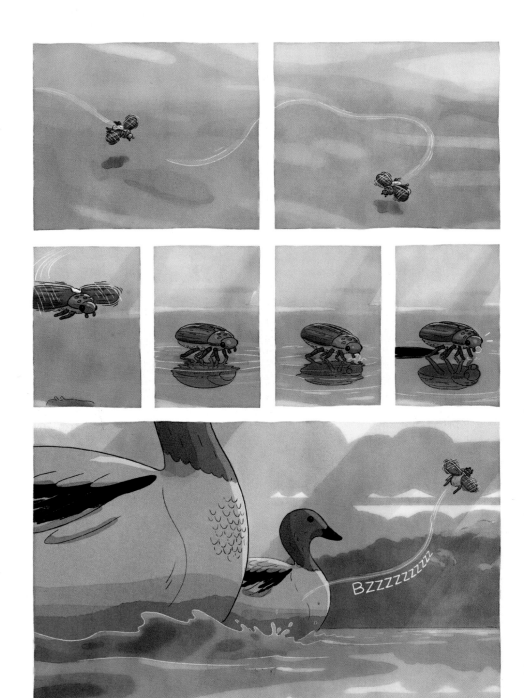

BZZZZZZZZZ

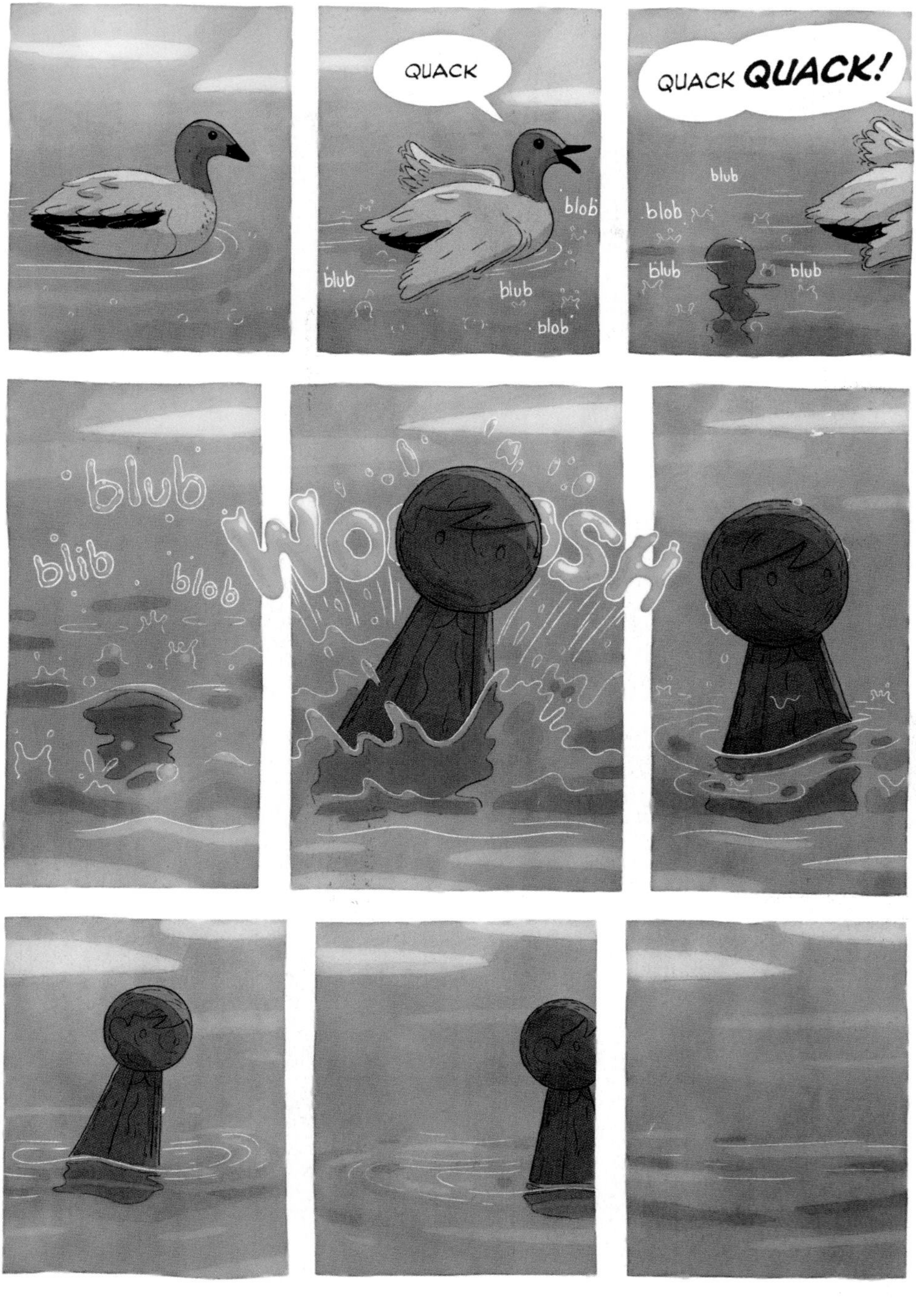
QUACK
blob
blub
blub
blob
QUACK QUACK!
blub
blob
blub
blub
blub
blib
blob

QUACK
QUACK
QUACK
tap
tap

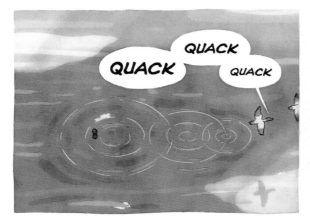

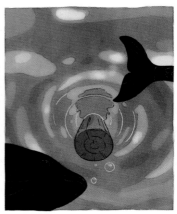

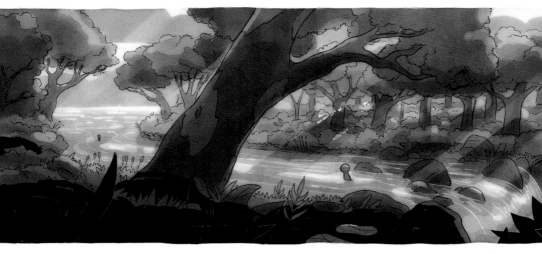

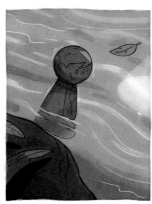

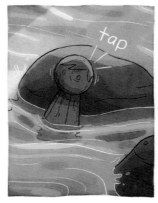

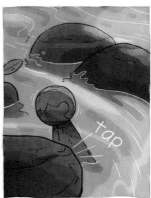

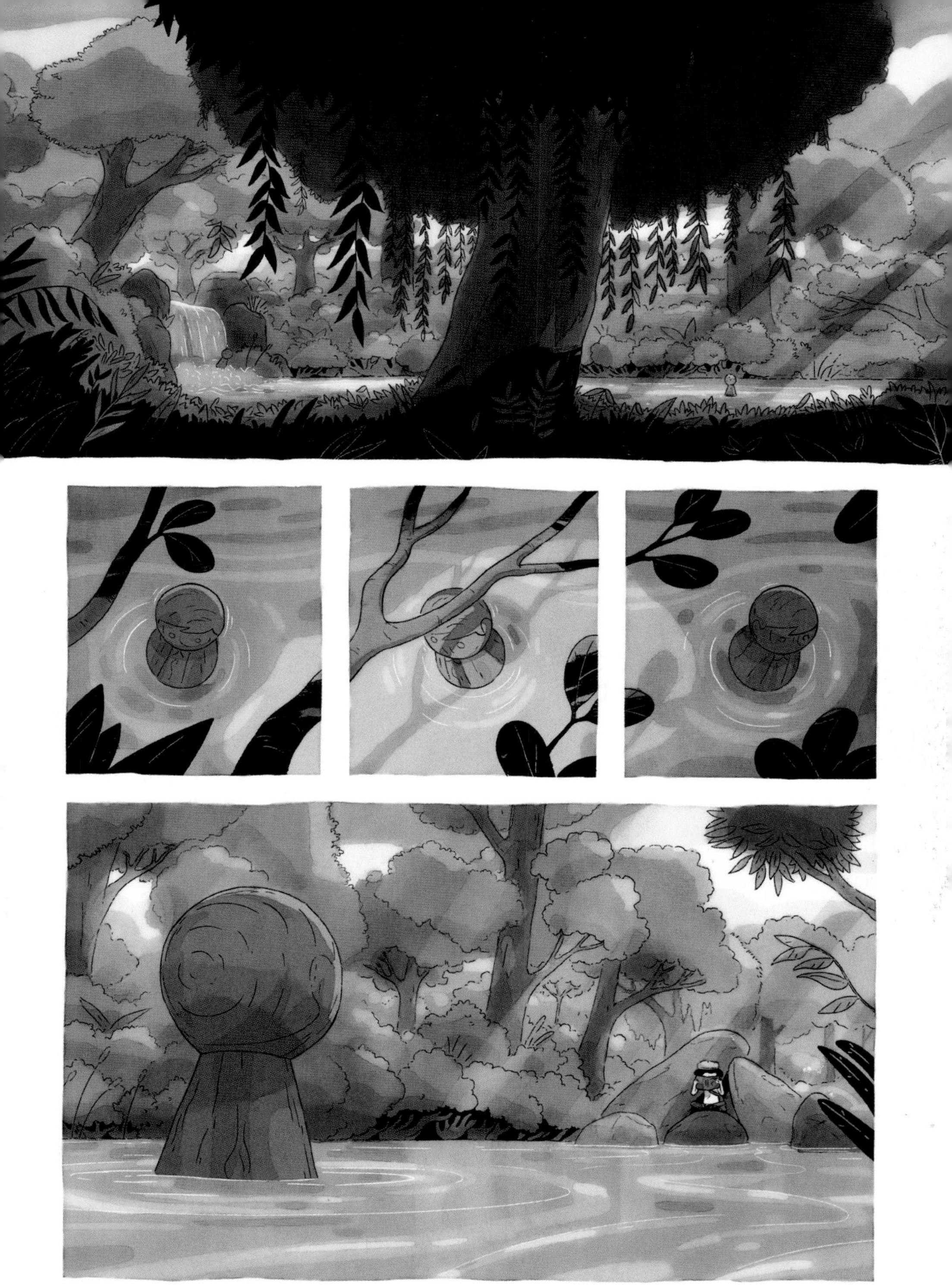

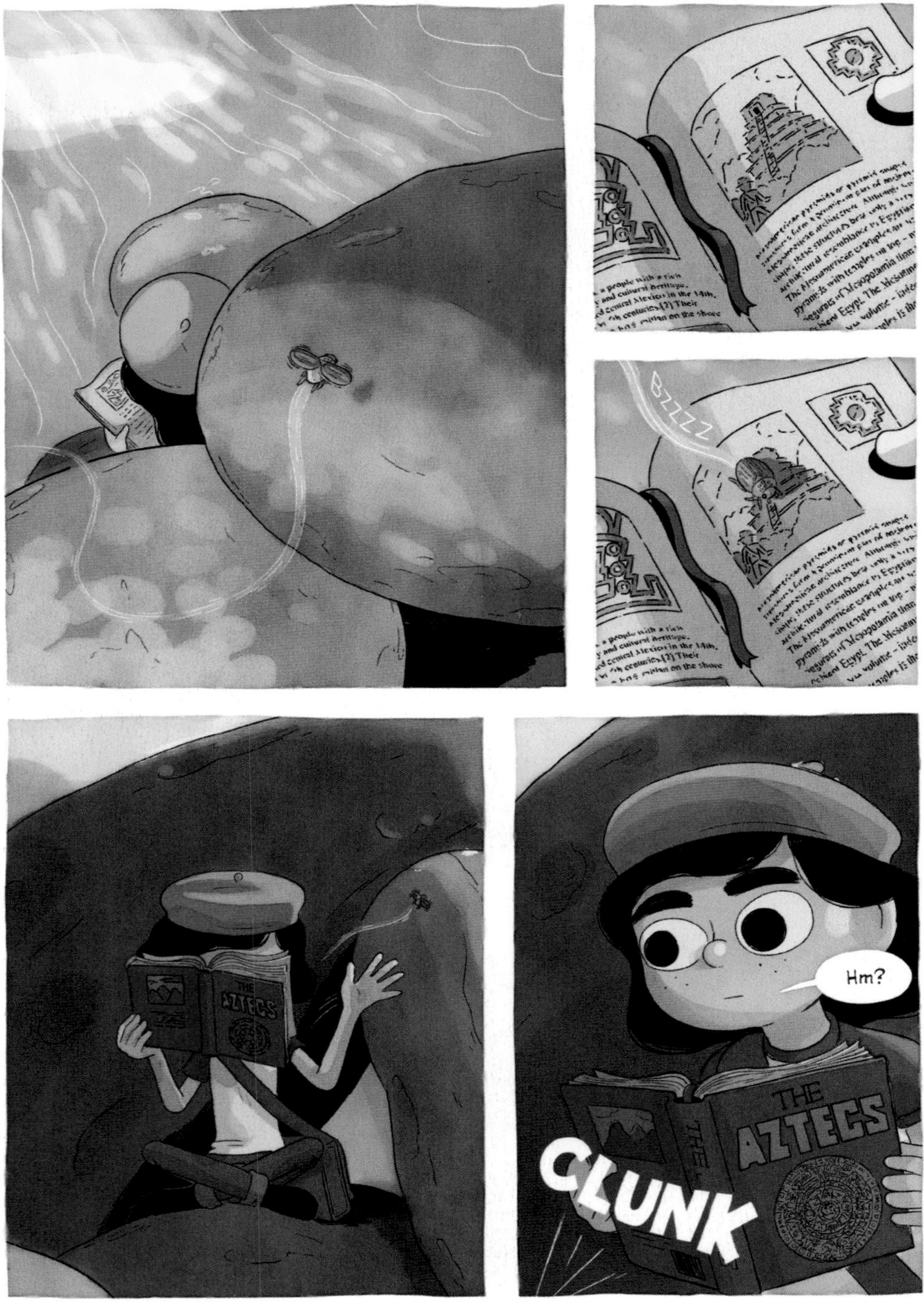
BZZZZ
THE AZTECS
Hm?
THE AZTECS
CLUNK

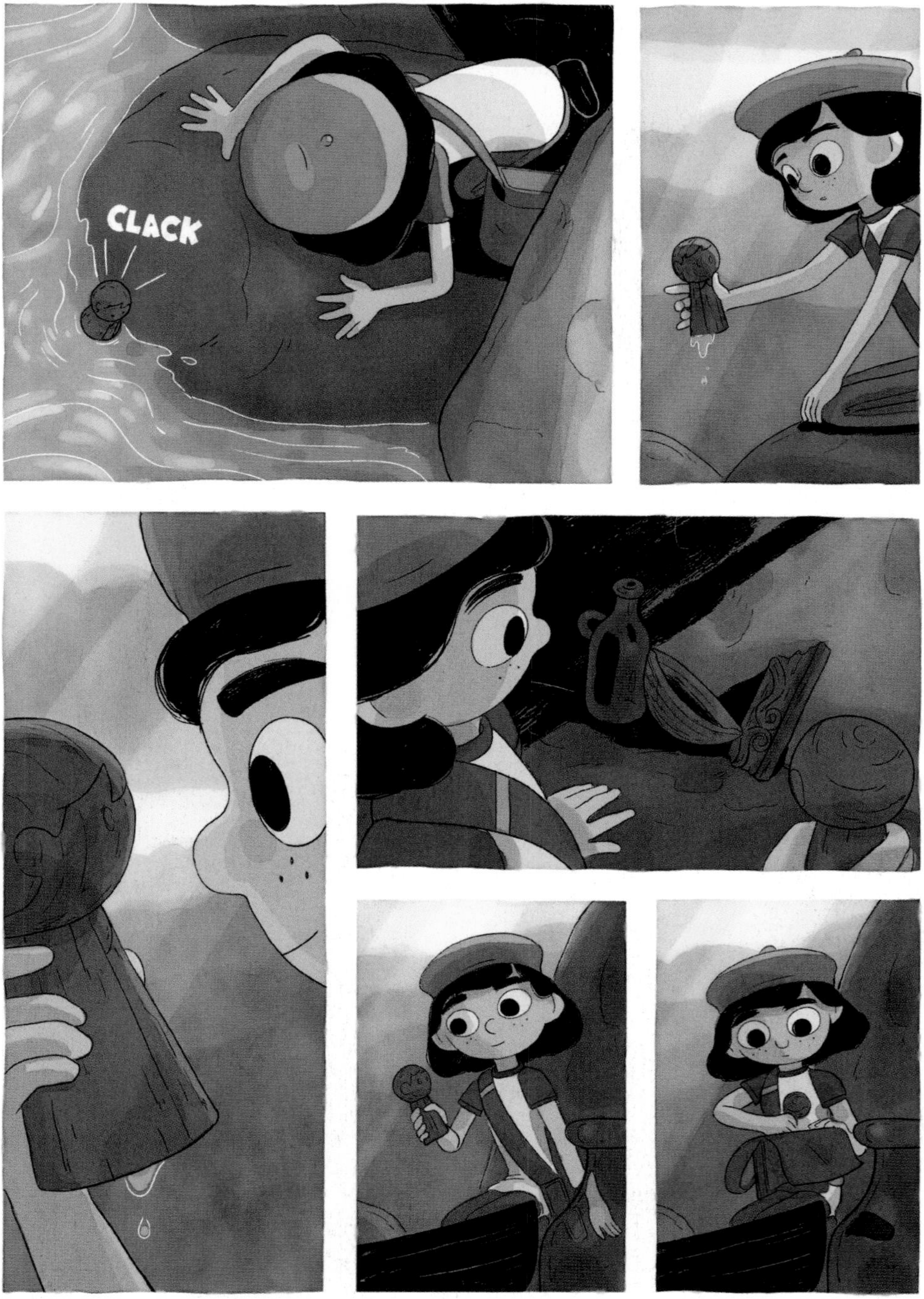
CLACK

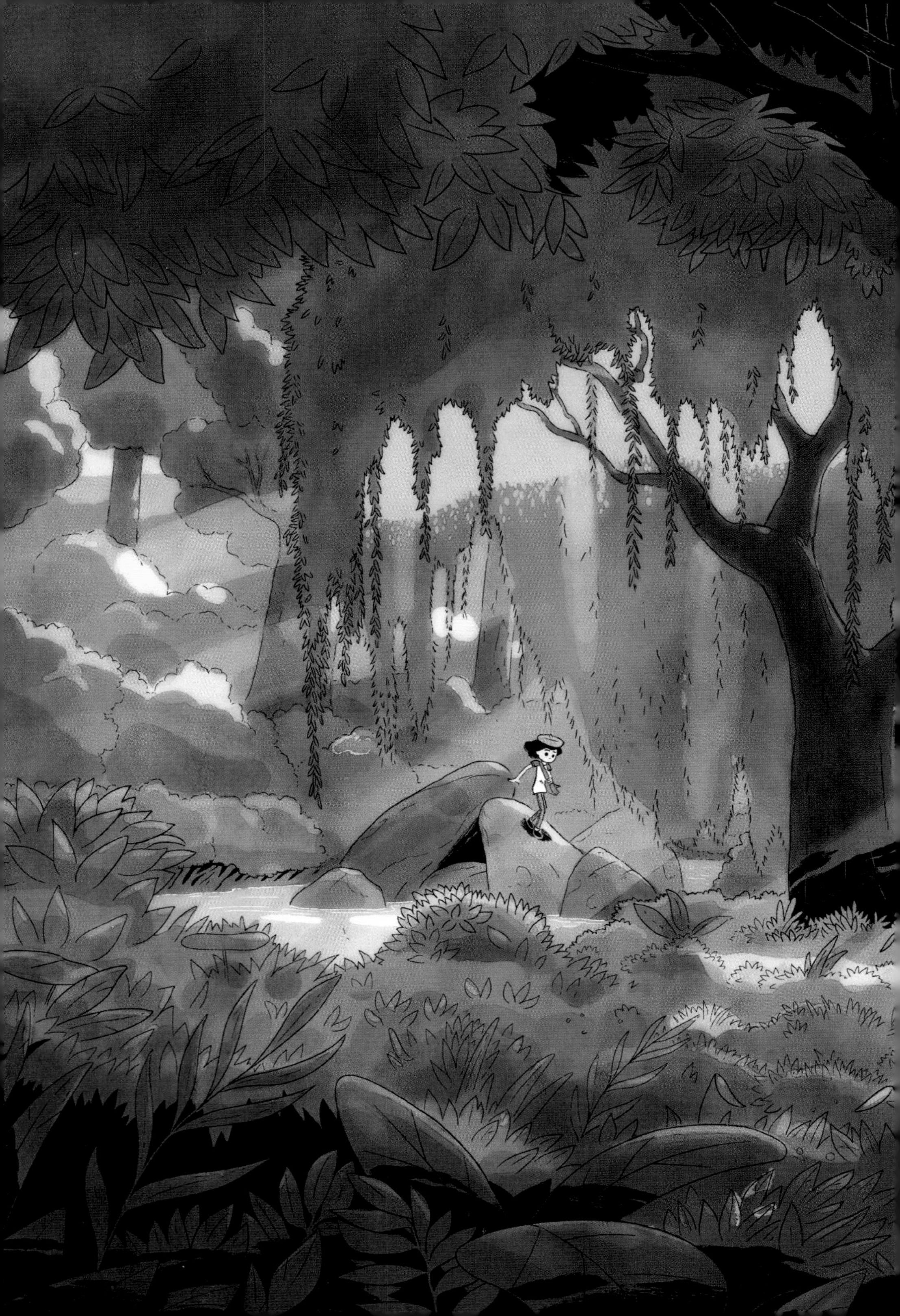

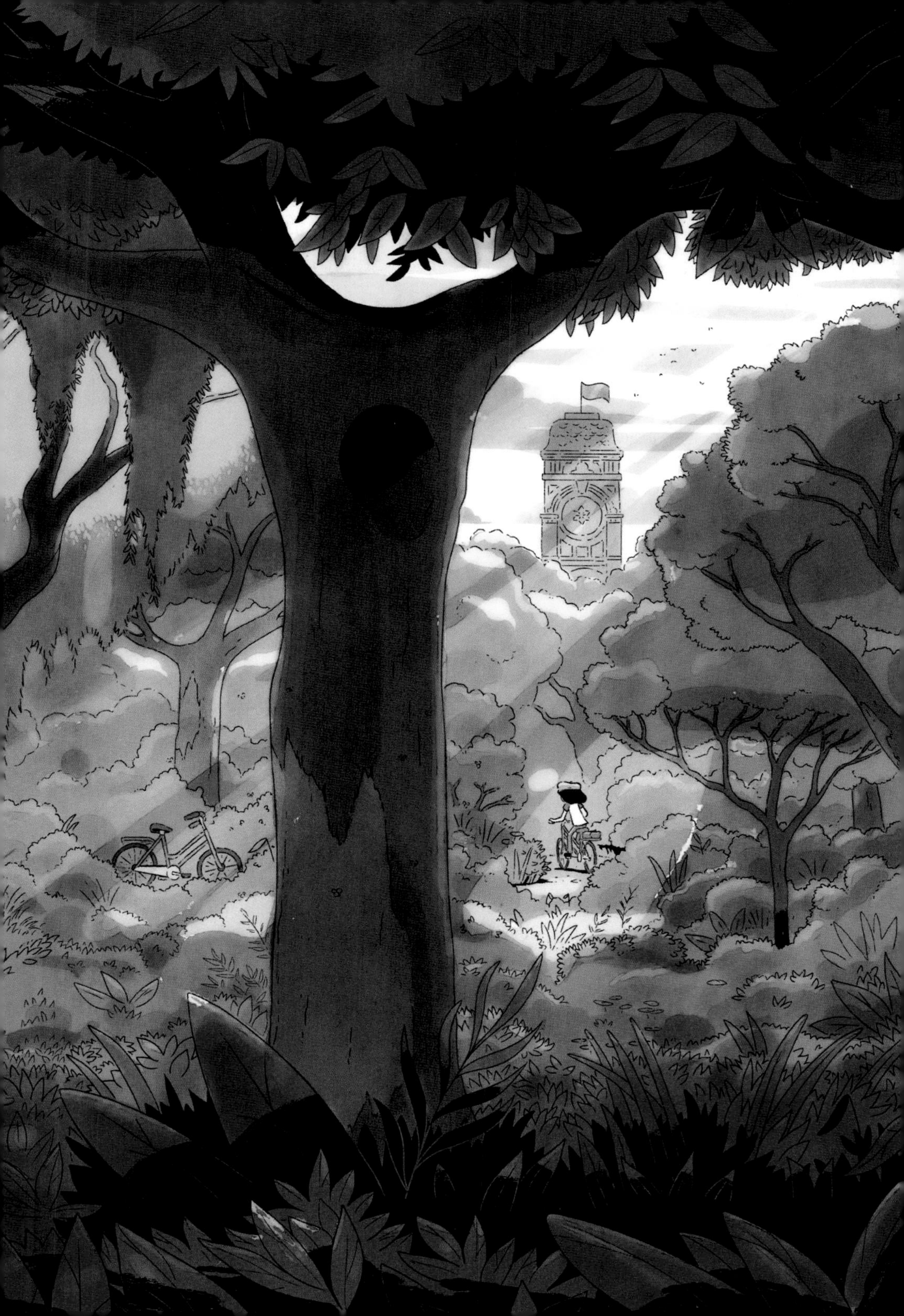

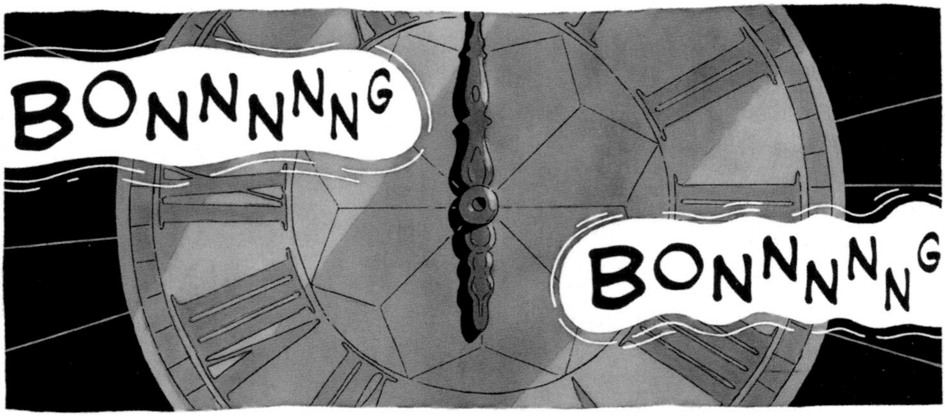
BONNNNNG
BONNNNNG

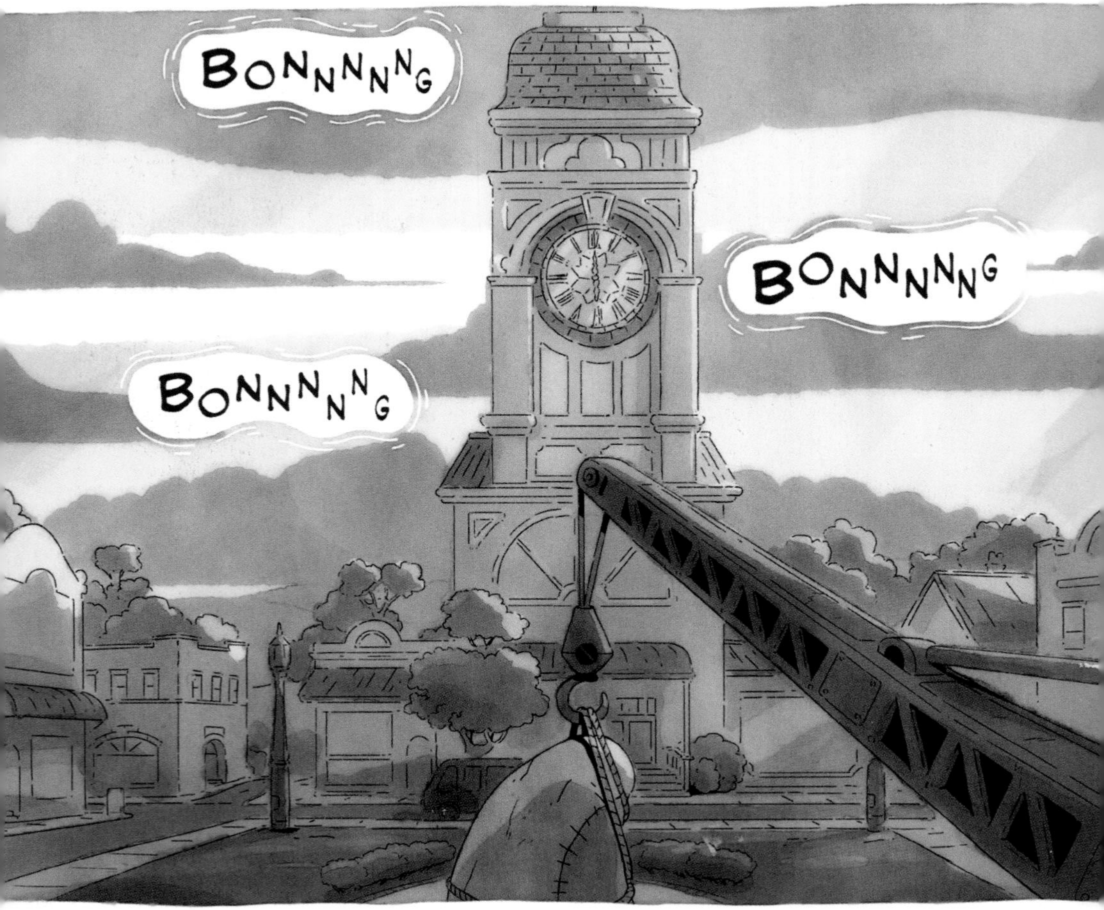
BONNNNNG
BONNNNNG
BONNNNNG

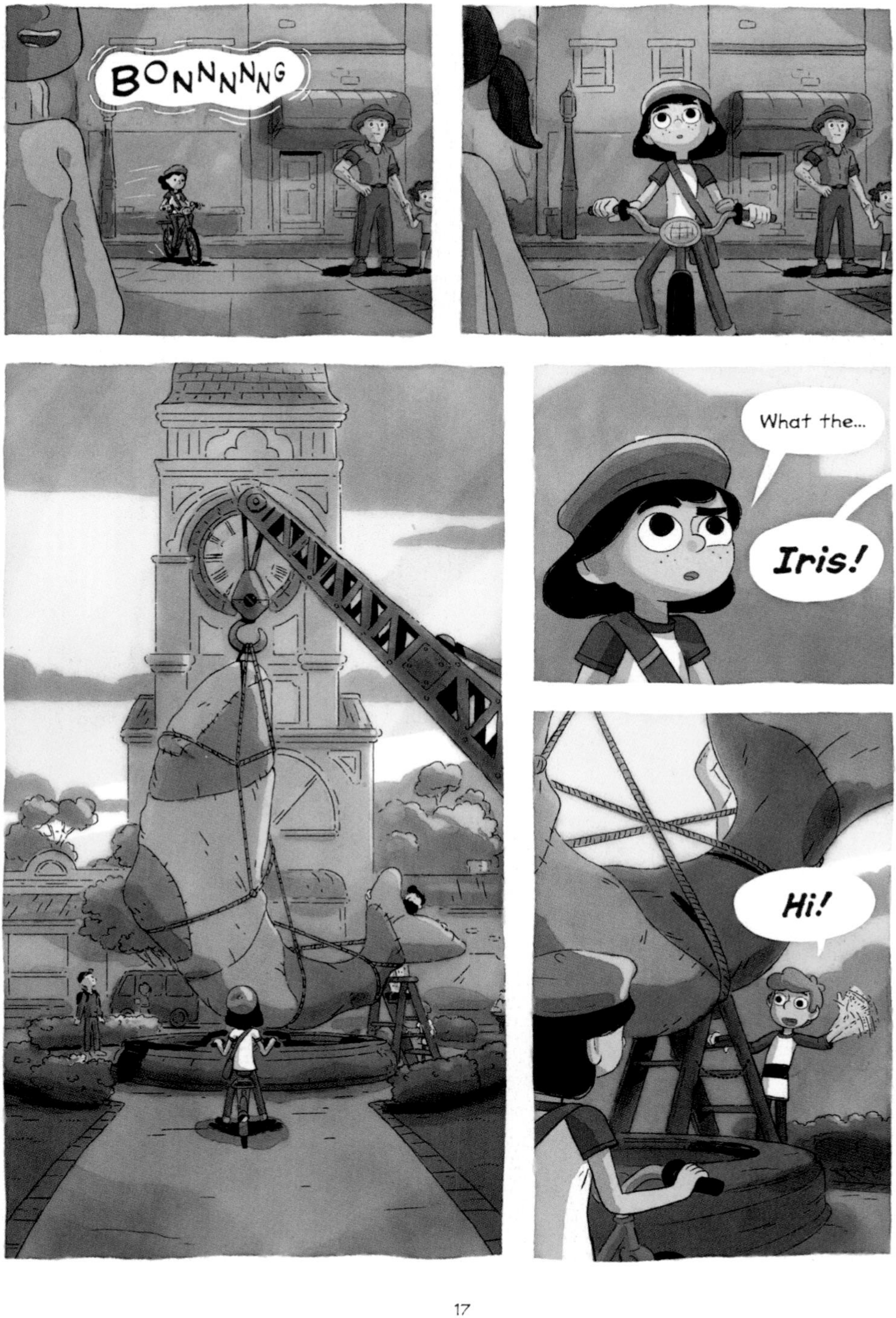
BONNNNNG
What the...
Iris!
Hi!

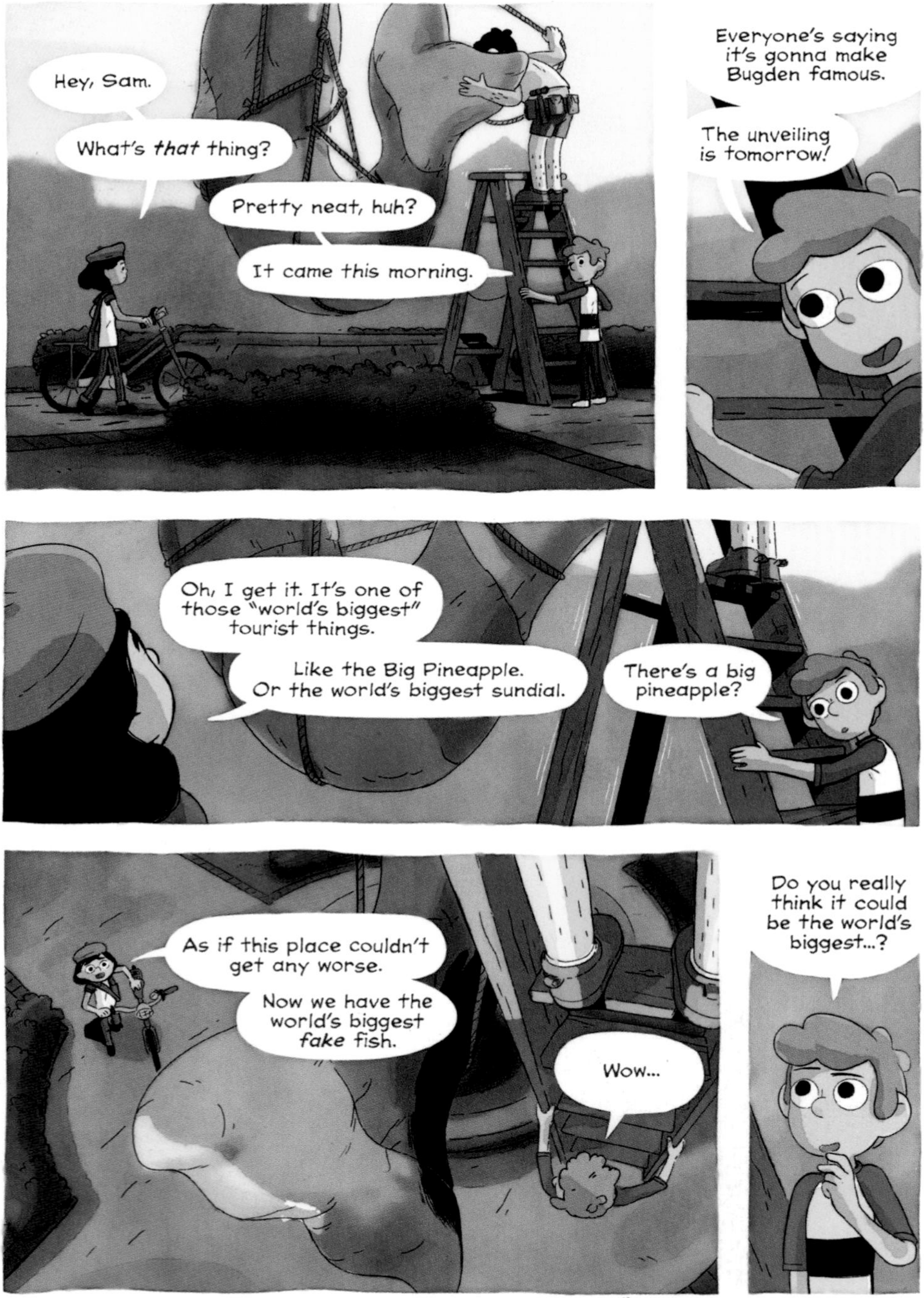
Hey, Sam.
What's *that* thing?
Pretty neat, huh?
It came this morning.
Everyone's saying it's gonna make Bugden famous.
The unveiling is tomorrow!
Oh, I get it. It's one of those "world's biggest" tourist things.
Like the Big Pineapple. Or the world's biggest sundial.
There's a big pineapple?
As if this place couldn't get any worse.
Now we have the world's biggest *fake* fish.
Wow...
Do you really think it could be the world's biggest...?

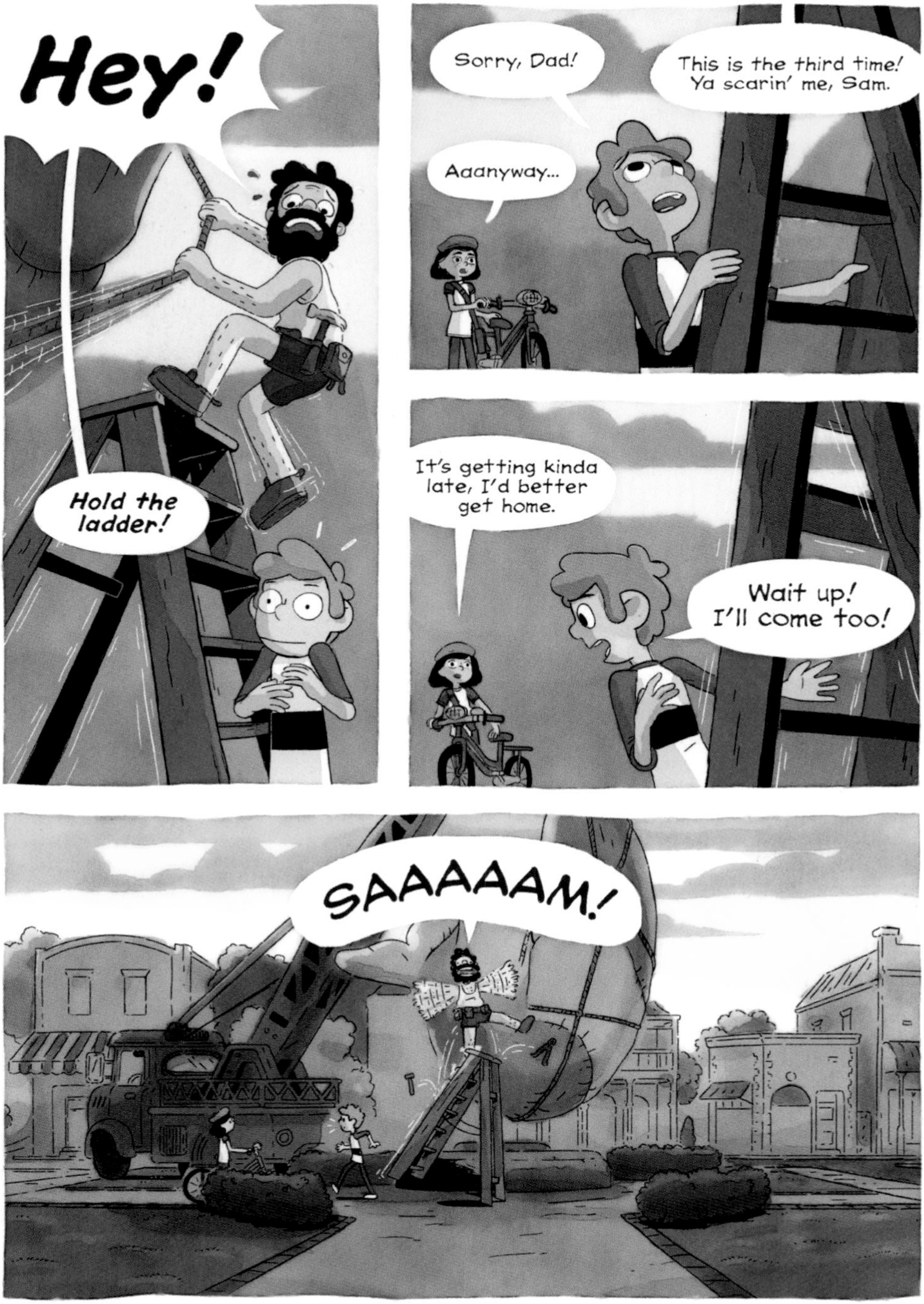

Hey!
Hold the ladder!
Sorry, Dad!
This is the third time! Ya scarin' me, Sam.
Aaanyway...
It's getting kinda late, I'd better get home.
Wait up! I'll come too!
SAAAAAM!

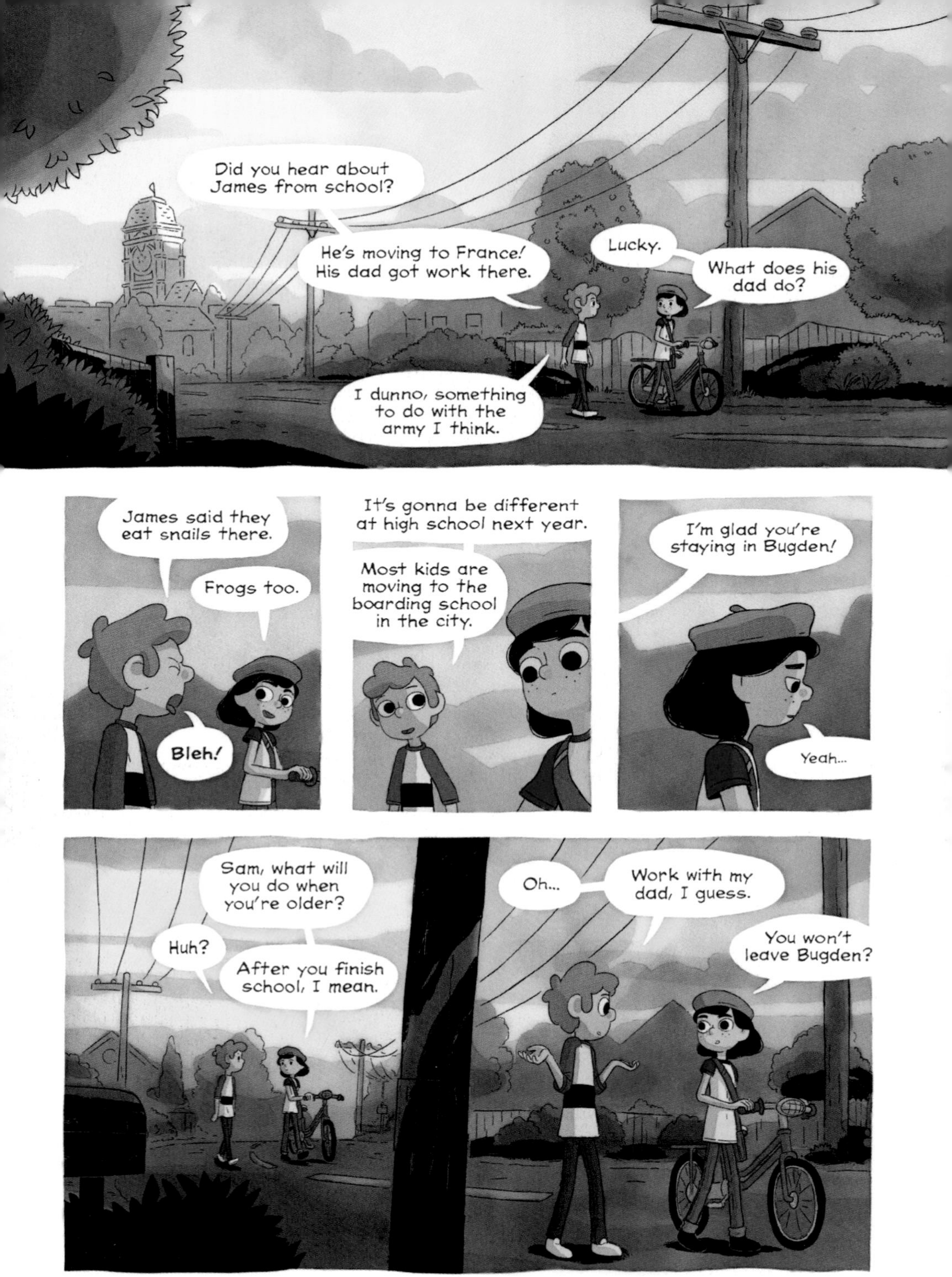

Did you hear about James from school?
He's moving to France! His dad got work there.
Lucky.
What does his dad do?
I dunno, something to do with the army I think.
James said they eat snails there.
Frogs too.
Bleh!
It's gonna be different at high school next year.
Most kids are moving to the boarding school in the city.
I'm glad you're staying in Bugden!
Yeah...
Sam, what will you do when you're older?
Huh?
After you finish school, I mean.
Oh...
Work with my dad, I guess.
You won't leave Bugden?

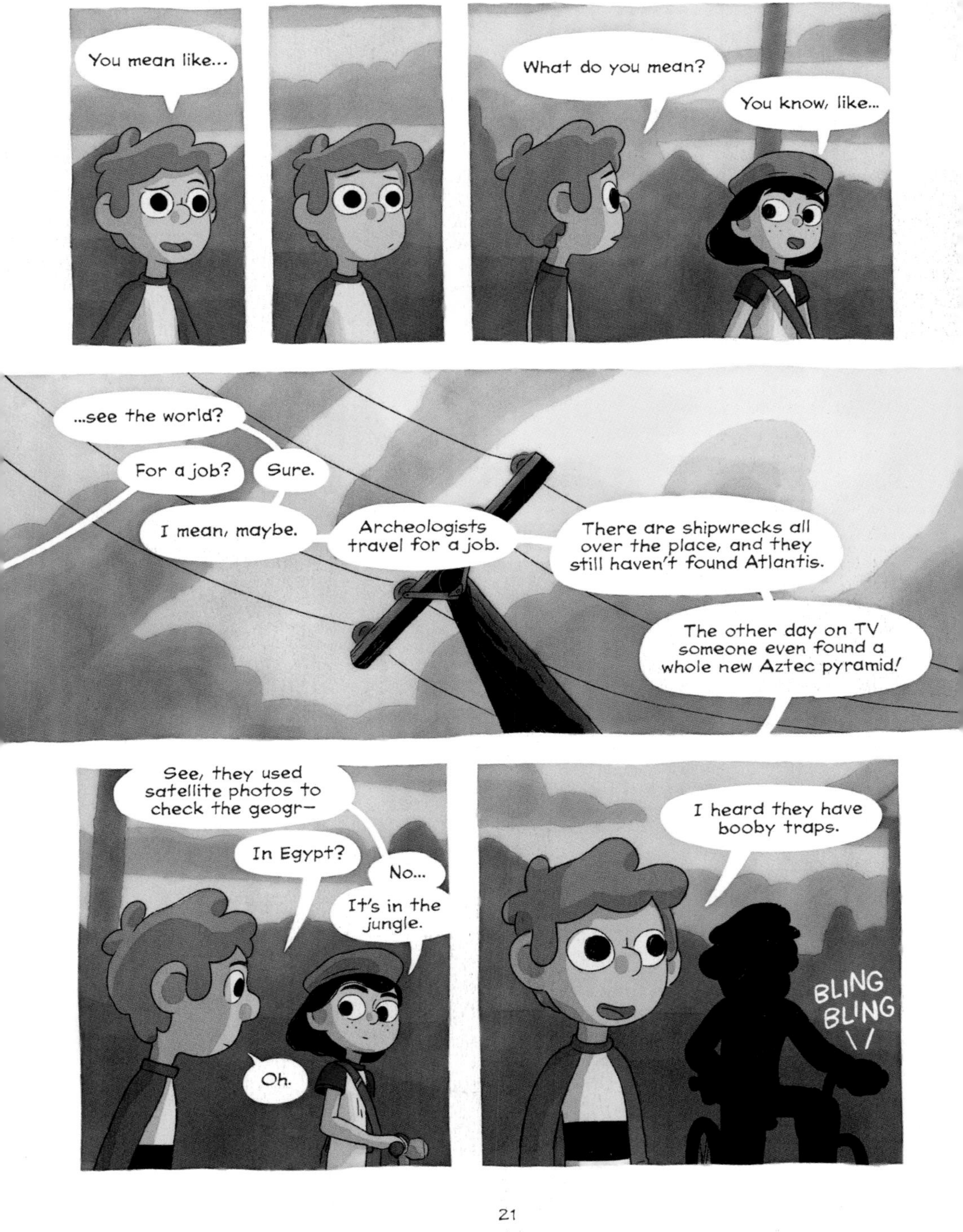
You mean like...
What do you mean?
You know, like...
...see the world?
For a job?
Sure.
I mean, maybe.
Archeologists travel for a job.
There are shipwrecks all over the place, and they still haven't found Atlantis.
The other day on TV someone even found a whole new Aztec pyramid!
See, they used satellite photos to check the geogr–
In Egypt?
No...
It's in the jungle.
Oh.
I heard they have booby traps.
BLING BLING

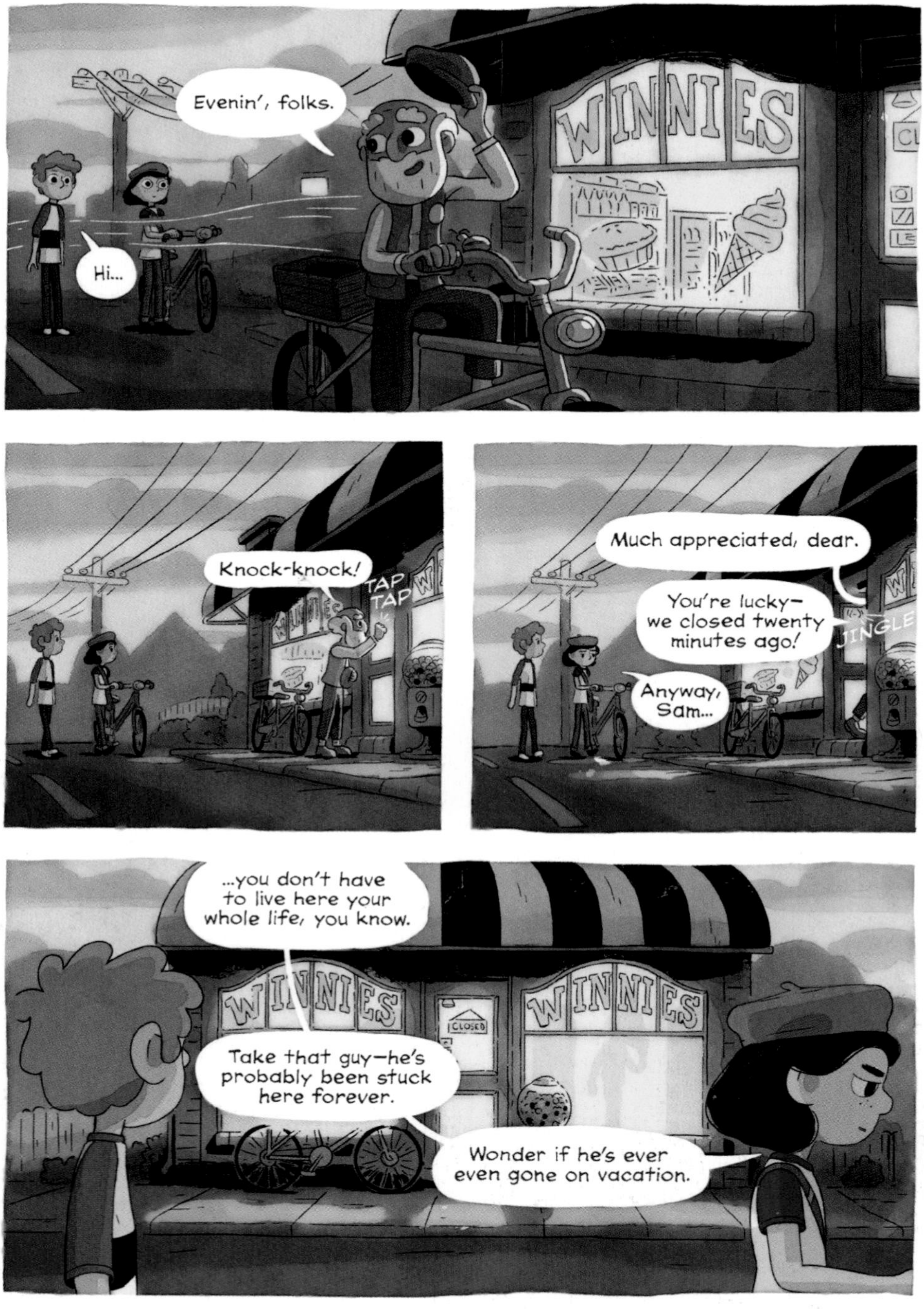
Evenin', folks.
Hi...
Knock-knock!
TAP TAP
Much appreciated, dear.
You're lucky—we closed twenty minutes ago!
JINGLE
Anyway, Sam...
...you don't have to live here your whole life, you know.
Take that guy—he's probably been stuck here forever.
Wonder if he's ever even gone on vacation.

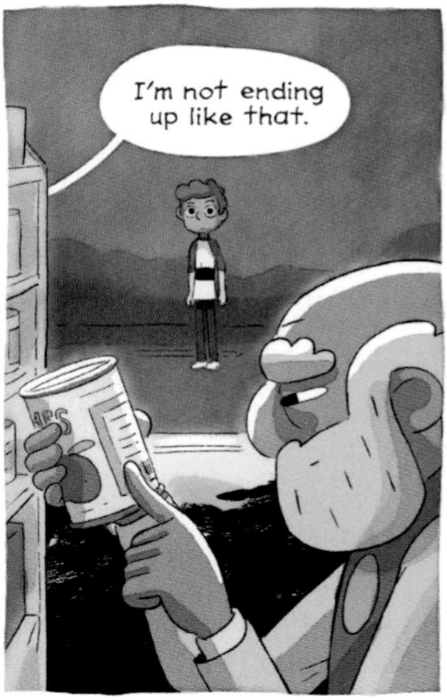
I'm not ending up like that.

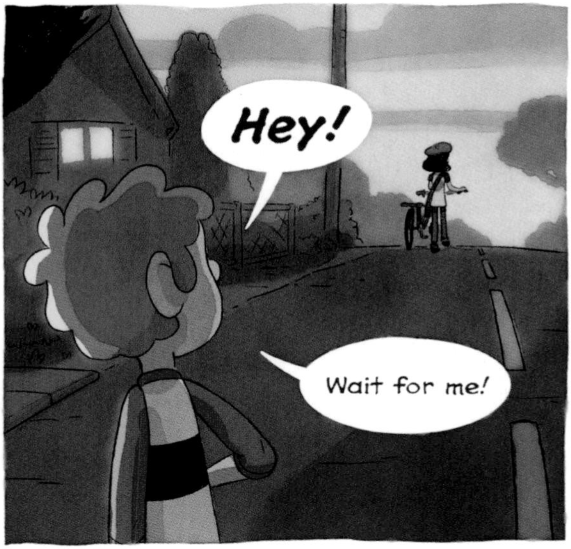
Hey!
Wait for me!

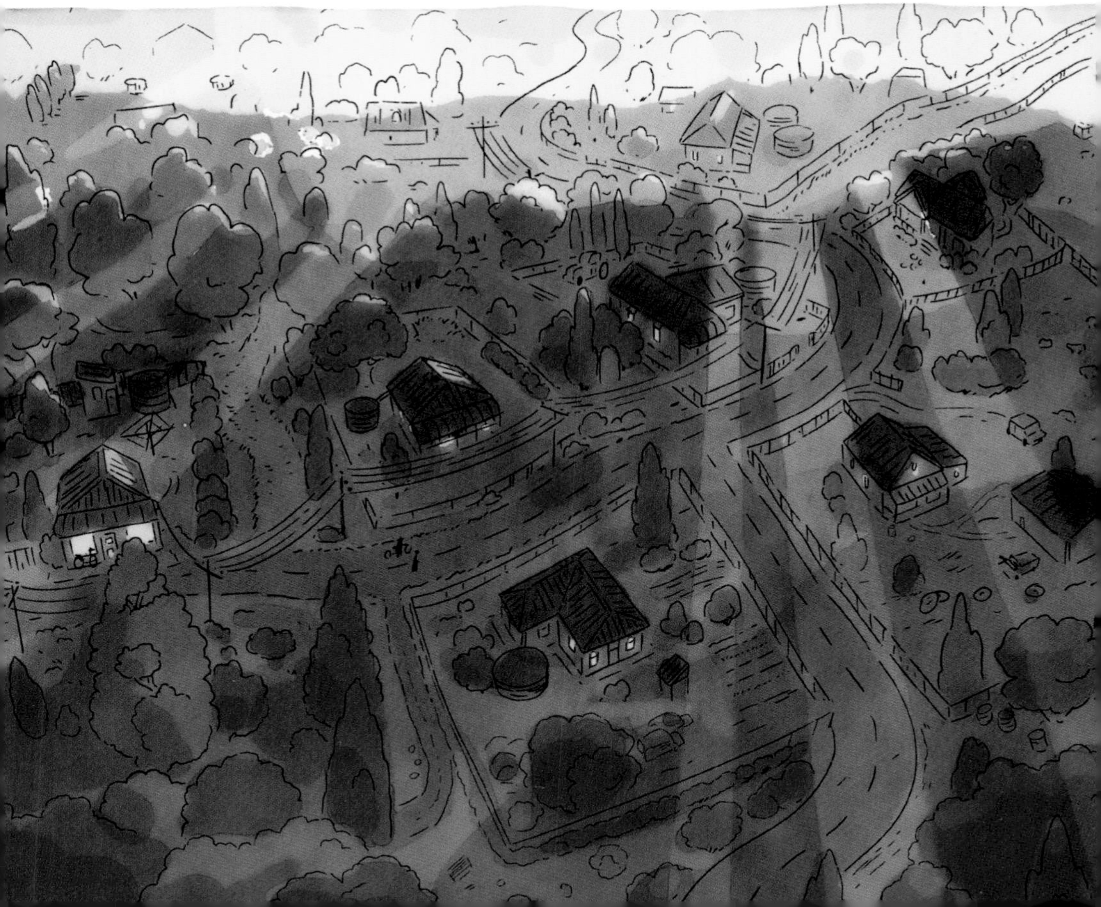

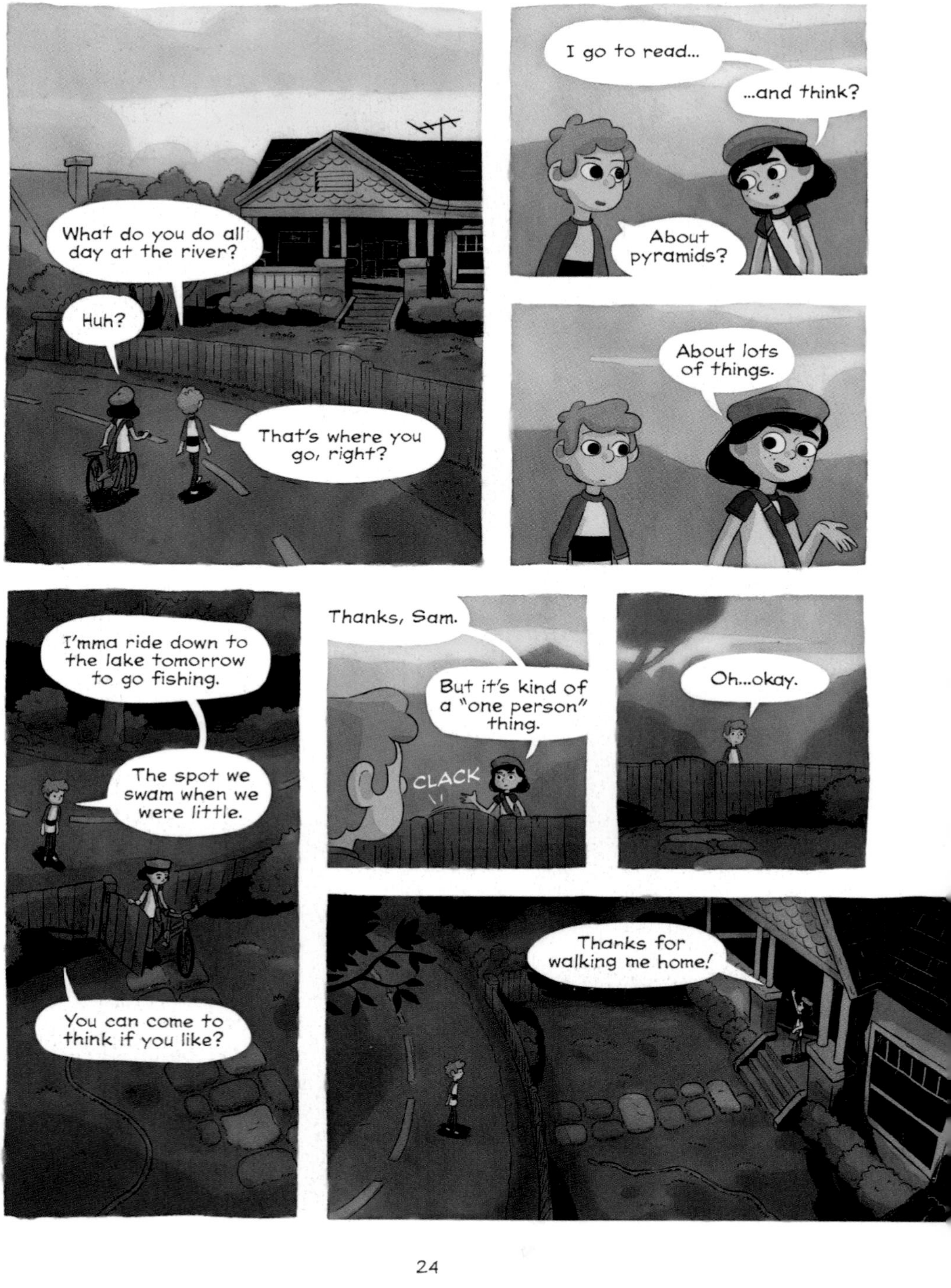
What do you do all day at the river?
Huh?
That's where you go, right?
I go to read...
...and think?
About pyramids?
About lots of things.
I'mma ride down to the lake tomorrow to go fishing.
The spot we swam when we were little.
You can come to think if you like?
Thanks, Sam.
But it's kind of a "one person" thing.
CLACK
Oh...okay.
Thanks for walking me home!

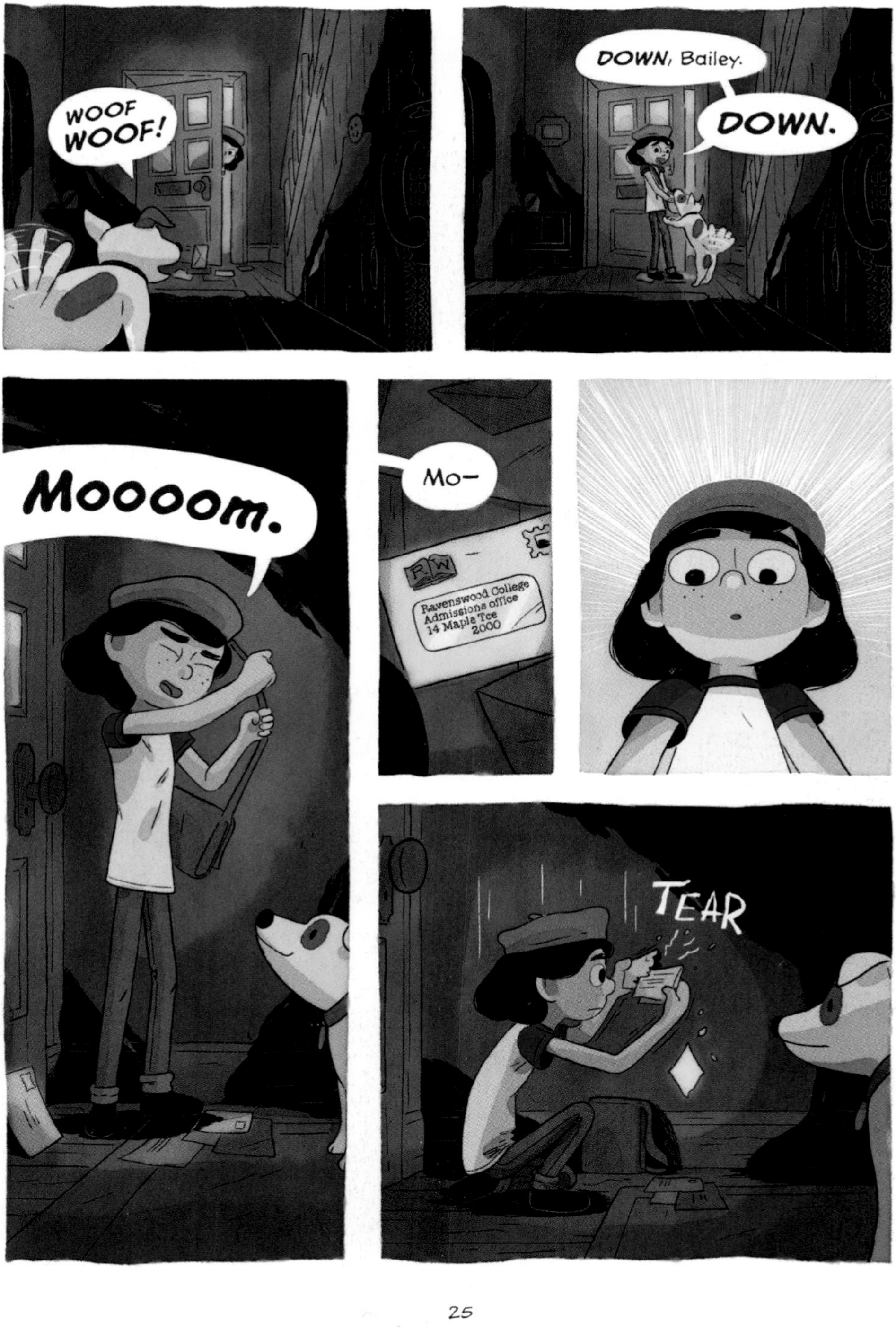
WOOF WOOF!
DOWN, Bailey.
DOWN.
Moooom.
Mo–
R W
Ravenswood College
Admissions office
14 Maple Tce
2000
TEAR

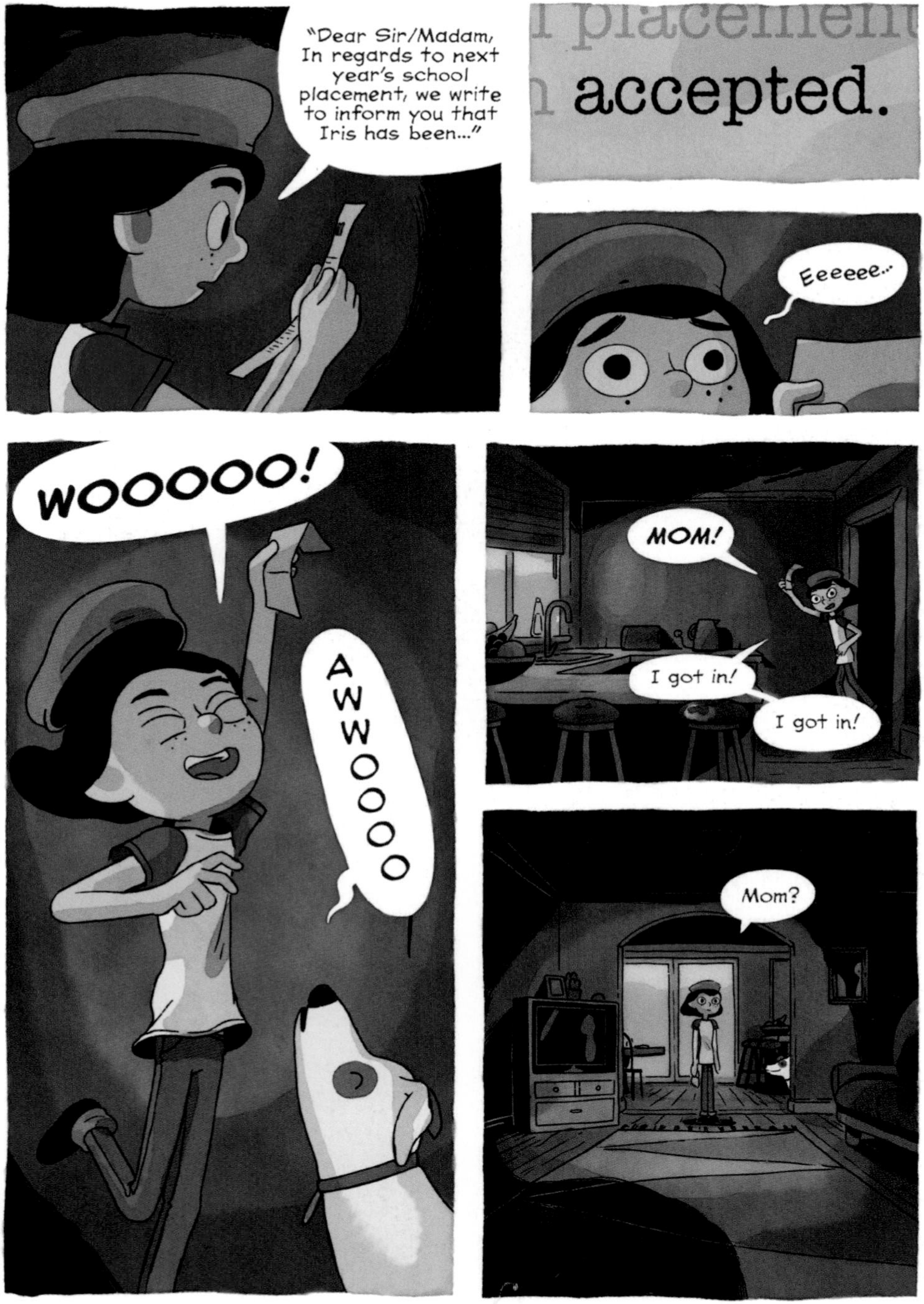
"Dear Sir/Madam, In regards to next year's school placement, we write to inform you that Iris has been..."
accepted.
Eeeeee...
WOOOOO!
AWWOOOOO
MOM!
I got in!
I got in!
Mom?

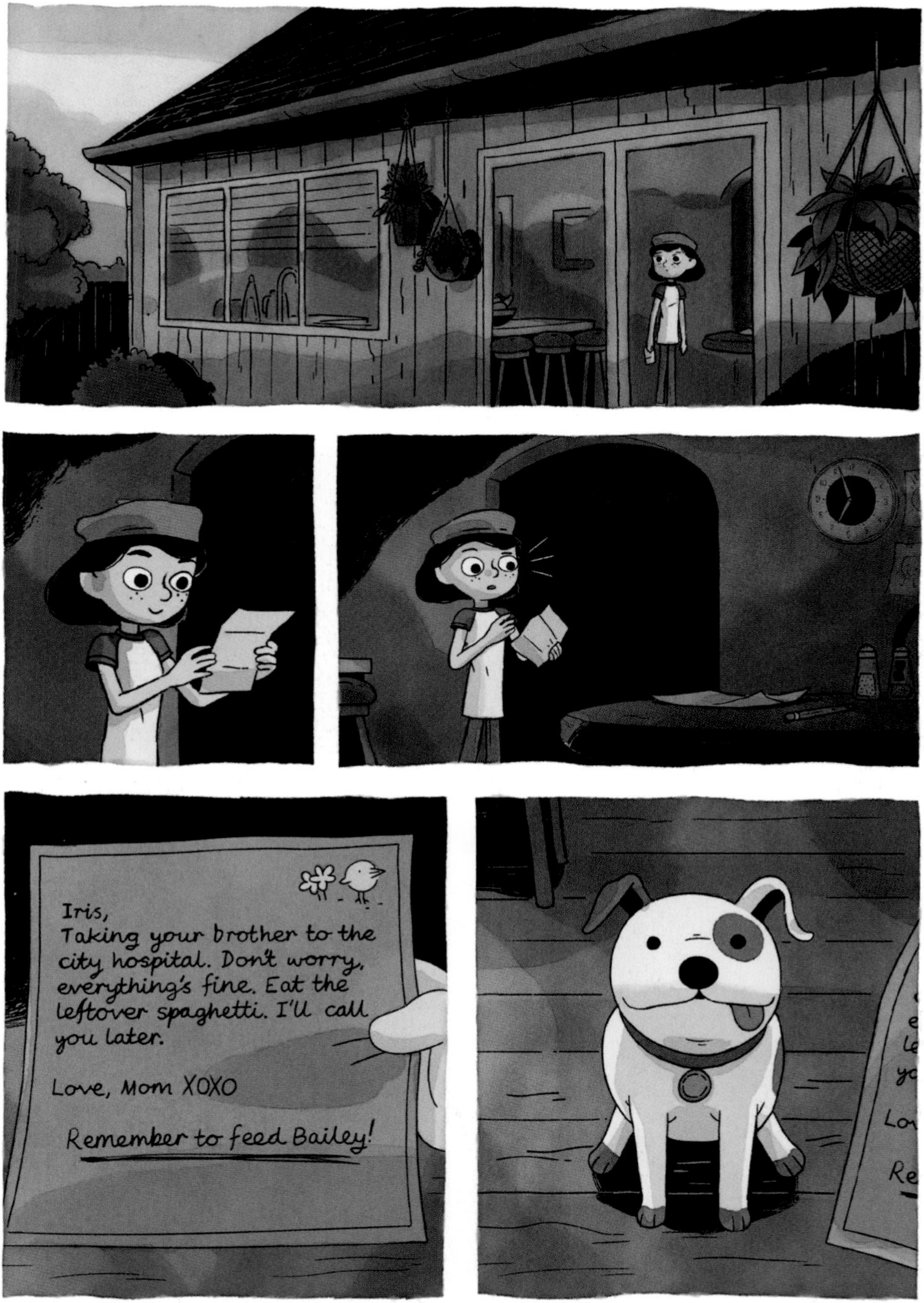
Iris,
Taking your brother to the city hospital. Don't worry, everything's fine. Eat the leftover spaghetti. I'll call you later.
Love, Mom XOXO
Remember to feed Bailey!

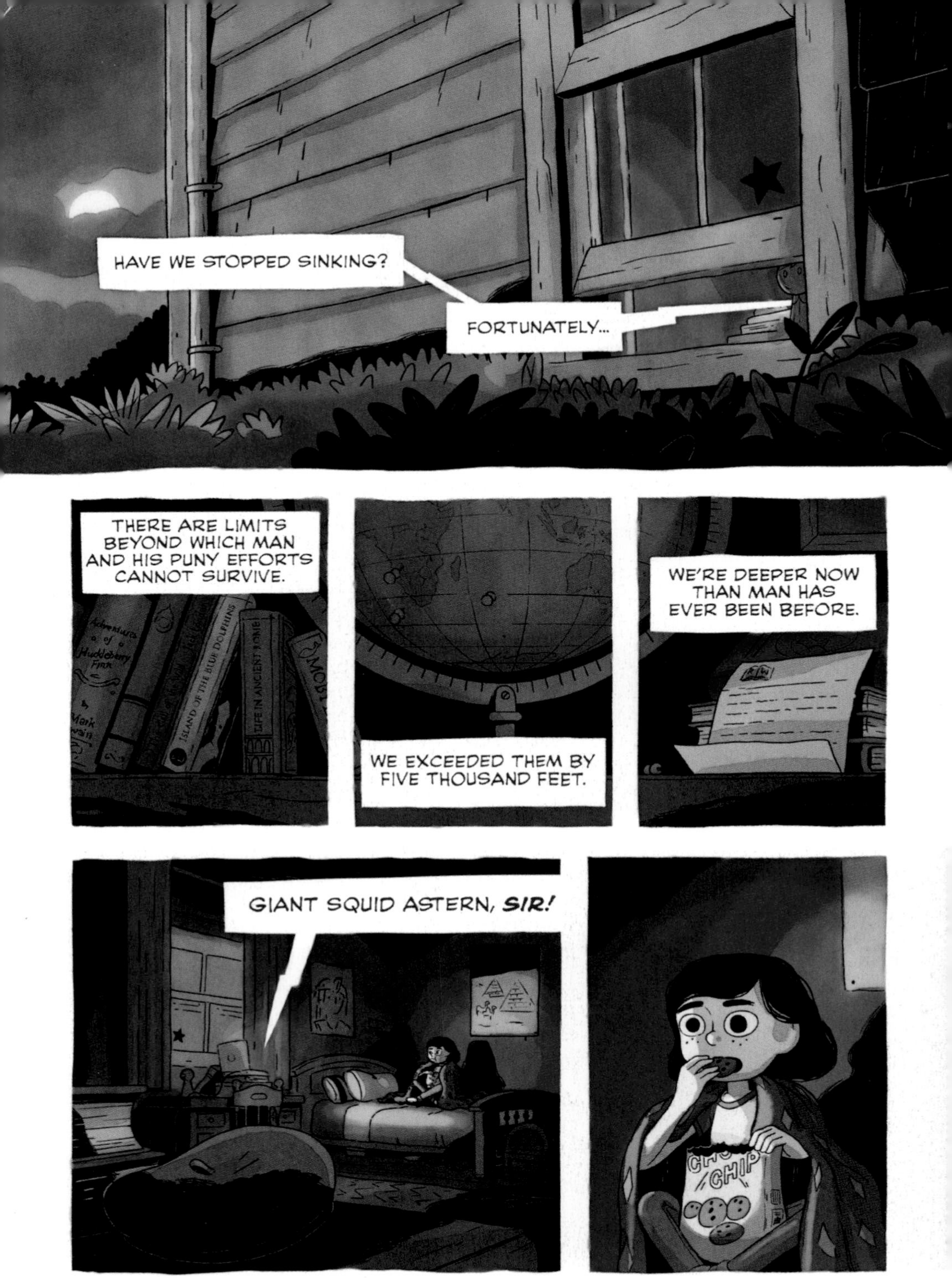
HAVE WE STOPPED SINKING?
FORTUNATELY...
THERE ARE LIMITS BEYOND WHICH MAN AND HIS PUNY EFFORTS CANNOT SURVIVE.
Adventures of Huckleberry Finn by Mark Twain
ISLAND OF THE BLUE DOLPHINS
LIFE IN ANCIENT ROME
WE EXCEEDED THEM BY FIVE THOUSAND FEET.
WE'RE DEEPER NOW THAN MAN HAS EVER BEEN BEFORE.
GIANT SQUID ASTERN, ***SIR!***
CHIP

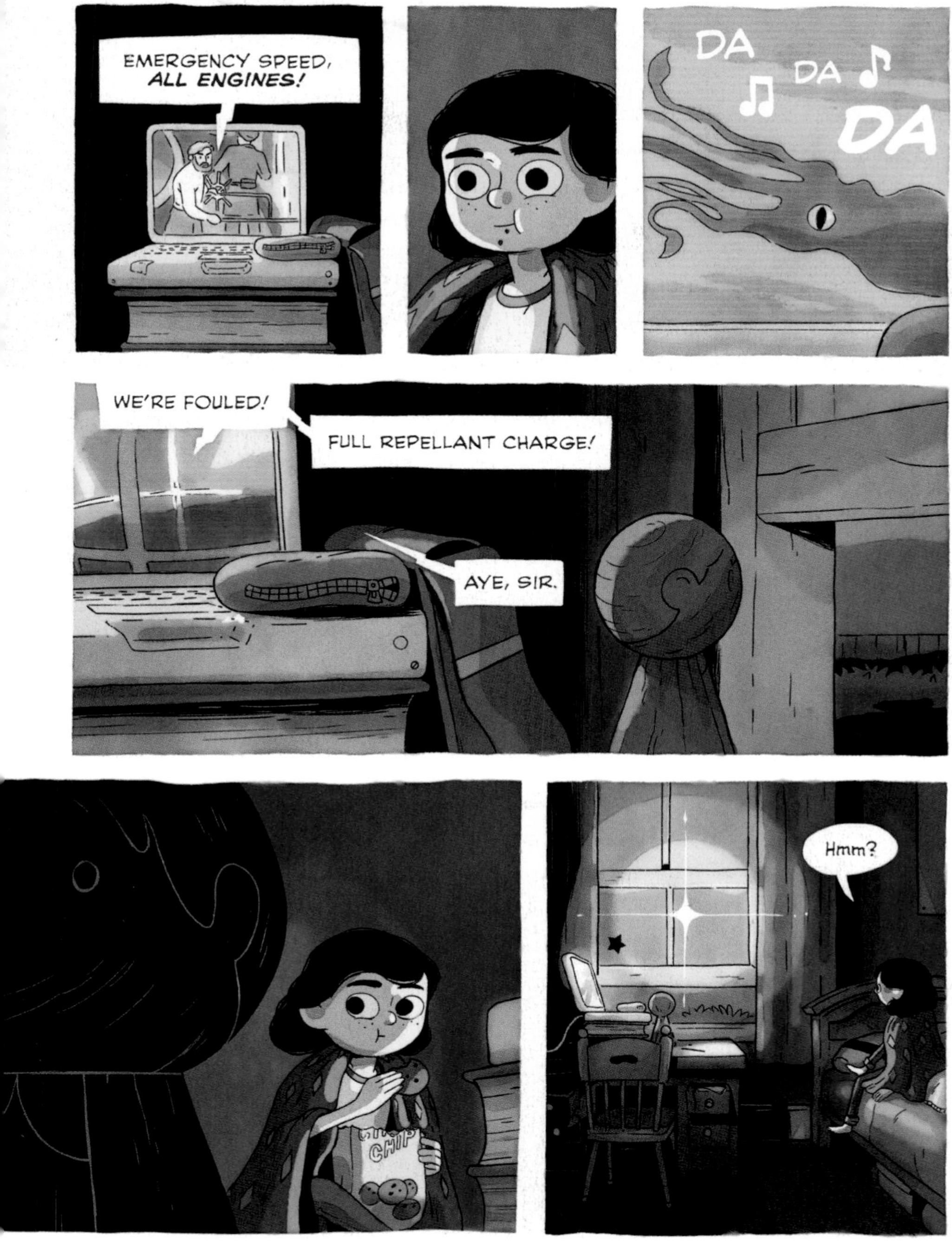
EMERGENCY SPEED, ALL ENGINES!
DA DA DA
WE'RE FOULED!
FULL REPELLANT CHARGE!
AYE, SIR.
CHIP
Hmm?

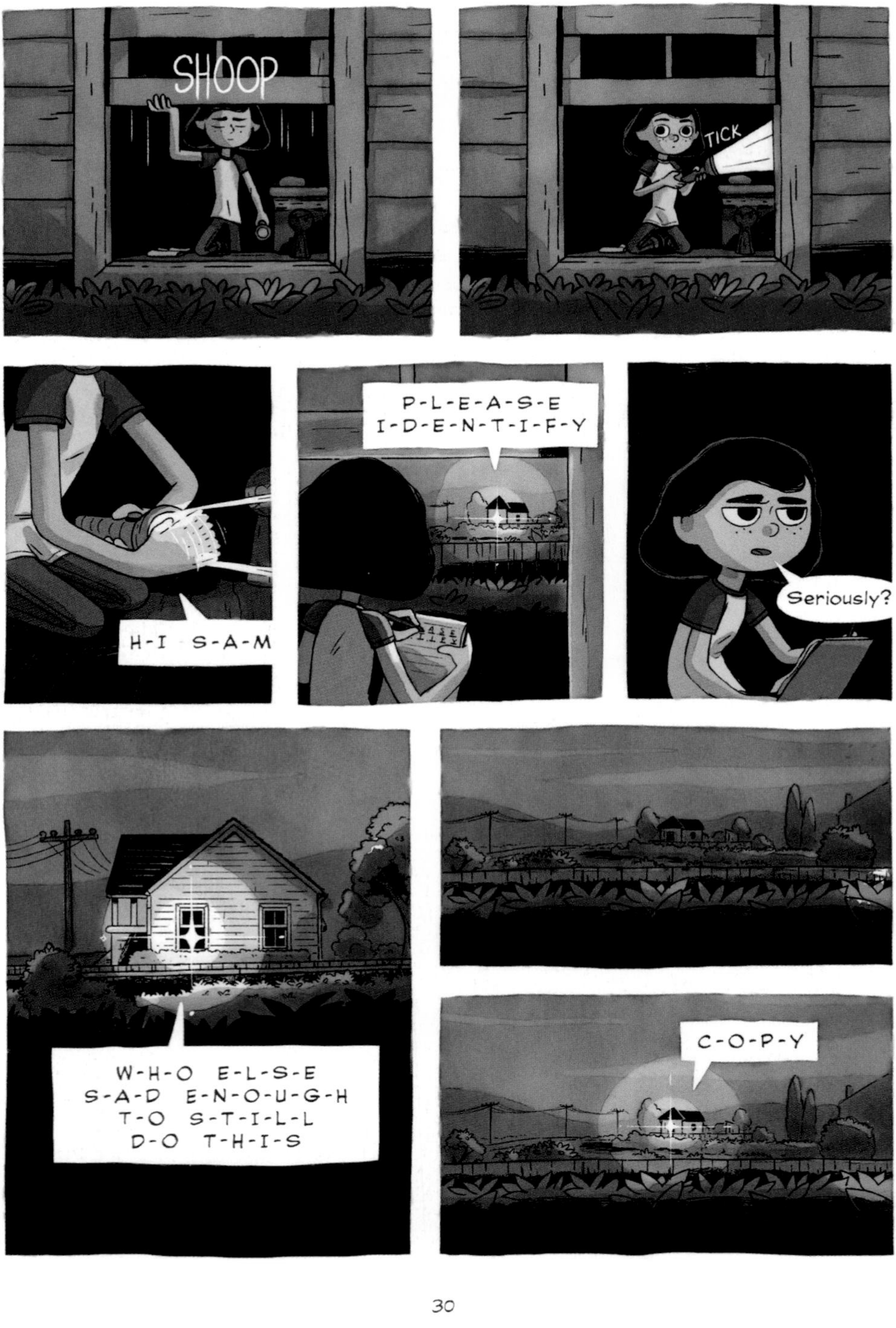
SHOOP
TICK
H-I S-A-M
P-L-E-A-S-E I-D-E-N-T-I-F-Y
Seriously?
W-H-O E-L-S-E S-A-D E-N-O-U-G-H T-O S-T-I-L-L D-O T-H-I-S
C-O-P-Y

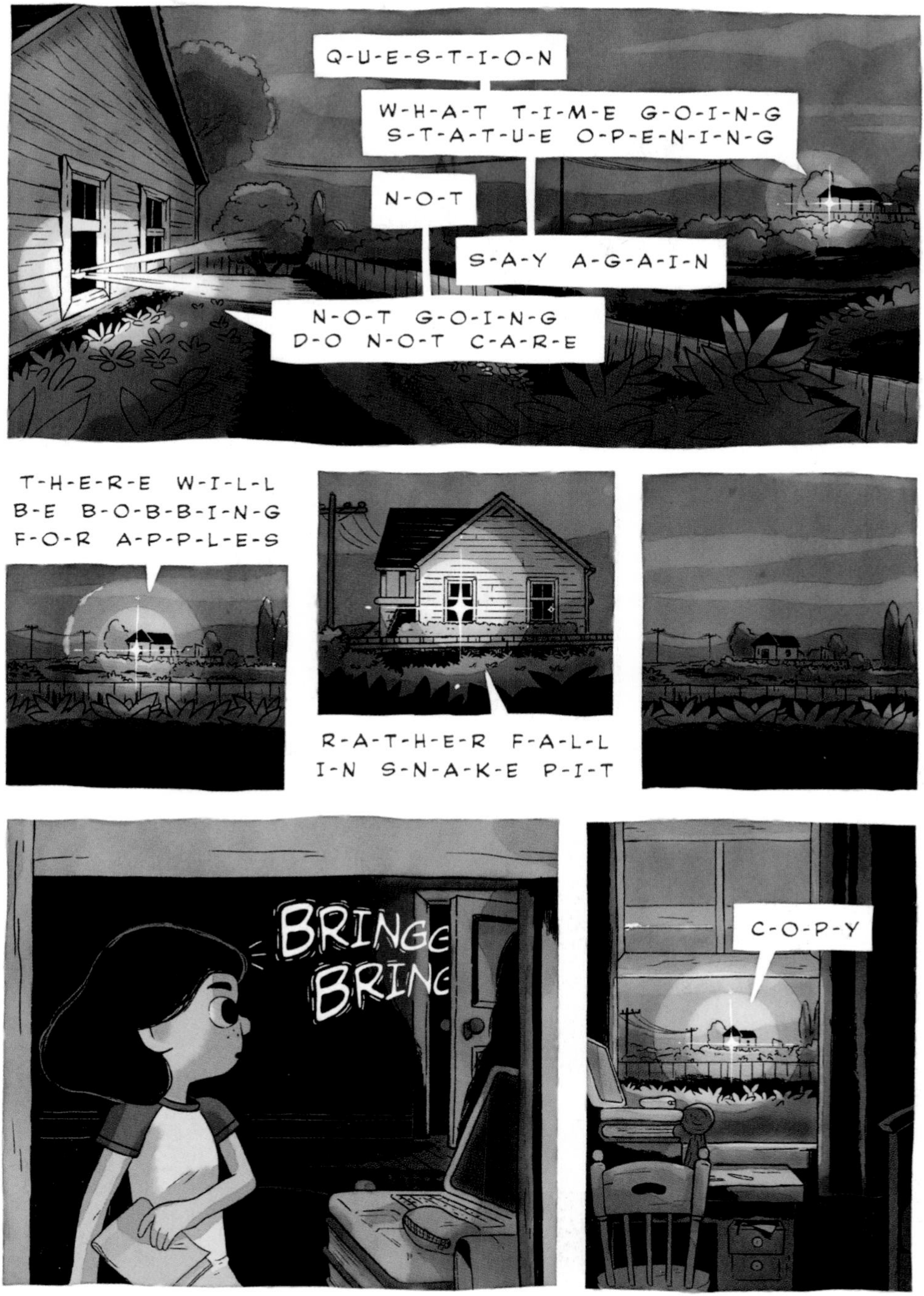
Q-U-E-S-T-I-O-N
W-H-A-T T-I-M-E G-O-I-N-G S-T-A-T-U-E O-P-E-N-I-N-G
N-O-T
S-A-Y A-G-A-I-N
N-O-T G-O-I-N-G D-O N-O-T C-A-R-E
T-H-E-R-E W-I-L-L B-E B-O-B-B-I-N-G F-O-R A-P-P-L-E-S
R-A-T-H-E-R F-A-L-L I-N S-N-A-K-E P-I-T
BRINGE
BRIN
C-O-P-Y

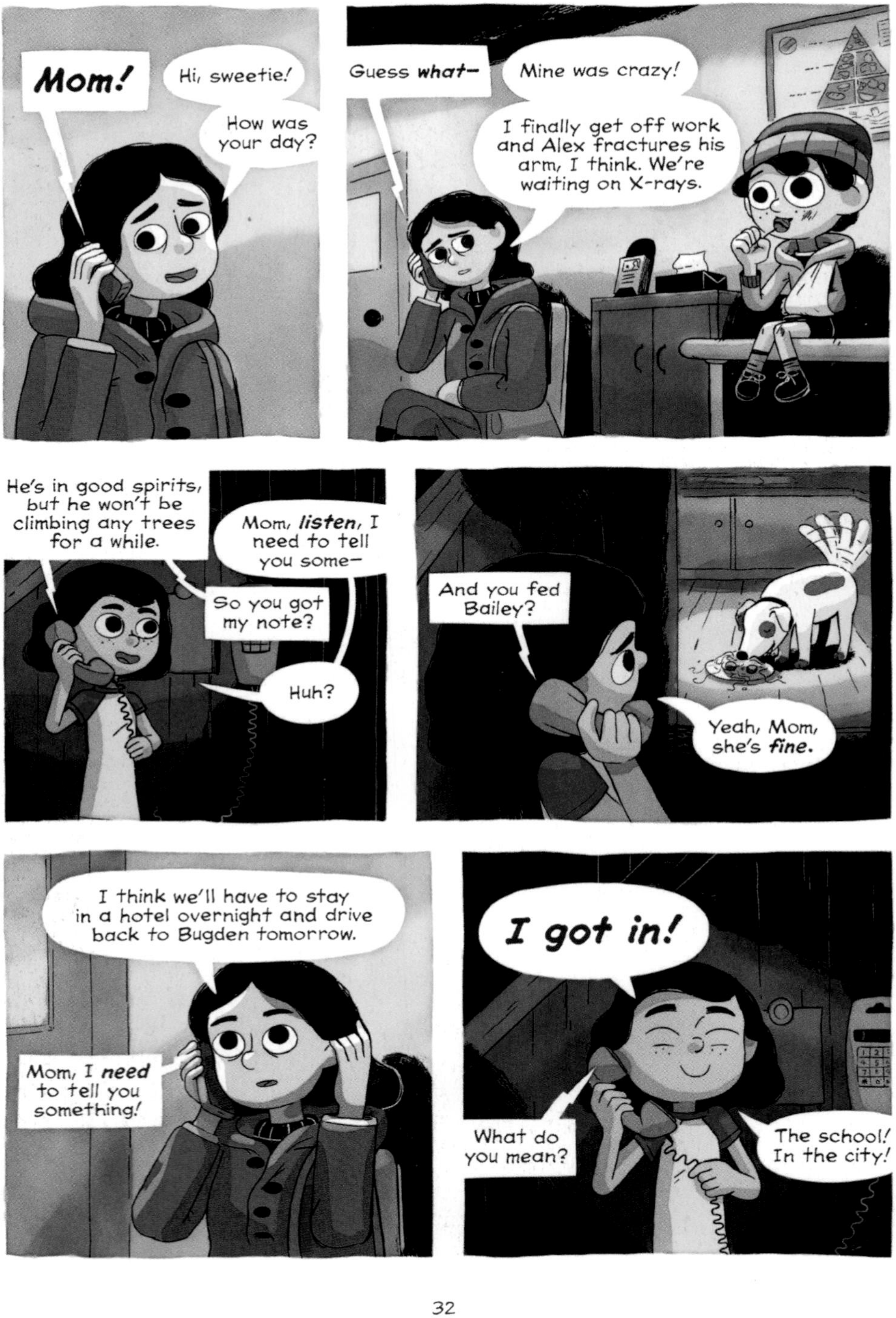

Mom!
Hi, sweetie!
How was your day?
Guess what—
Mine was crazy!
I finally get off work and Alex fractures his arm, I think. We're waiting on X-rays.
He's in good spirits, but he won't be climbing any trees for a while.
Mom, listen, I need to tell you some—
So you got my note?
Huh?
And you fed Bailey?
Yeah, Mom, she's fine.
I think we'll have to stay in a hotel overnight and drive back to Bugden tomorrow.
Mom, I need to tell you something!
I got in!
What do you mean?
The school! In the city!

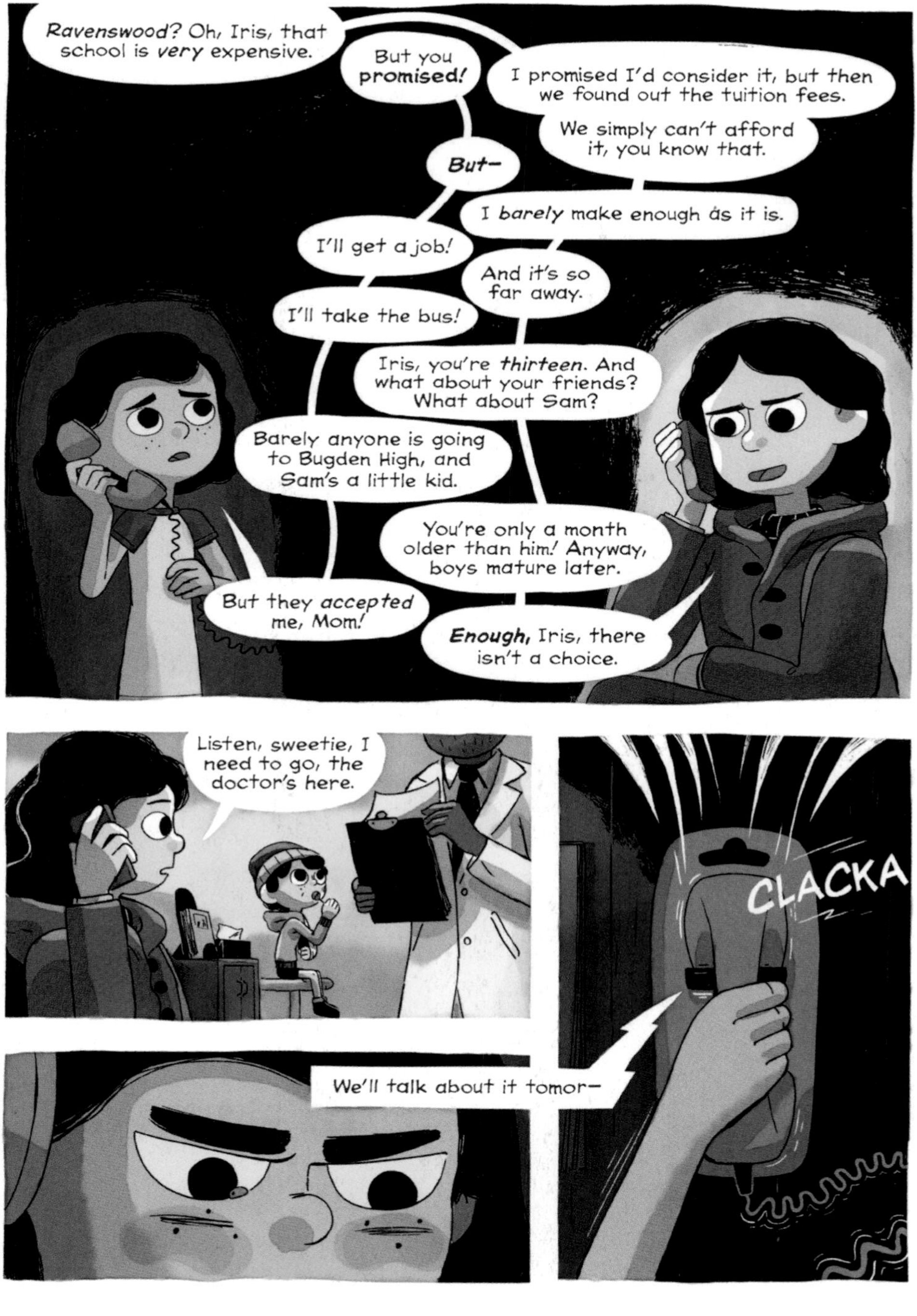
Ravenswood? Oh, Iris, that school is very expensive.
But you promised!
I promised I'd consider it, but then we found out the tuition fees.
We simply can't afford it, you know that.
But–
I barely make enough as it is.
I'll get a job!
And it's so far away.
I'll take the bus!
Iris, you're thirteen. And what about your friends? What about Sam?
Barely anyone is going to Bugden High, and Sam's a little kid.
You're only a month older than him! Anyway, boys mature later.
But they accepted me, Mom!
Enough, Iris, there isn't a choice.
Listen, sweetie, I need to go, the doctor's here.
We'll talk about it tomor–
CLACKA

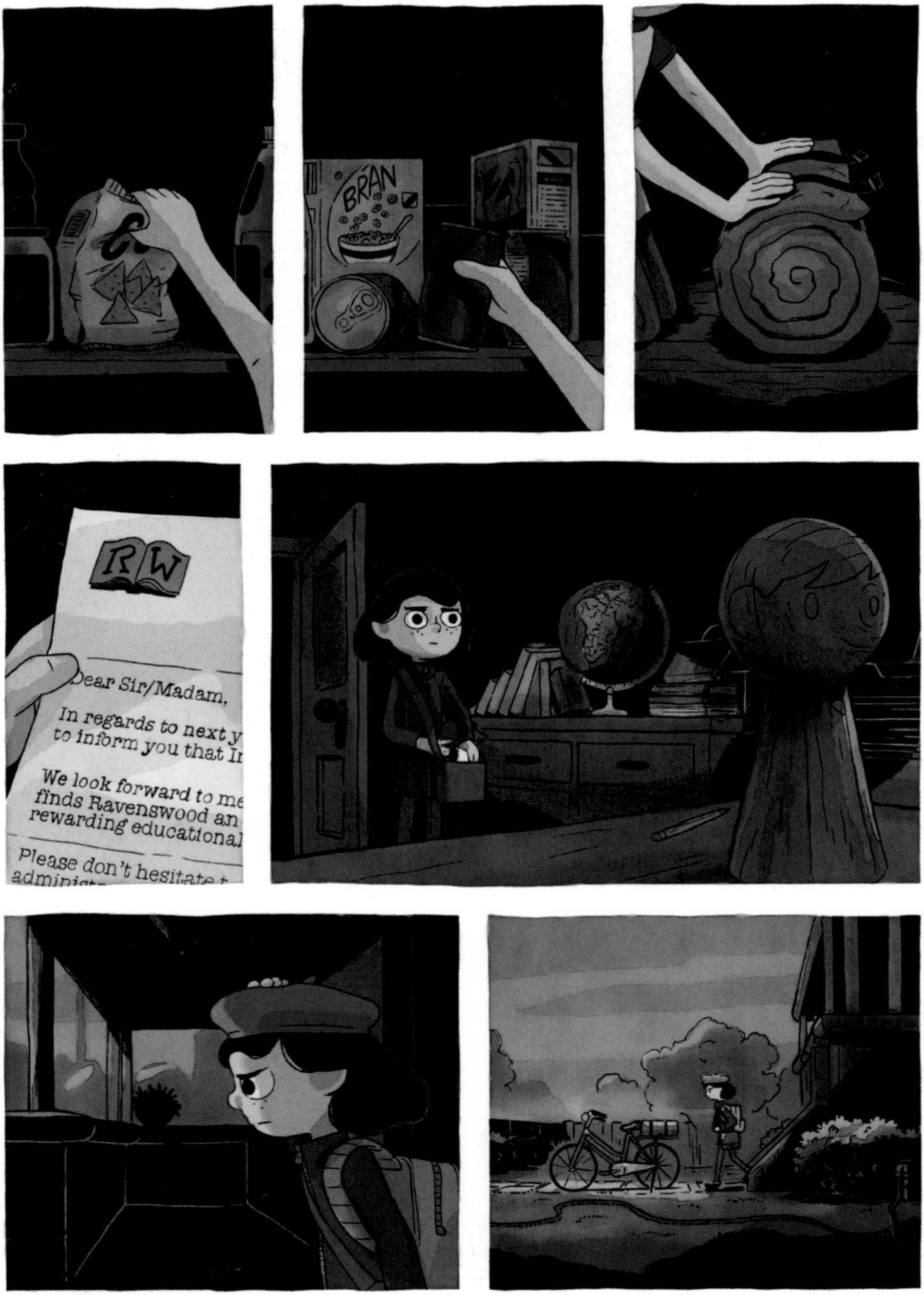
BRAN
RW
Dear Sir/Madam,
In regards to next y
to inform you that I
We look forward to me
finds Ravenswood an
rewarding educational
Please don't hesitate t

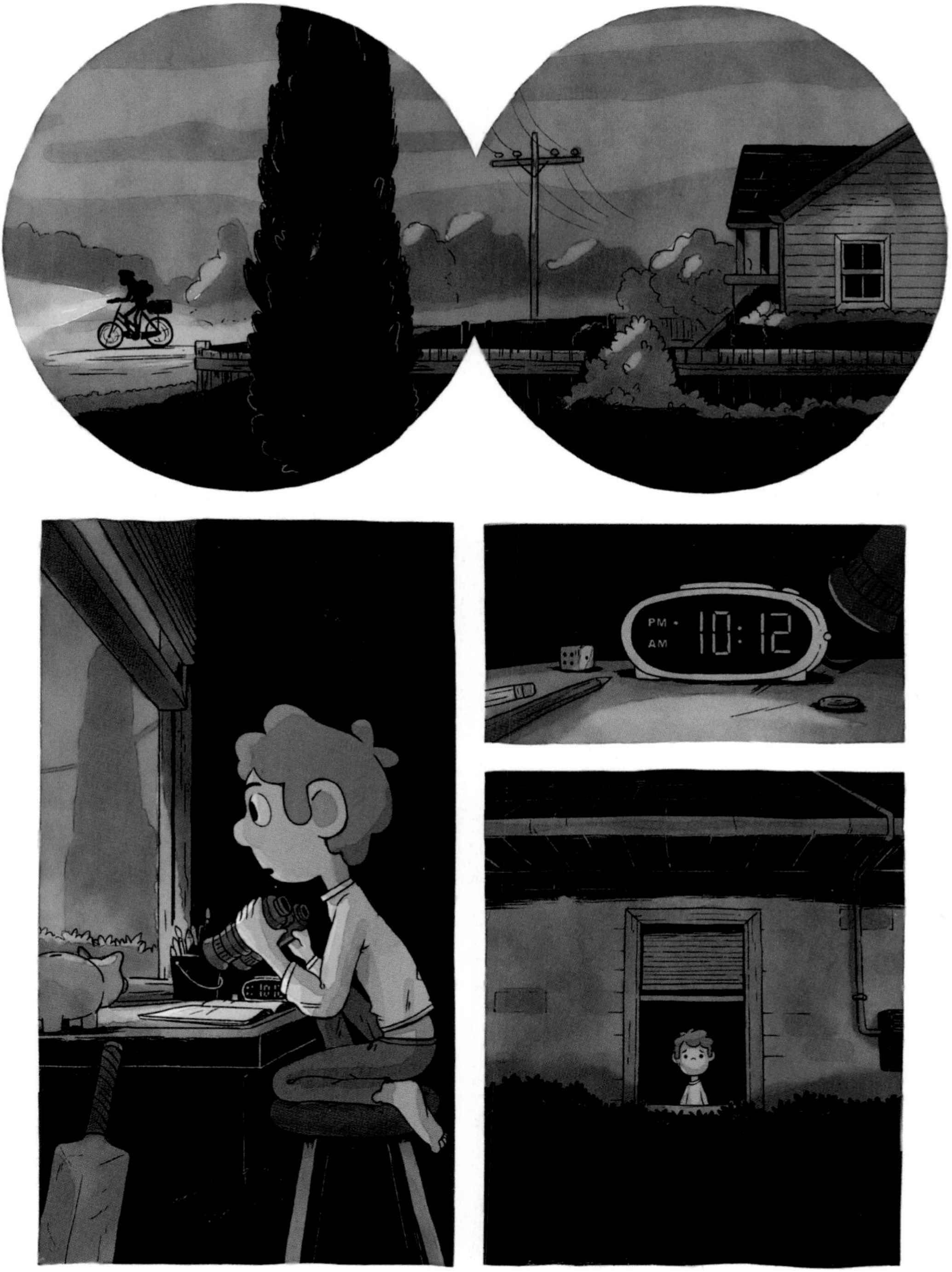
PM
AM
10:12

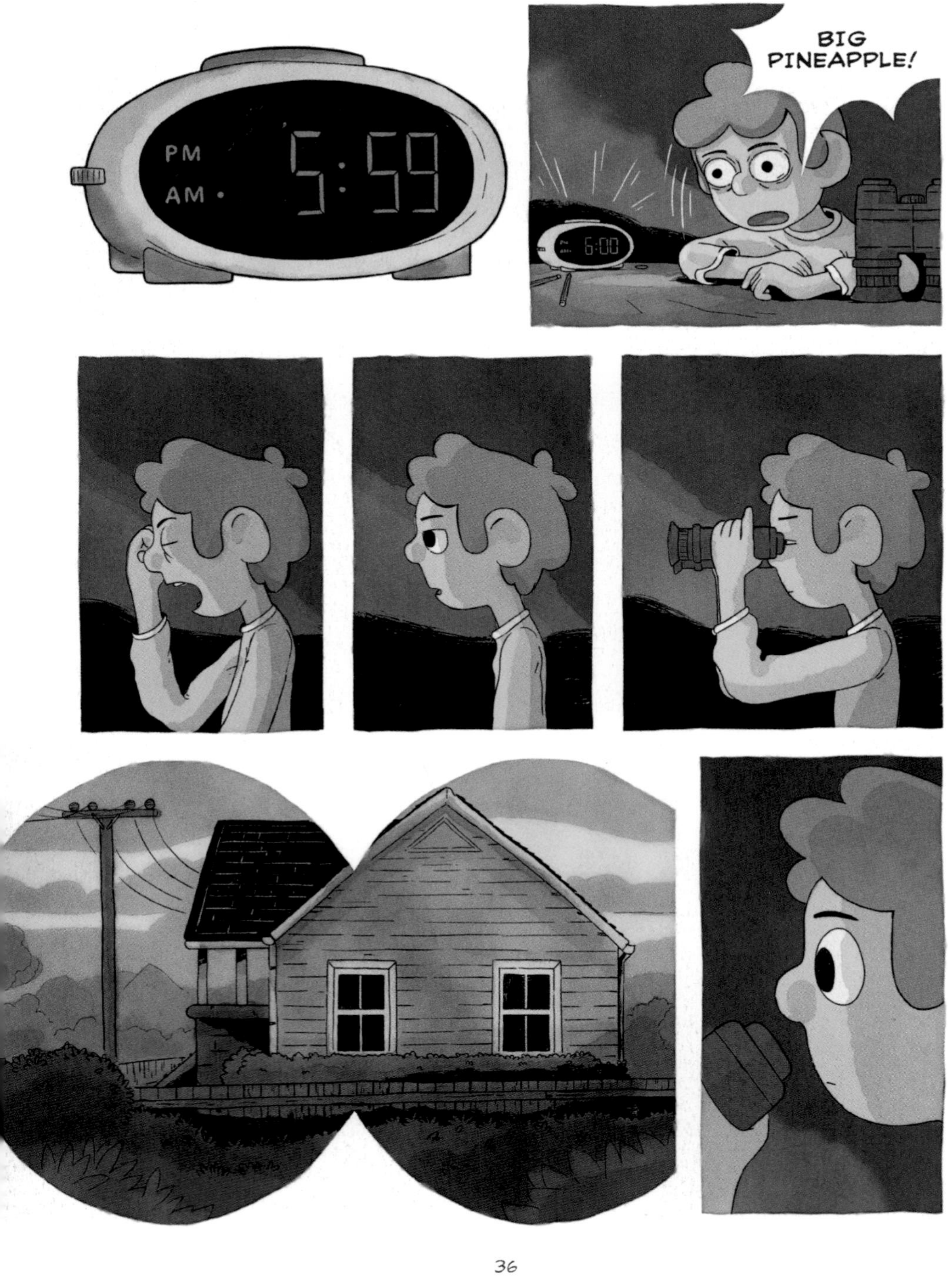
PM
AM
5:59
BIG PINEAPPLE!

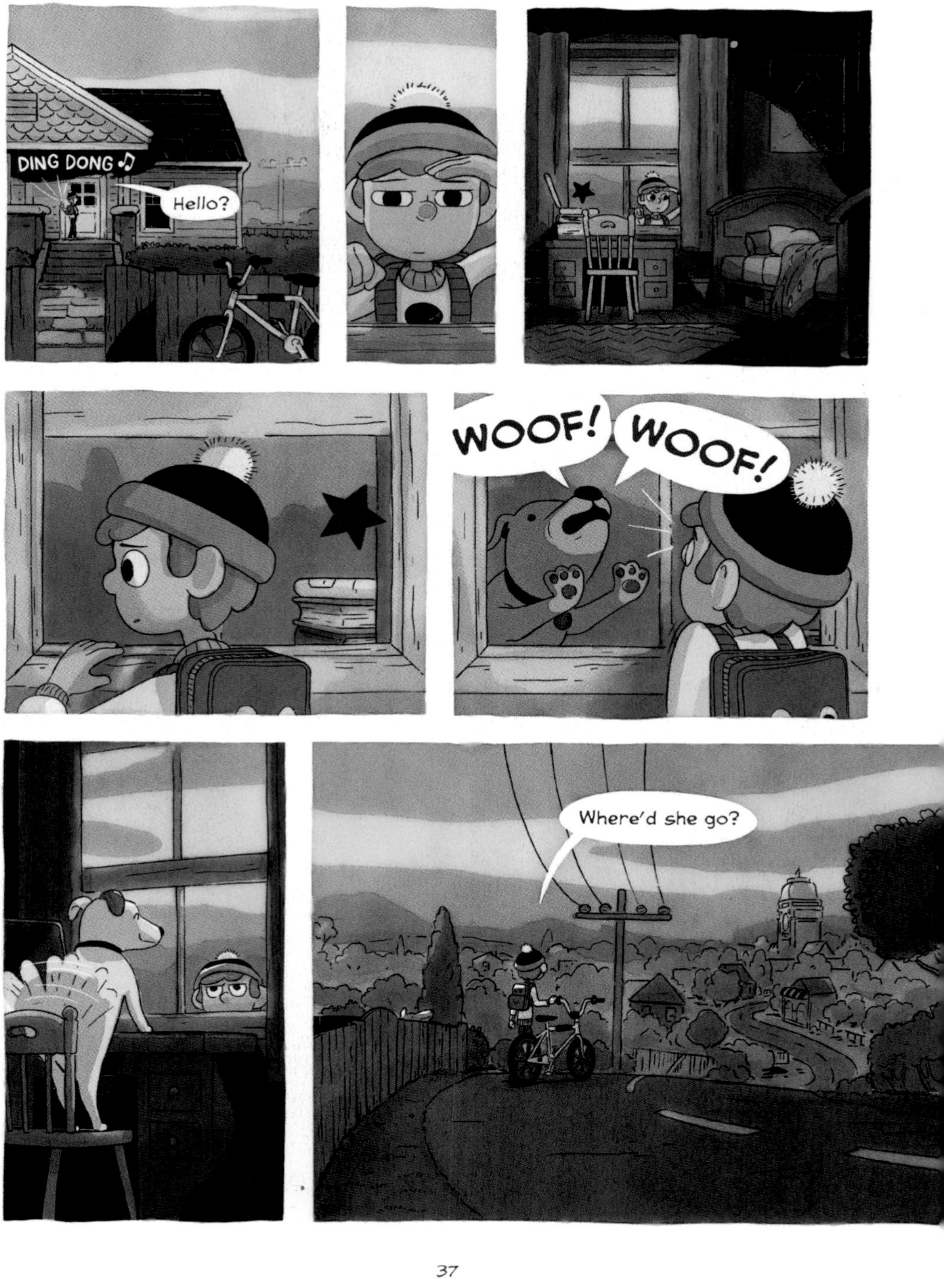
DING DONG ♫
Hello?
WOOF!
WOOF!
Where'd she go?

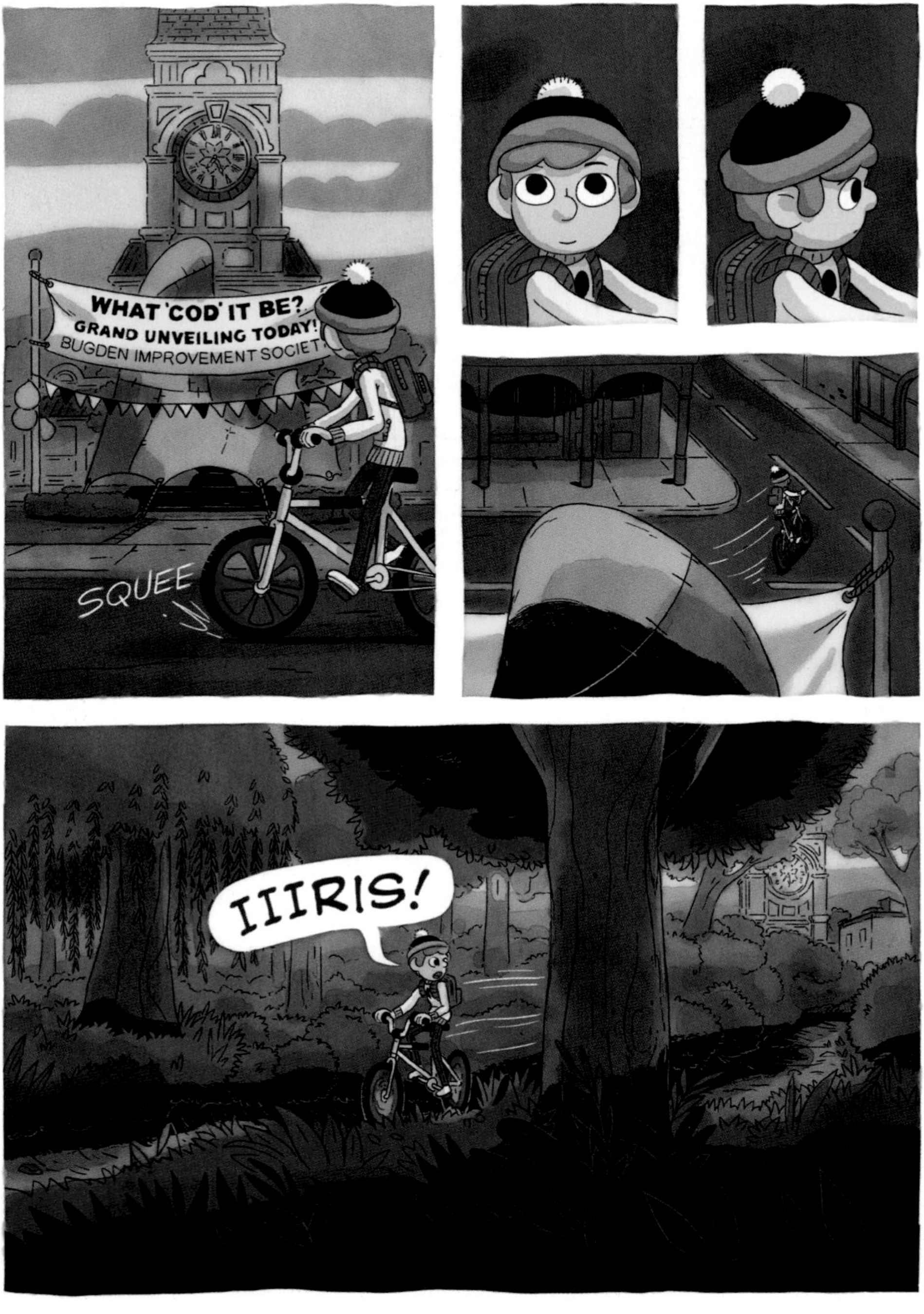
WHAT 'COD' IT BE?
GRAND UNVEILING TODAY!
BUGDEN IMPROVEMENT SOCIET
SQUEE
IIIRIS!

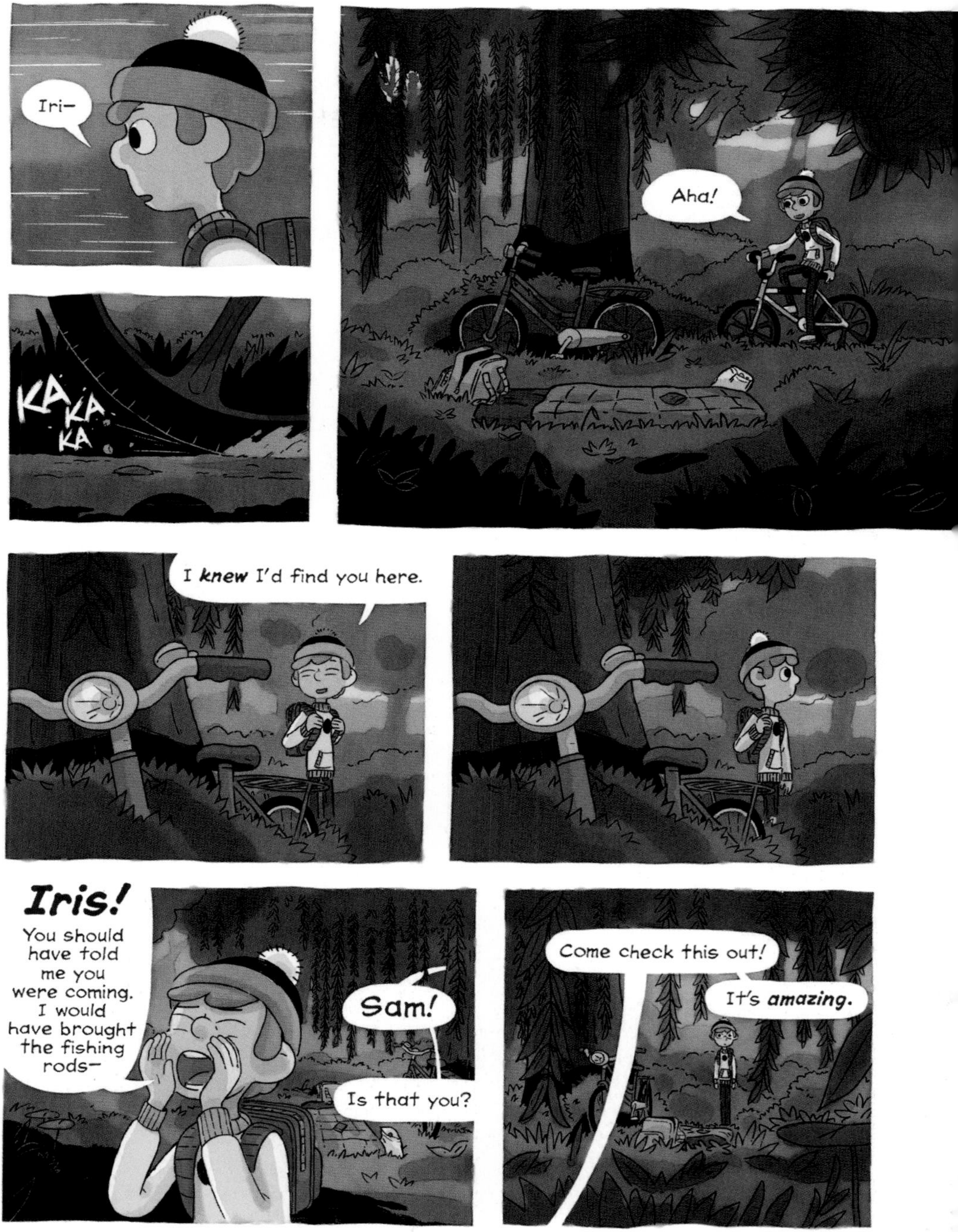
Iri–
KA KA KA
Aha!
I knew I'd find you here.
Iris!
You should have told me you were coming. I would have brought the fishing rods–
Sam!
Is that you?
Come check this out!
It's amazing.

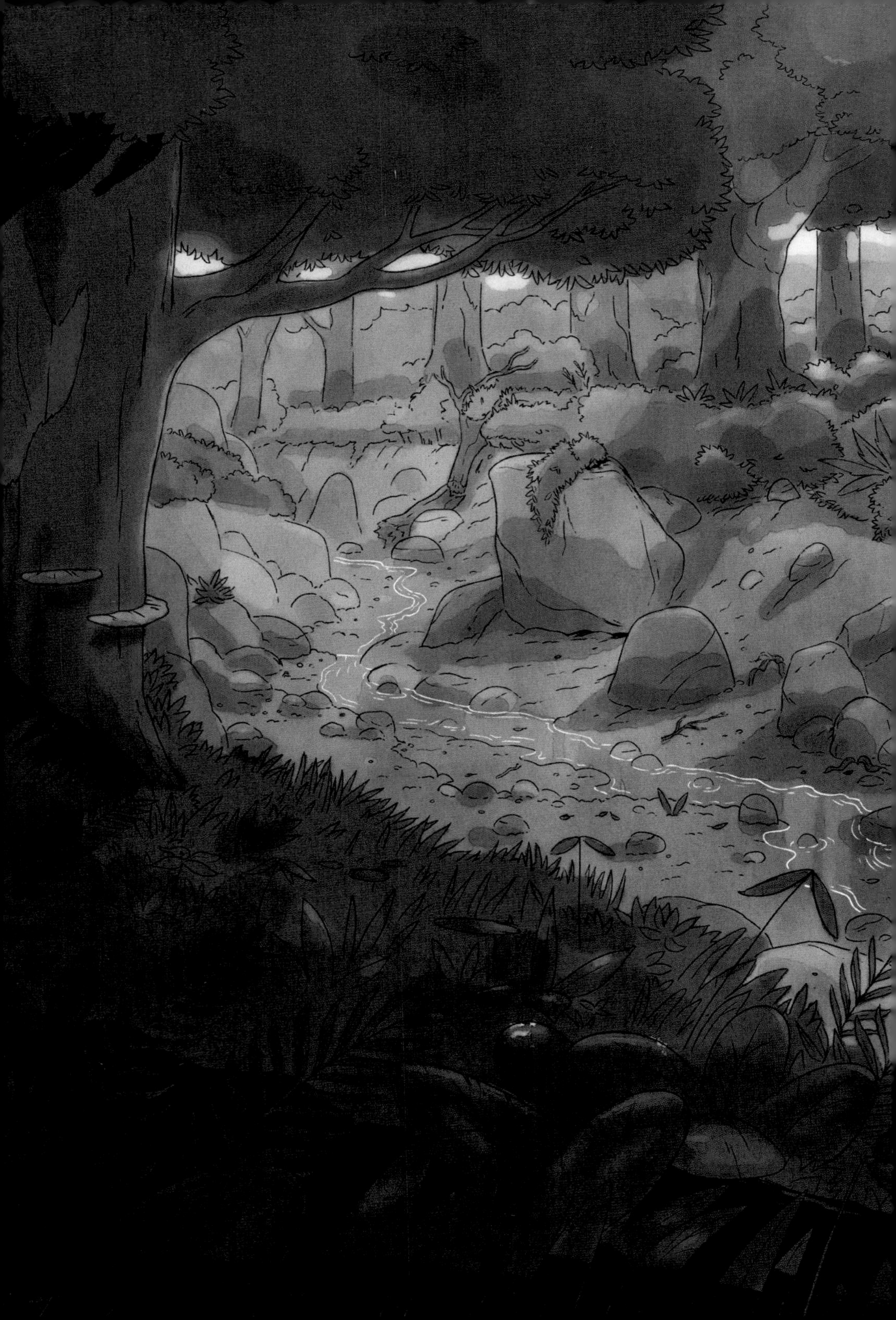

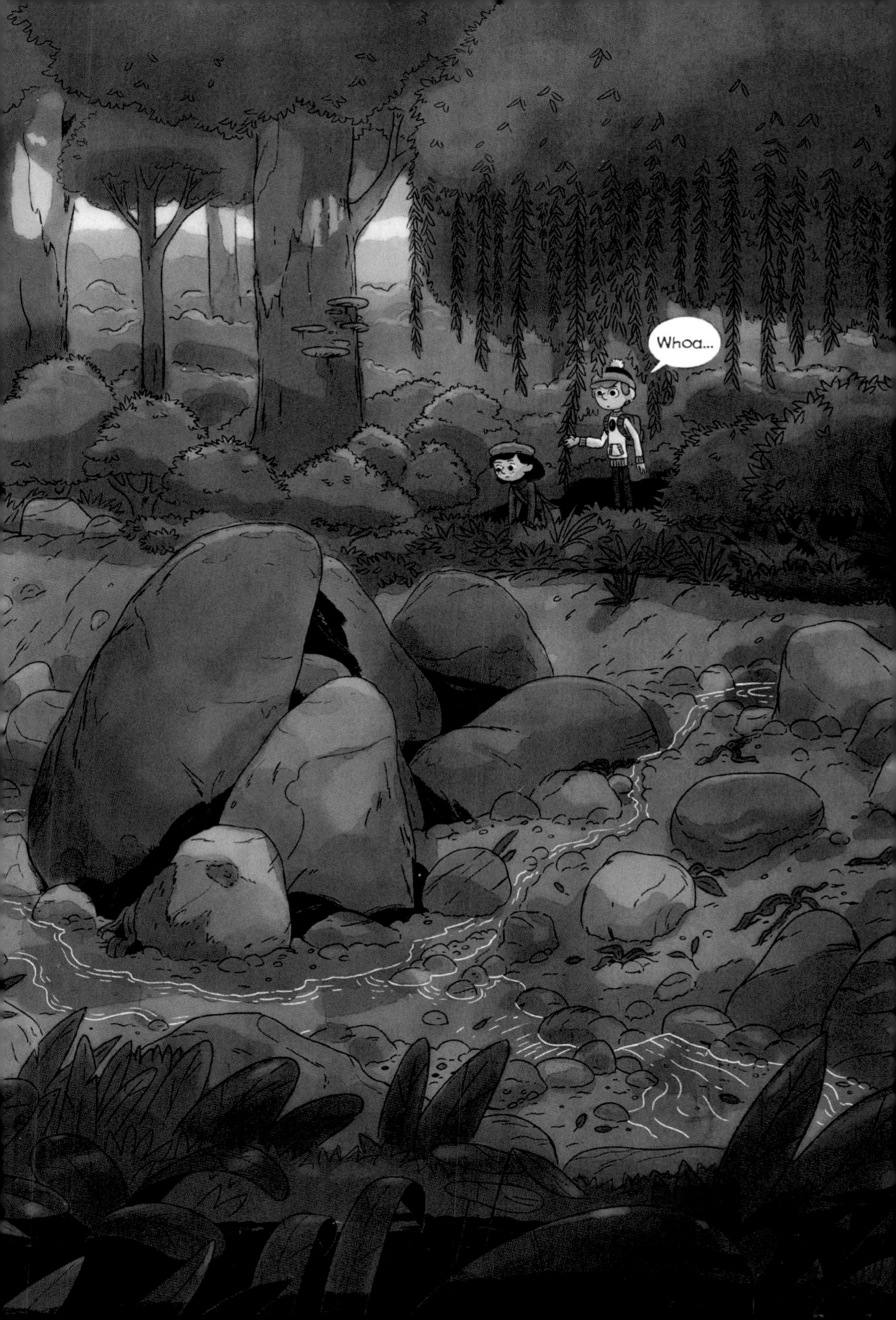
Whoa...

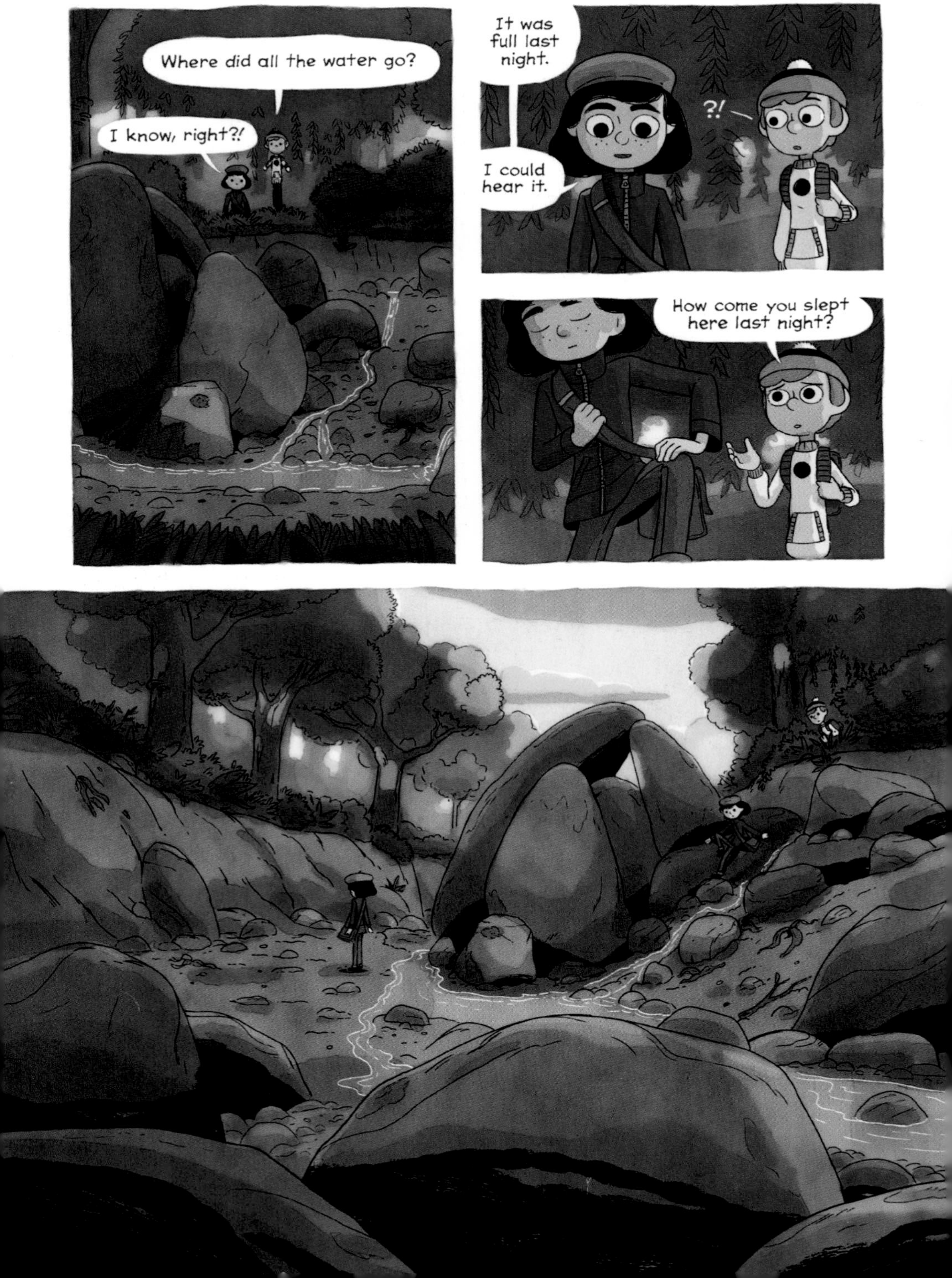
Where did all the water go?
I know, right?!
It was full last night.
I could hear it.
?!
How come you slept here last night?

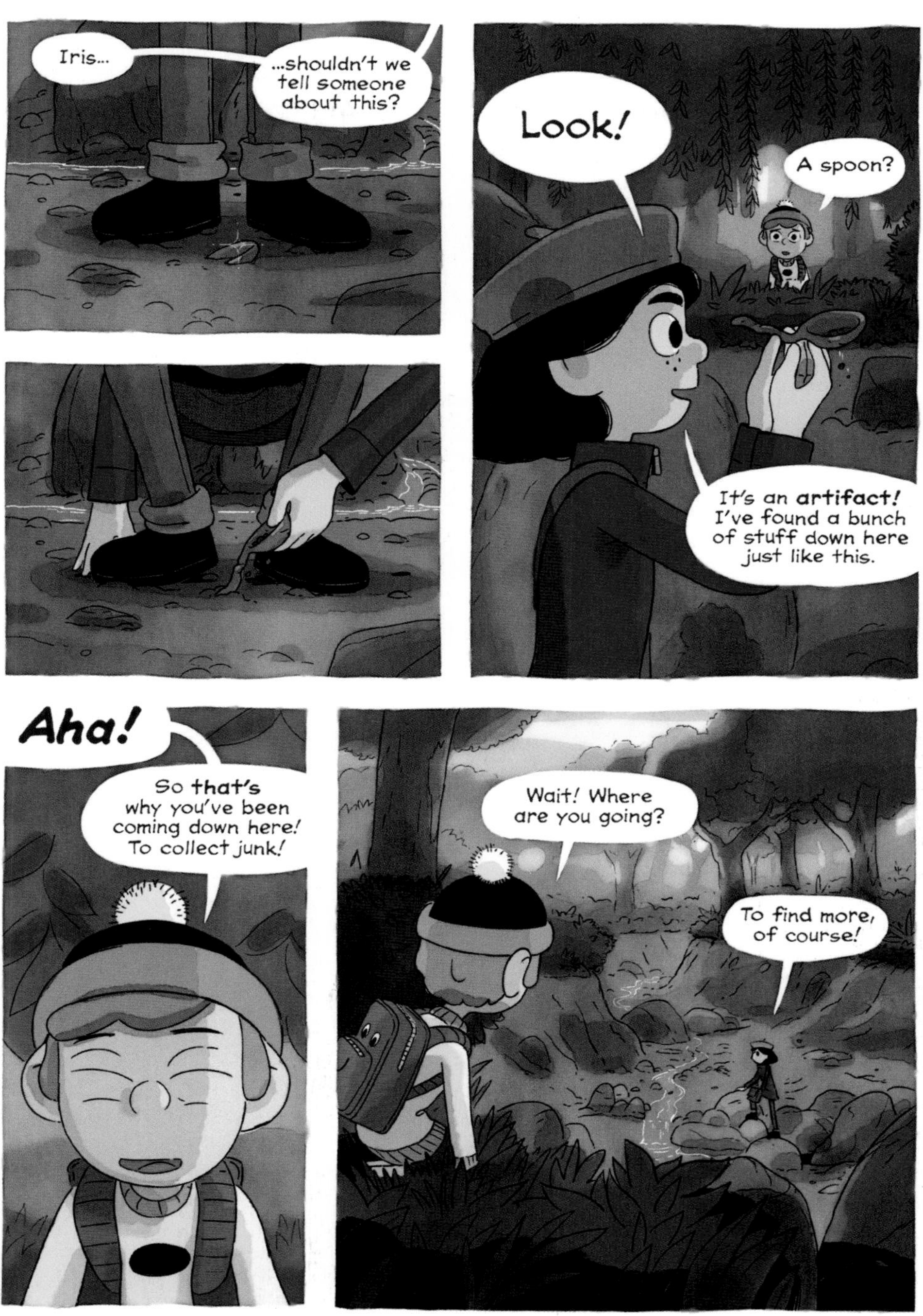
Iris...
...shouldn't we tell someone about this?
Look!
A spoon?
It's an **artifact!** I've found a bunch of stuff down here just like this.
Aha!
So **that's** why you've been coming down here! To collect junk!
Wait! Where are you going?
To find more, of course!

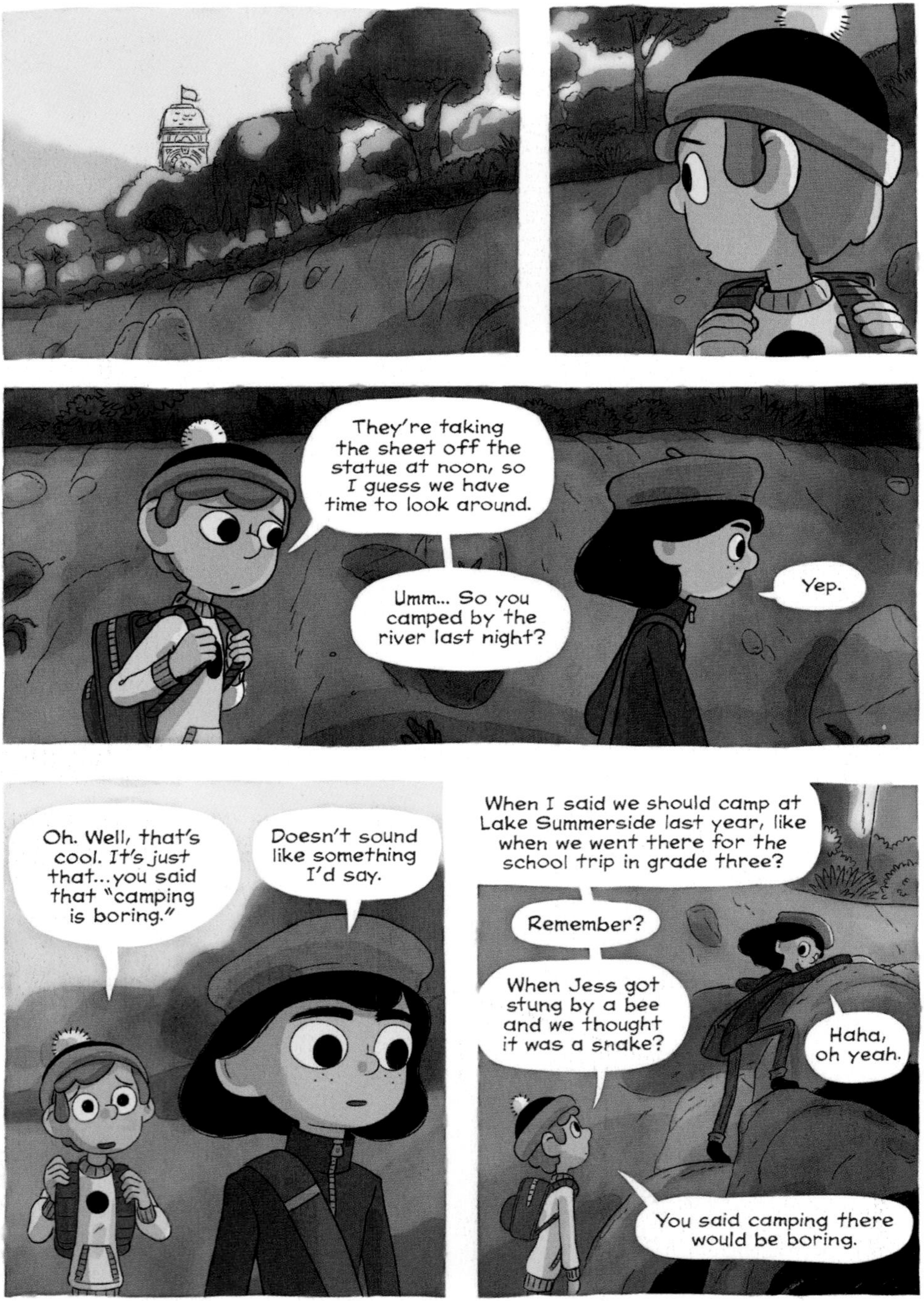
They're taking the sheet off the statue at noon, so I guess we have time to look around.
Umm... So you camped by the river last night?
Yep.
Oh. Well, that's cool. It's just that...you said that "camping is boring."
Doesn't sound like something I'd say.
When I said we should camp at Lake Summerside last year, like when we went there for the school trip in grade three?
Remember?
When Jess got stung by a bee and we thought it was a snake?
Haha, oh yeah.
You said camping there would be boring.

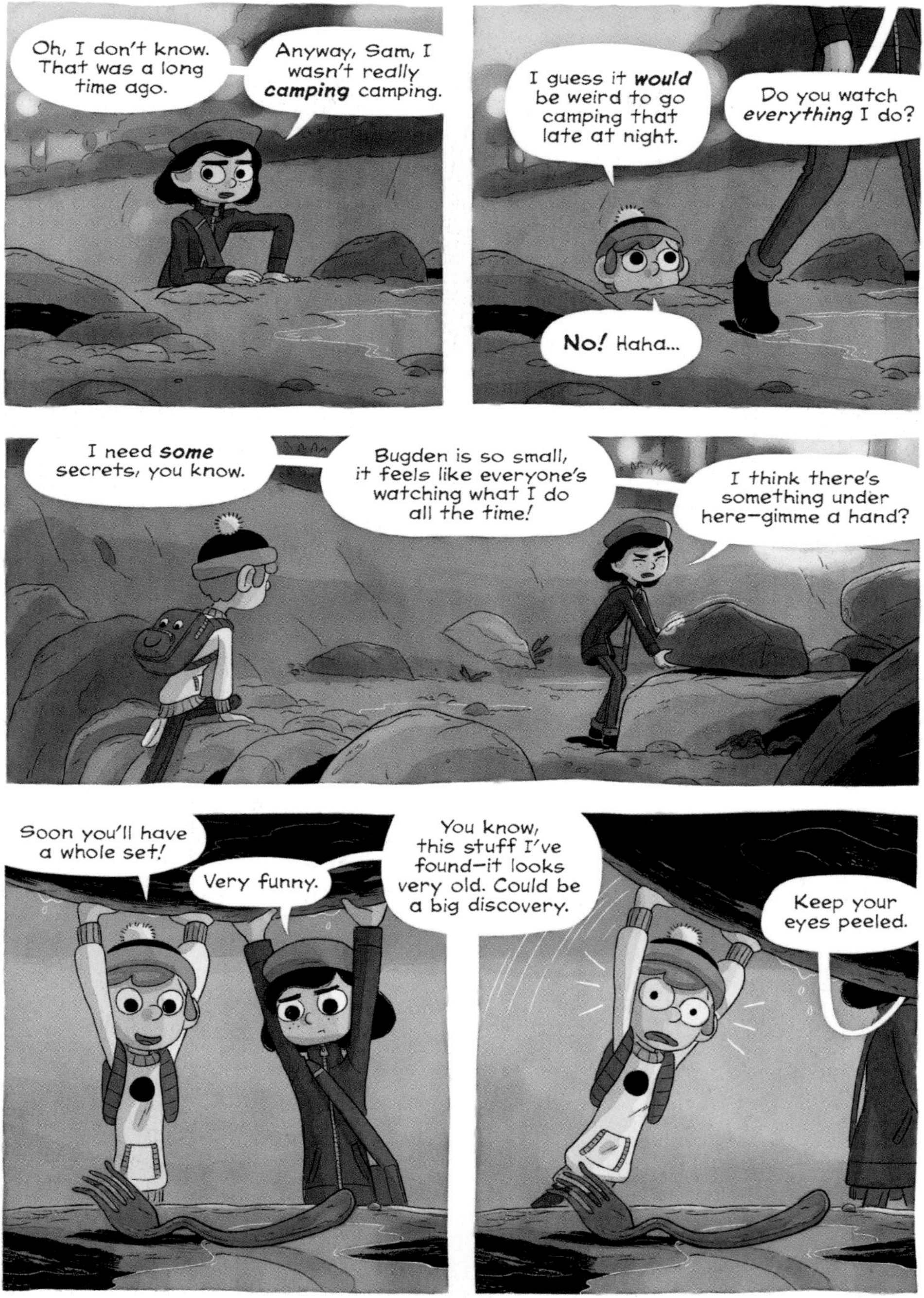
Oh, I don't know. That was a long time ago.
Anyway, Sam, I wasn't really **camping** camping.
I guess it **would** be weird to go camping that late at night.
Do you watch *everything* I do?
No! Haha...
I need **some** secrets, you know.
Bugden is so small, it feels like everyone's watching what I do all the time!
I think there's something under here—gimme a hand?
Soon you'll have a whole set!
Very funny.
You know, this stuff I've found—it looks very old. Could be a big discovery.
Keep your eyes peeled.

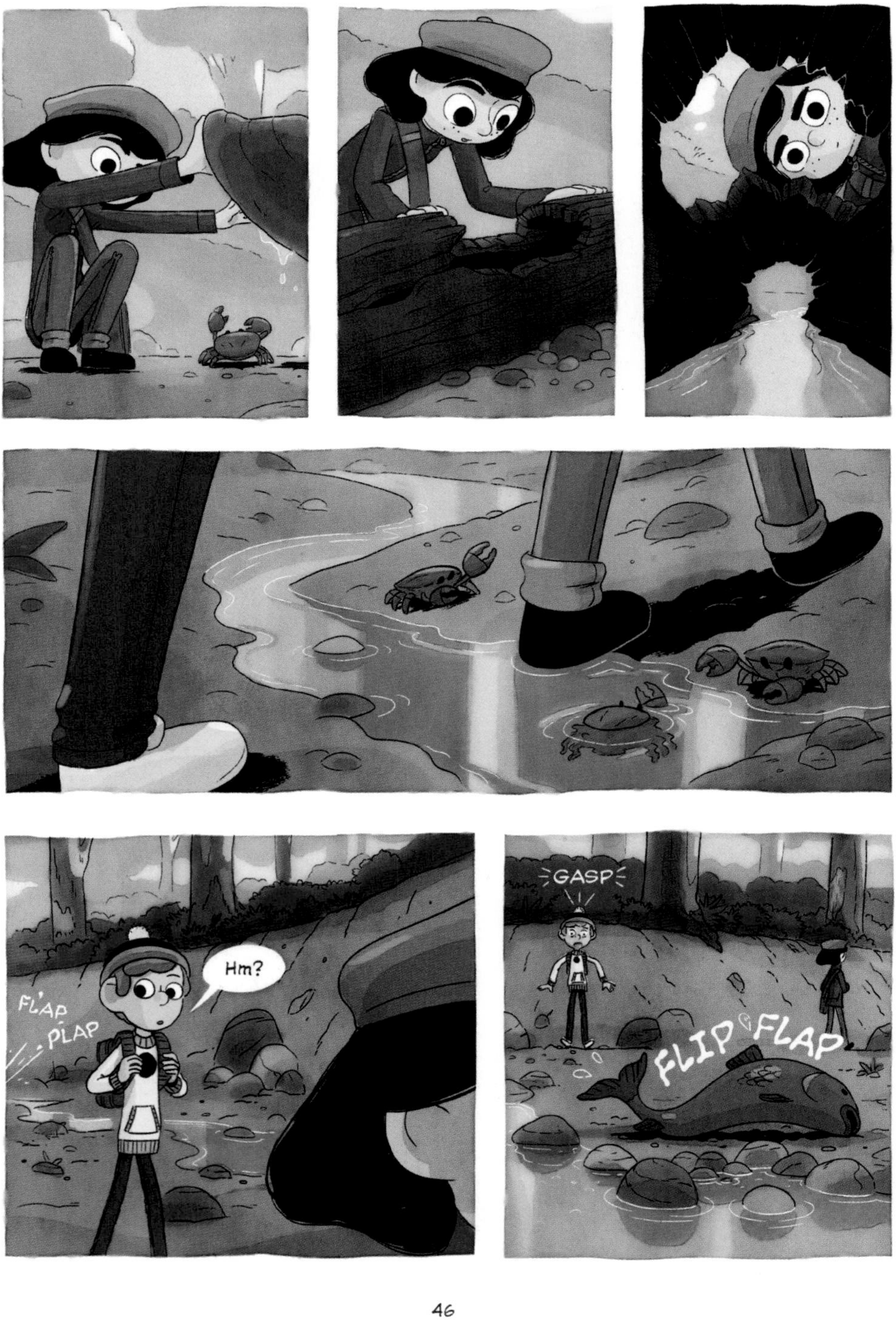
FL'AP
PLAP
Hm?
GASP
FLIP FLAP

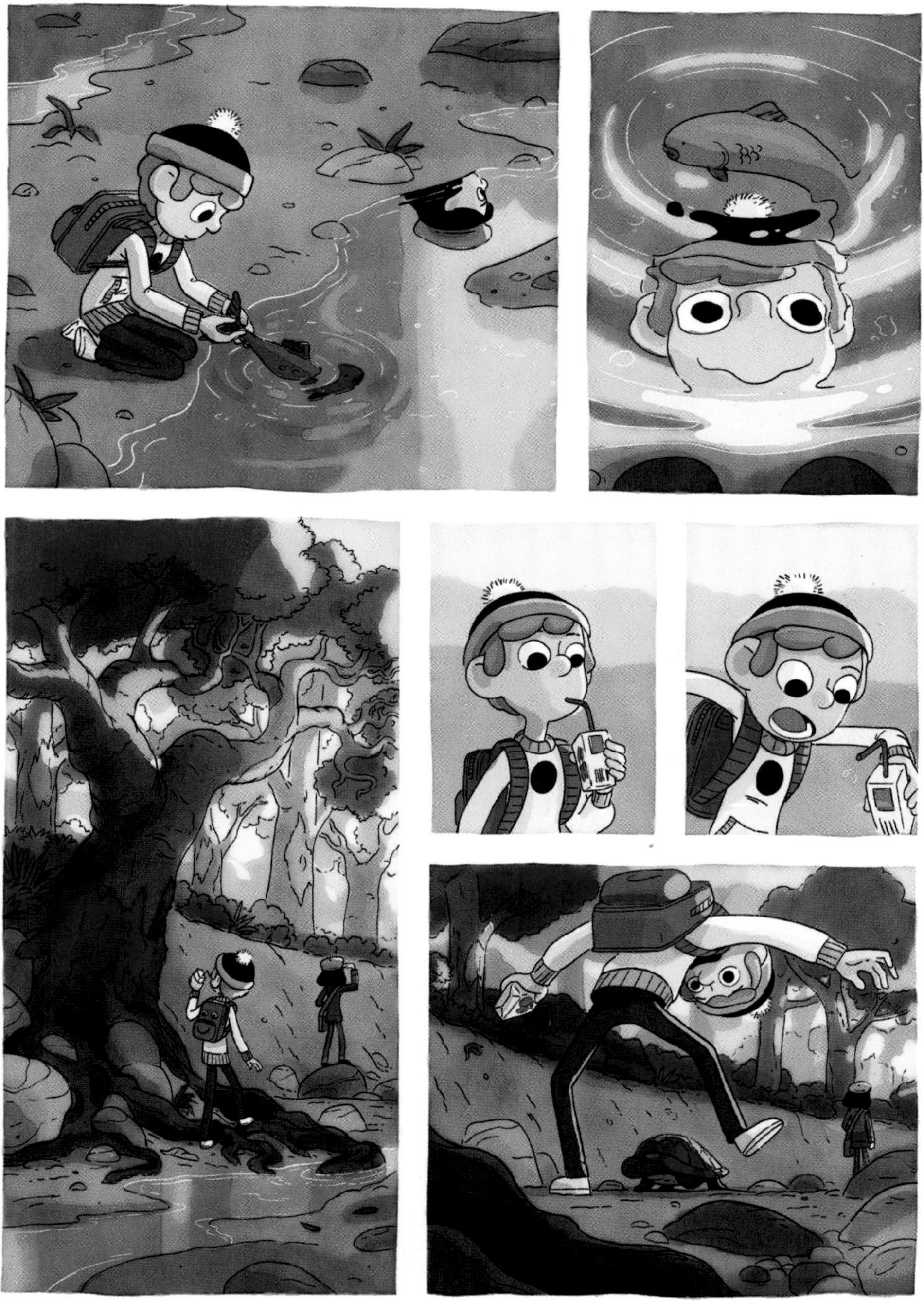

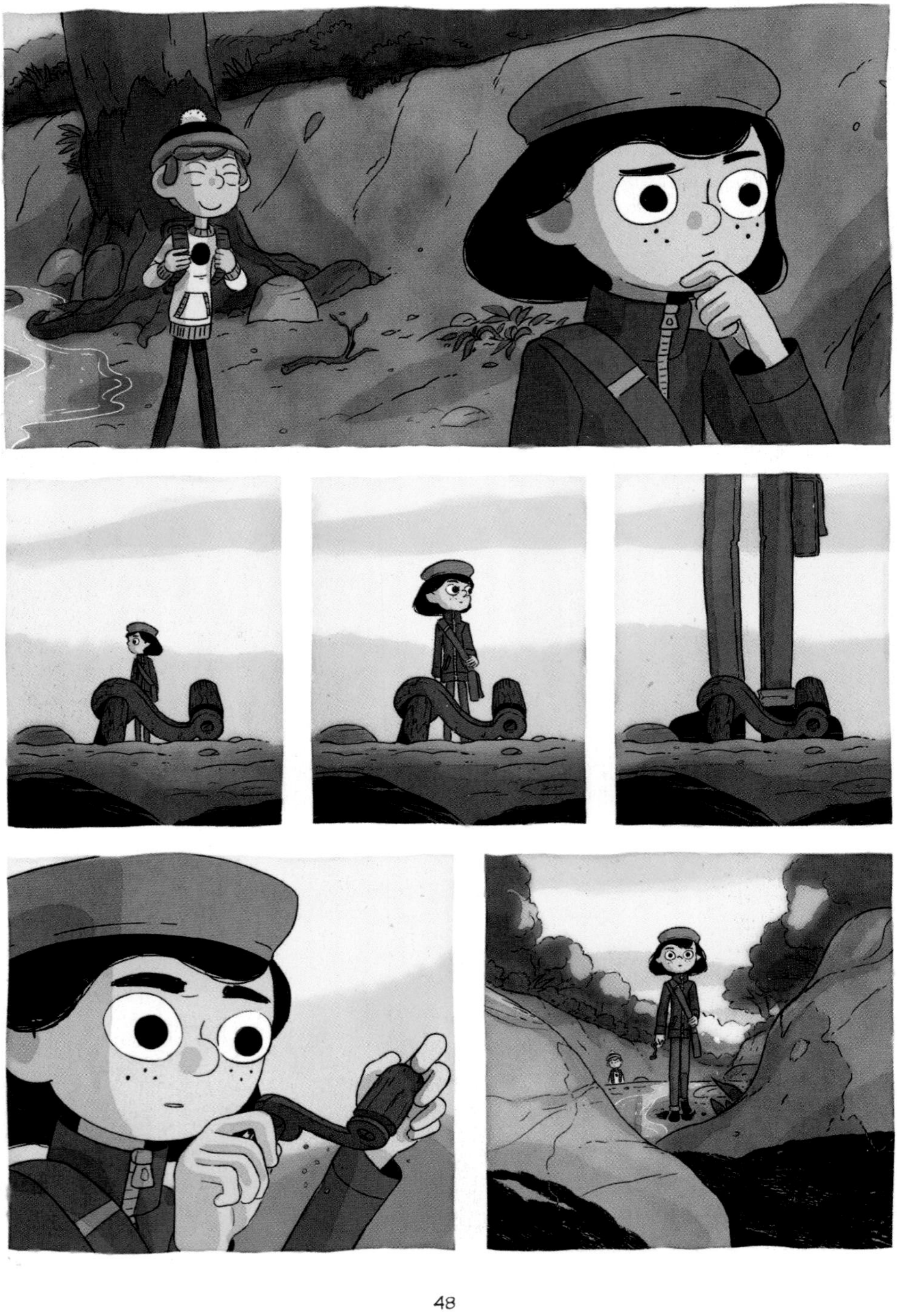

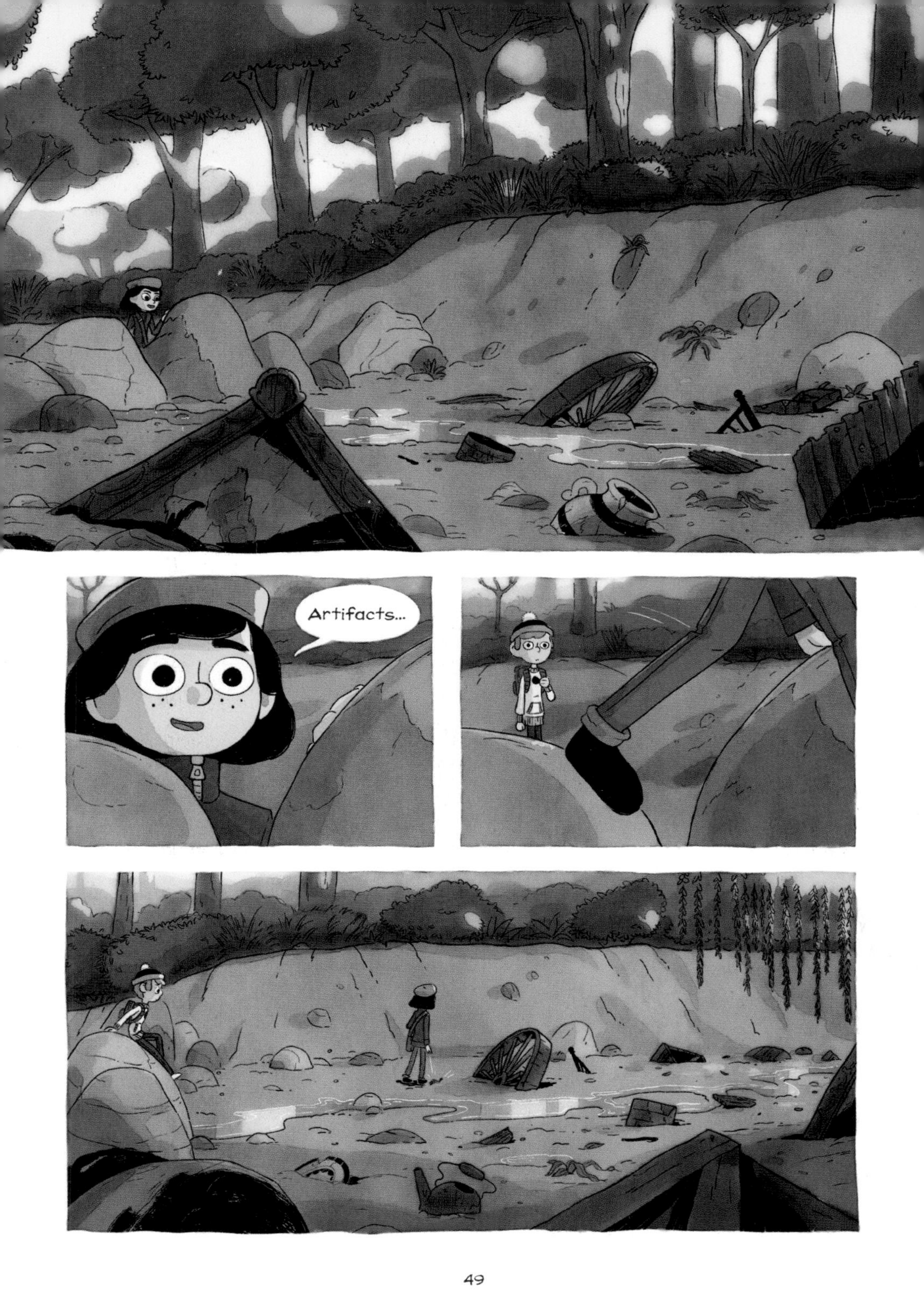
Artifacts...

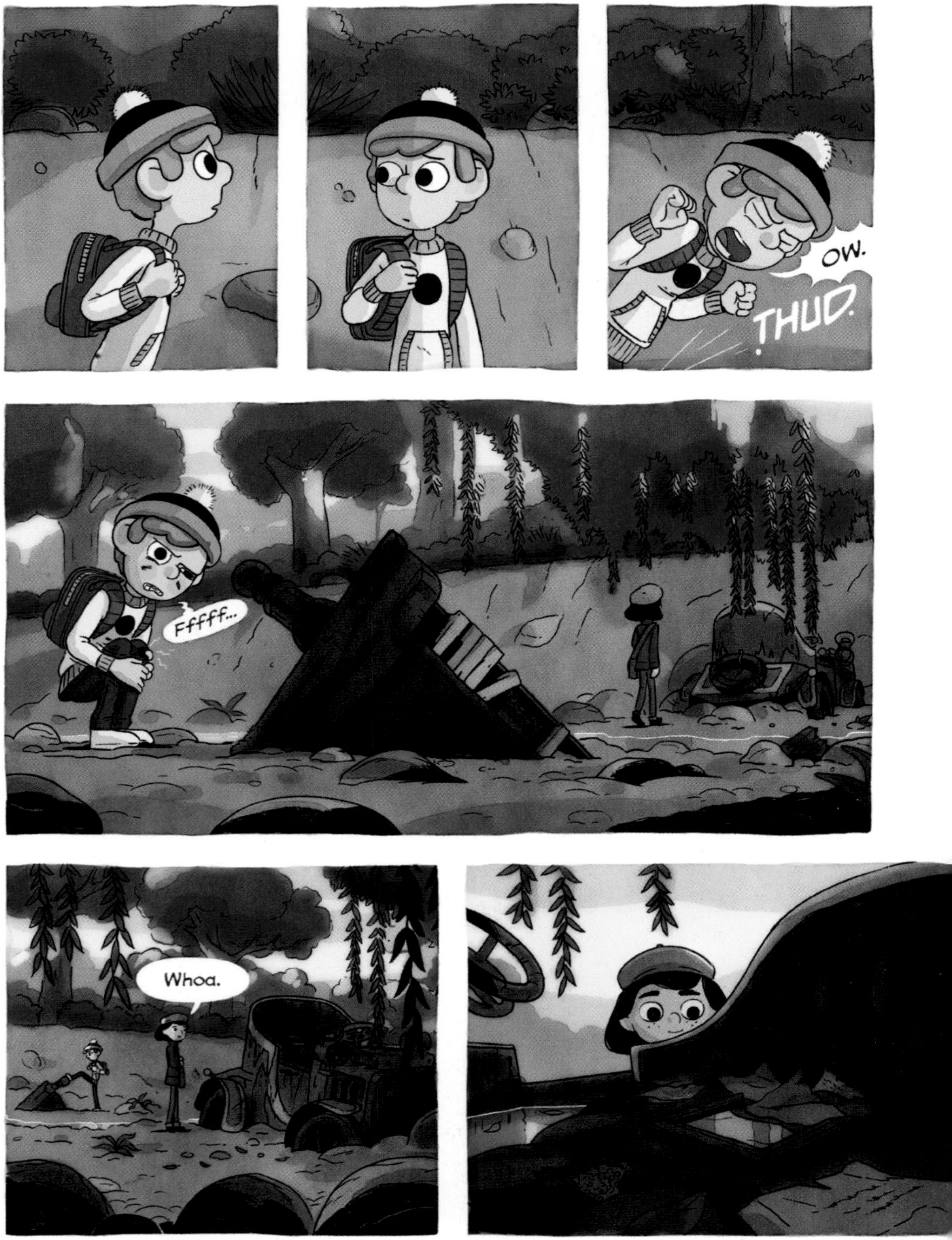
OW.
THUD.
Fffff...
Whoa.

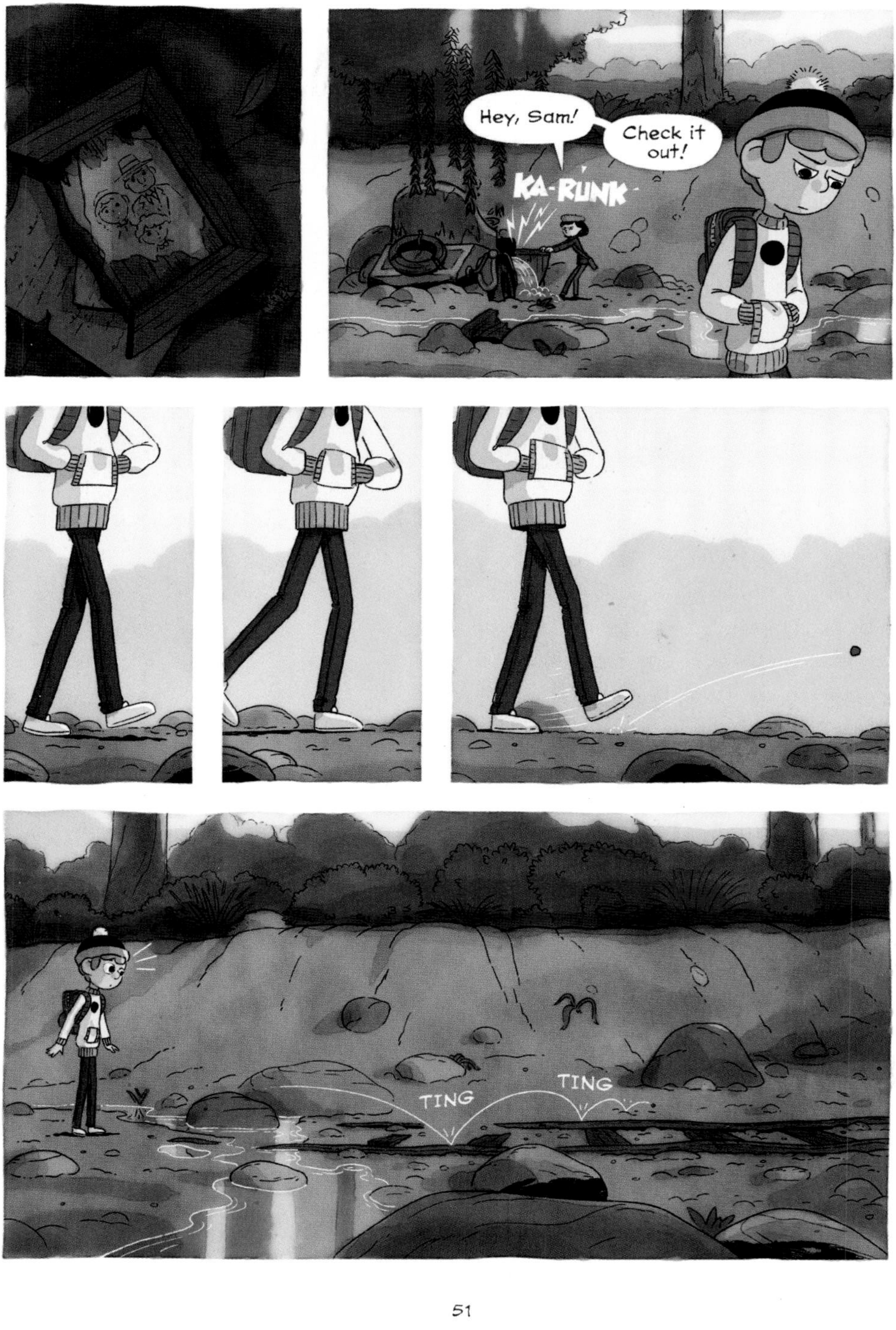

Hey, Sam!
Check it out!
KA-RUNK
TING
TING

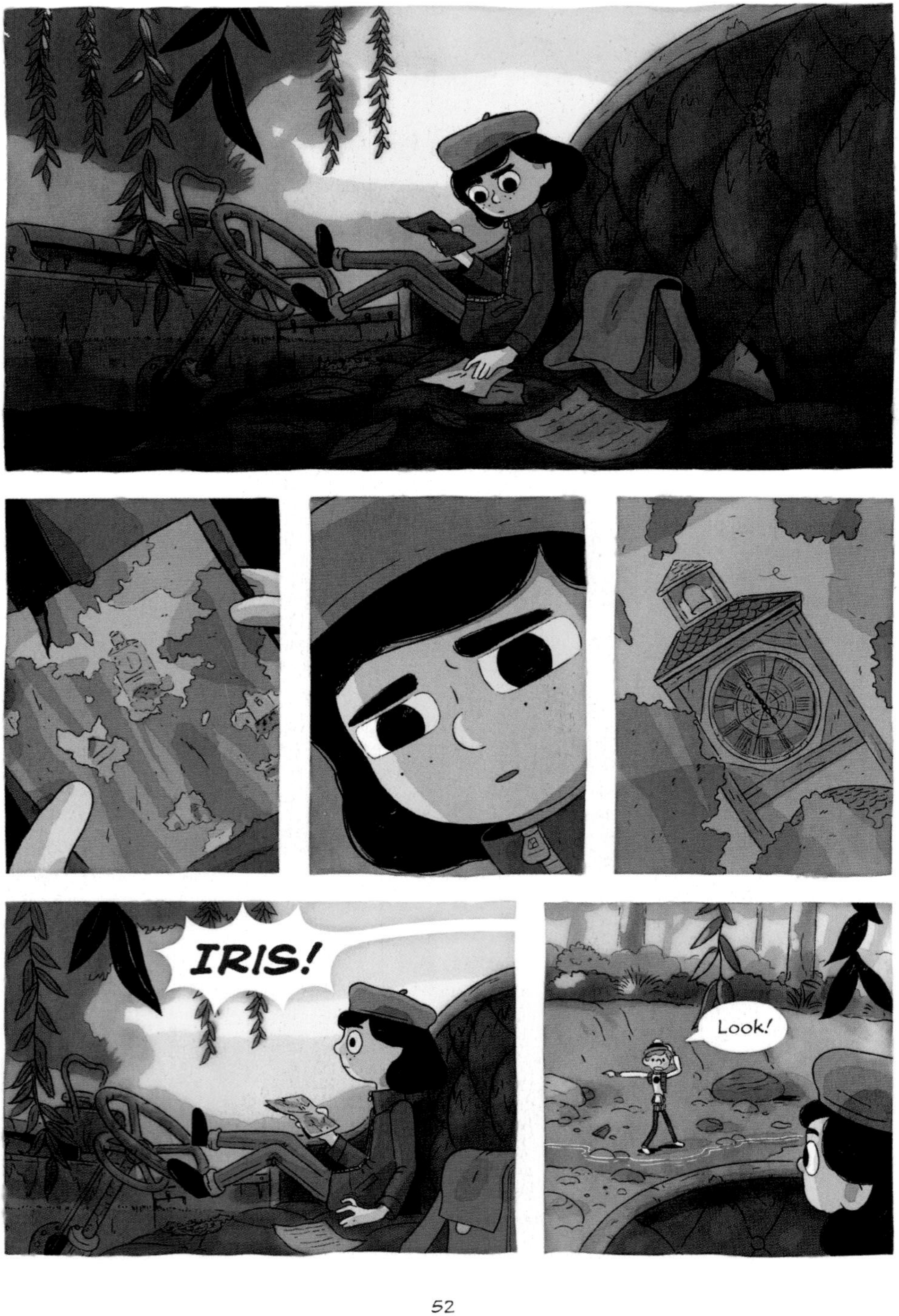
IRIS!
Look!

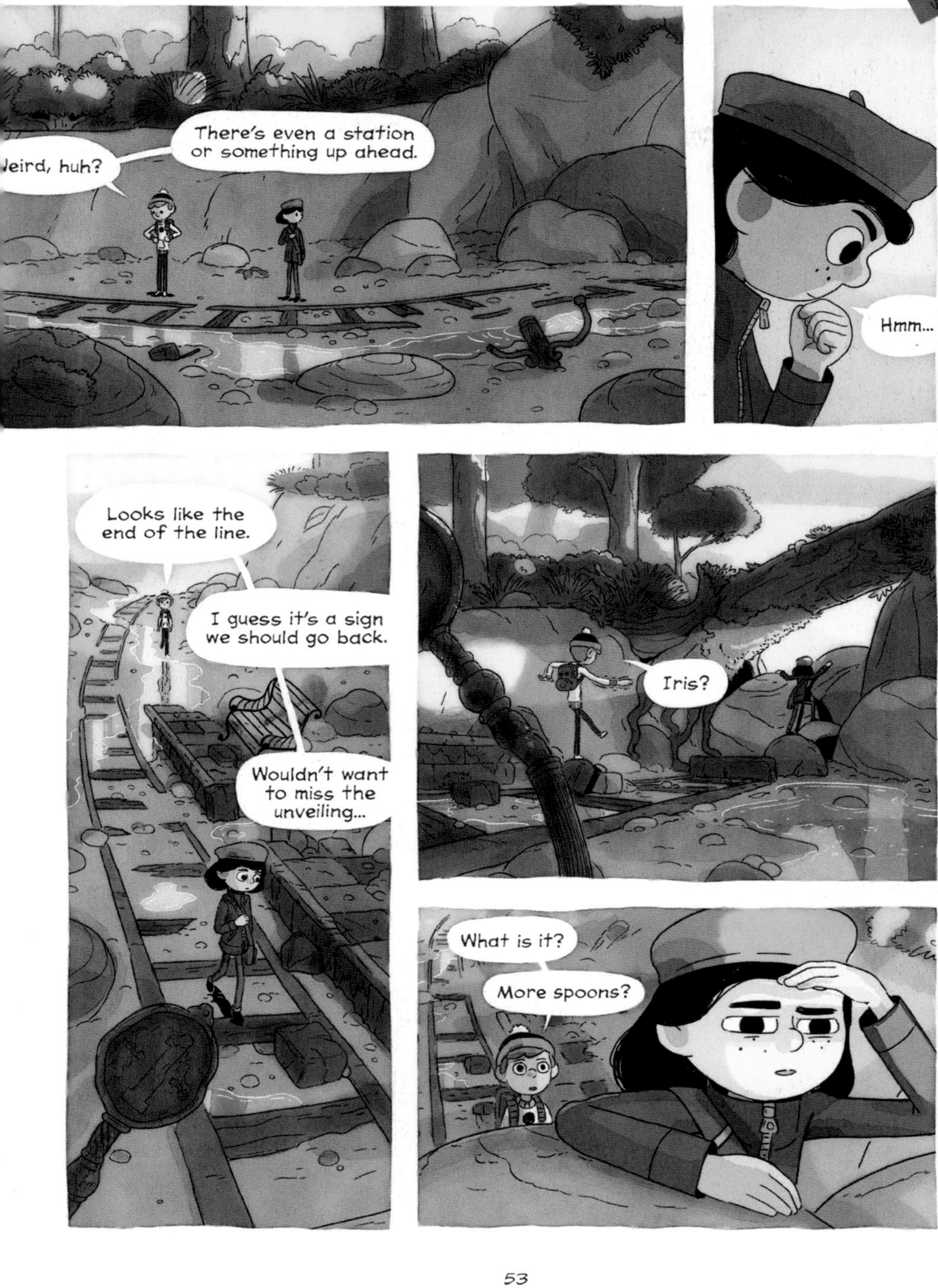
Weird, huh?
There's even a station or something up ahead.
Hmm...
Looks like the end of the line.
I guess it's a sign we should go back.
Wouldn't want to miss the unveiling...
Iris?
What is it?
More spoons?

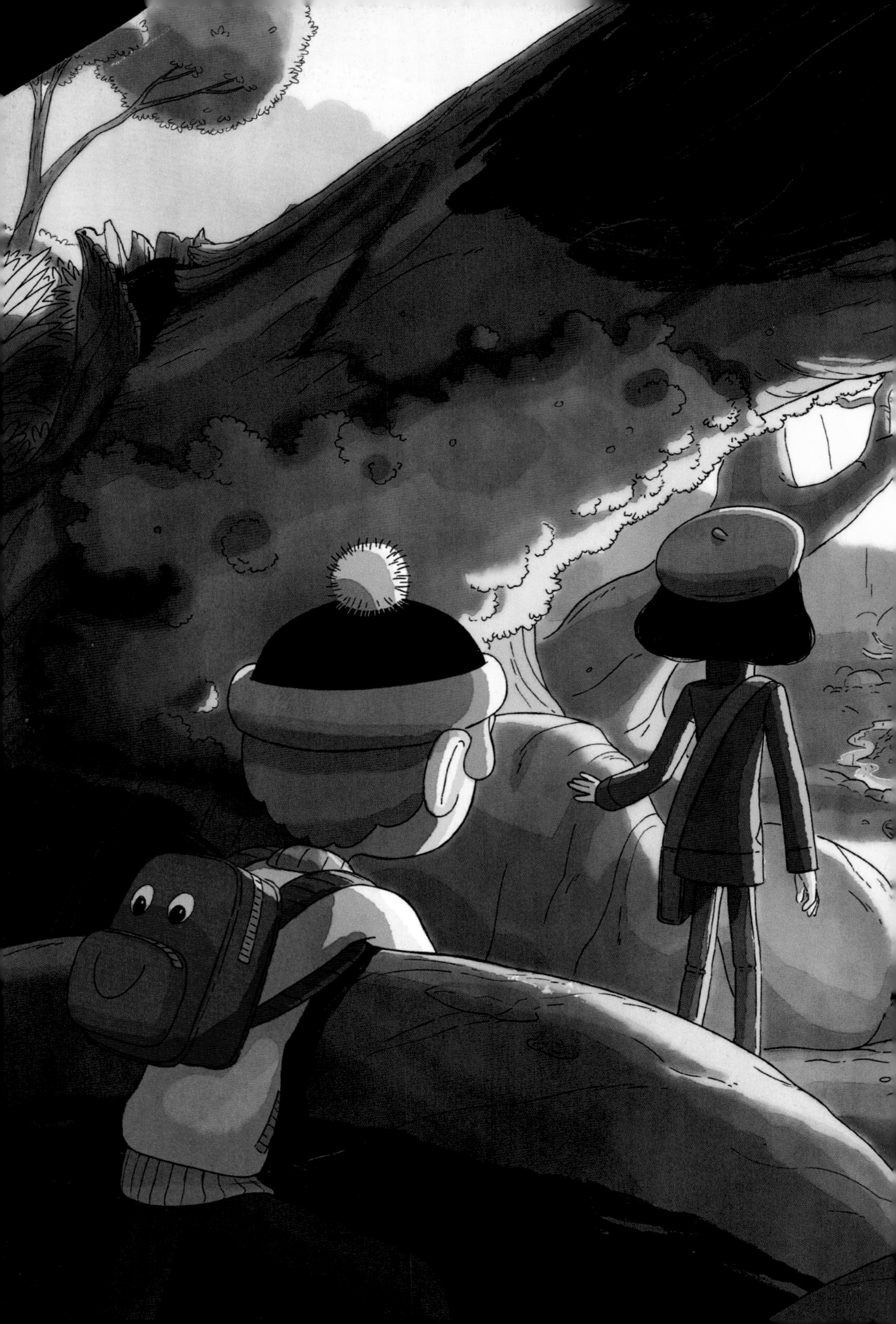

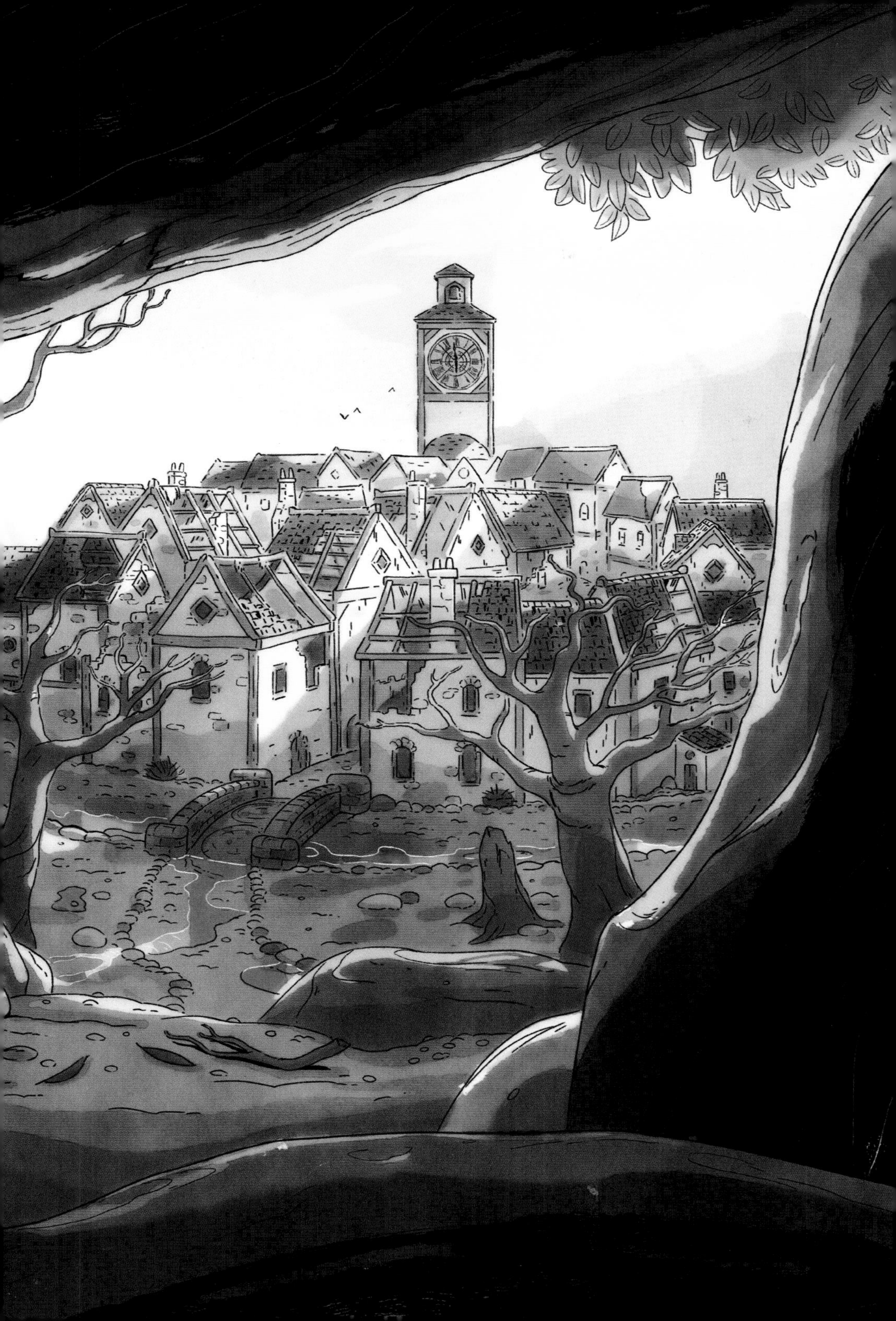

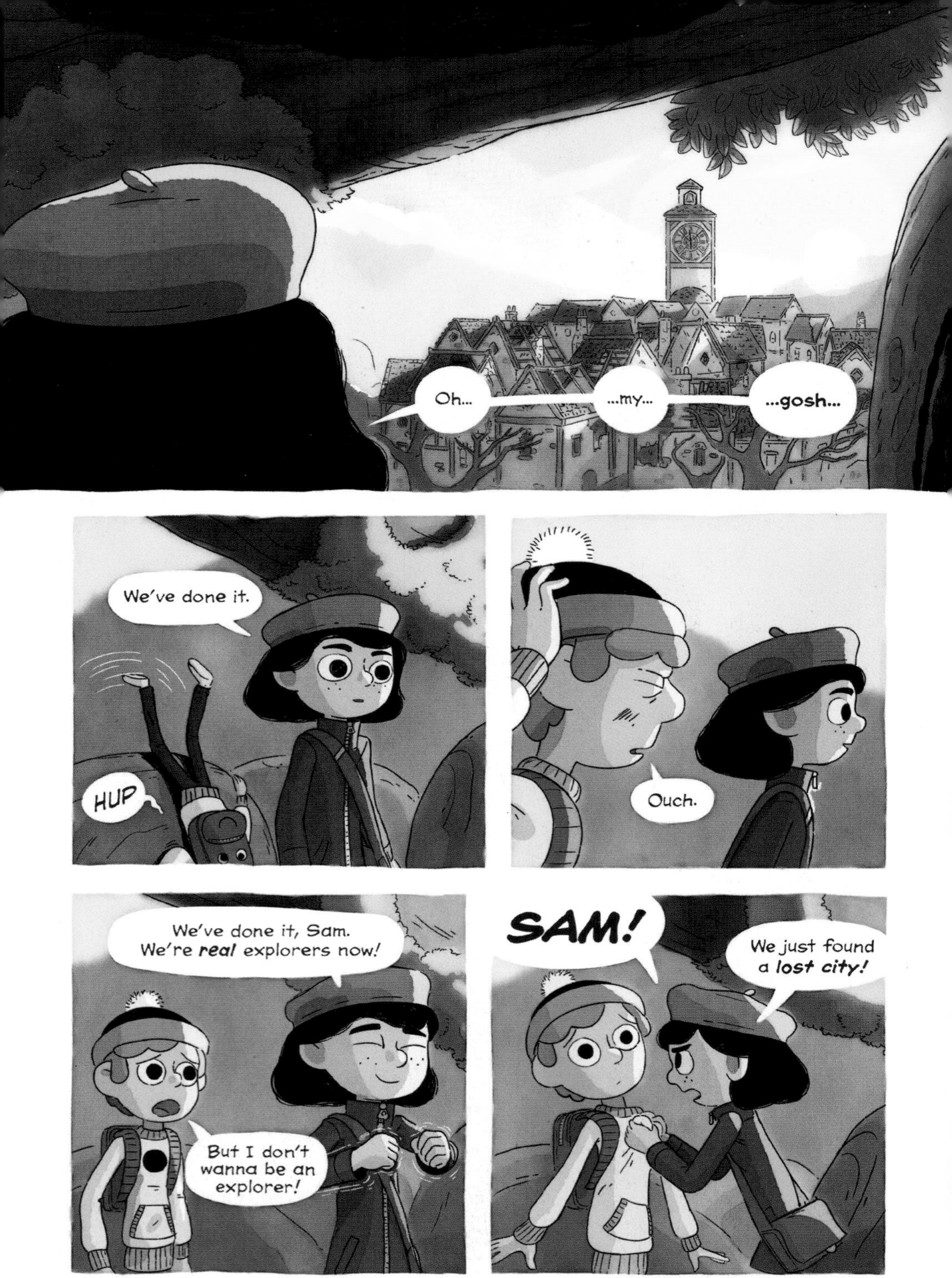
Oh...
...my...
...gosh...
We've done it.
HUP
Ouch.
We've done it, Sam. We're *real* explorers now!
But I don't wanna be an explorer!
SAM!
We just found a **lost city!**

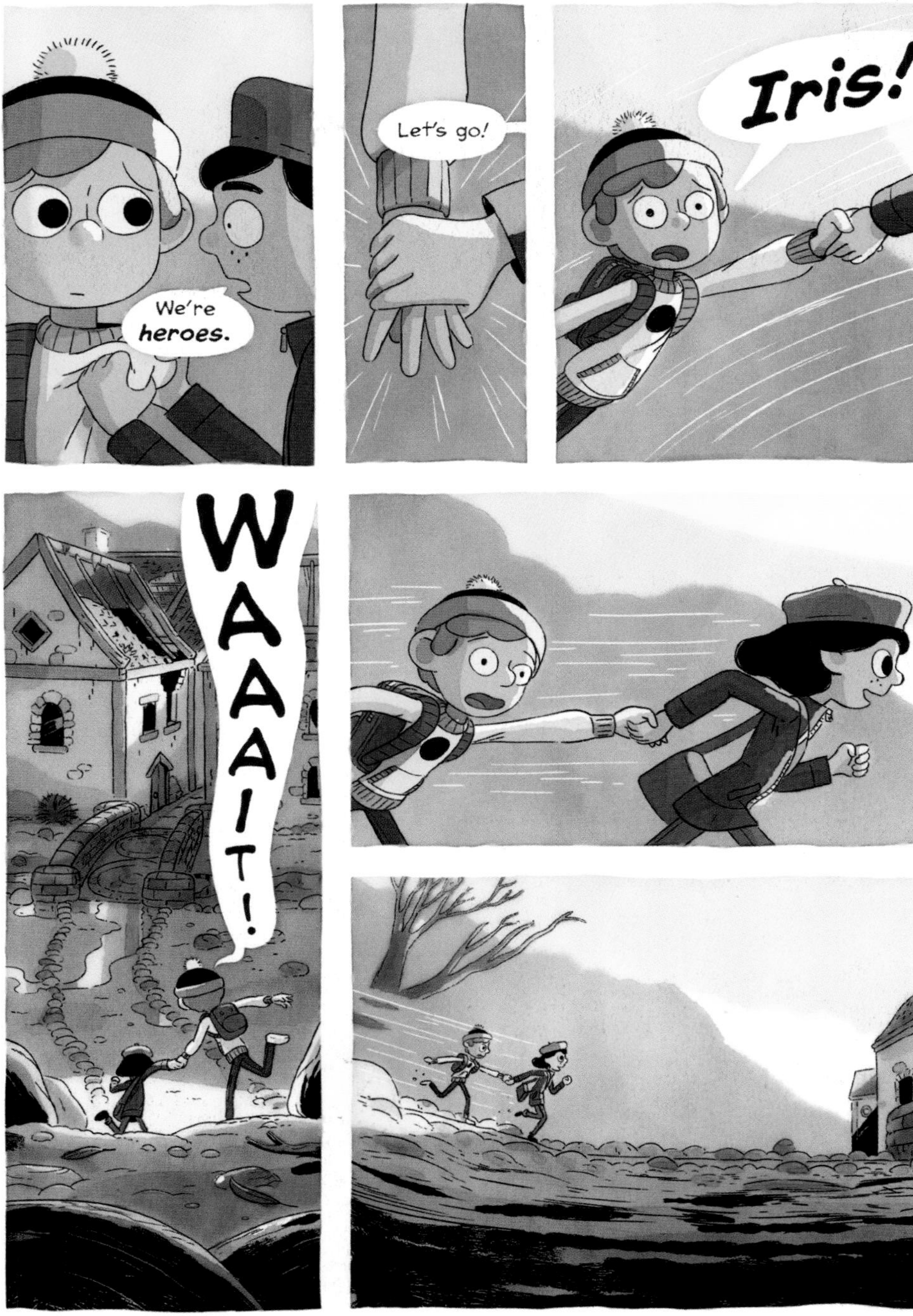
We're **heroes.**
Let's go!
Iris!
WAAAIT!

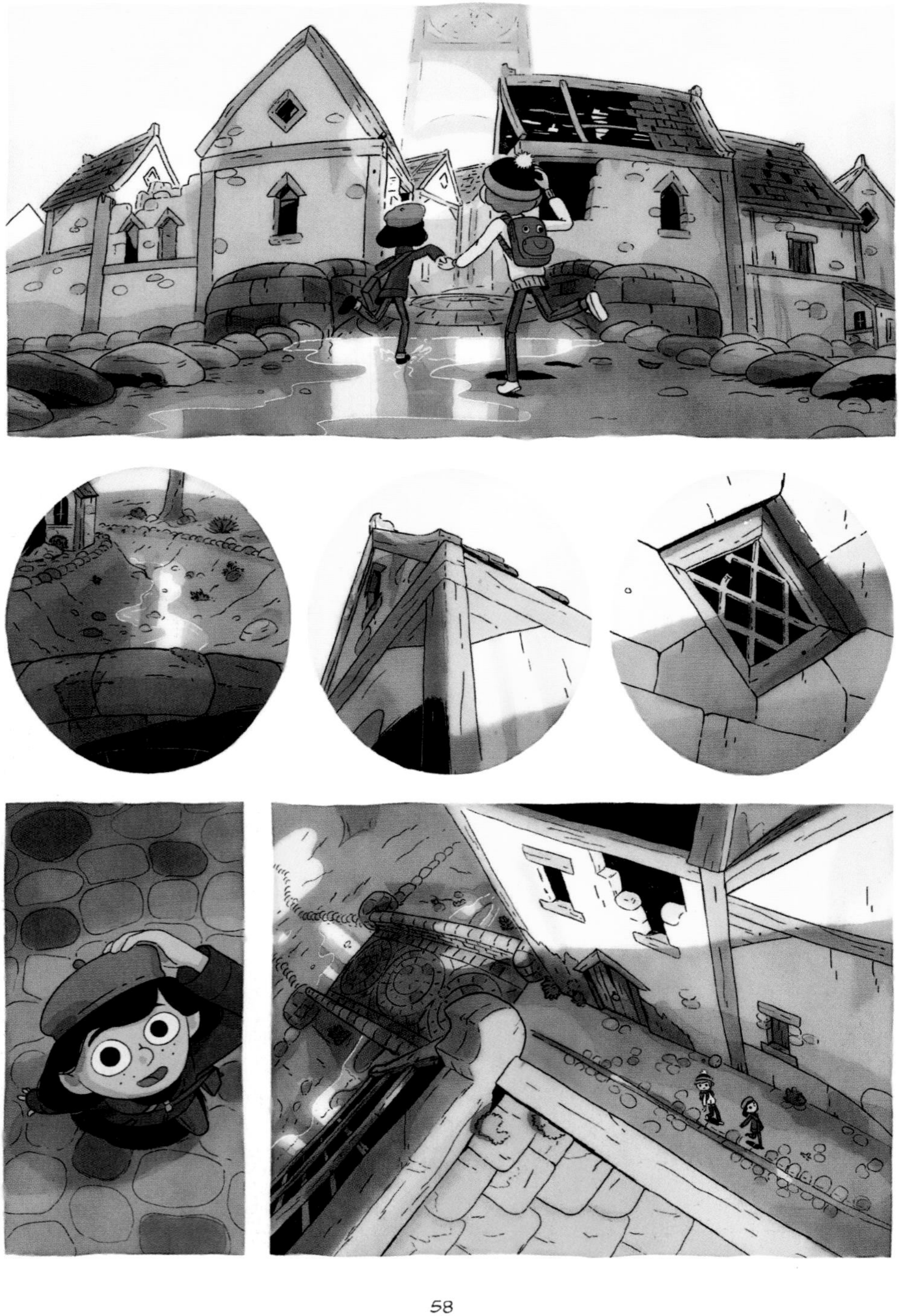

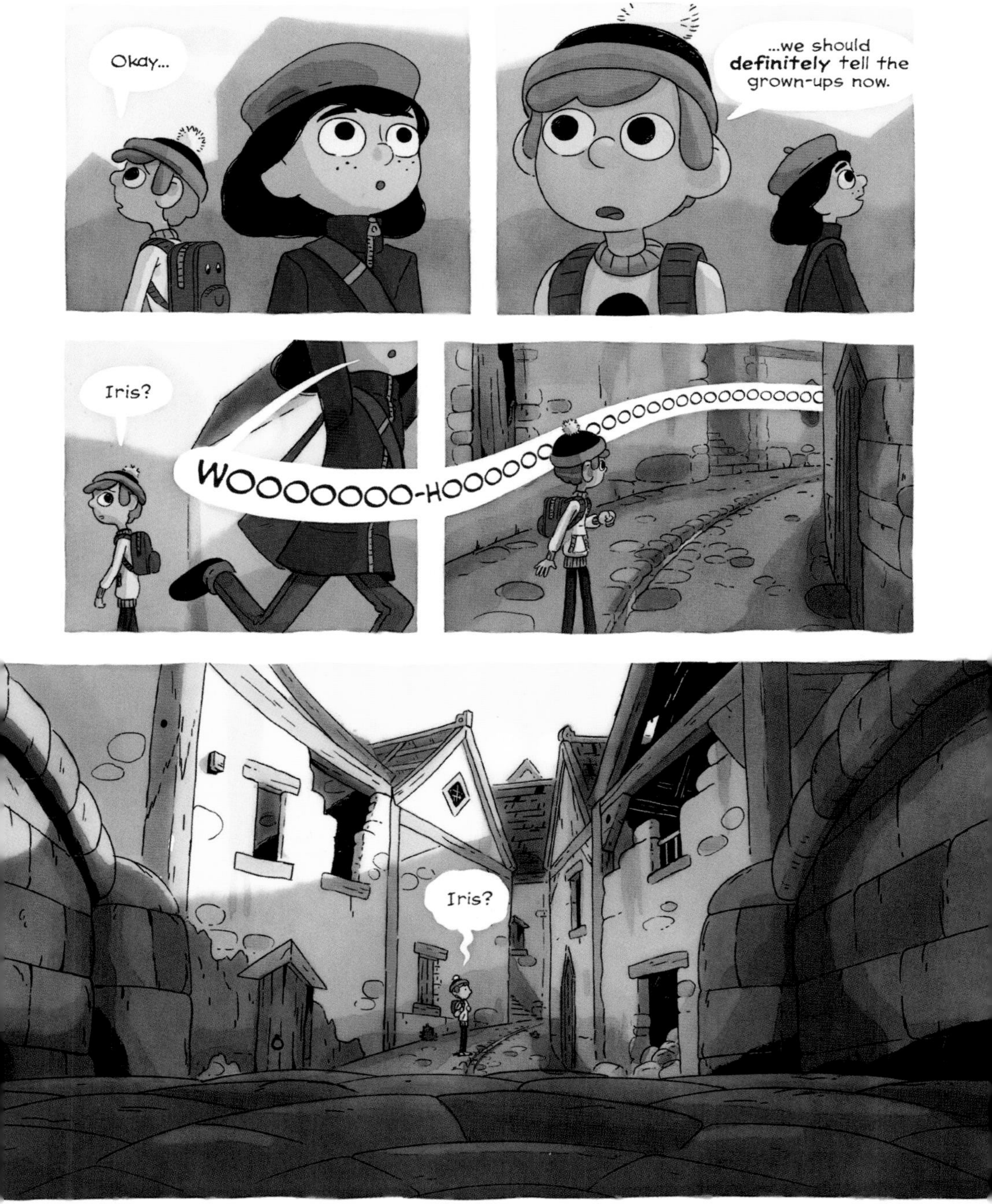
Okay...
...we should **definitely** tell the grown-ups now.
Iris?
WOOOOOOO-HOOOOOOOOOOOOOOOOOOOOOOOOOOOOOOO
Iris?

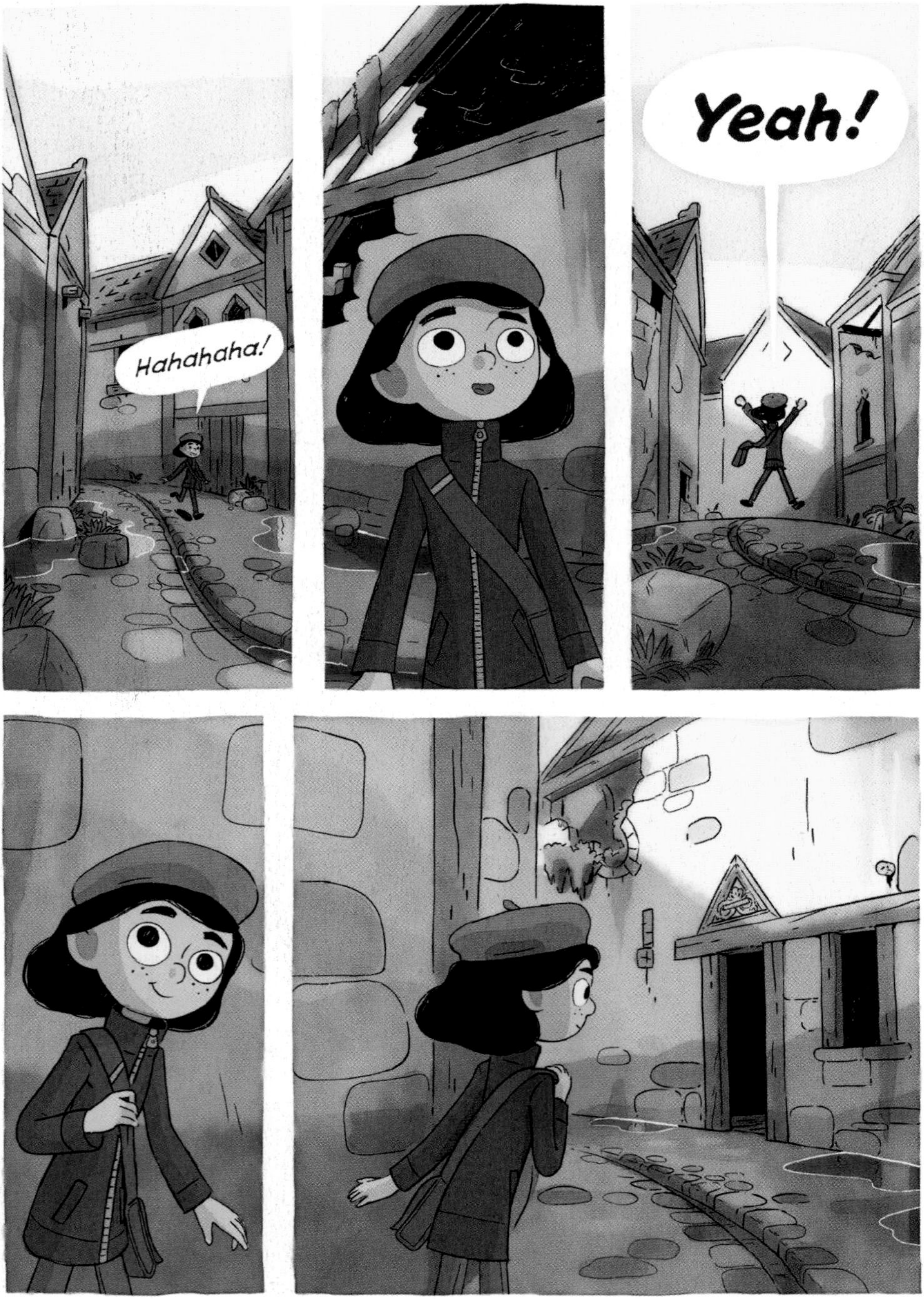
Hahahaha!
Yeah!

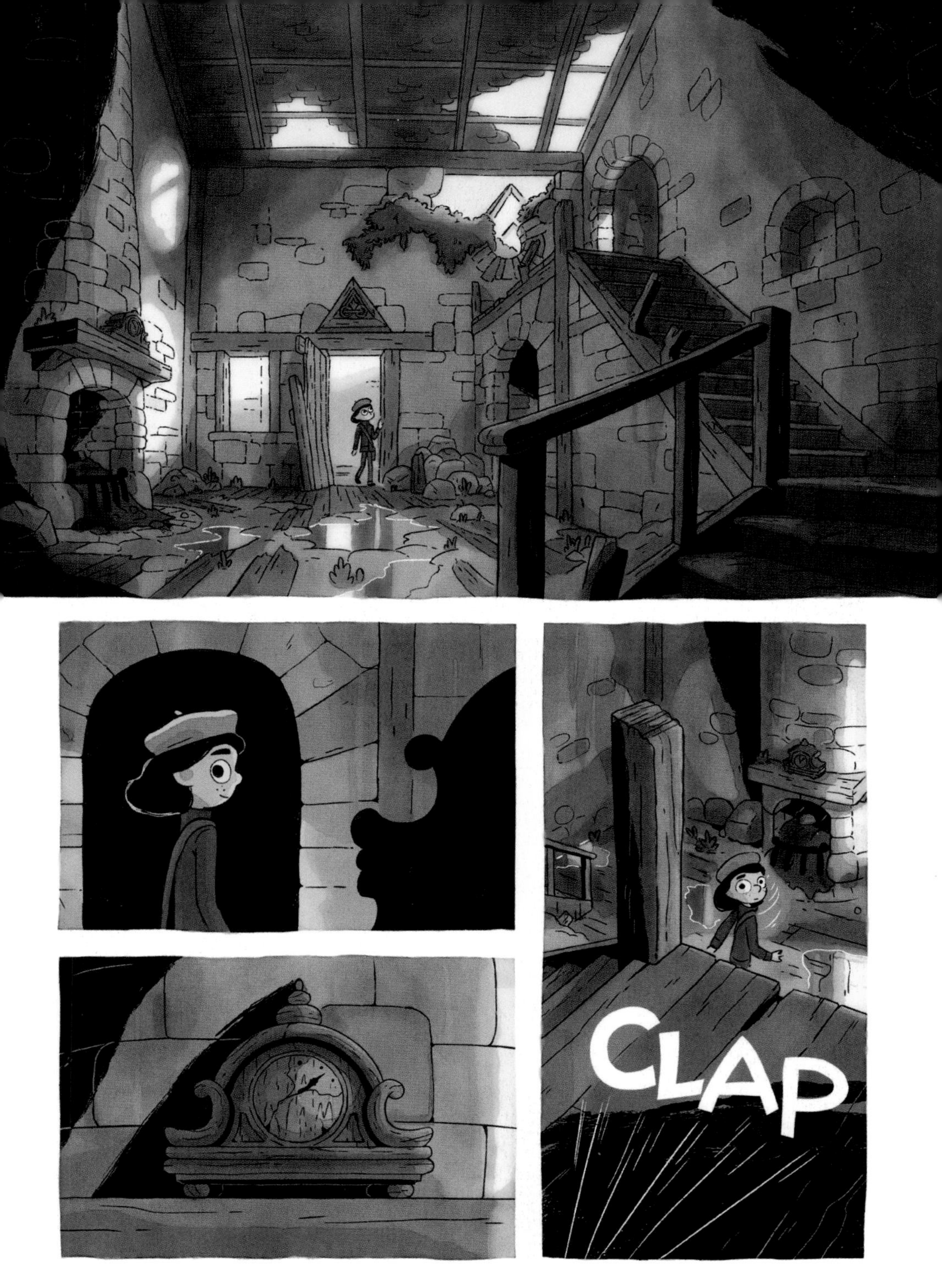
CLAP

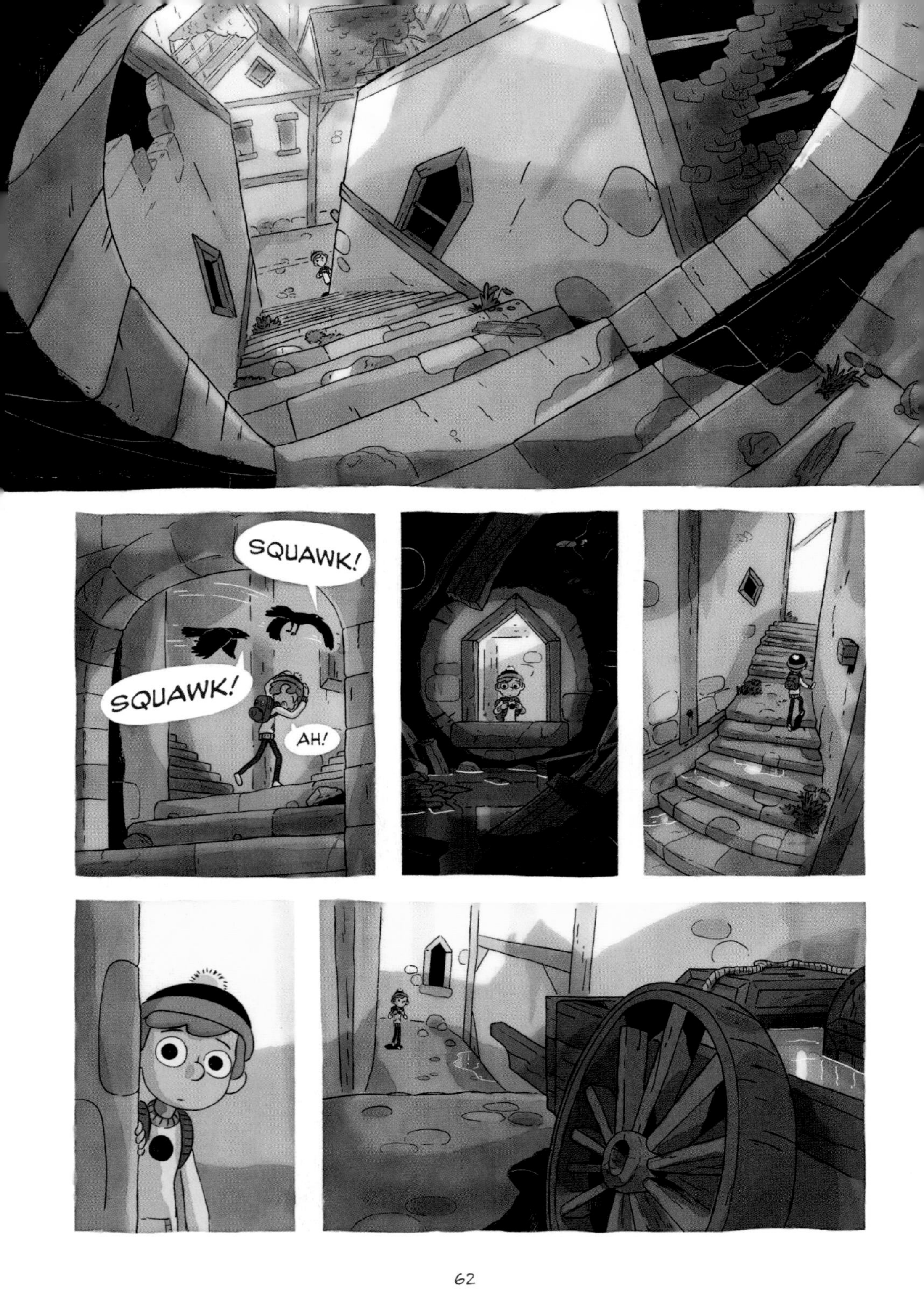
SQUAWK!
SQUAWK!
AH!

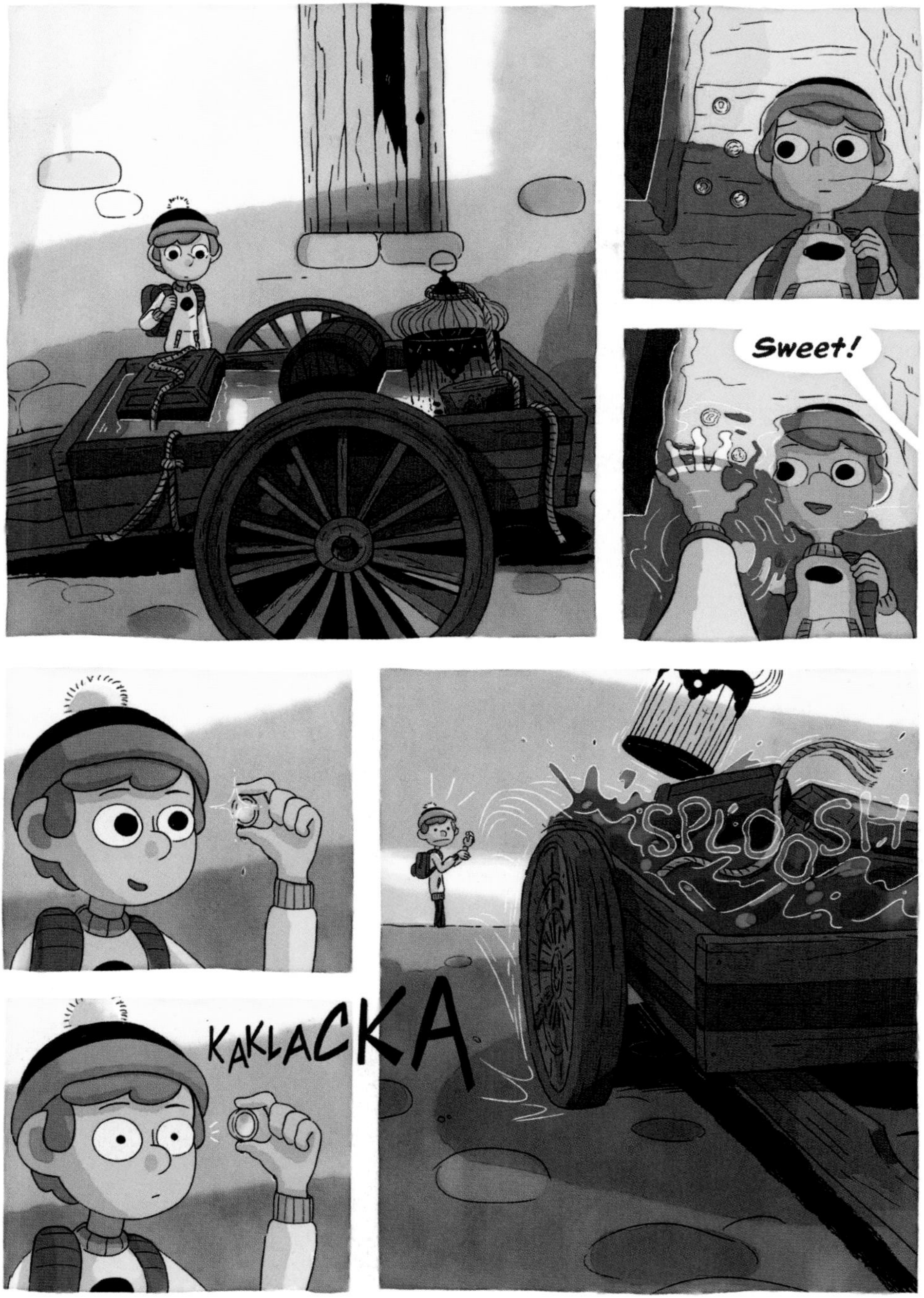
Sweet!
KAKLACKA
SPLOOSH

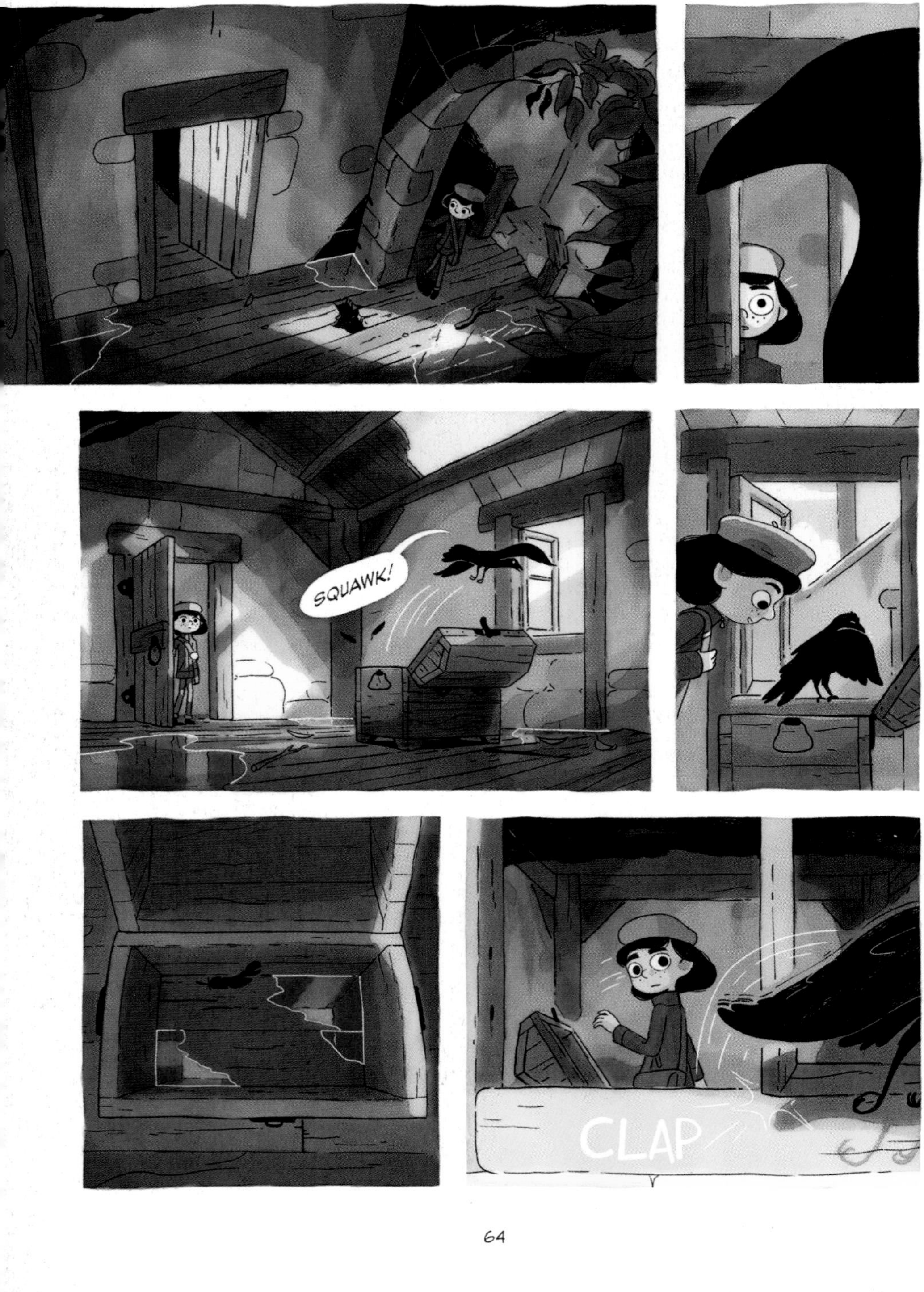
SQUAWK!
CLAP

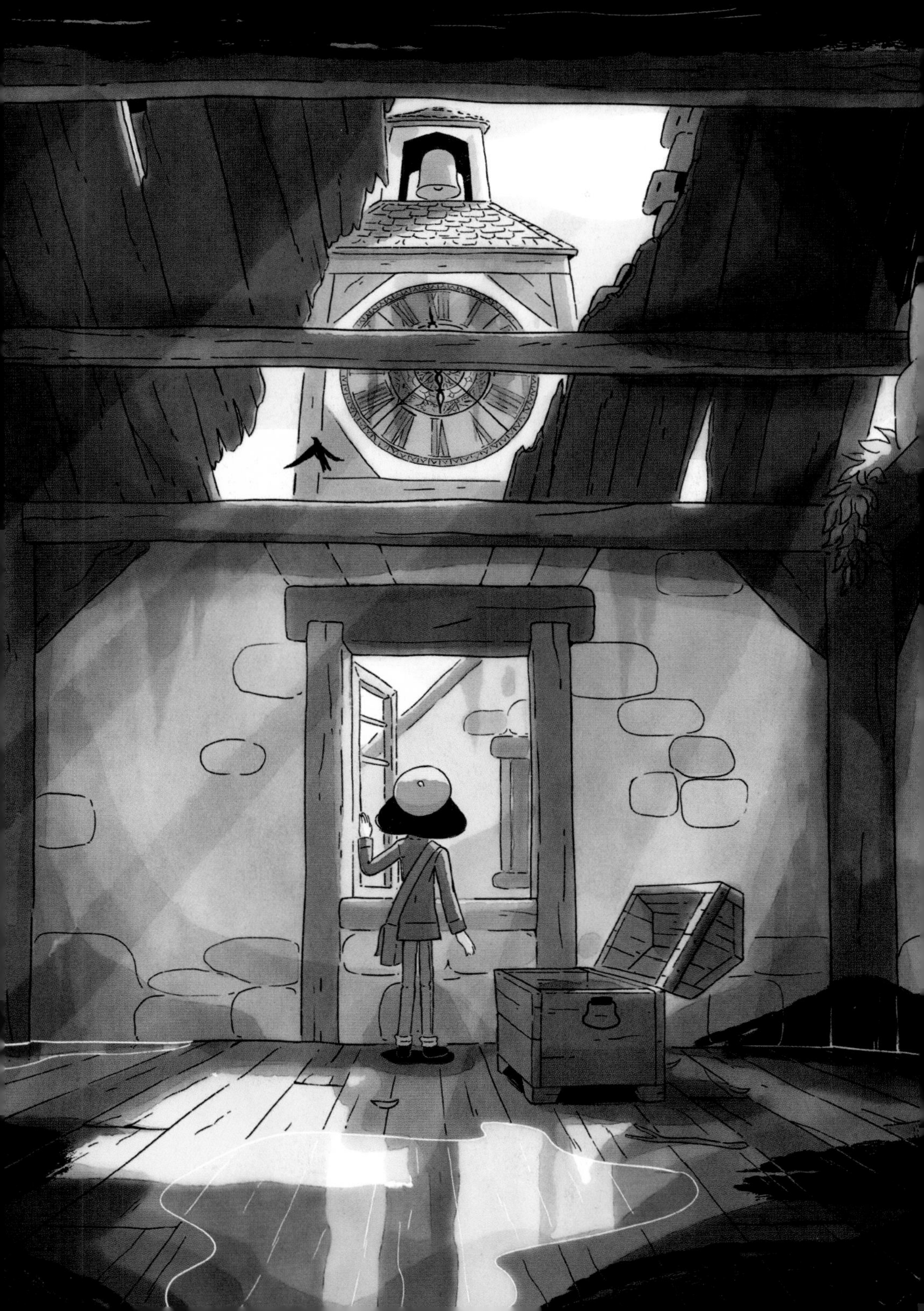

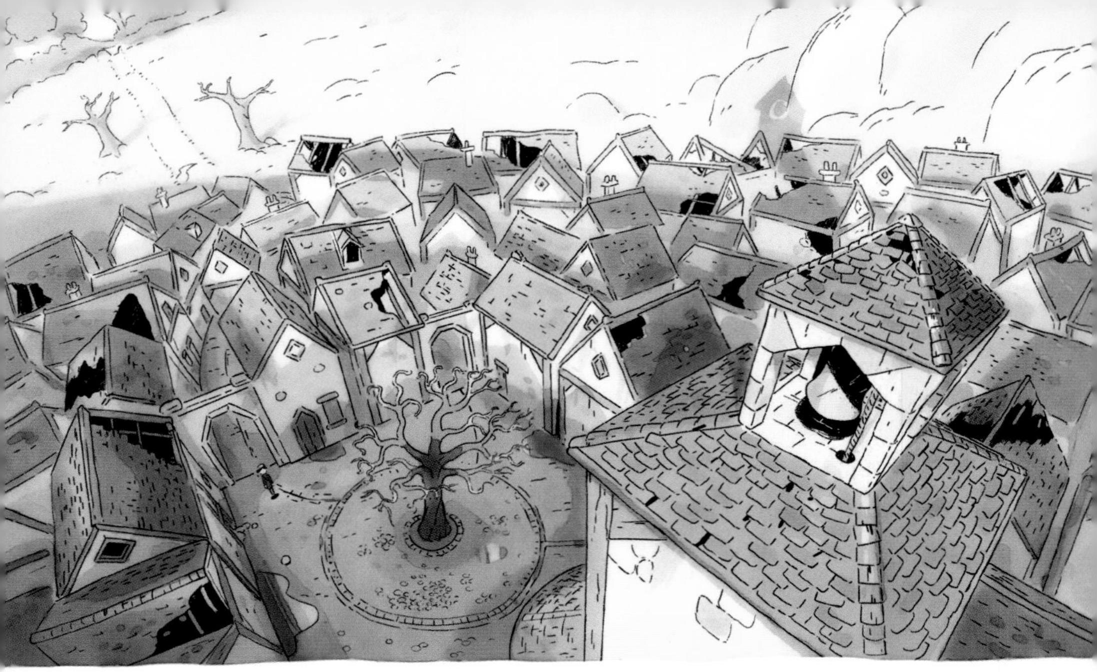

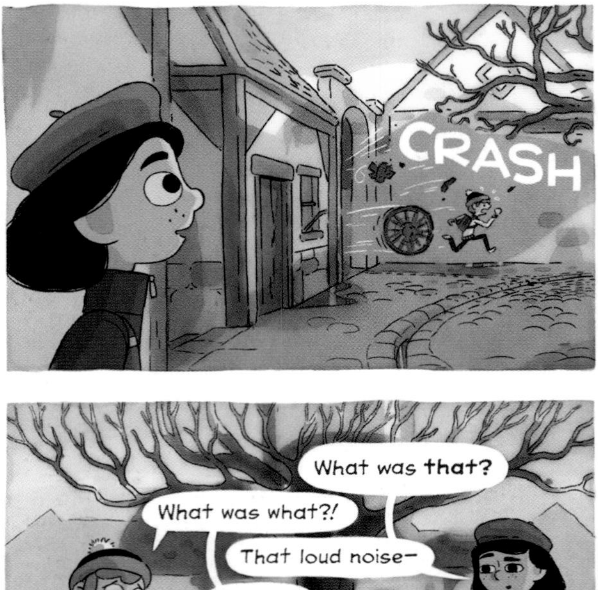
CRASH

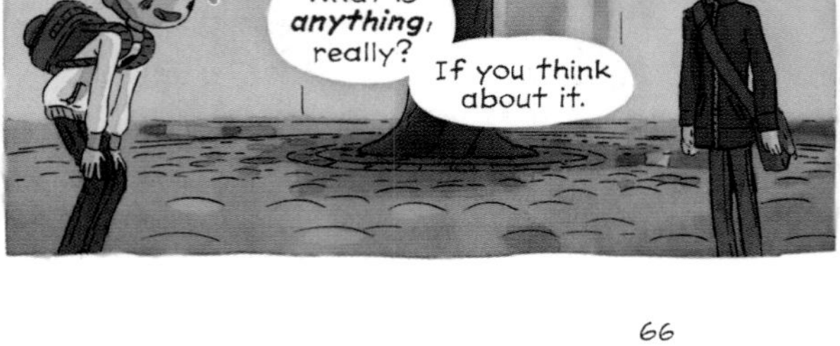
What was **that**?
What was what?!
That loud noise—
What is **anything**, really?
If you think about it.

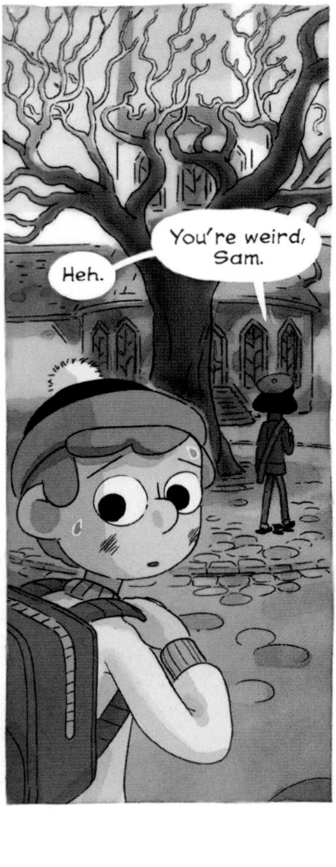
You're weird, Sam.
Heh.

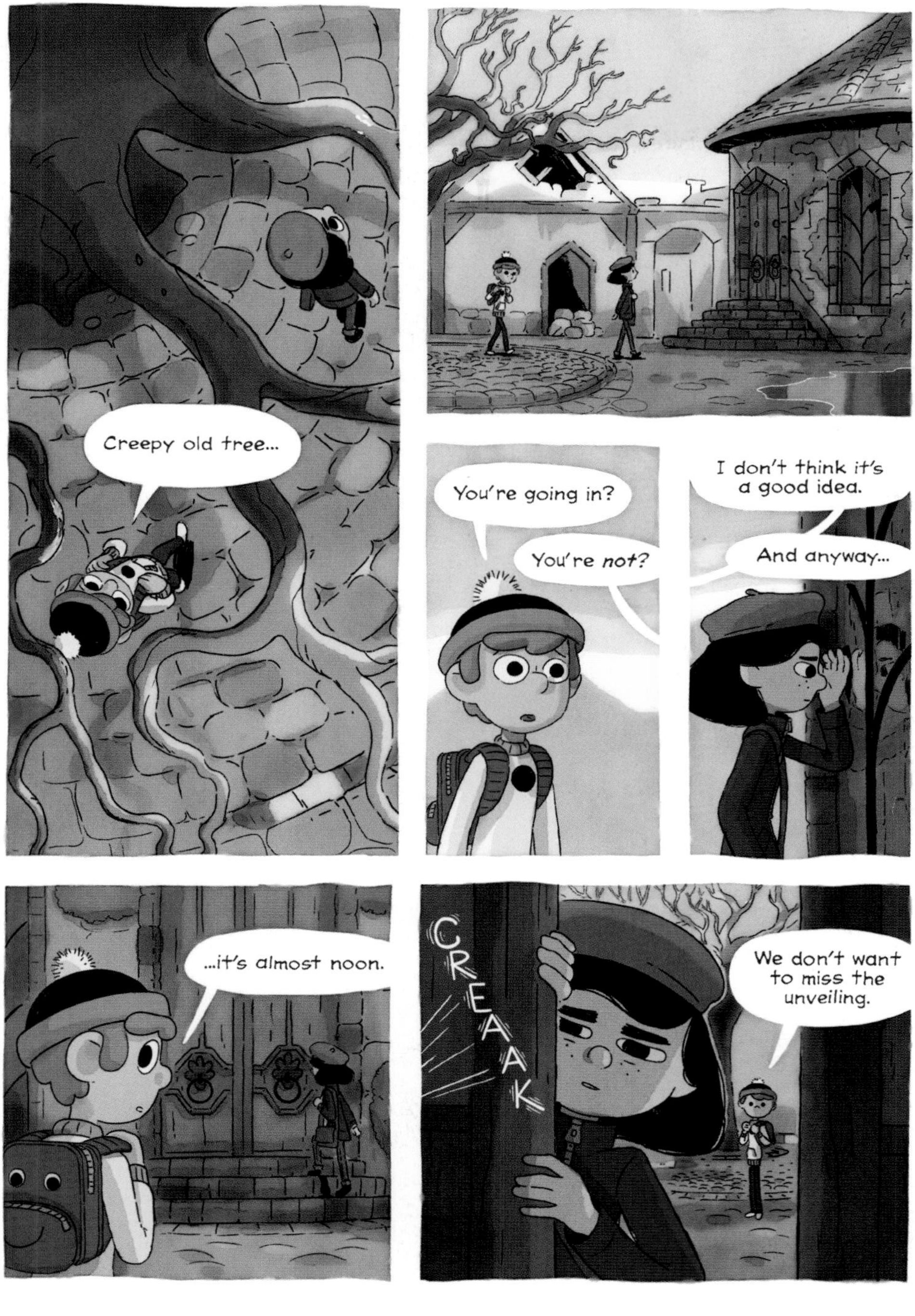
Creepy old tree...
You're going in?
You're *not*?
I don't think it's a good idea.
And anyway...
...it's almost noon.
CREAAK
We don't want to miss the unveiling.

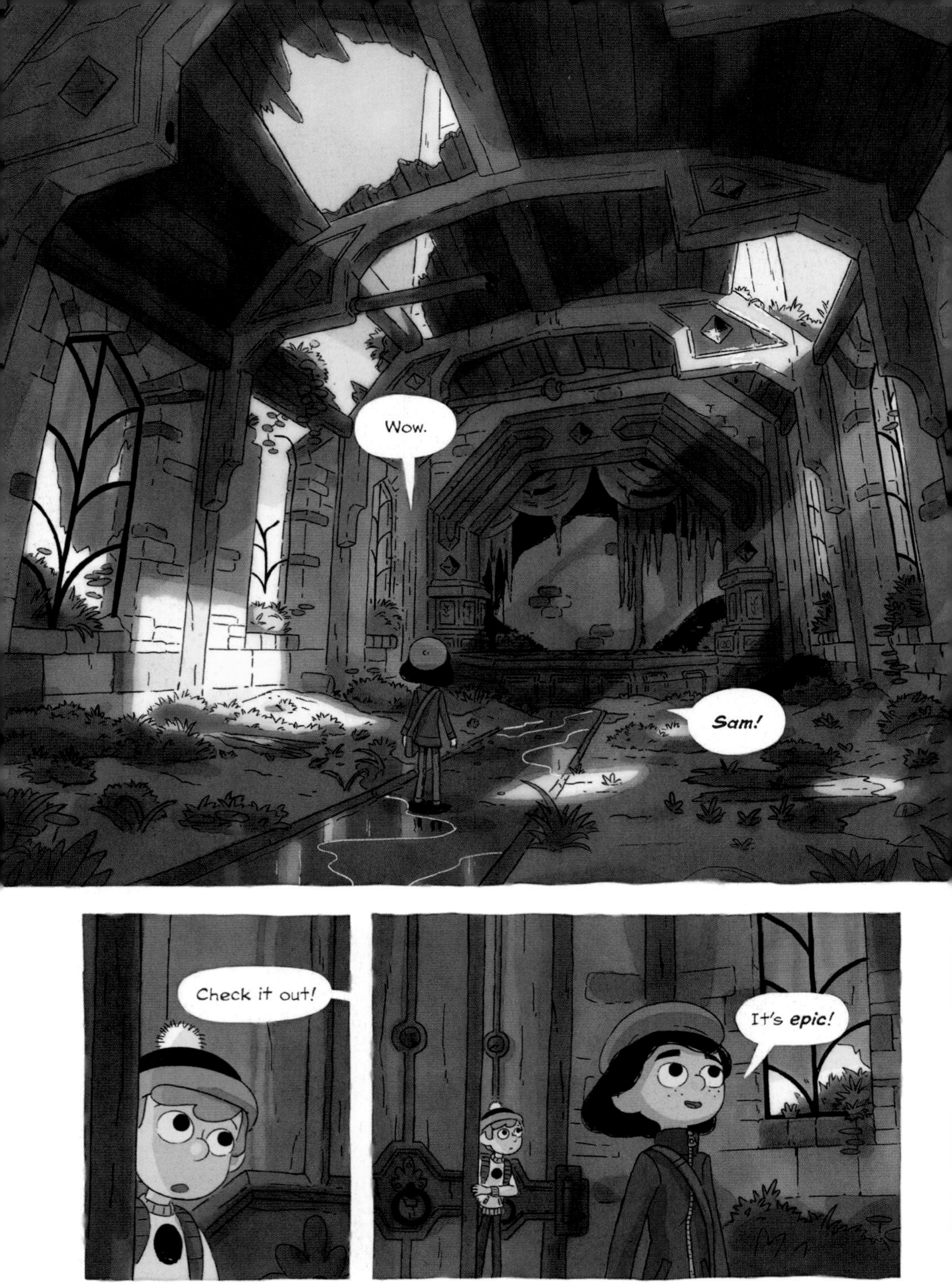
Wow.
Sam!
Check it out!
It's *epic!*

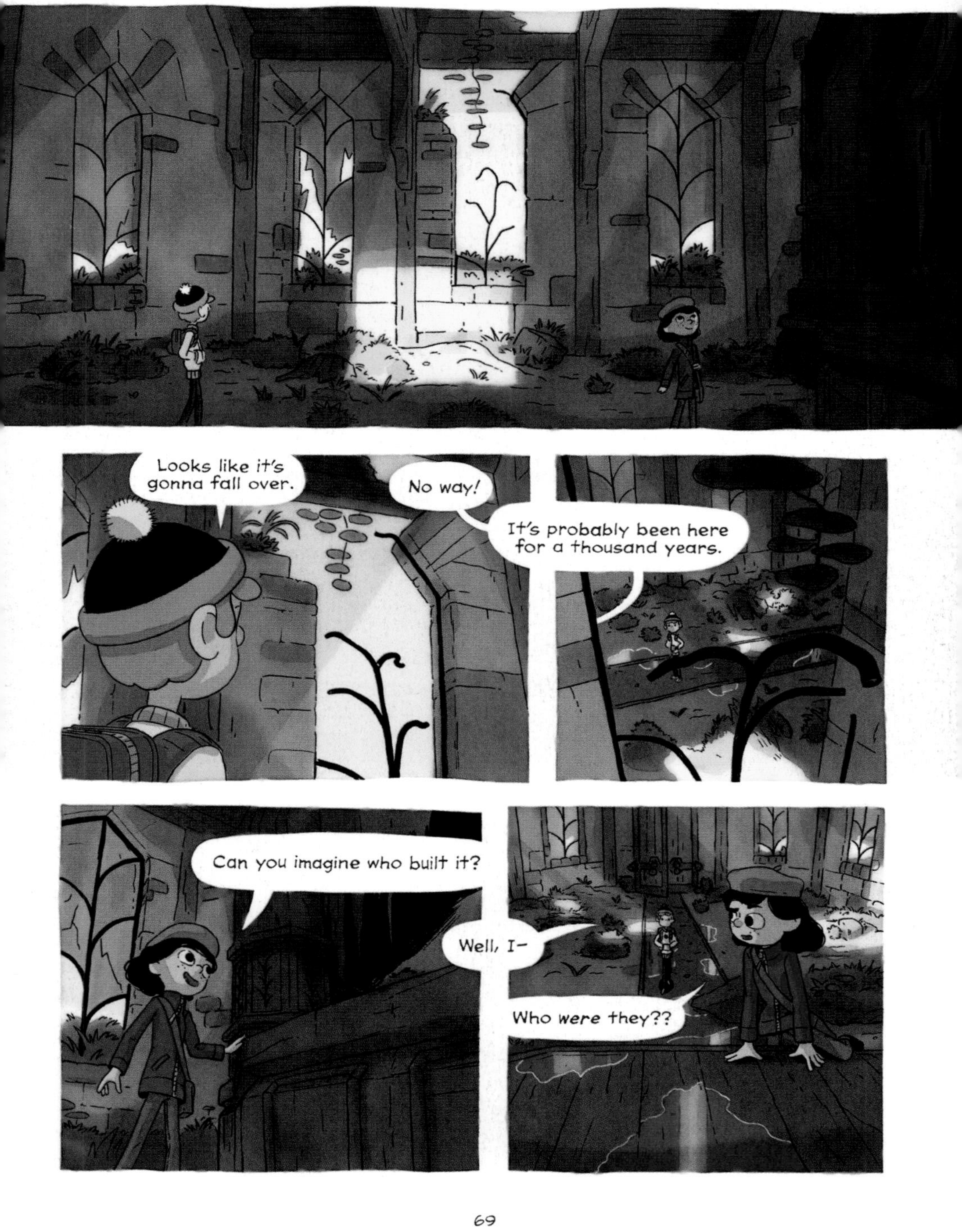
Looks like it's gonna fall over.
No way!
It's probably been here for a thousand years.
Can you imagine who built it?
Well, I-
Who *were* they??

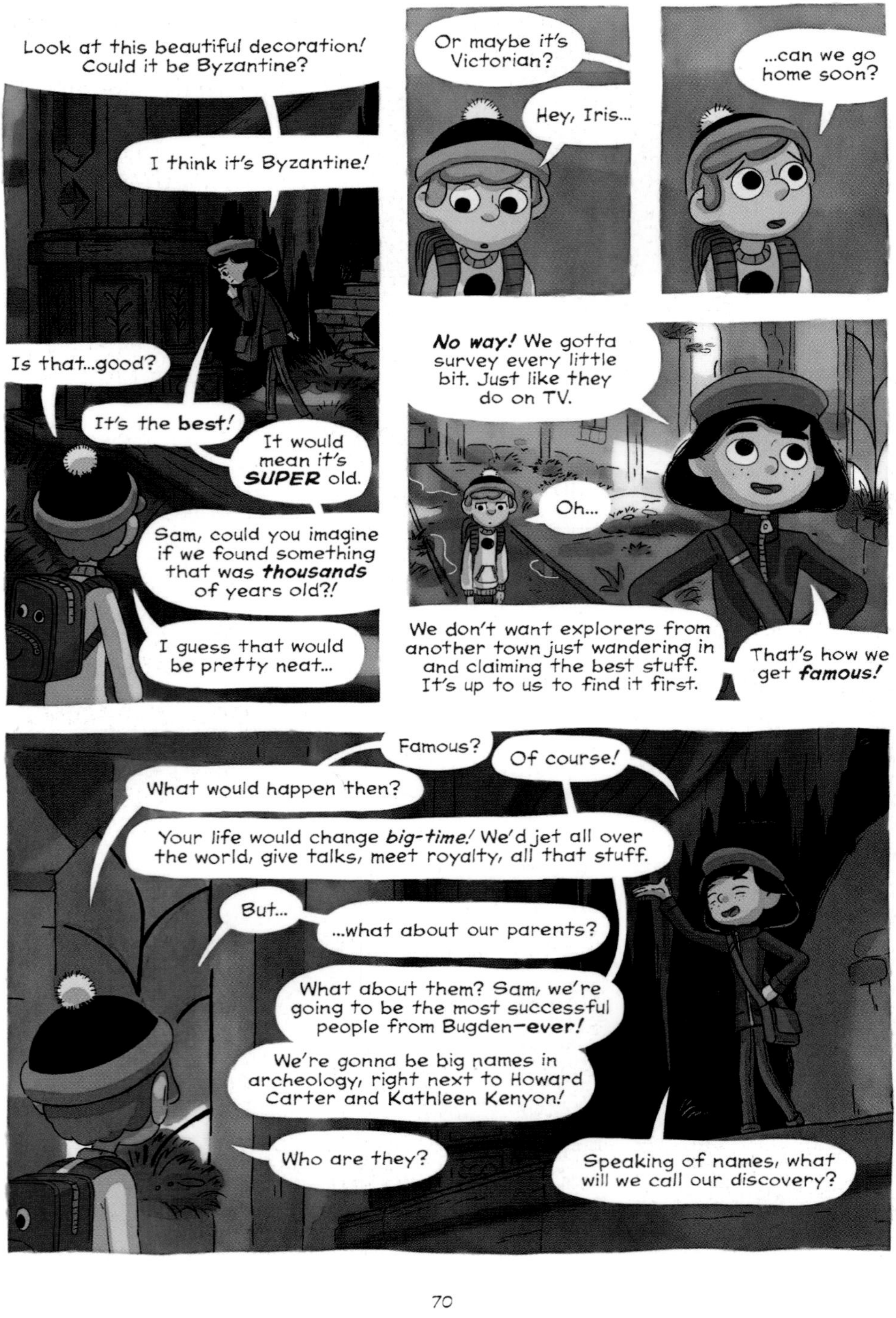

Look at this beautiful decoration! Could it be Byzantine?
I think it's Byzantine!
Is that...good?
It's the **best!**
It would mean it's ***SUPER*** old.
Sam, could you imagine if we found something that was ***thousands*** of years old?!
I guess that would be pretty neat...
Or maybe it's Victorian?
Hey, Iris...
...can we go home soon?
No way! We gotta survey every little bit. Just like they do on TV.
Oh...
We don't want explorers from another town just wandering in and claiming the best stuff. It's up to us to find it first.
That's how we get ***famous!***
Famous?
Of course!
What would happen then?
Your life would change ***big-time!*** We'd jet all over the world, give talks, meet royalty, all that stuff.
But...
...what about our parents?
What about them? Sam, we're going to be the most successful people from Bugden—**ever!**
We're gonna be big names in archeology, right next to Howard Carter and Kathleen Kenyon!
Who are they?
Speaking of names, what will we call our discovery?

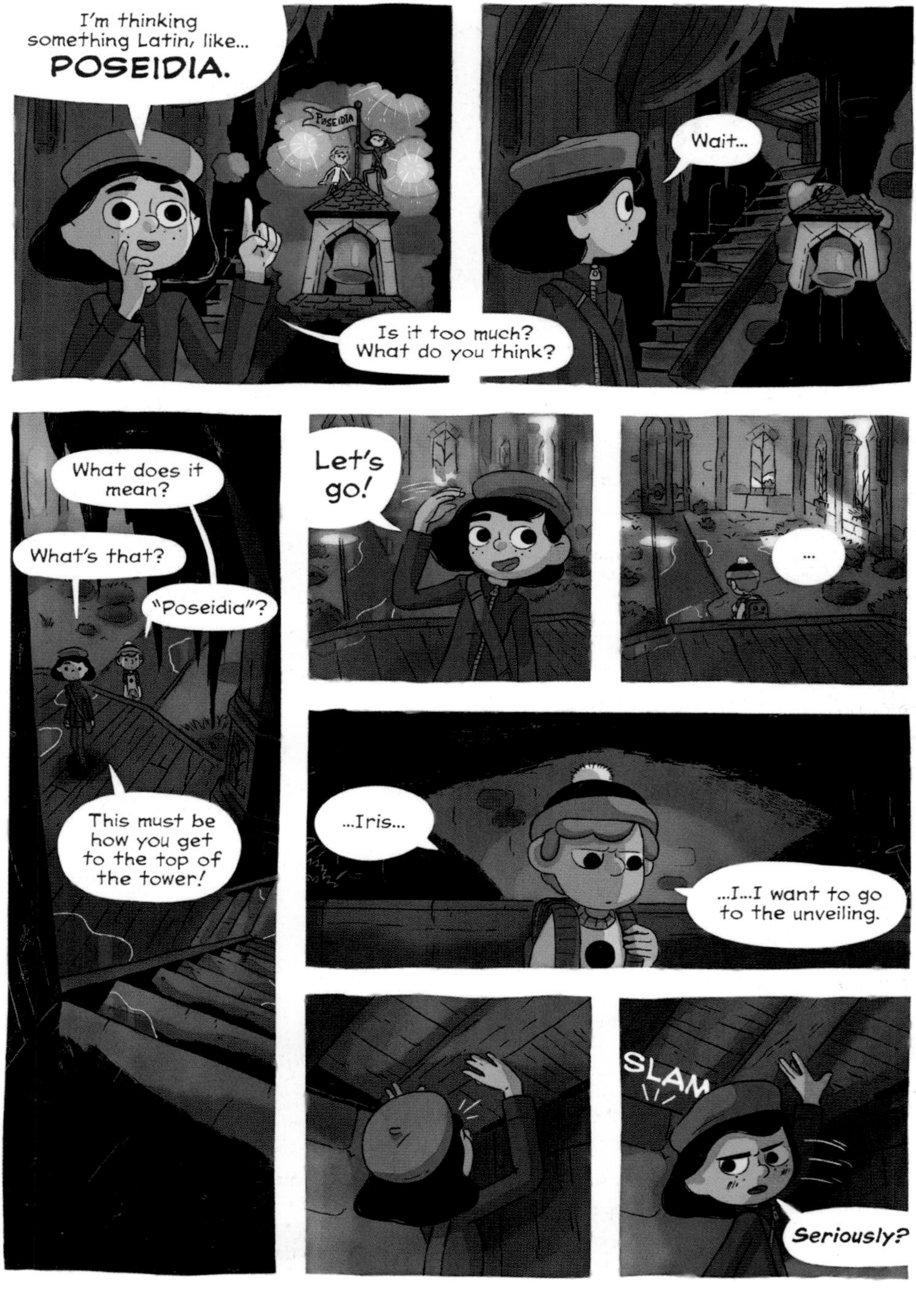
I'm thinking something Latin, like... POSEIDIA.
POSEIDIA
Is it too much? What do you think?
Wait...
What does it mean?
What's that?
"Poseidia"?
This must be how you get to the top of the tower!
Let's go!
...
...Iris...
...I...I want to go to the unveiling.
SLAM
Seriously?

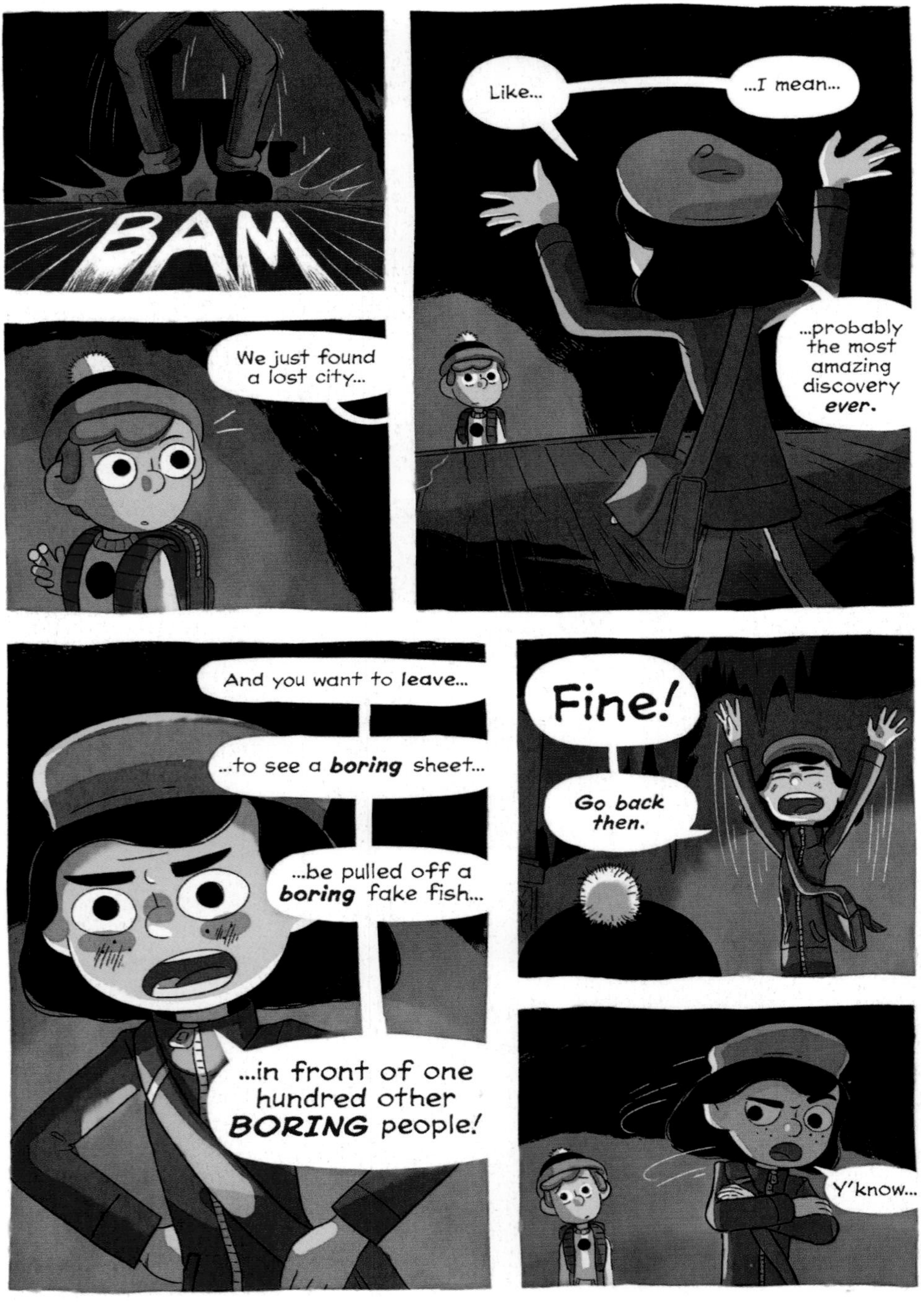
BAM
We just found a lost city...
Like...
...I mean...
...probably the most amazing discovery ever.
And you want to leave...
...to see a boring sheet...
...be pulled off a boring fake fish...
...in front of one hundred other BORING people!
Fine!
Go back then.
Y'know...

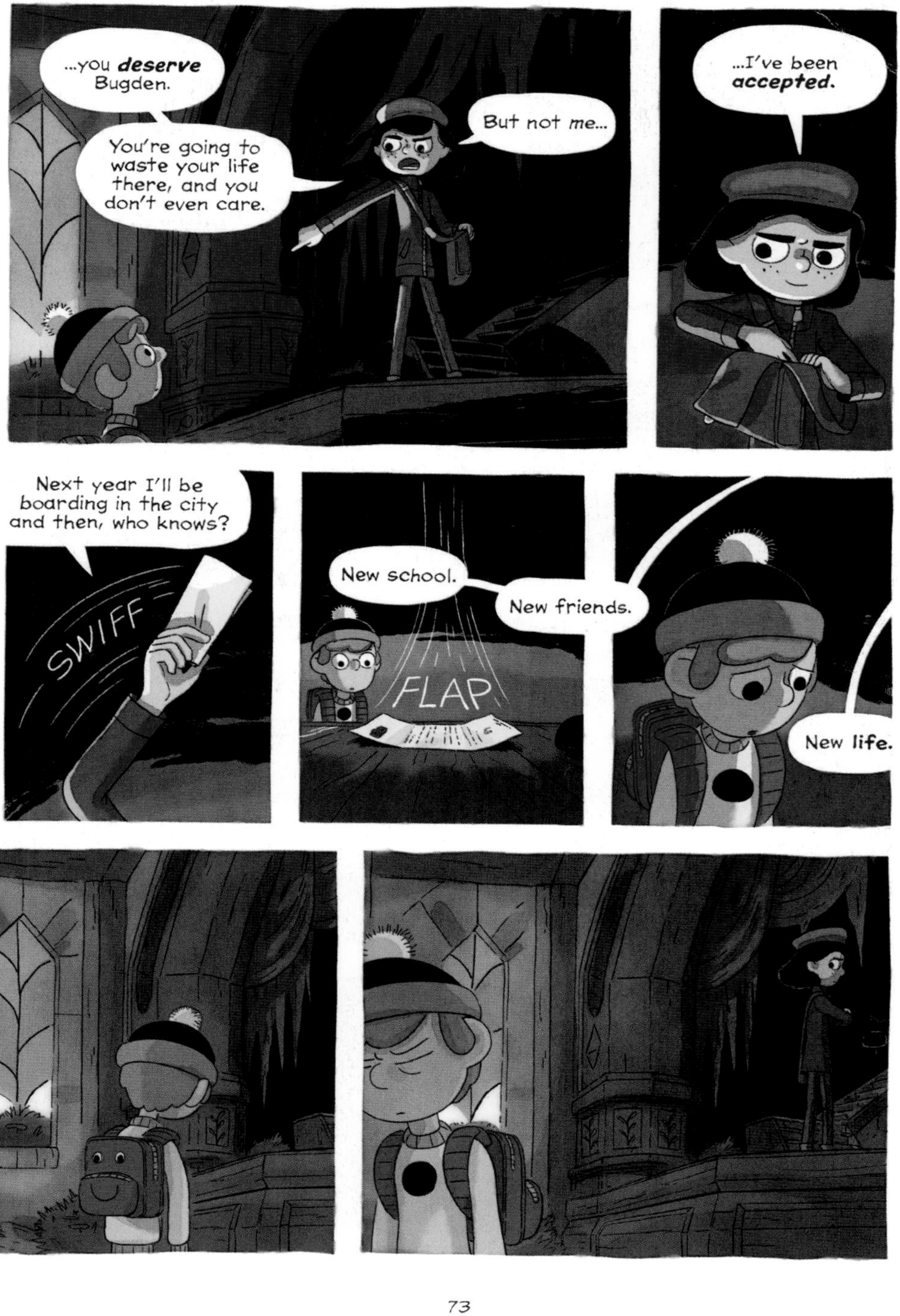
...you **deserve** Bugden.
You're going to waste your life there, and you don't even care.
But not *me*...
...I've been ***accepted.***
Next year I'll be boarding in the city and then, who knows?
SWIFF
New school.
New friends.
FLAP
New **life.**

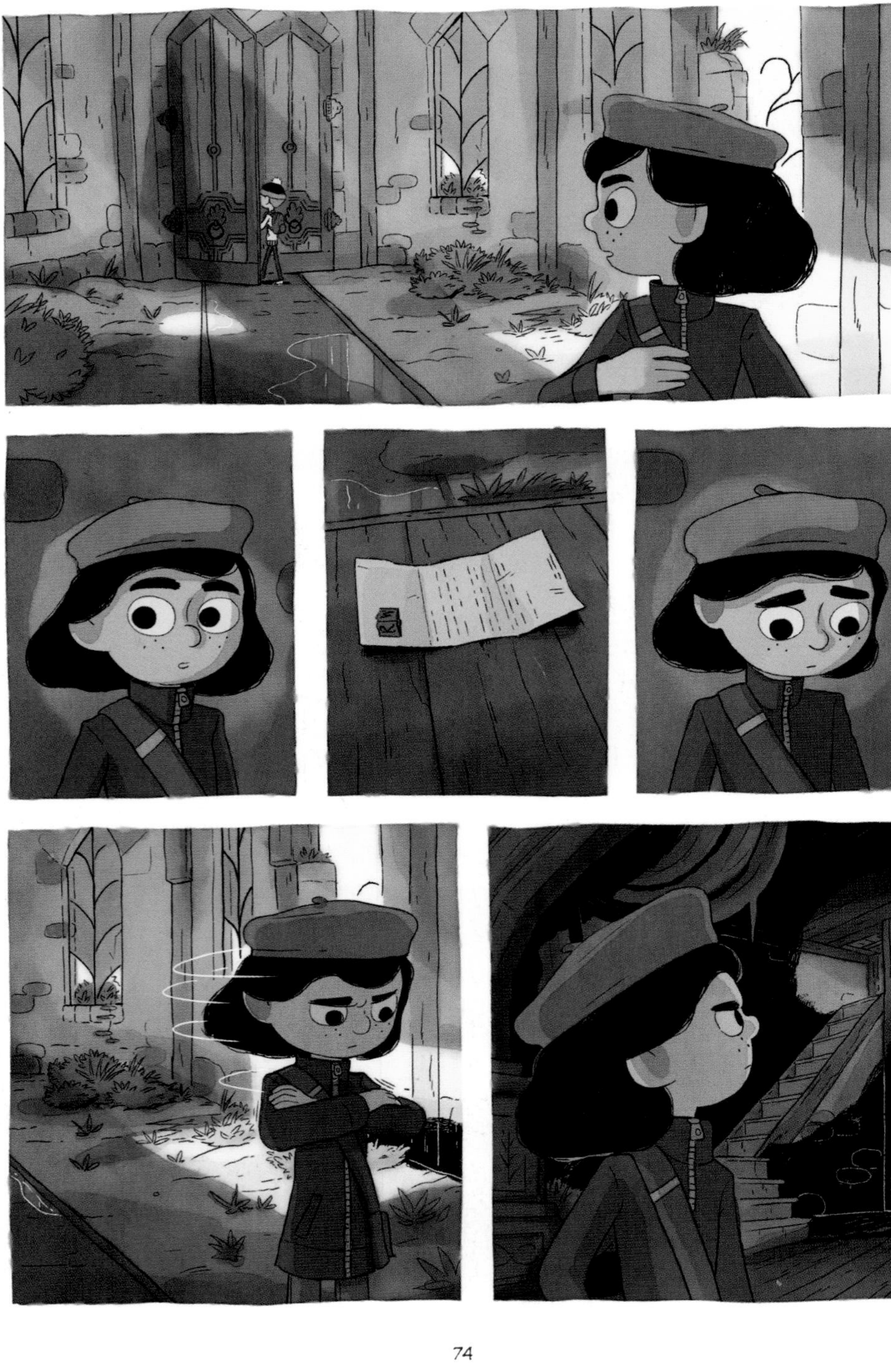

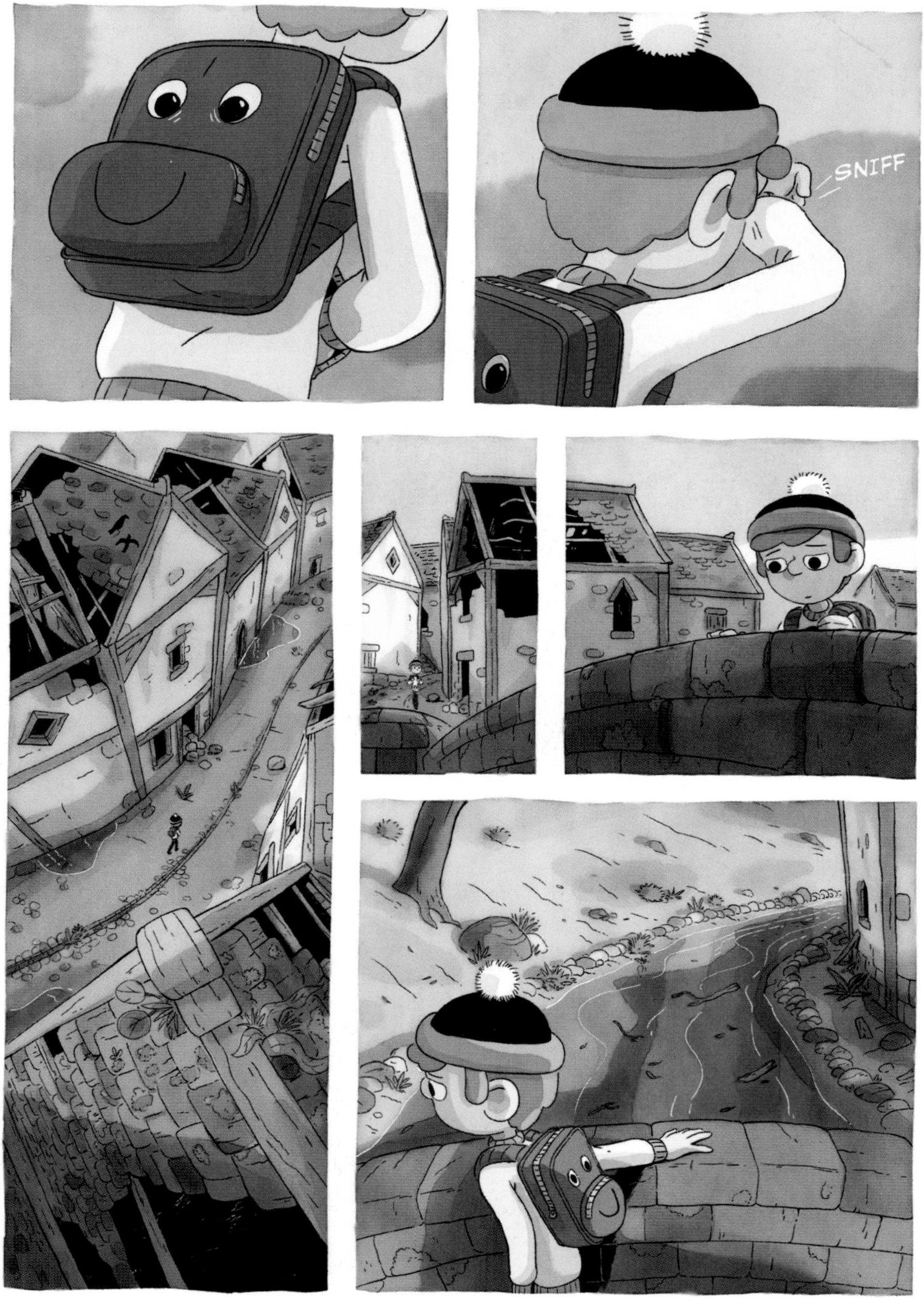
SNIFF

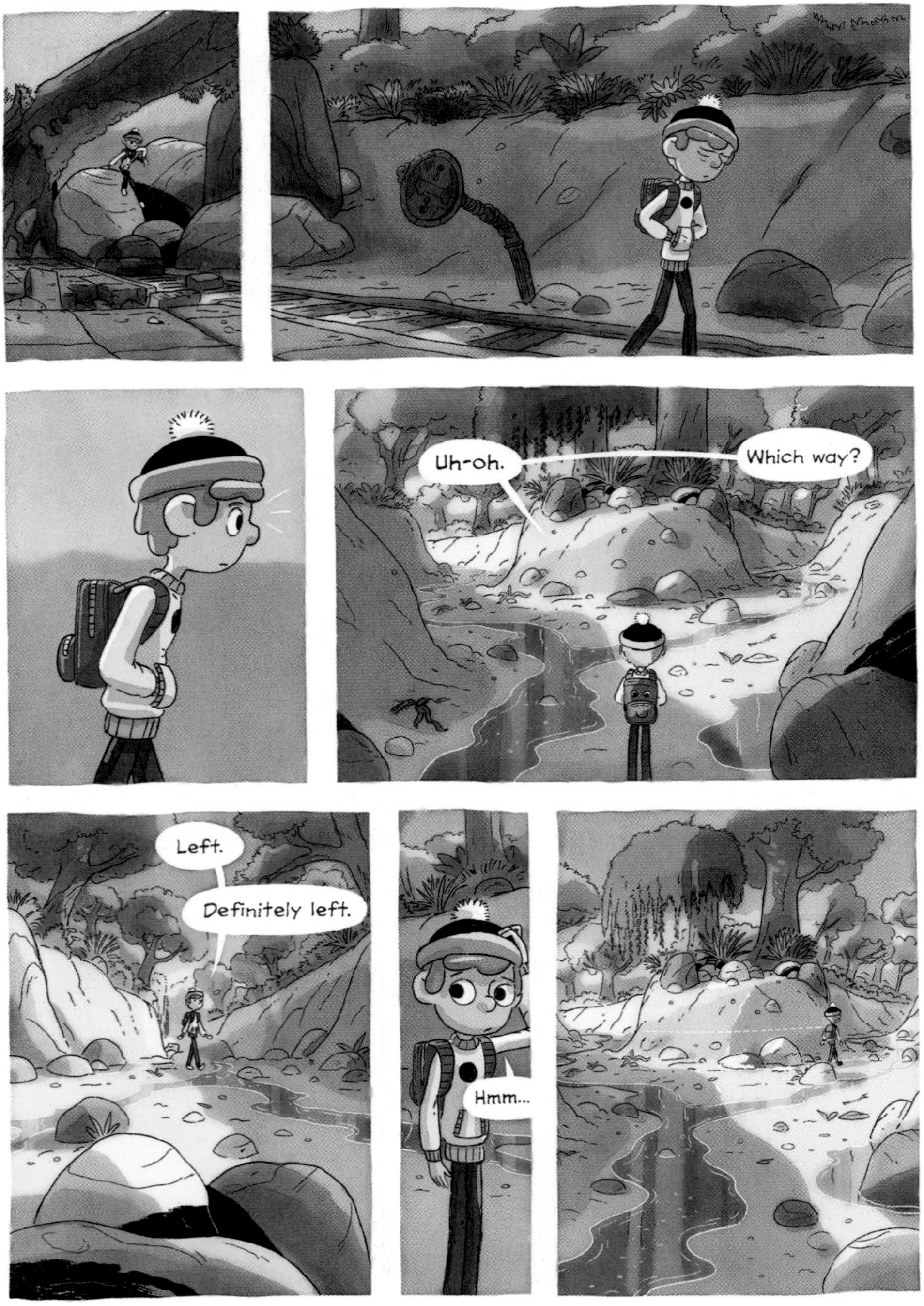
Uh-oh.
Which way?
Left.
Definitely left.
Hmm...

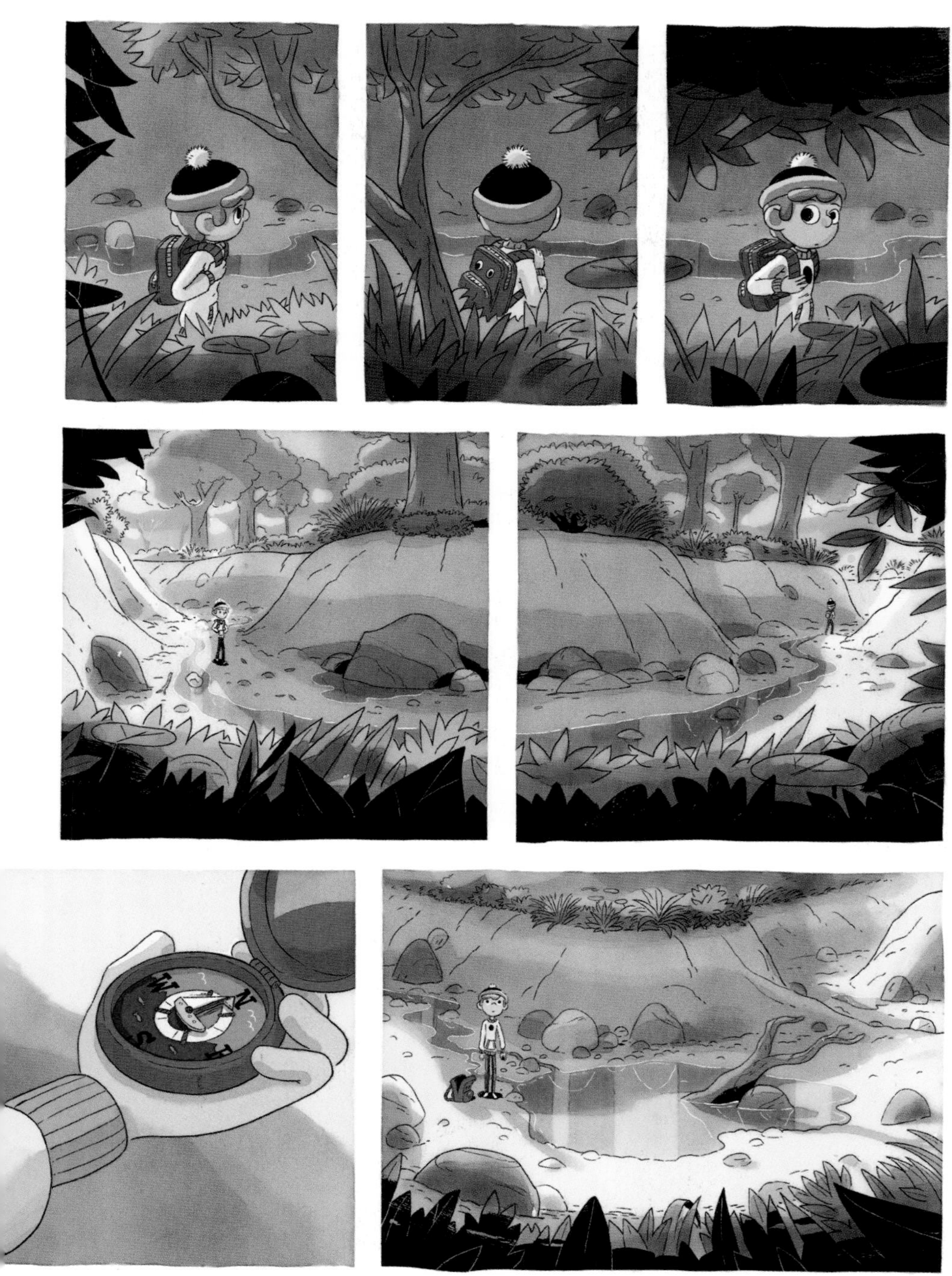

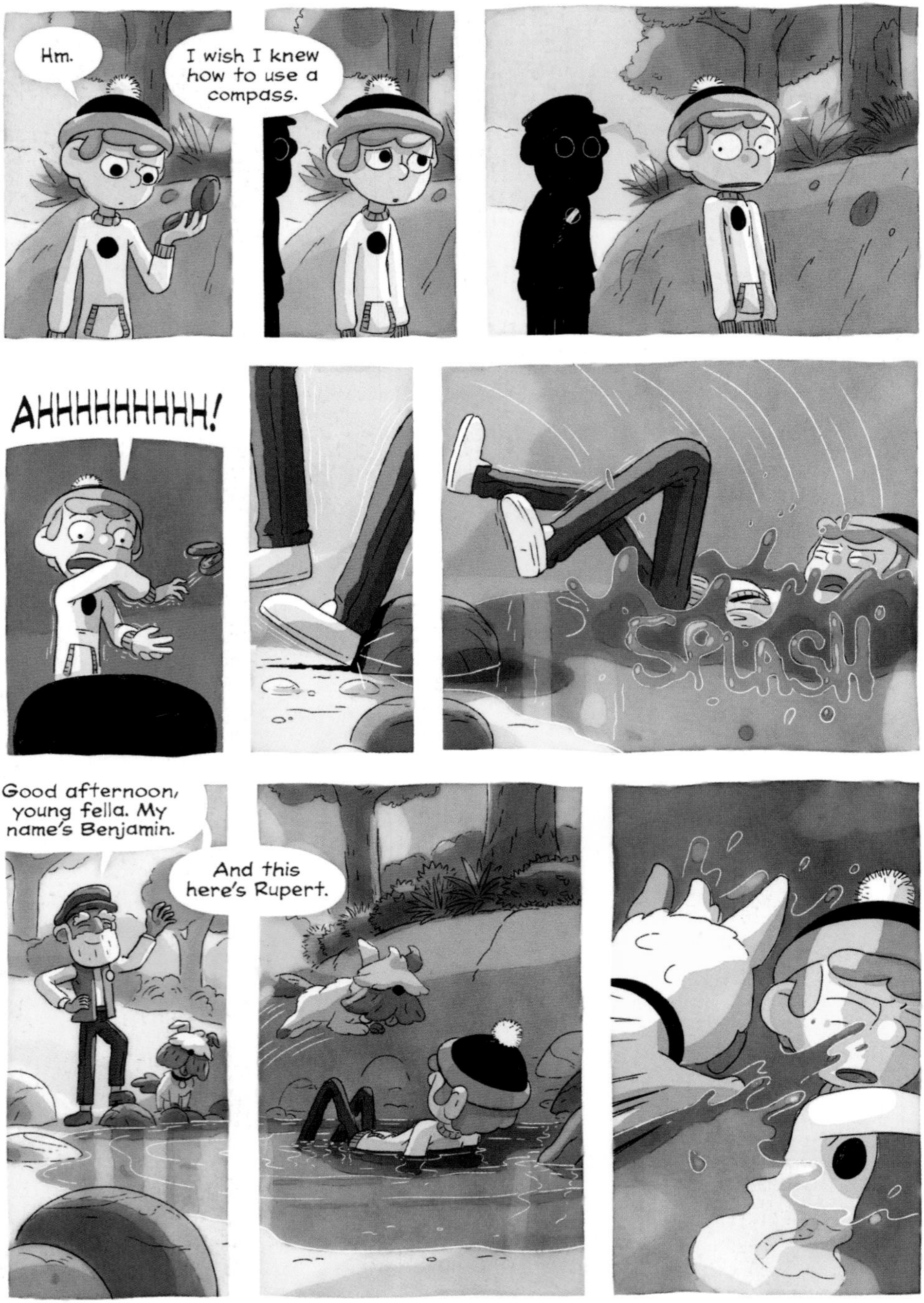

Hm.
I wish I knew how to use a compass.
AHHHHHHHHH!
SPLASH
Good afternoon, young fella. My name's Benjamin.
And this here's Rupert.

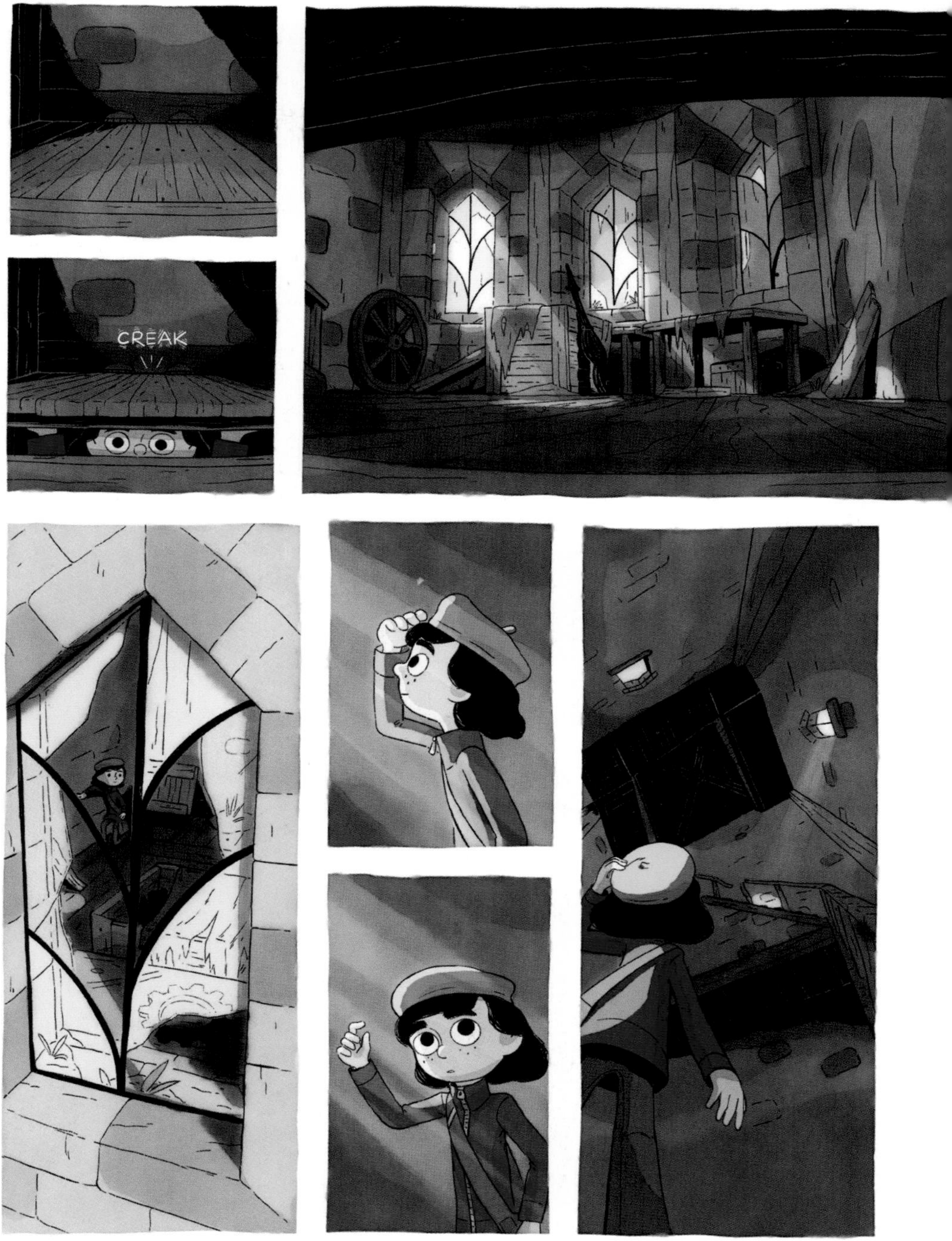
CREAK

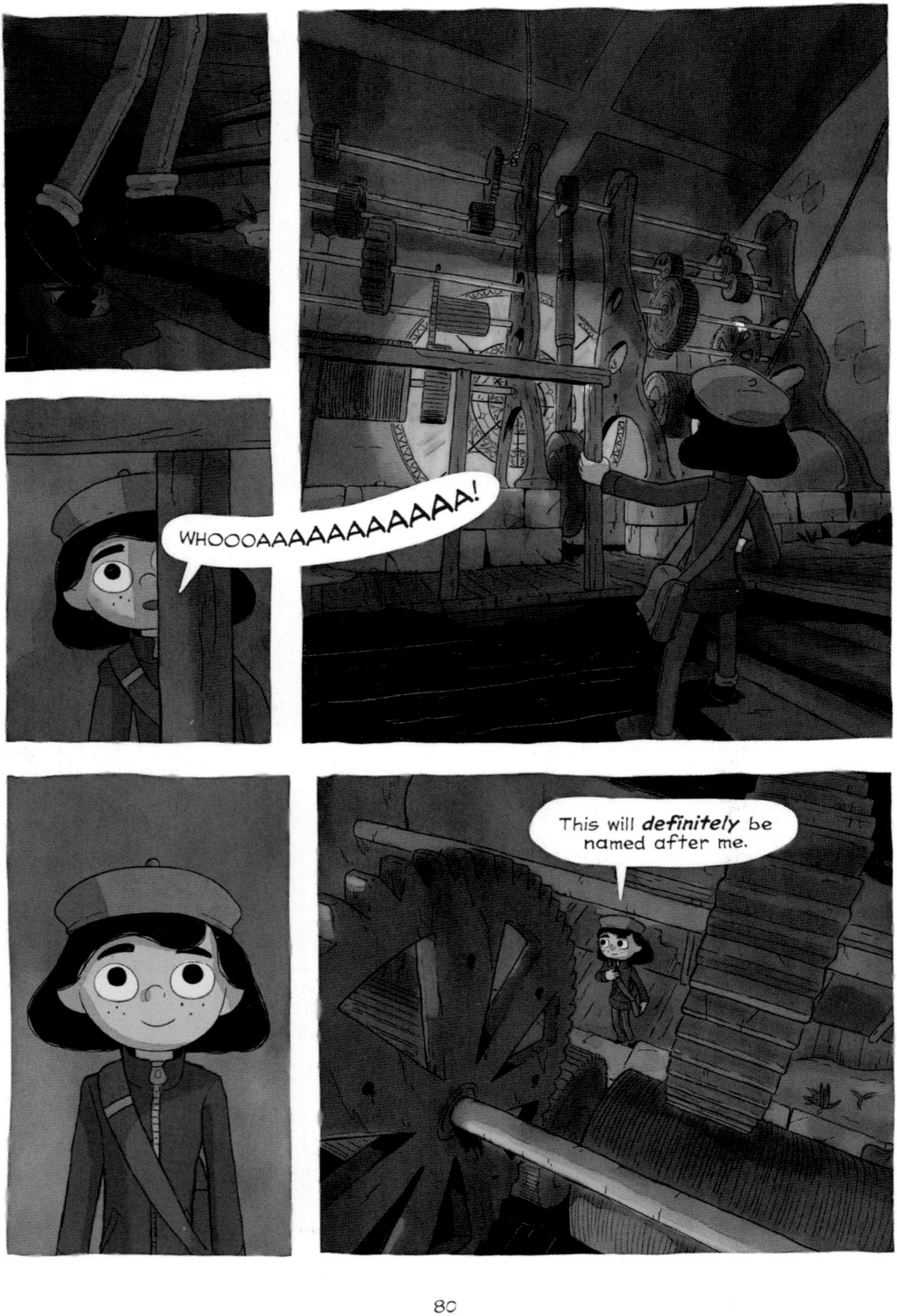
WHOOOAAAAAAAAAAA!
This will **definitely** be named after me.

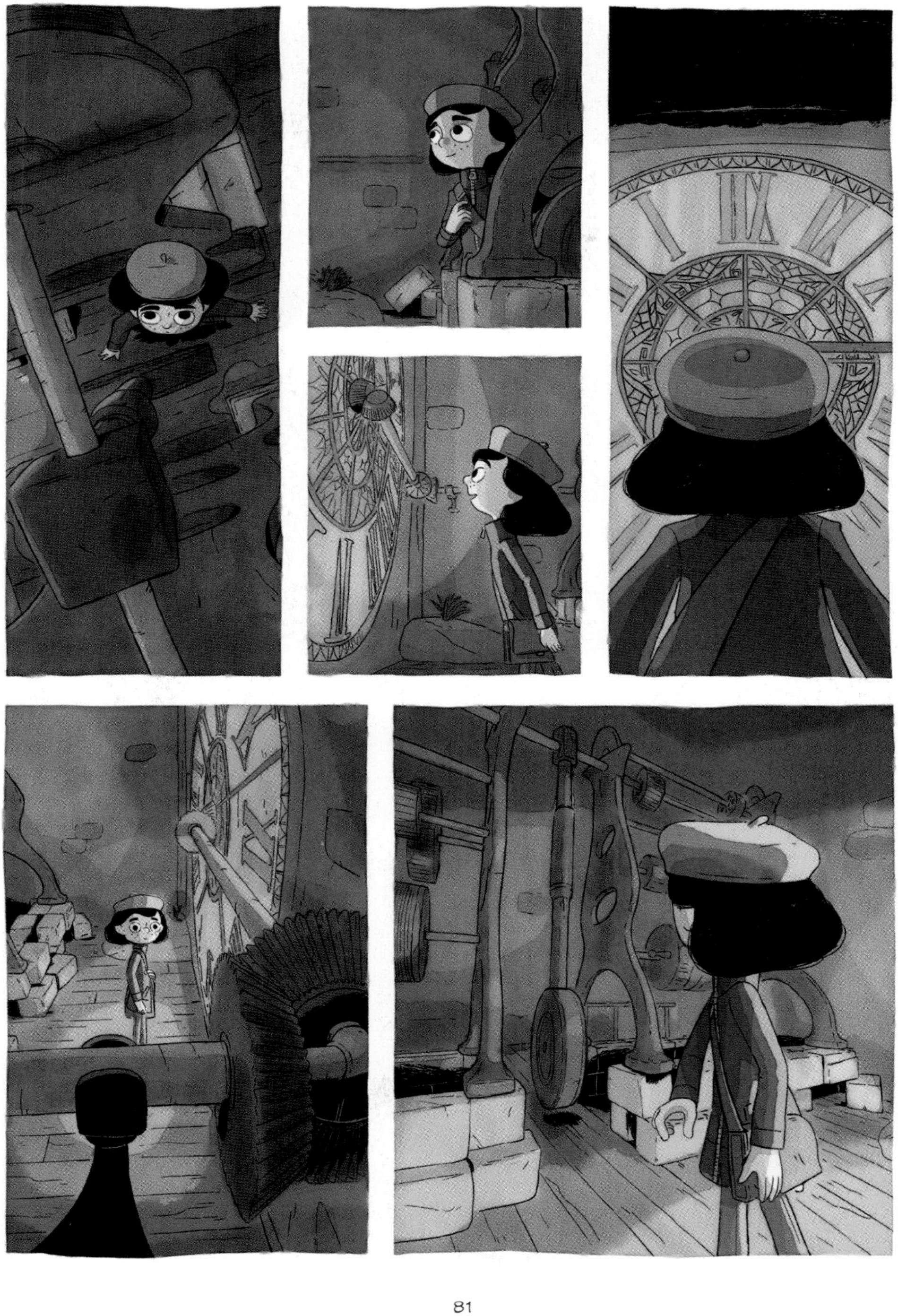

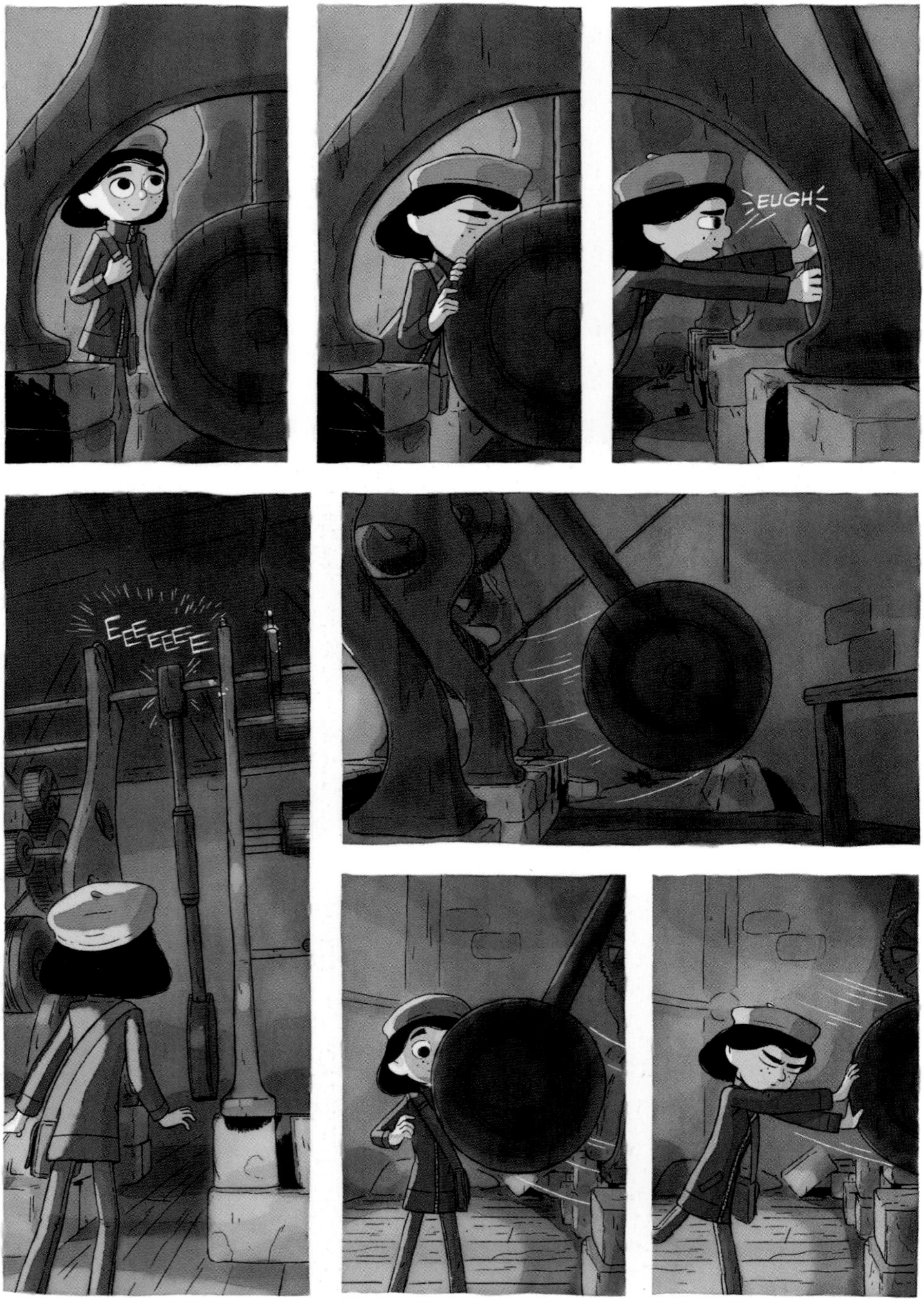
EUGH
EEEEEEE

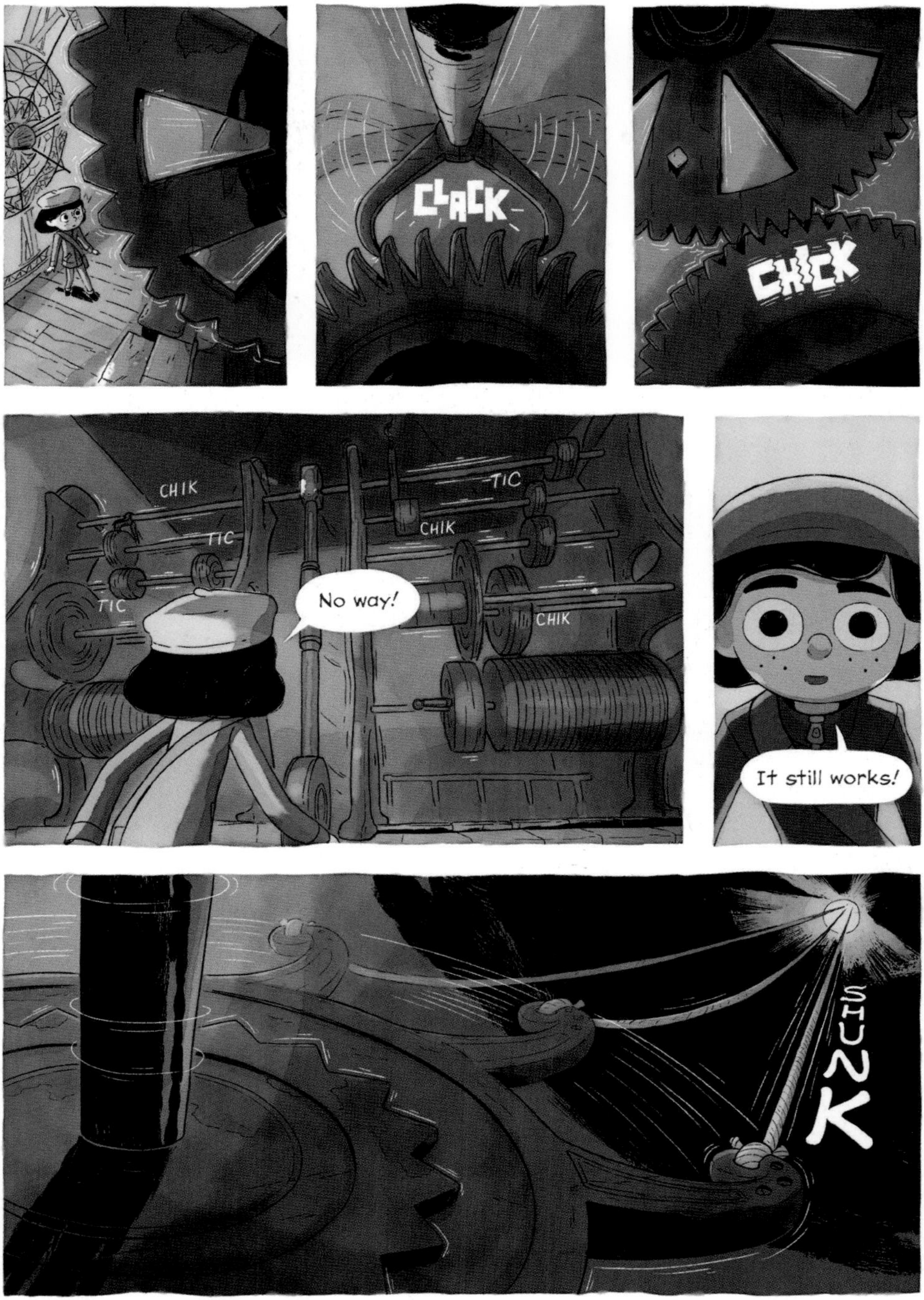
CLACK
CHICK
CHIK
TIC
CHIK
TIC
TIC
No way!
CHIK
It still works!
SHUNK

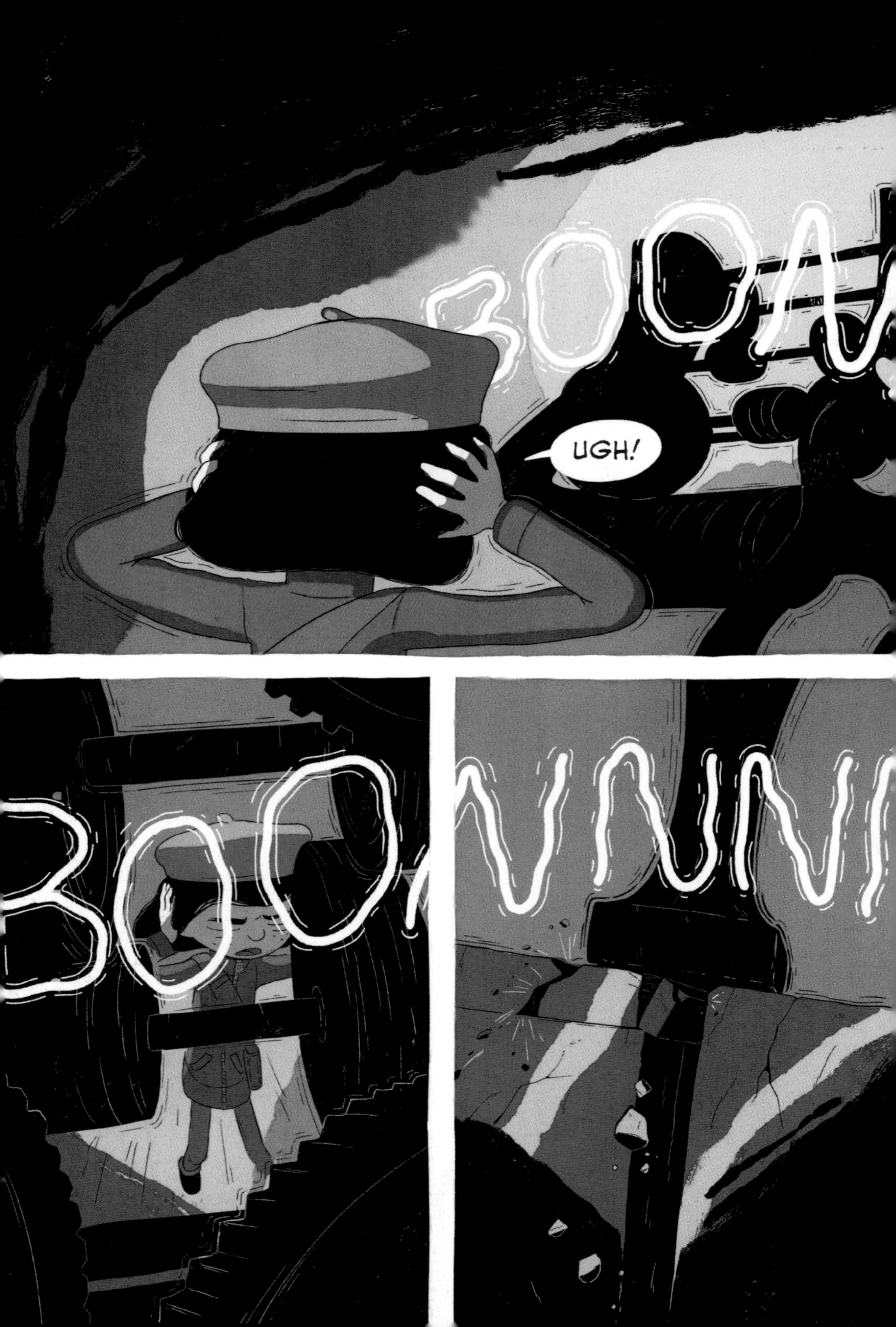
UGH!

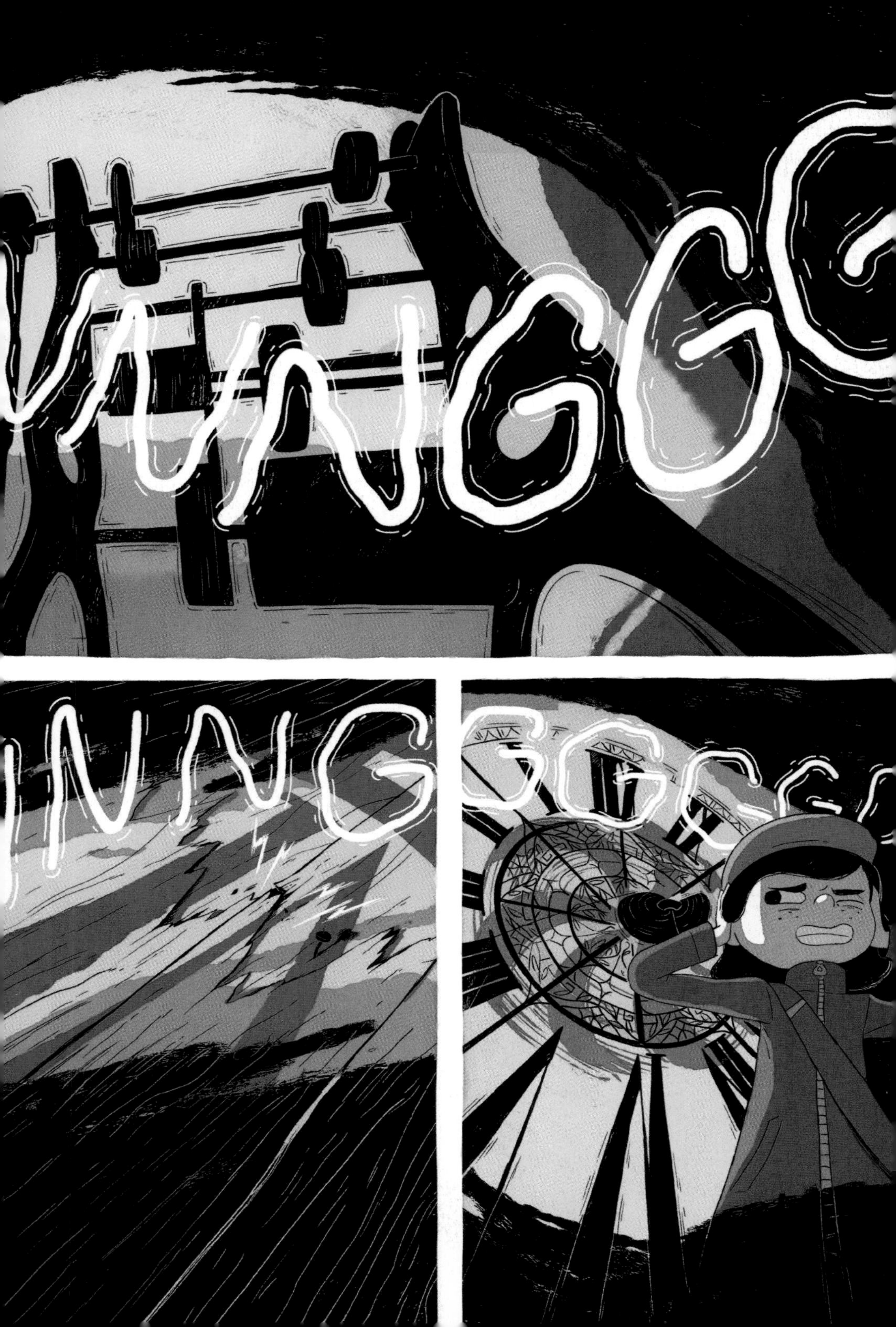

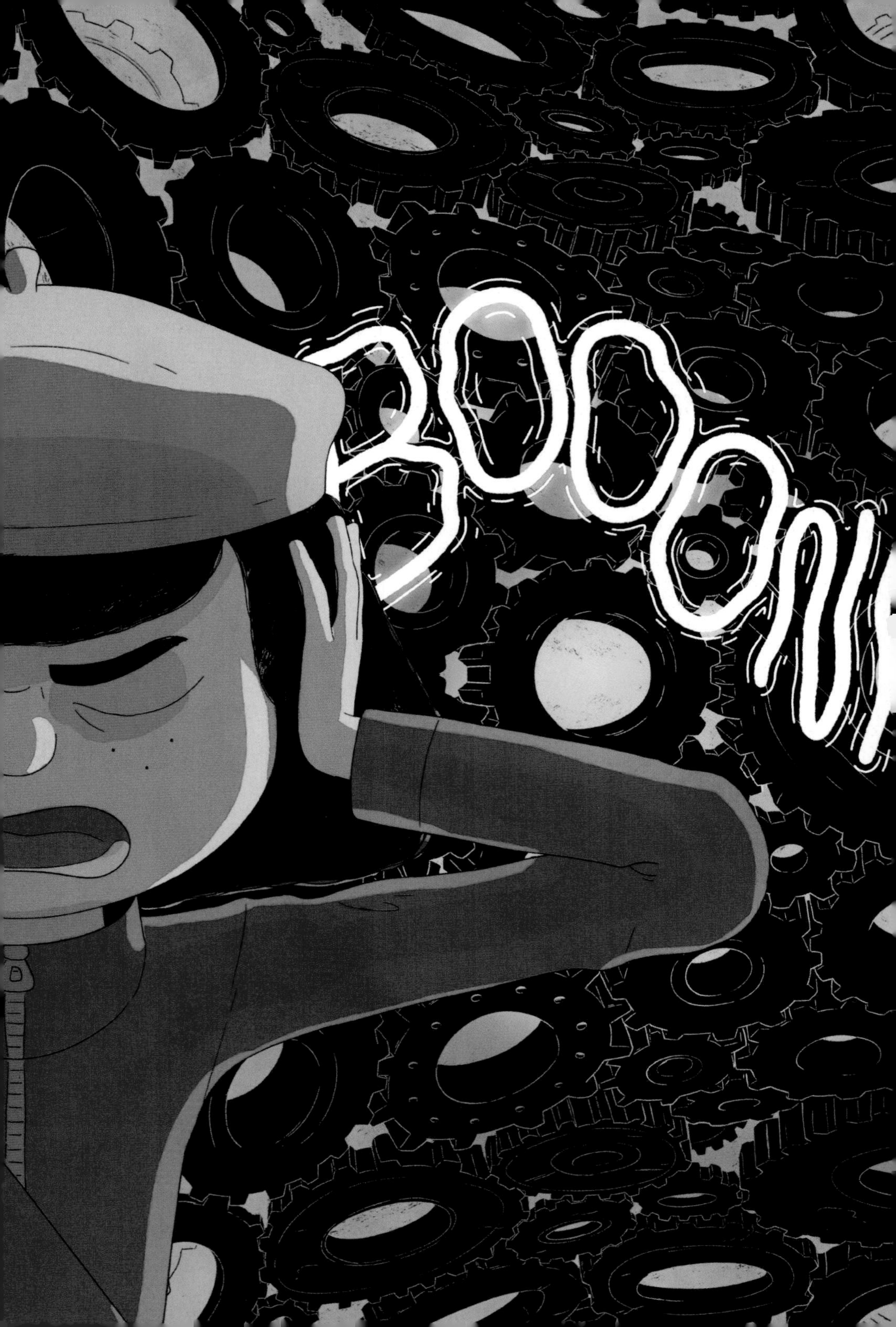
BOOO

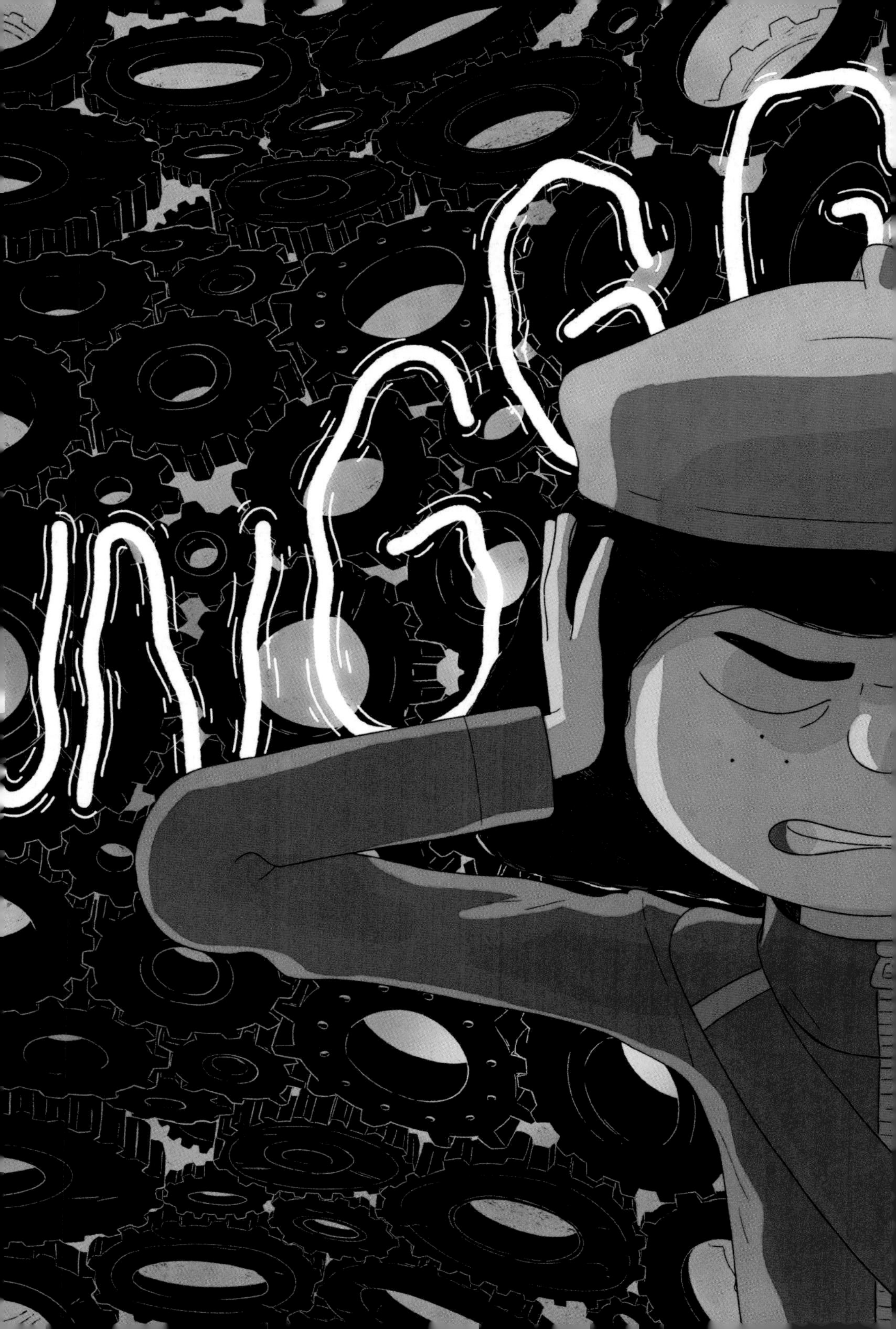

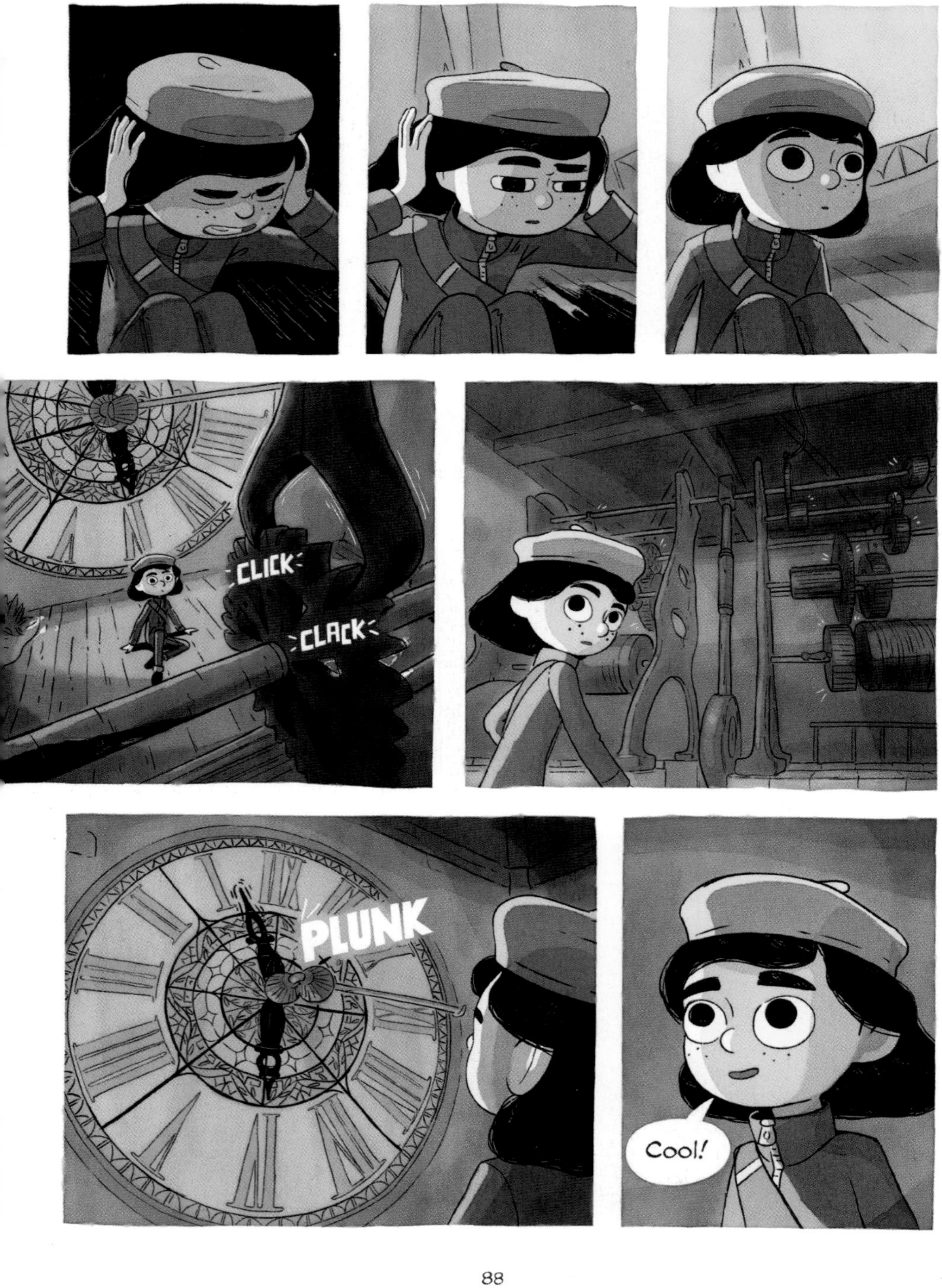
CLICK
CLACK
PLUNK
Cool!

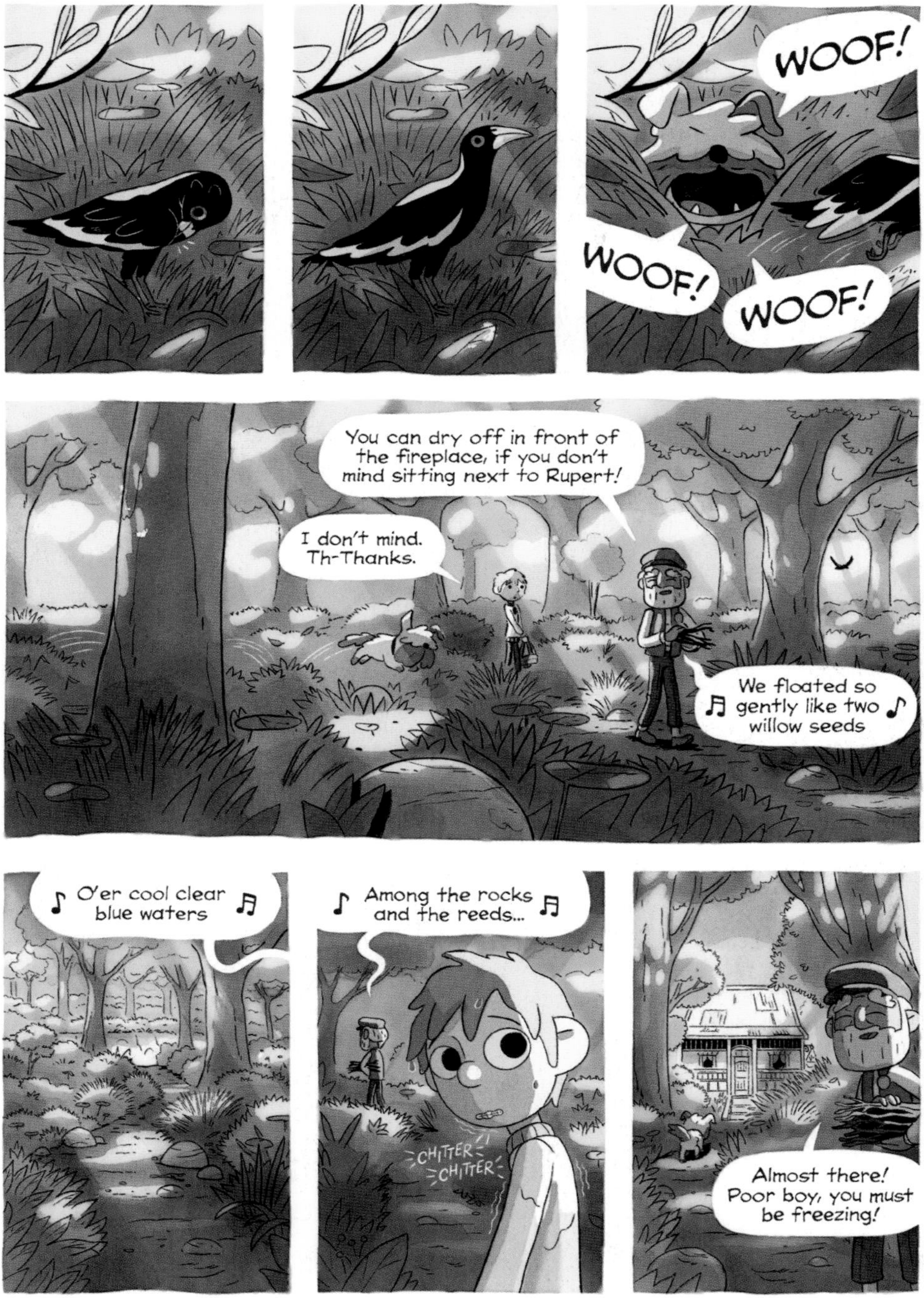
WOOF!
WOOF!
WOOF!
You can dry off in front of the fireplace, if you don't mind sitting next to Rupert!
I don't mind. Th-Thanks.
♫ We floated so gently like two willow seeds ♪
♪ O'er cool clear blue waters ♫
♪ Among the rocks and the reeds... ♫
CHITTER CHITTER
Almost there! Poor boy, you must be freezing!

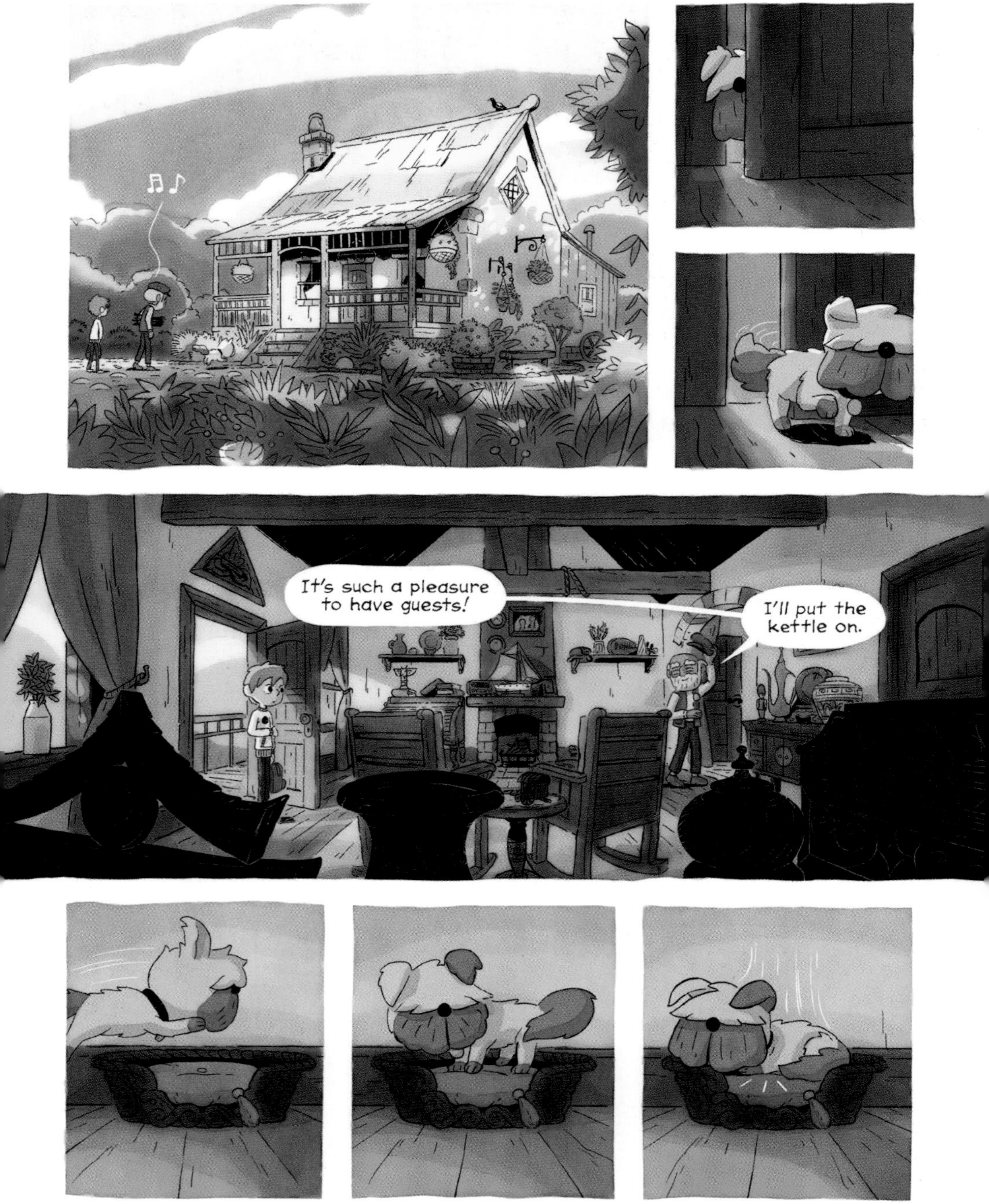
It's such a pleasure to have guests!
I'll put the kettle on.

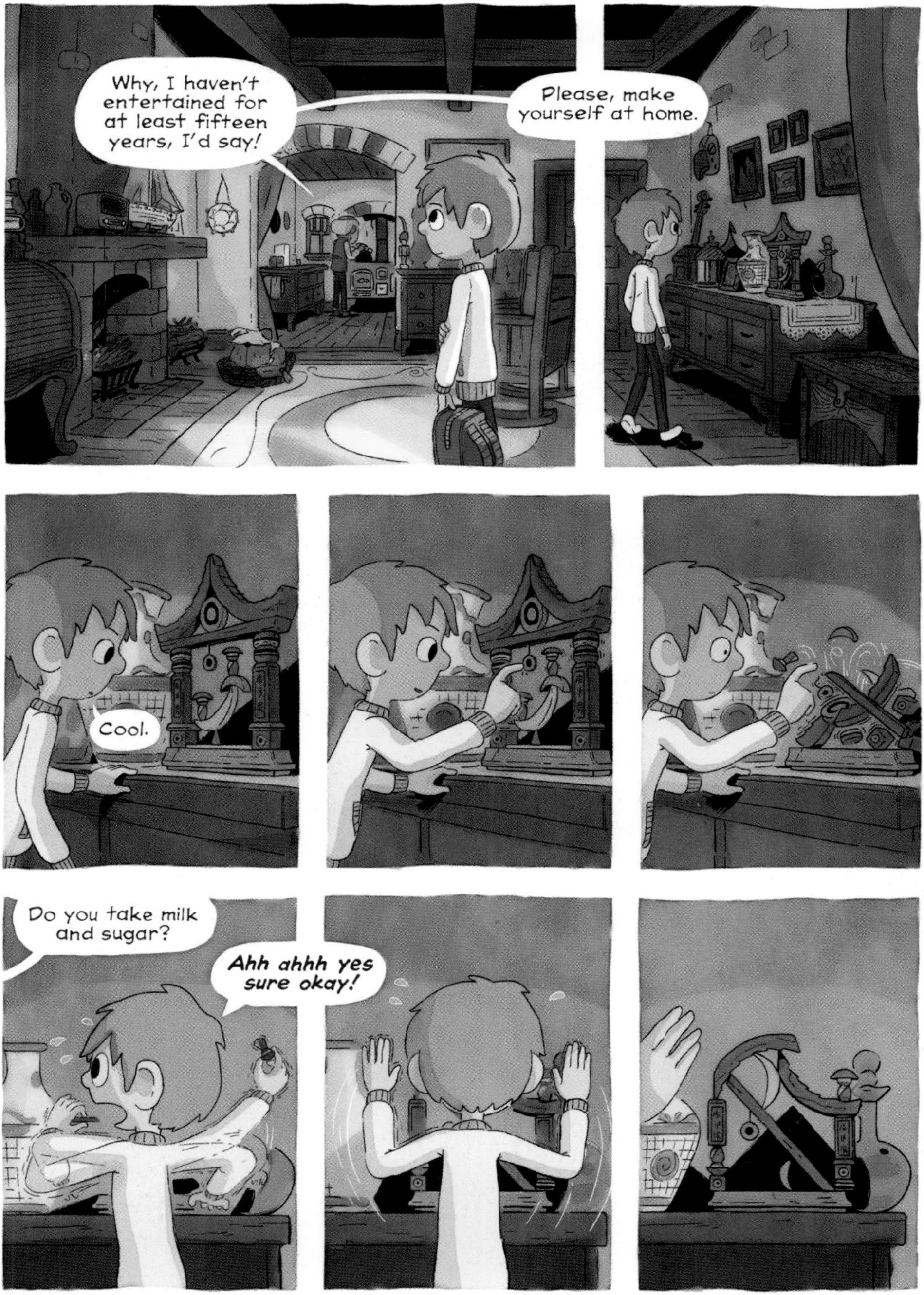
Why, I haven't entertained for at least fifteen years, I'd say!
Please, make yourself at home.
Cool.
Do you take milk and sugar?
Ahh ahhh yes sure okay!

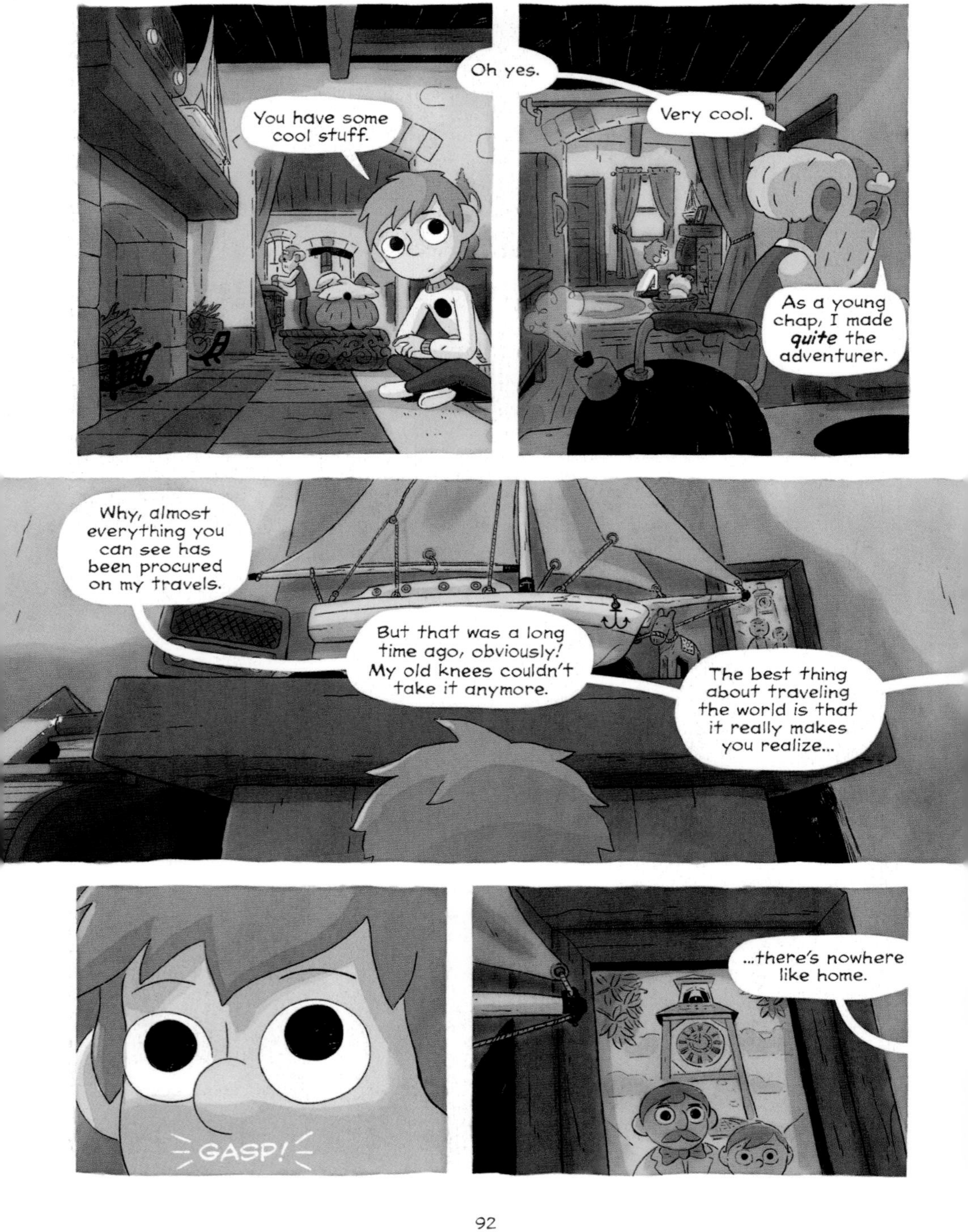

You have some cool stuff.
Oh yes.
Very cool.
As a young chap, I made *quite* the adventurer.
Why, almost everything you can see has been procured on my travels.
But that was a long time ago, obviously! My old knees couldn't take it anymore.
The best thing about traveling the world is that it really makes you realize...
GASP!
...there's nowhere like home.

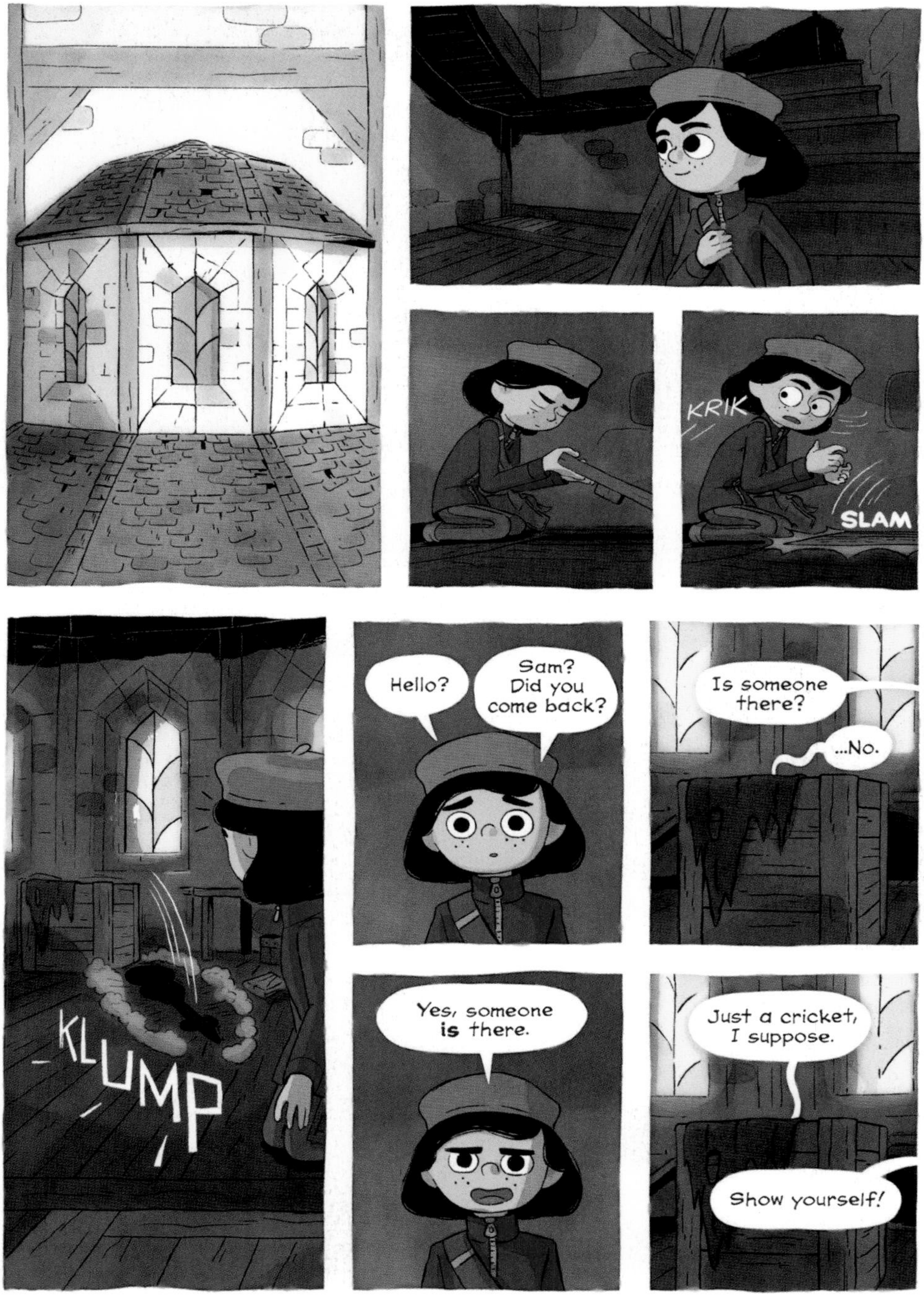
KRIK
SLAM
KLUMP
Hello?
Sam? Did you come back?
Is someone there?
...No.
Yes, someone **is** there.
Just a cricket, I suppose.
Show yourself!

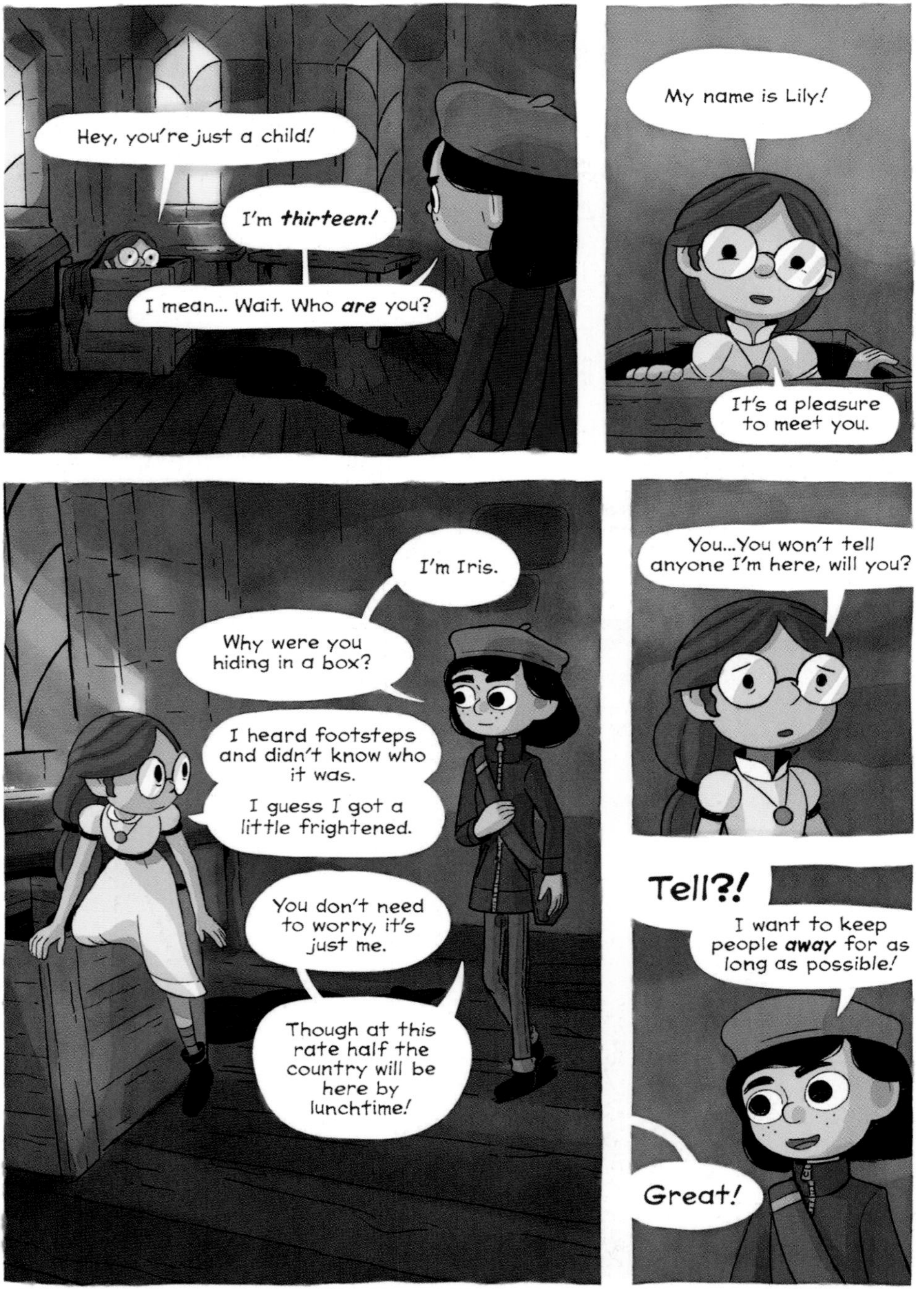
Hey, you're just a child!
I'm **thirteen!**
I mean... Wait. Who **are** you?
My name is Lily!
It's a pleasure to meet you.
I'm Iris.
Why were you hiding in a box?
I heard footsteps and didn't know who it was.
I guess I got a little frightened.
You don't need to worry, it's just me.
Though at this rate half the country will be here by lunchtime!
You...You won't tell anyone I'm here, will you?
Tell?!
I want to keep people **away** for as long as possible!
Great!

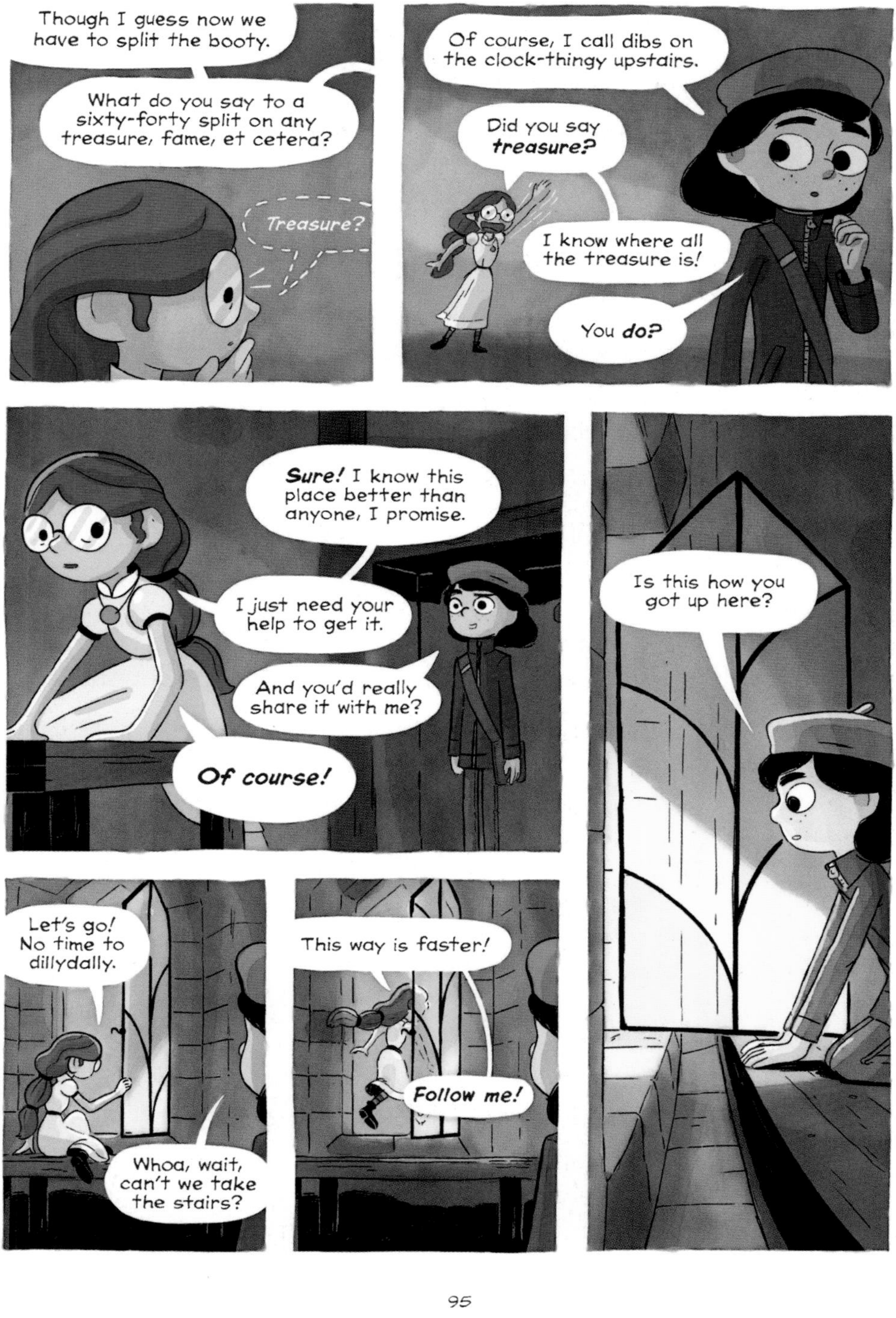

Though I guess now we have to split the booty.
What do you say to a sixty-forty split on any treasure, fame, et cetera?
Treasure?
Of course, I call dibs on the clock-thingy upstairs.
Did you say ***treasure?***
I know where all the treasure is!
You ***do?***
Sure! I know this place better than anyone, I promise.
I just need your help to get it.
And you'd really share it with me?
Of course!
Is this how you got up here?
Let's go! No time to dillydally.
Whoa, wait, can't we take the stairs?
This way is faster!
Follow me!

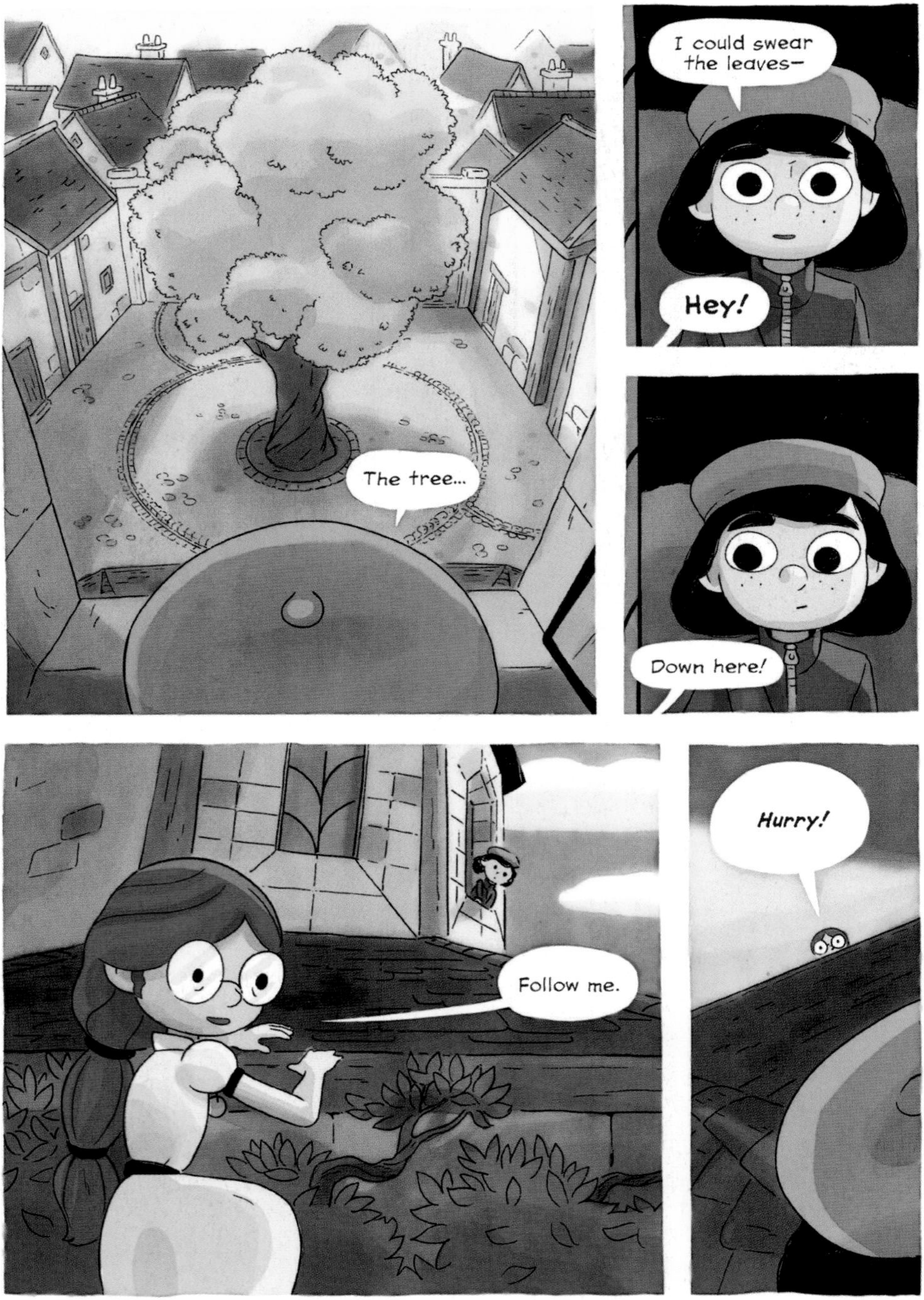
The tree...
I could swear the leaves—
Hey!
Down here!
Follow me.
Hurry!

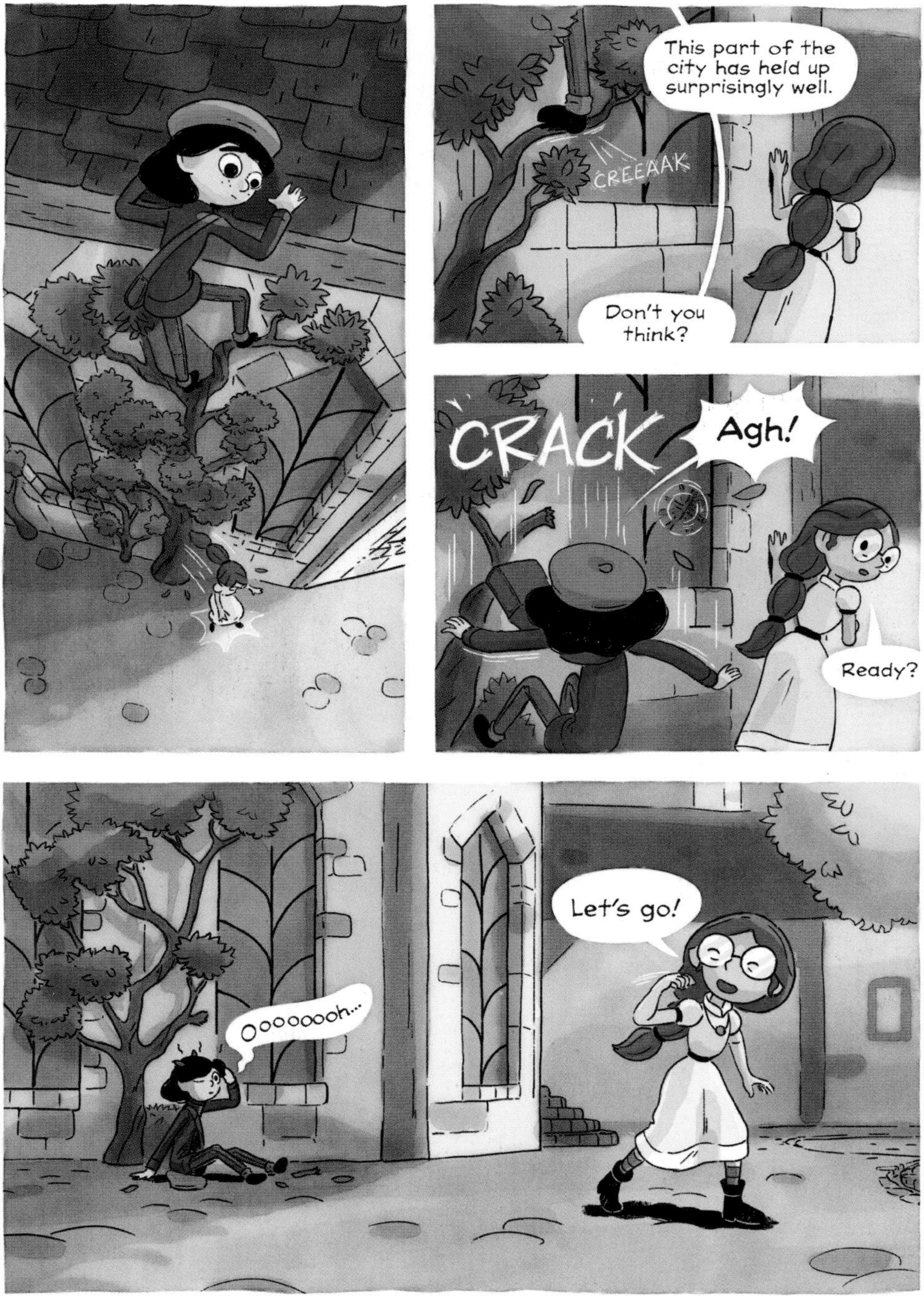
This part of the city has held up surprisingly well.
CREEAAK
Don't you think?
CRACK
Agh!
Ready?
Let's go!
Oooooooh...

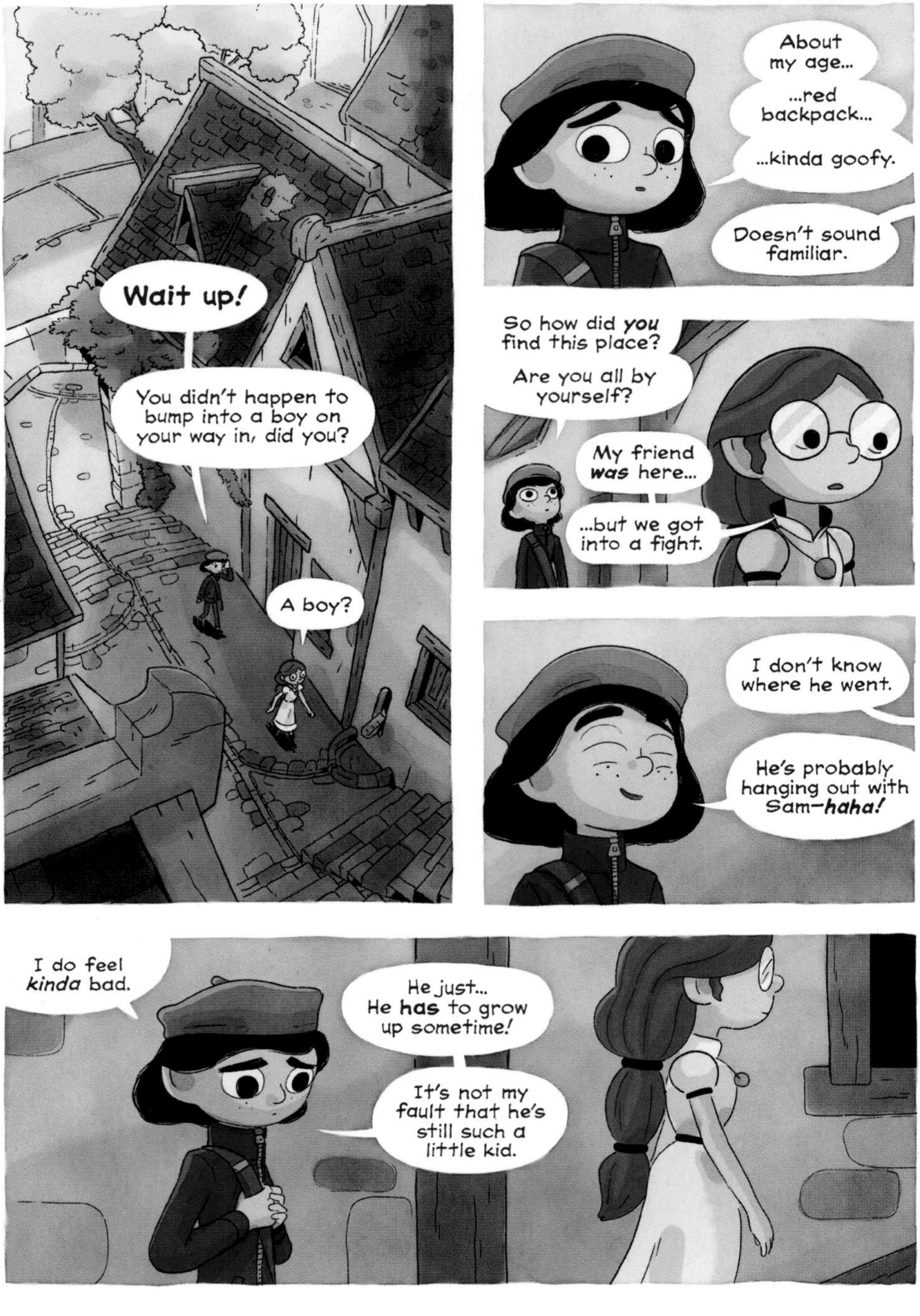

Wait up!
You didn't happen to bump into a boy on your way in, did you?
A boy?
About my age...
...red backpack...
...kinda goofy.
Doesn't sound familiar.
So how did *you* find this place?
Are you all by yourself?
My friend *was* here...
...but we got into a fight.
I don't know where he went.
He's probably hanging out with Sam—*haha!*
I do feel *kinda* bad.
He just...
He **has** to grow up sometime!
It's not my fault that he's still such a little kid.

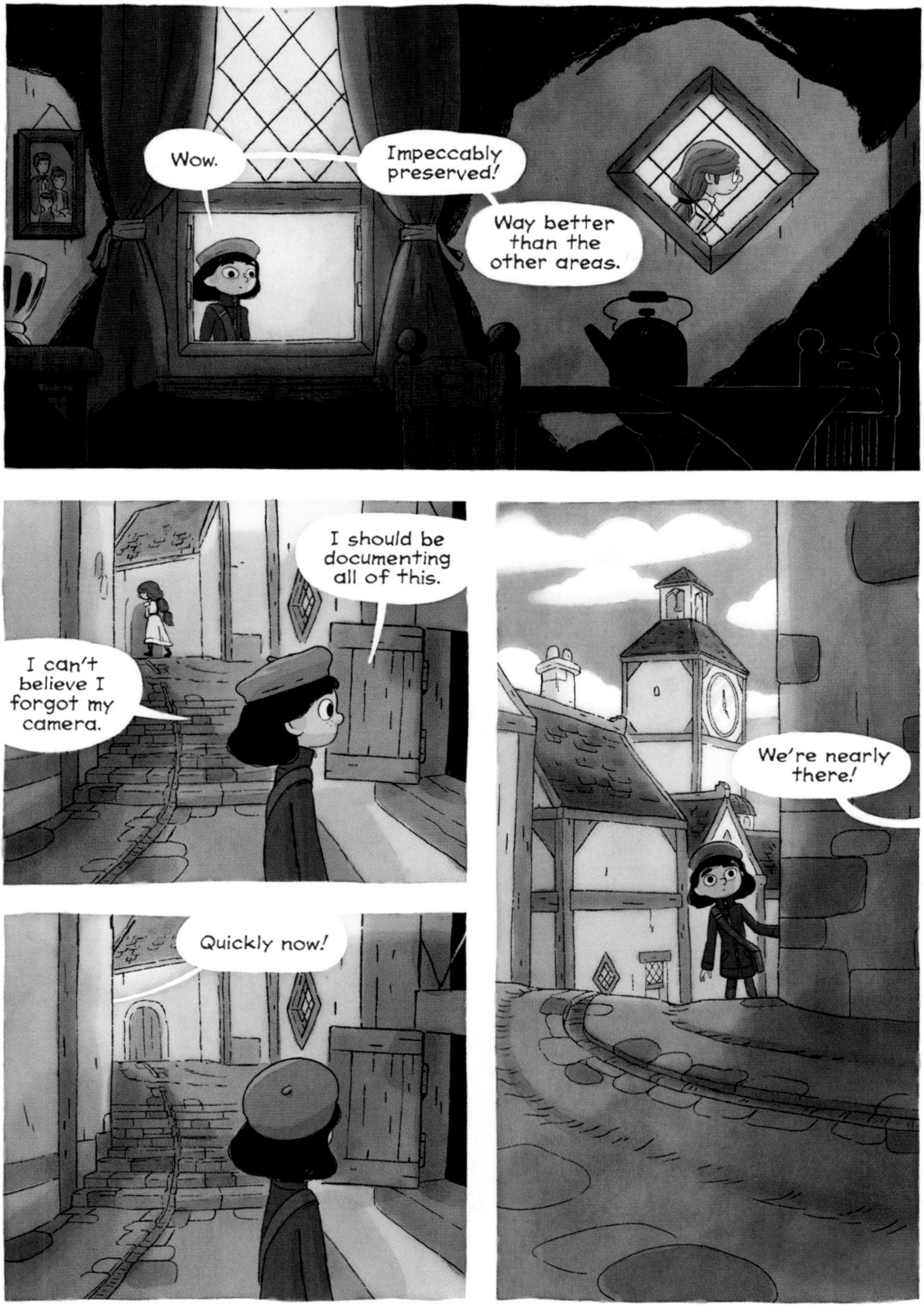
Wow.
Impeccably preserved!
Way better than the other areas.
I should be documenting all of this.
I can't believe I forgot my camera.
Quickly now!
We're nearly there!

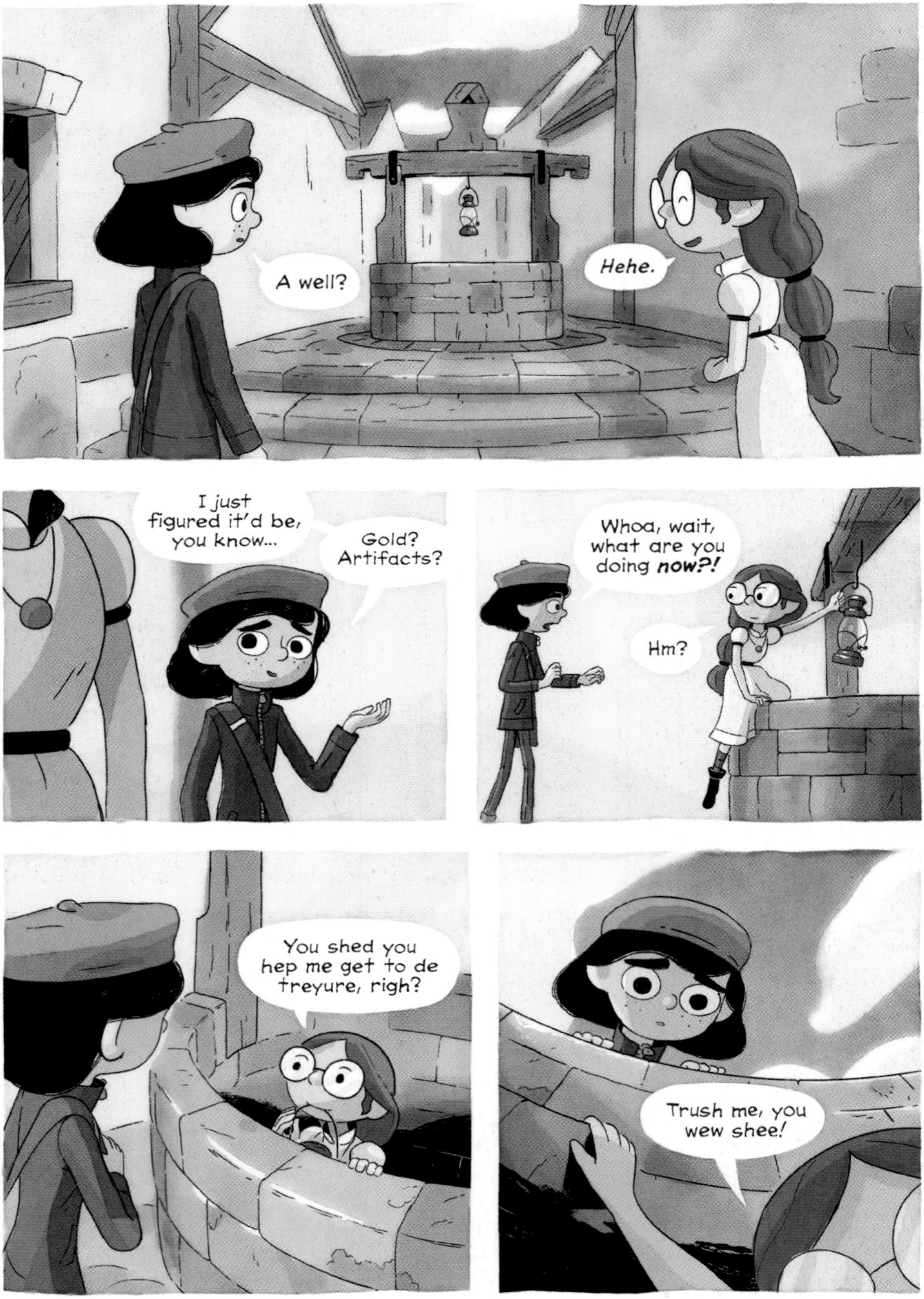
A well?
Hehe.
I just figured it'd be, you know...
Gold? Artifacts?
Whoa, wait, what are you doing **now?!**
Hm?
You shed you hep me get to de treyure, righ?
Trush me, you wew shee!

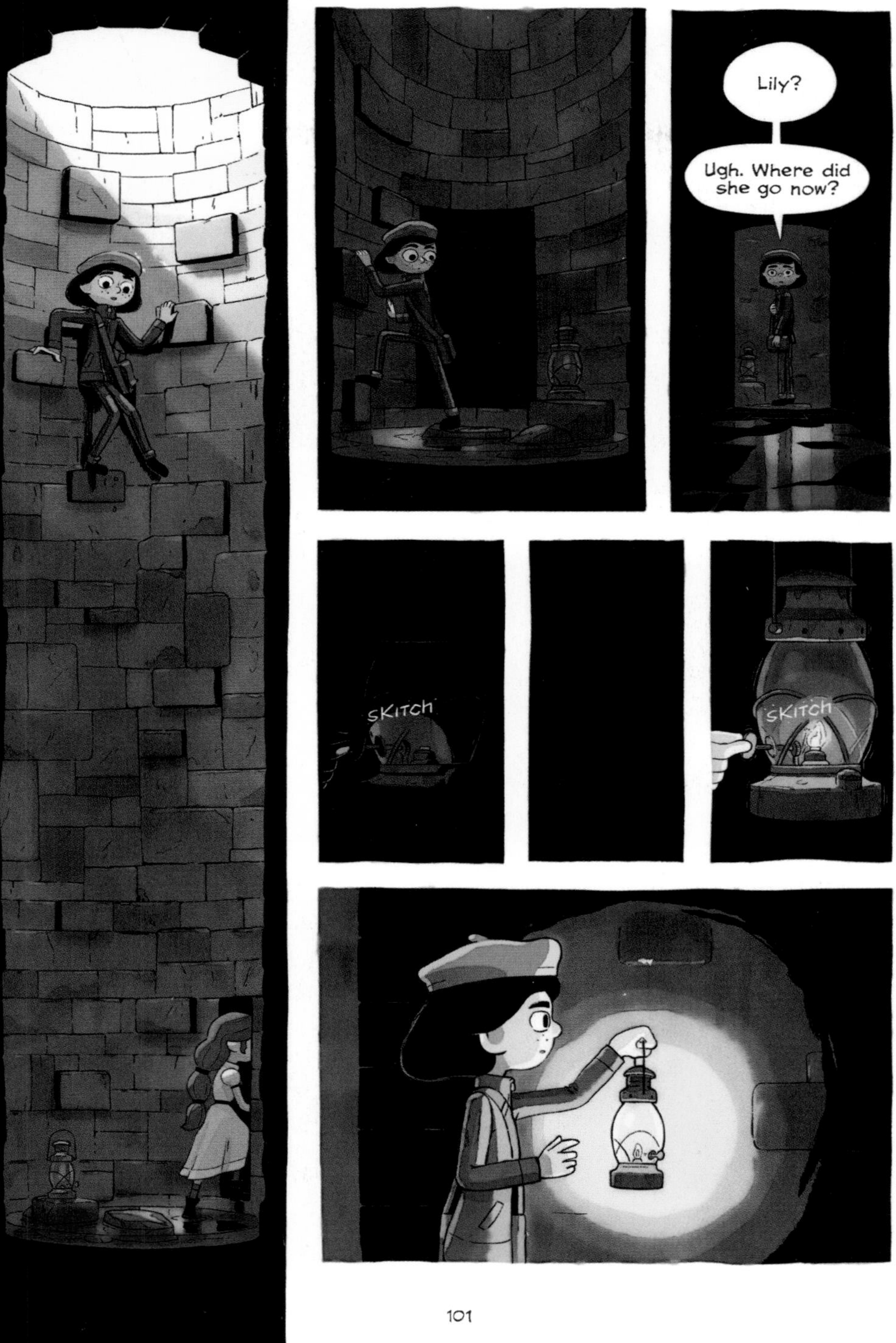
Lily?
Ugh. Where did she go now?
SKITCH
SKITCH

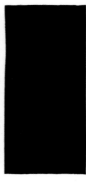

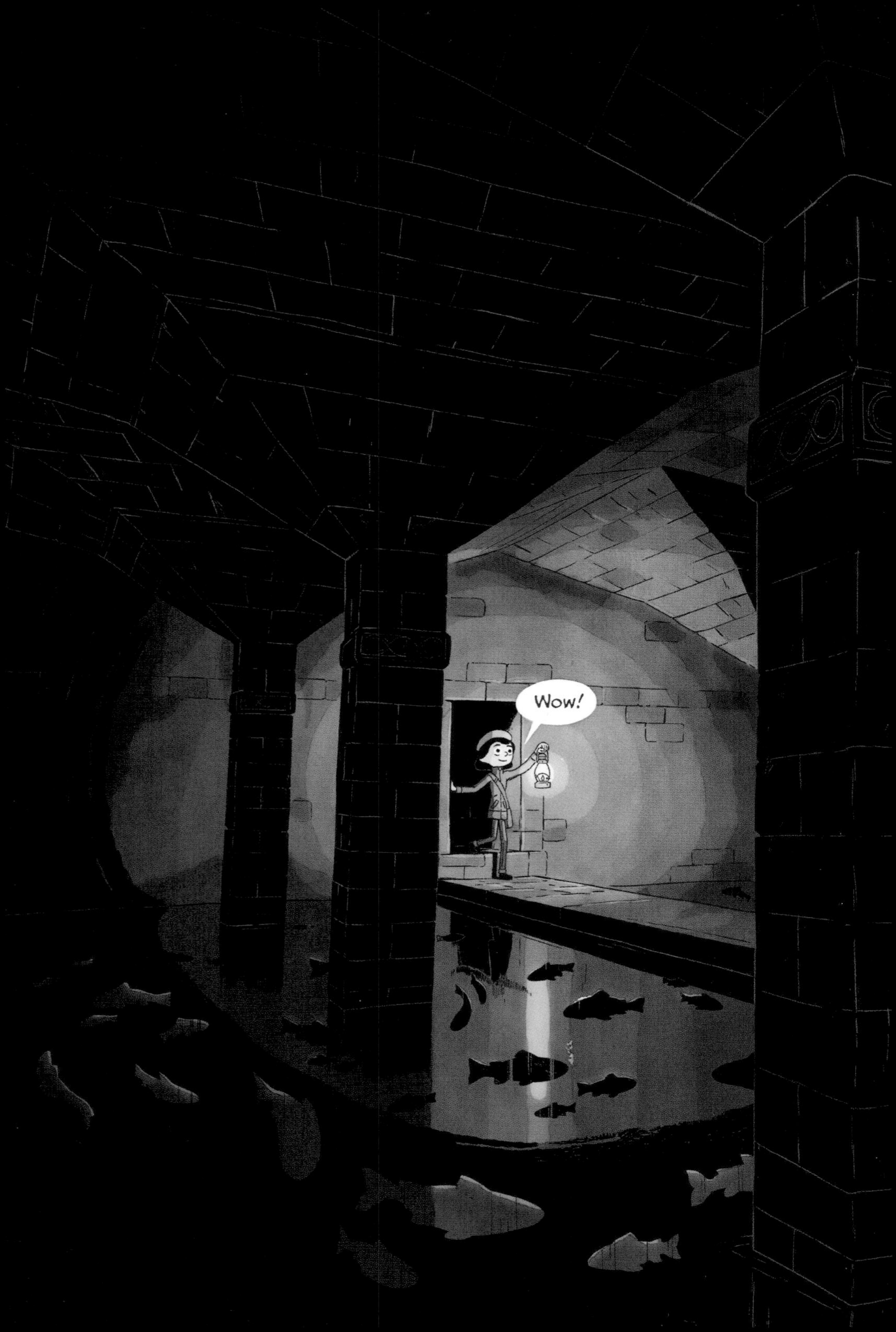
Wow!

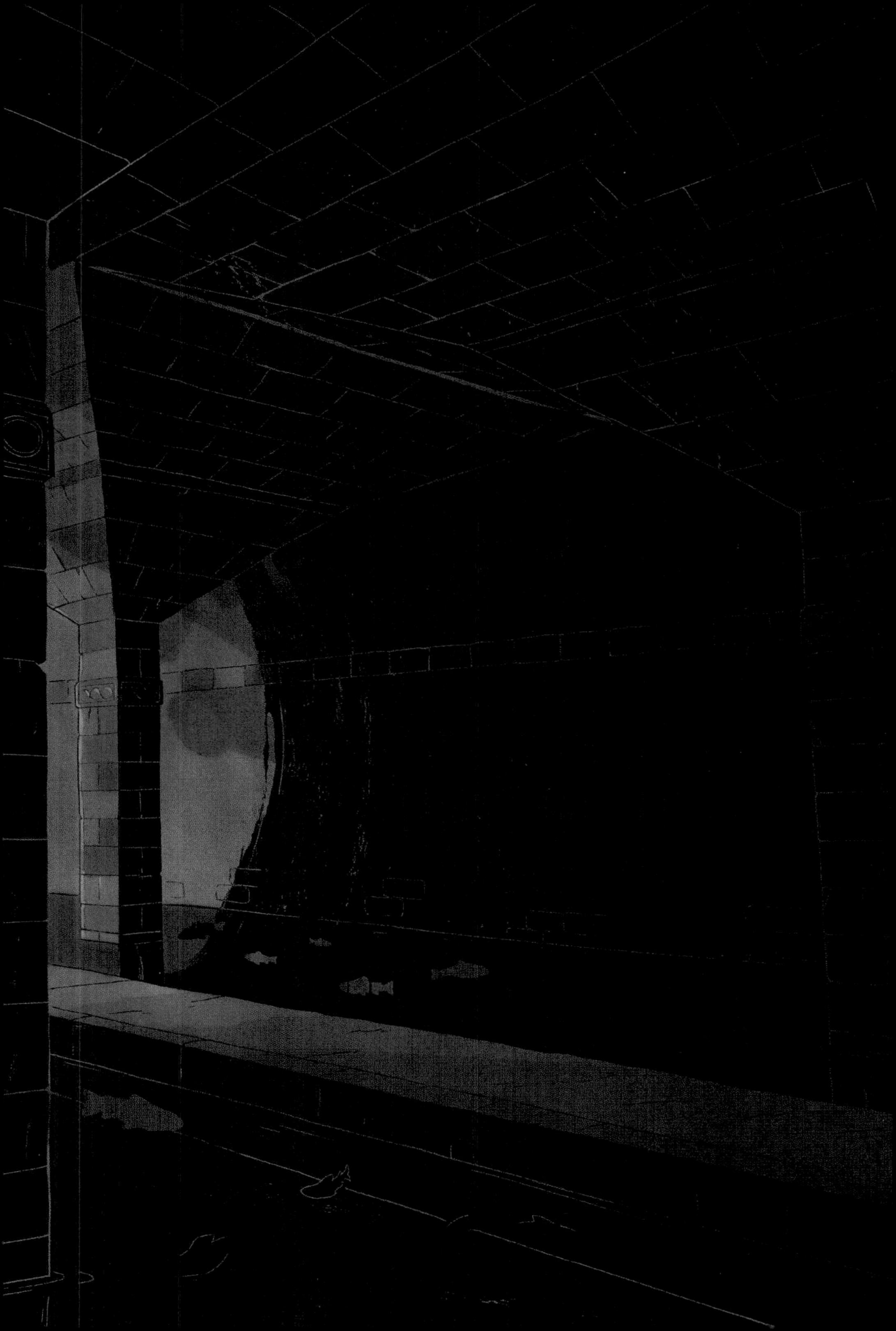

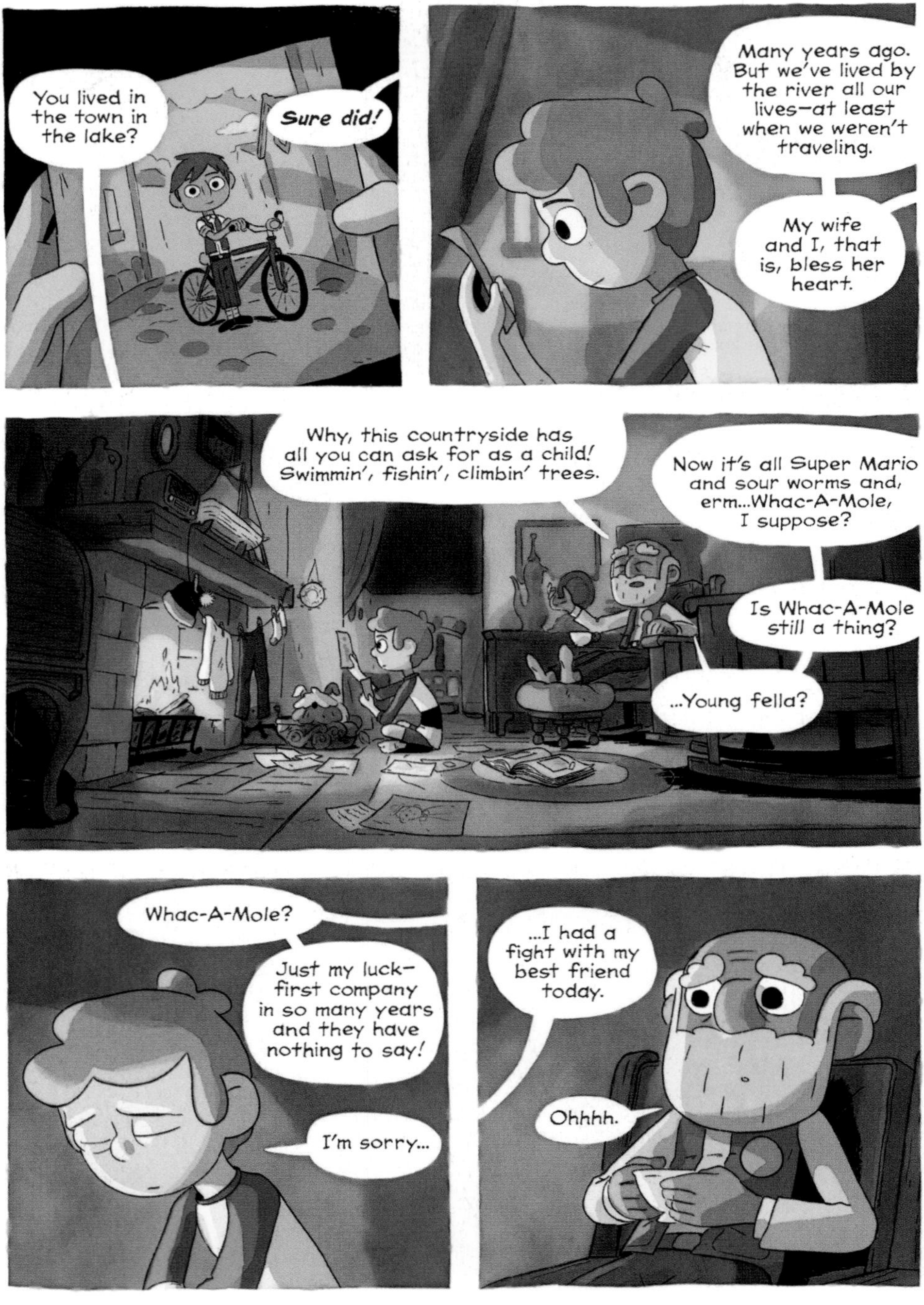
You lived in the town in the lake?
Sure did!
Many years ago. But we've lived by the river all our lives—at least when we weren't traveling.
My wife and I, that is, bless her heart.
Why, this countryside has all you can ask for as a child! Swimmin', fishin', climbin' trees.
Now it's all Super Mario and sour worms and, erm...Whac-A-Mole, I suppose?
Is Whac-A-Mole still a thing?
...Young fella?
Whac-A-Mole?
Just my luck—first company in so many years and they have nothing to say!
I'm sorry...
...I had a fight with my best friend today.
Ohhhh.

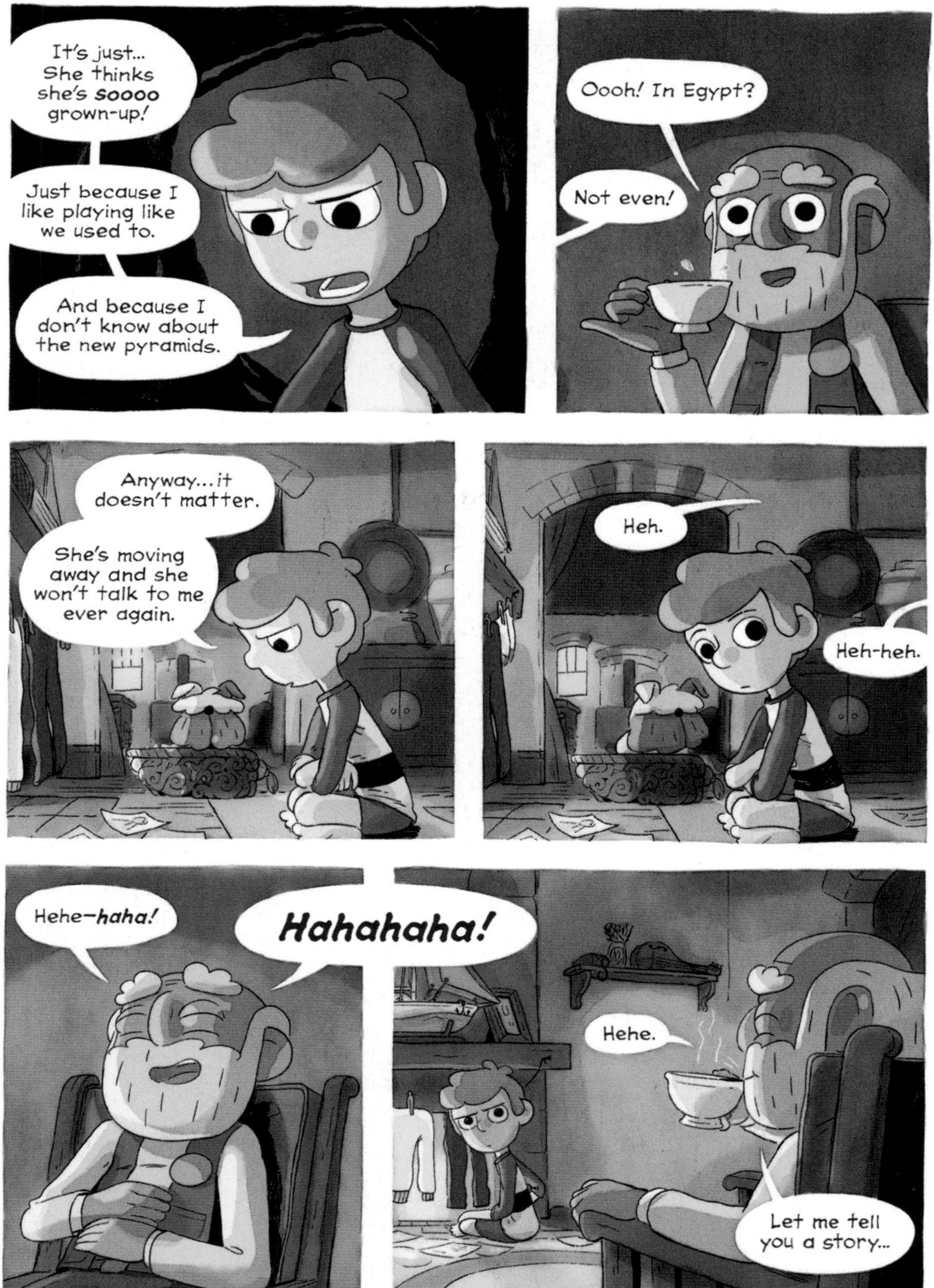
It's just... She thinks she's **soooo** grown-up!
Just because I like playing like we used to.
And because I don't know about the new pyramids.
Oooh! In Egypt?
Not even!
Anyway...it doesn't matter.
She's moving away and she won't talk to me ever again.
Heh.
Heh-heh.
Hehe-*haha!*
Hahahaha!
Hehe.
Let me tell you a story...

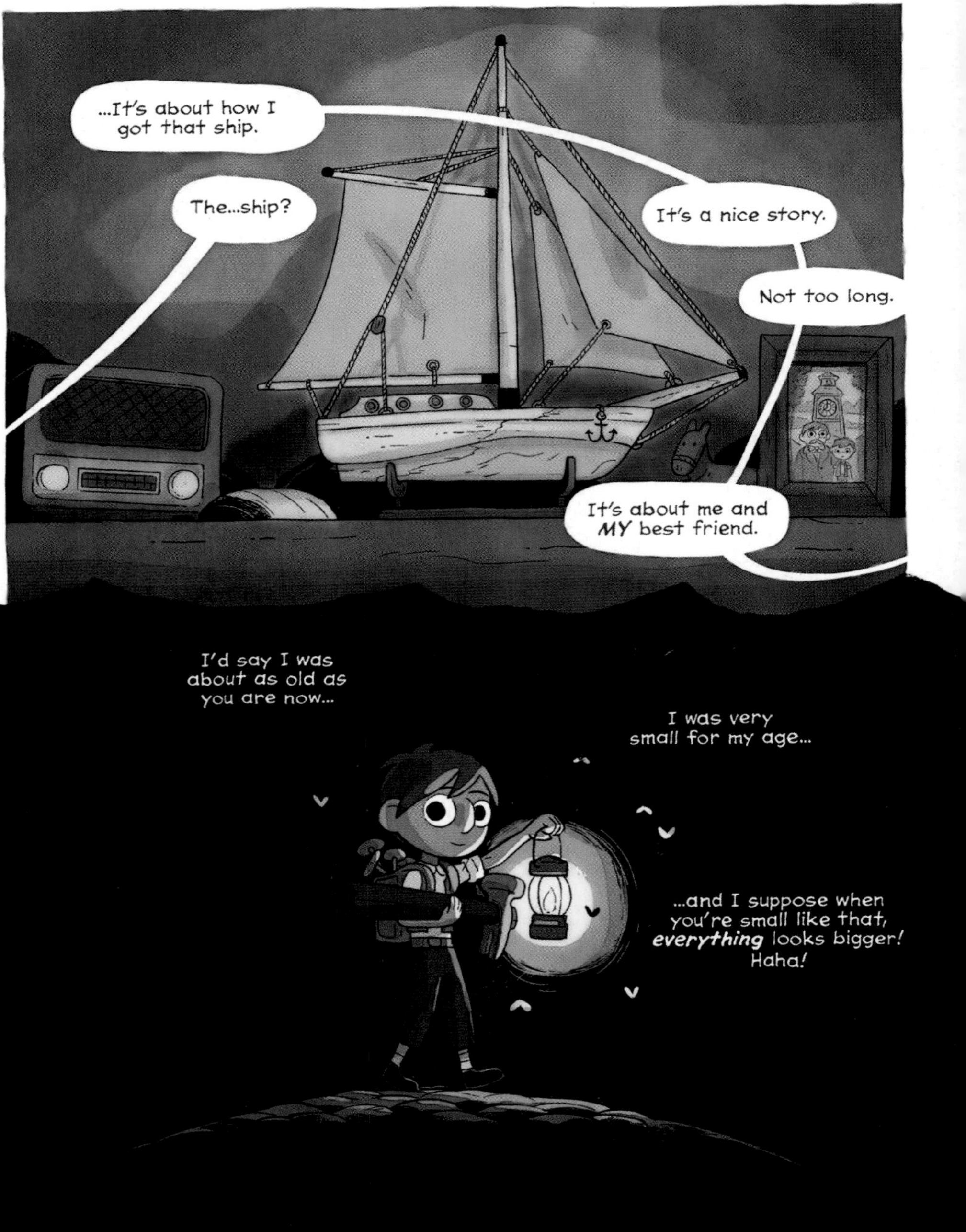
...It's about how I got that ship.
The...ship?
It's a nice story.
Not too long.
It's about me and MY best friend.
I'd say I was about as old as you are now...
I was very small for my age...
...and I suppose when you're small like that, everything looks bigger! Haha!

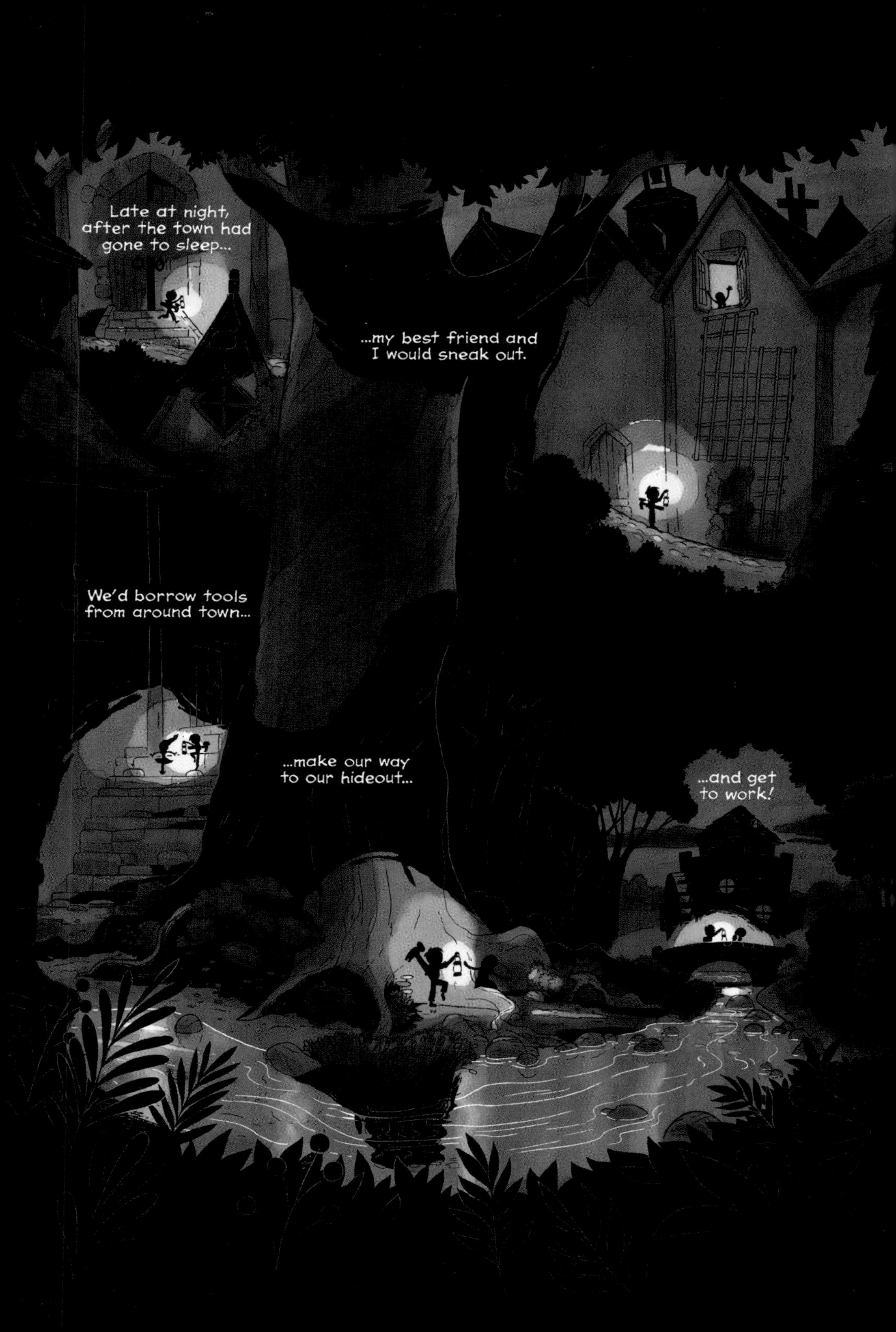
Late at night, after the town had gone to sleep...
...my best friend and I would sneak out.
We'd borrow tools from around town...
...make our way to our hideout...
...and get to work!

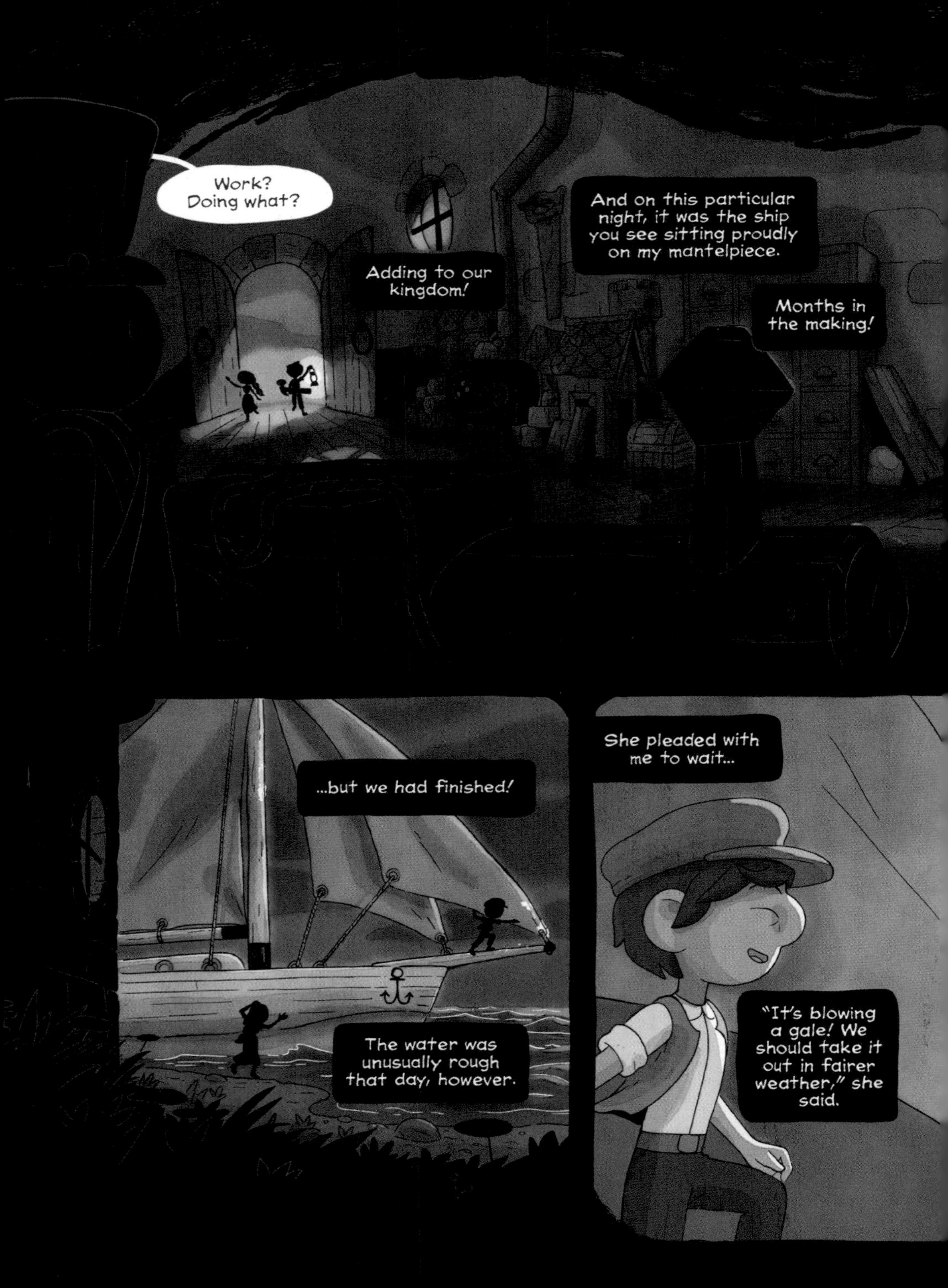

Work? Doing what?
Adding to our kingdom!
And on this particular night, it was the ship you see sitting proudly on my mantelpiece.
Months in the making!
...but we had finished!
The water was unusually rough that day, however.
She pleaded with me to wait...
"It's blowing a gale! We should take it out in fairer weather," she said.

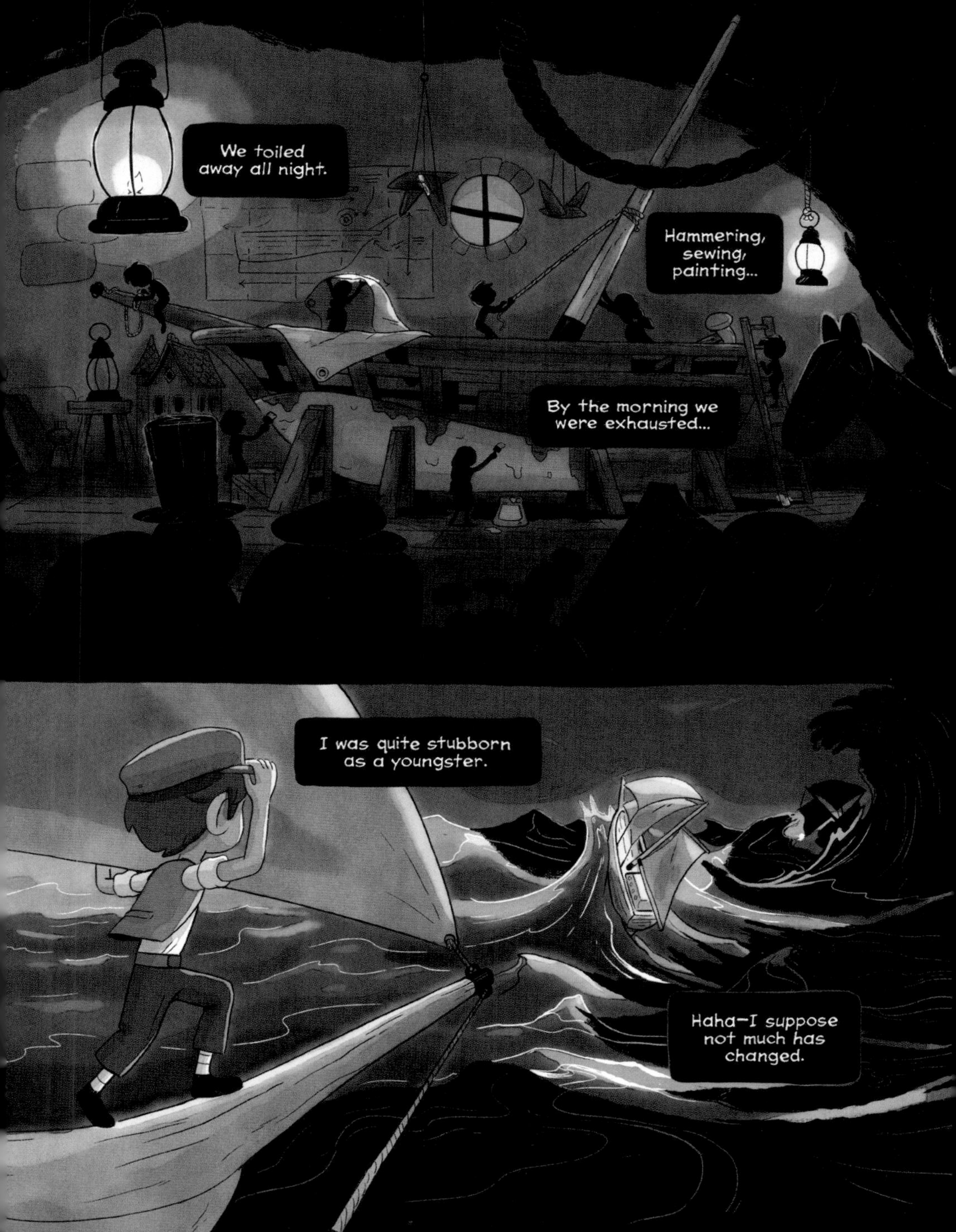
We toiled away all night.
Hammering, sewing, painting...
By the morning we were exhausted...
I was quite stubborn as a youngster.
Haha—I suppose not much has changed.

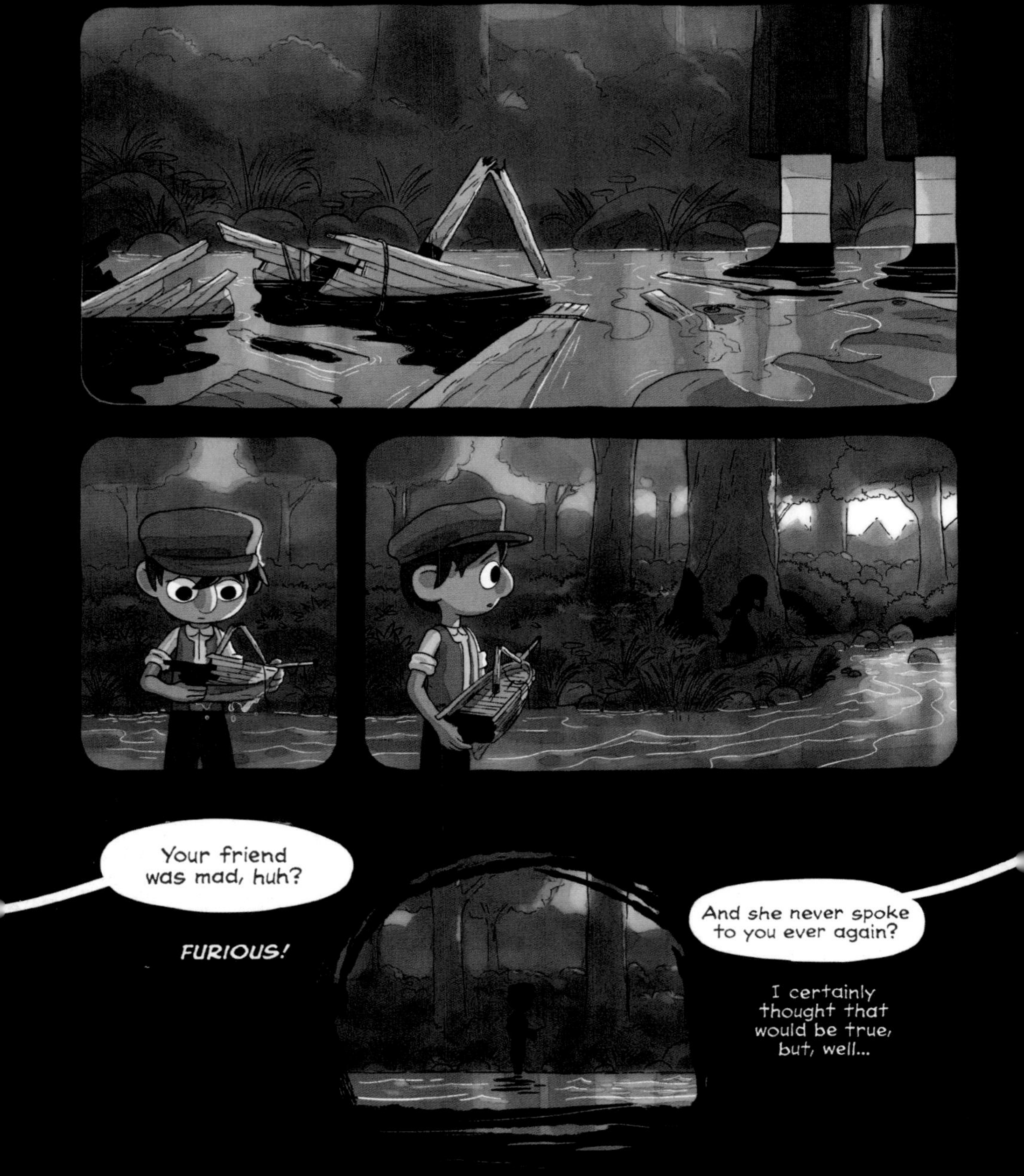
Your friend was mad, huh?
FURIOUS!
And she never spoke to you ever again?
I certainly thought that would be true, but, well...

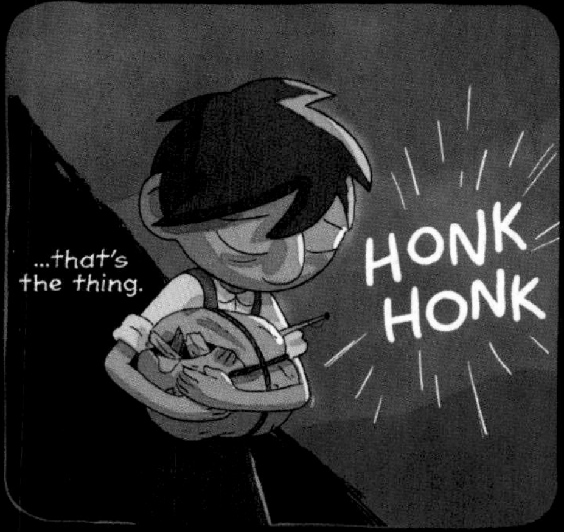
...that's the thing.
HONK HONK

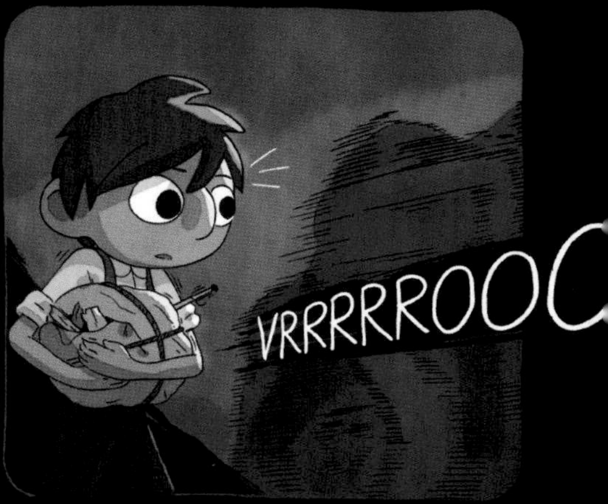
VRRRRROOO

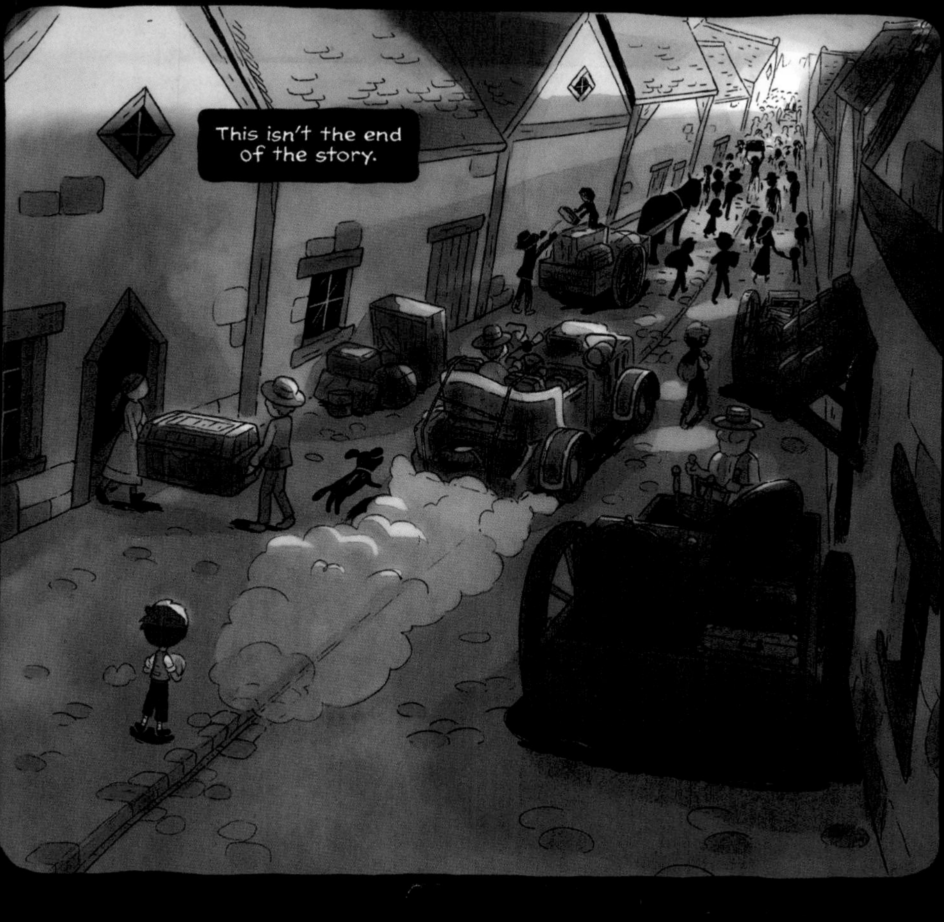
This isn't the end of the story.

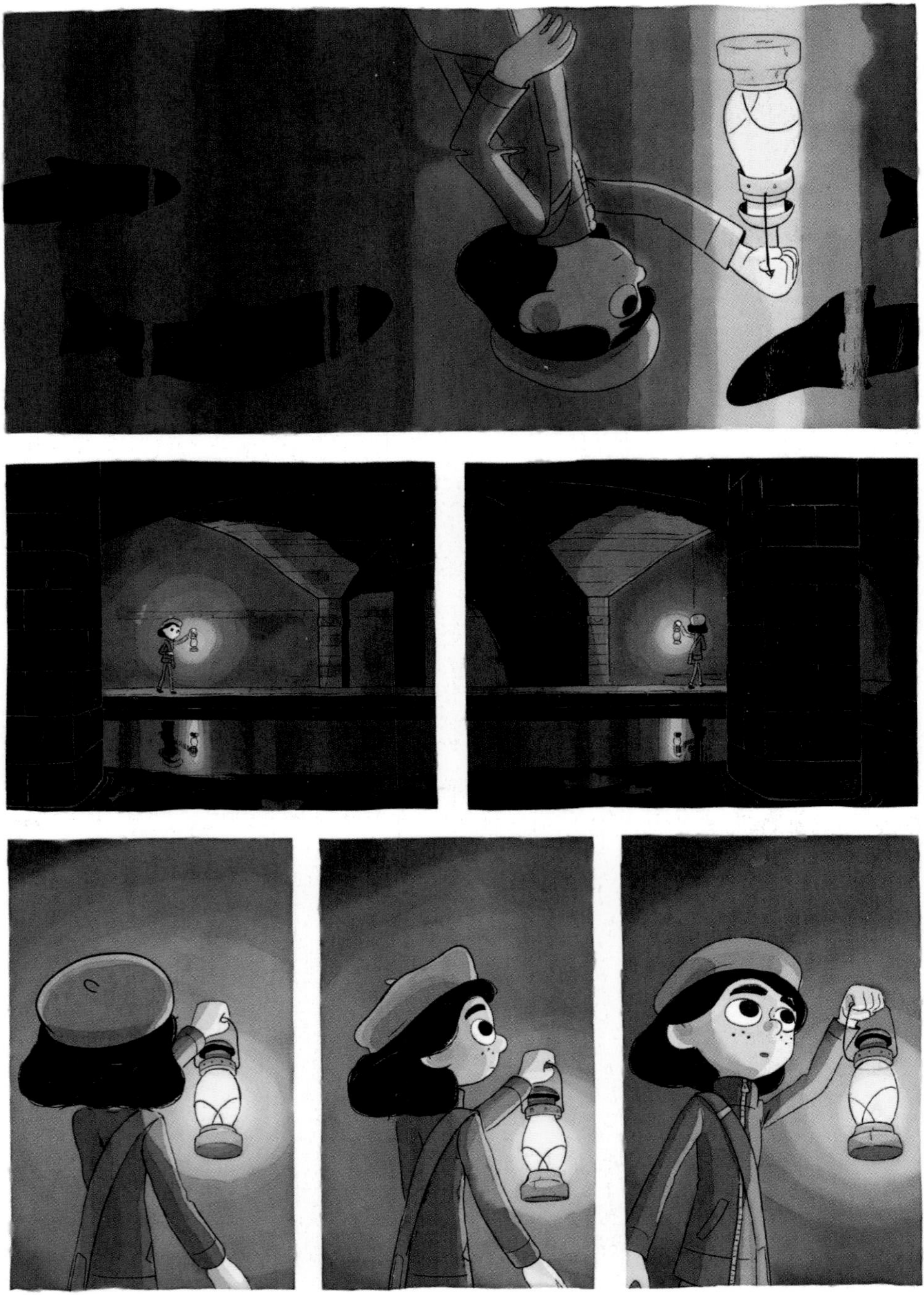

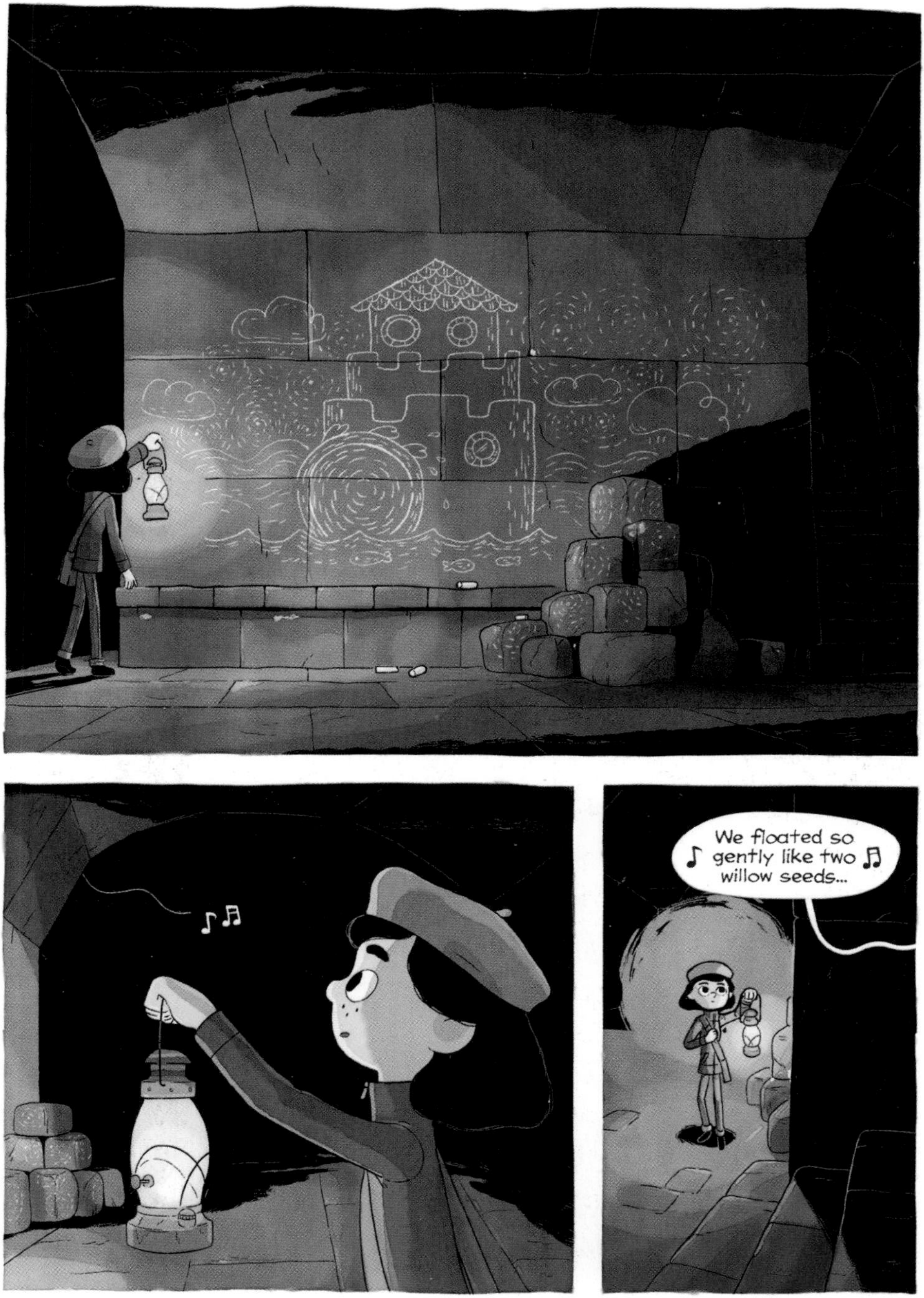
We floated so ♪ gently like two ♫ willow seeds...

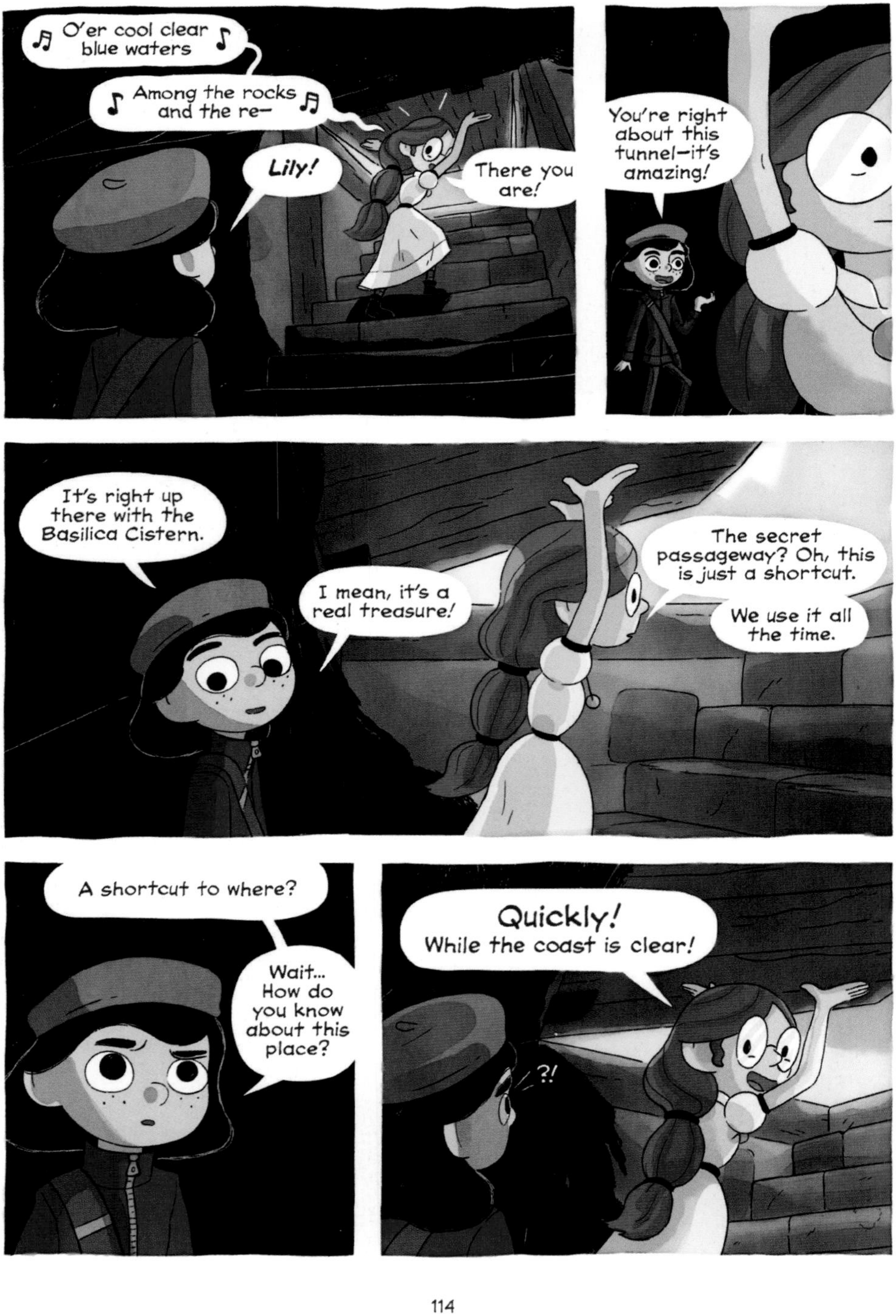

♫ O'er cool clear blue waters ♪
♪ Among the rocks and the re— ♫
Lily!
There you are!
You're right about this tunnel—it's amazing!
It's right up there with the Basilica Cistern.
I mean, it's a real treasure!
The secret passageway? Oh, this is just a shortcut.
We use it all the time.
A shortcut to where?
Wait... How do you know about this place?
Quickly! While the coast is clear!
?!

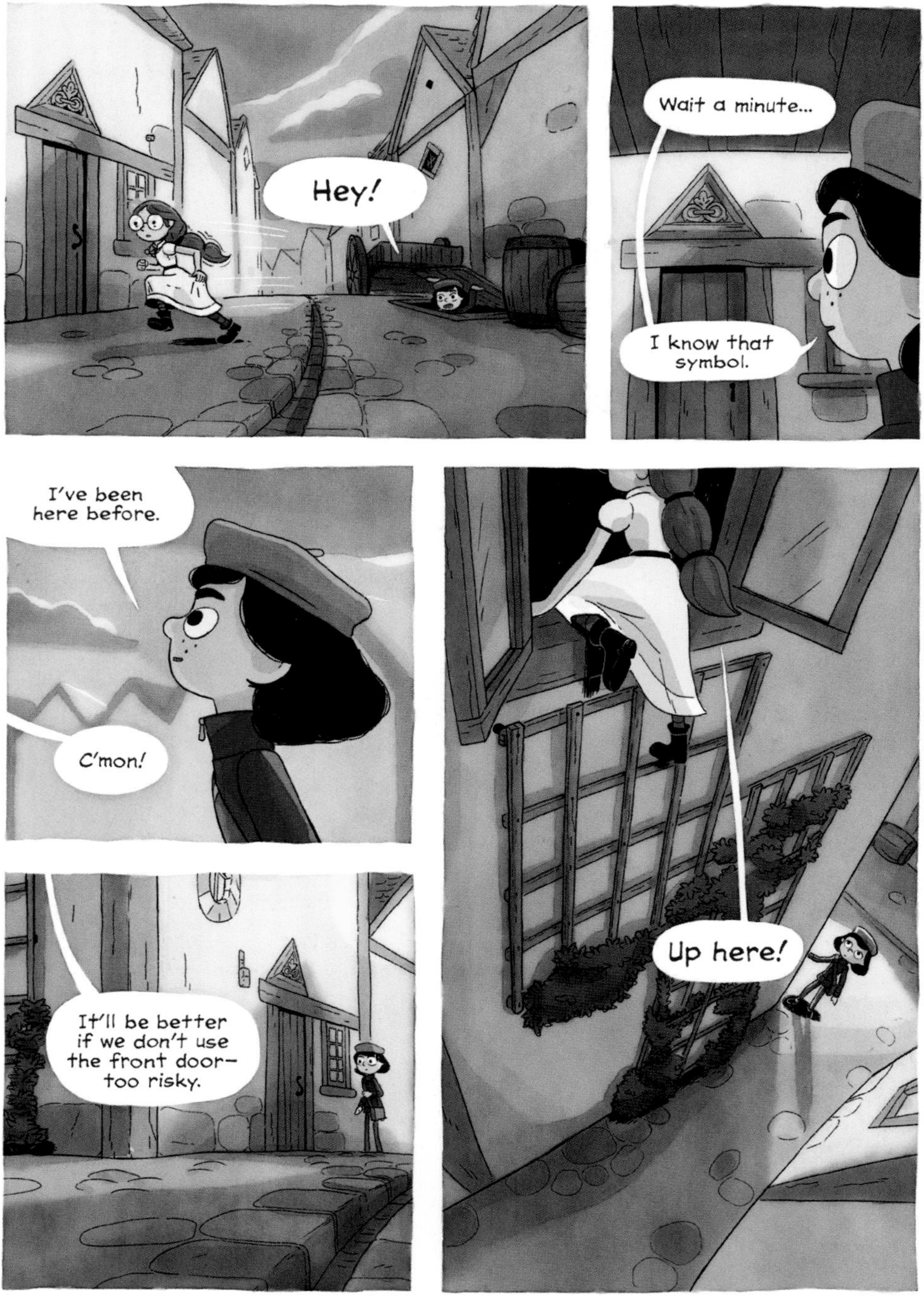
Hey!
Wait a minute...
I know that symbol.
I've been here before.
C'mon!
It'll be better if we don't use the front door—too risky.
Up here!

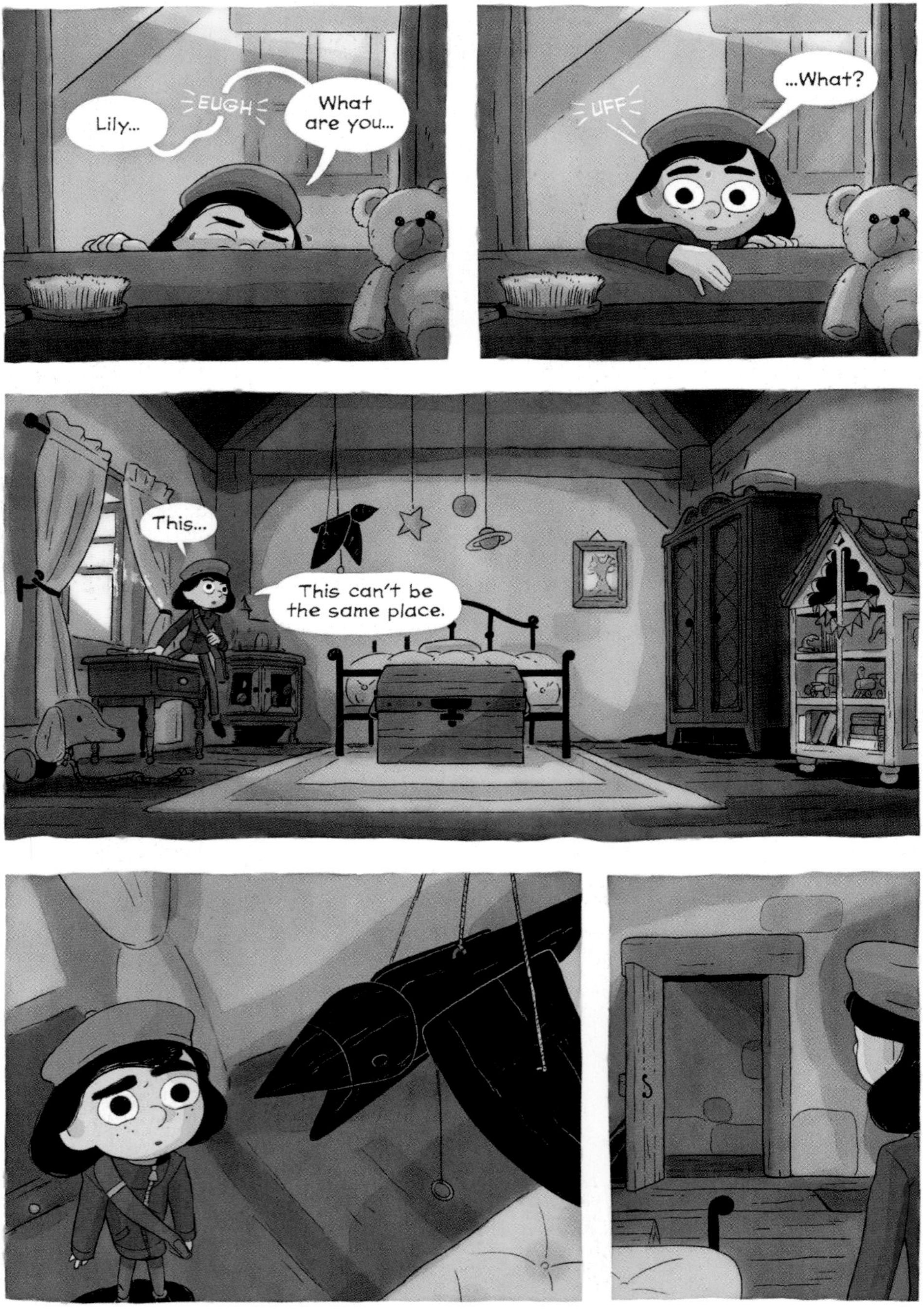
Lily...
EUGH
What are you...
UFF
...What?
This...
This can't be the same place.

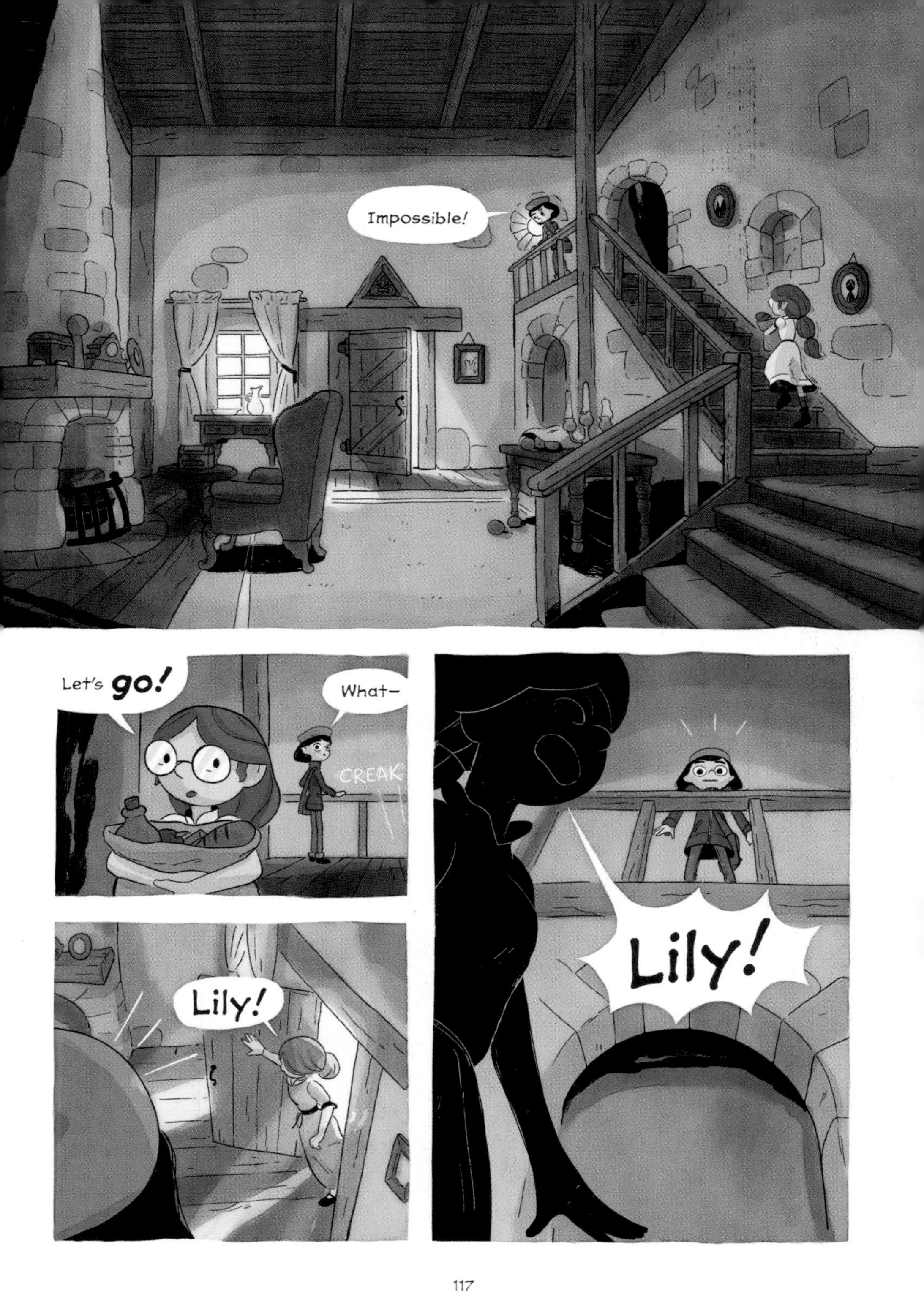
Impossible!
Let's go!
What–
CREAK
Lily!
Lily!

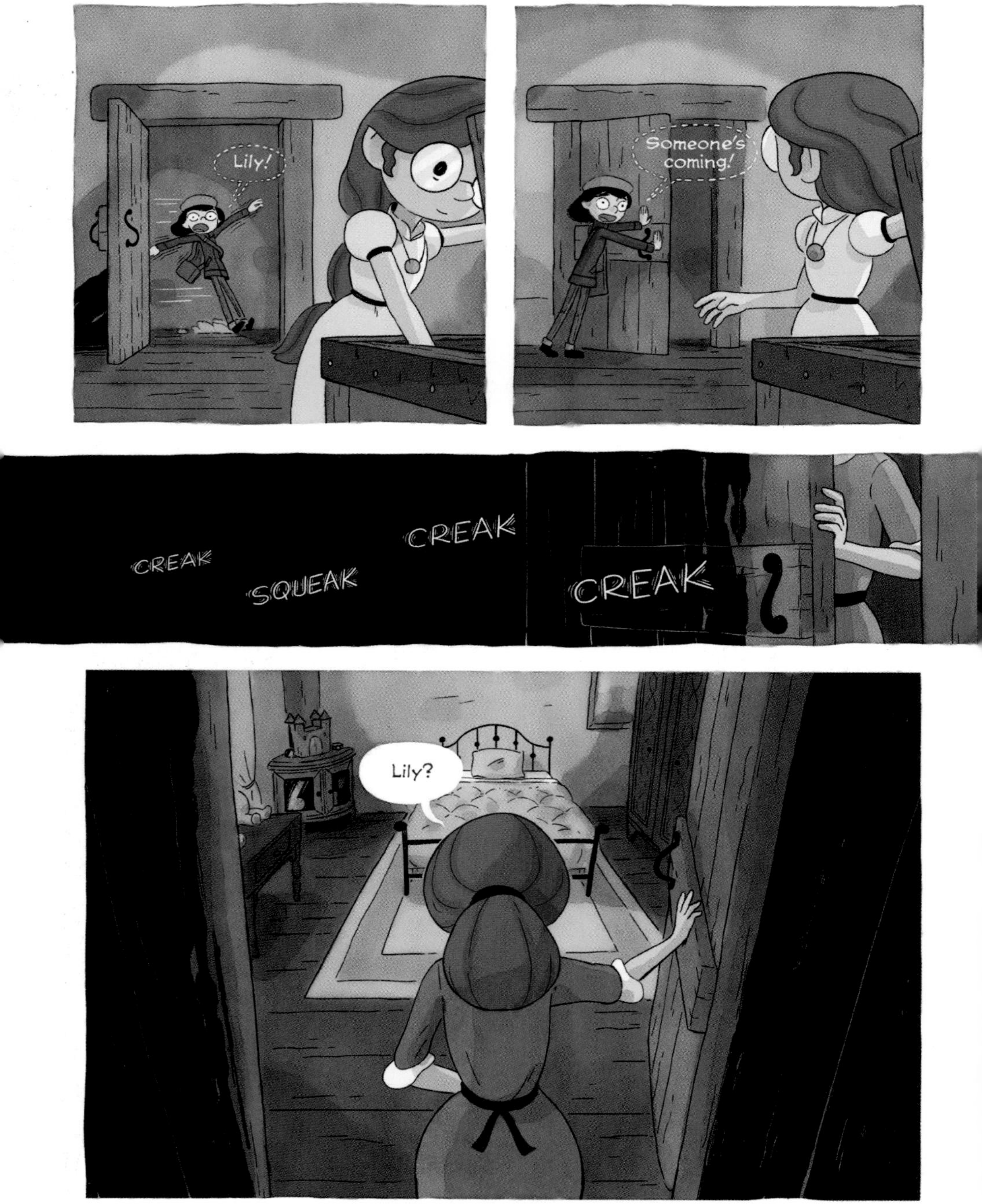
Lily!
Someone's coming!
CREAK
SQUEAK
CREAK
CREAK
Lily?

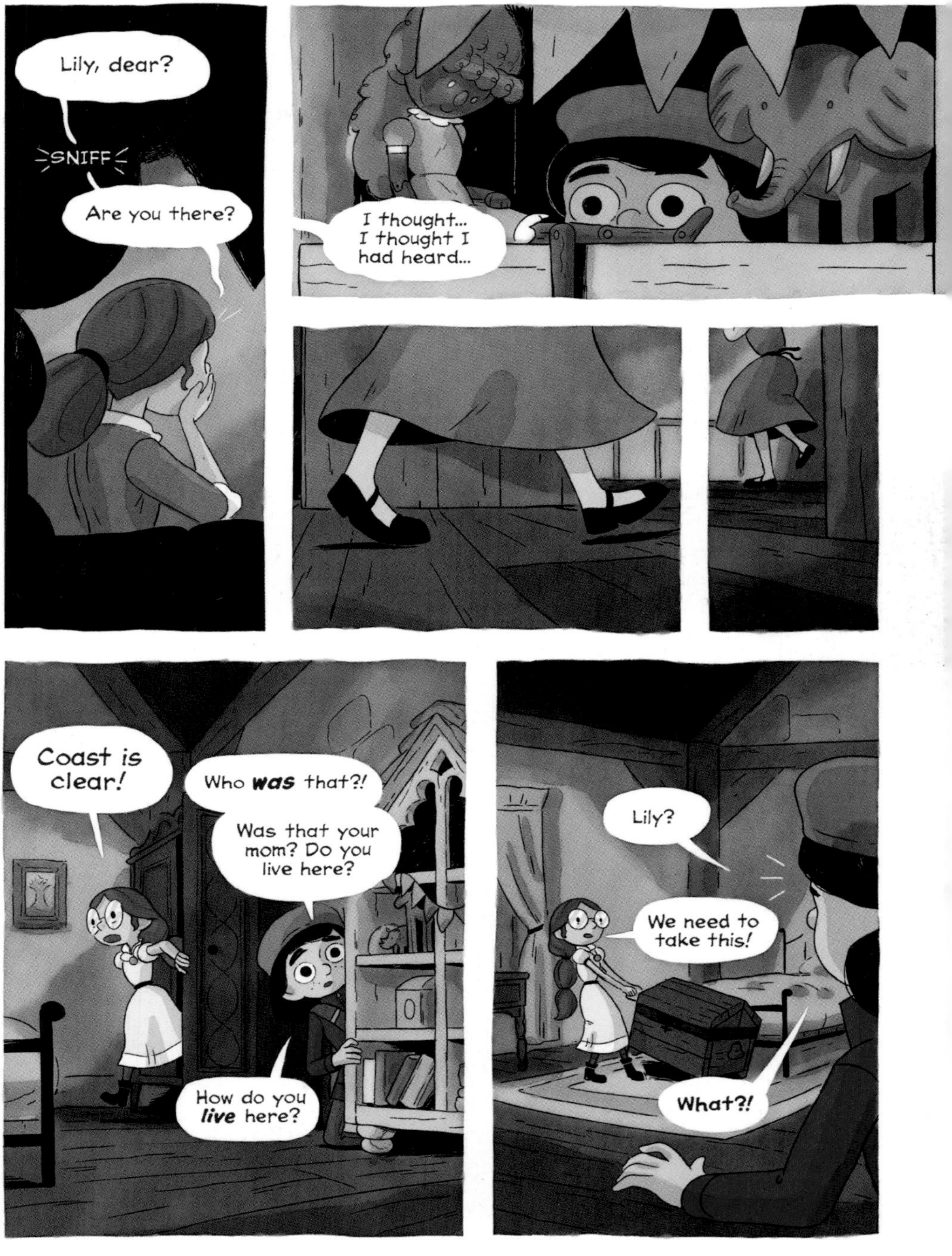
Lily, dear?
SNIFF
Are you there?
I thought... I thought I had heard...
Coast is clear!
Who **was** that?!
Was that your mom? Do you live here?
How do you ***live*** here?
Lily?
We need to take this!
What?!

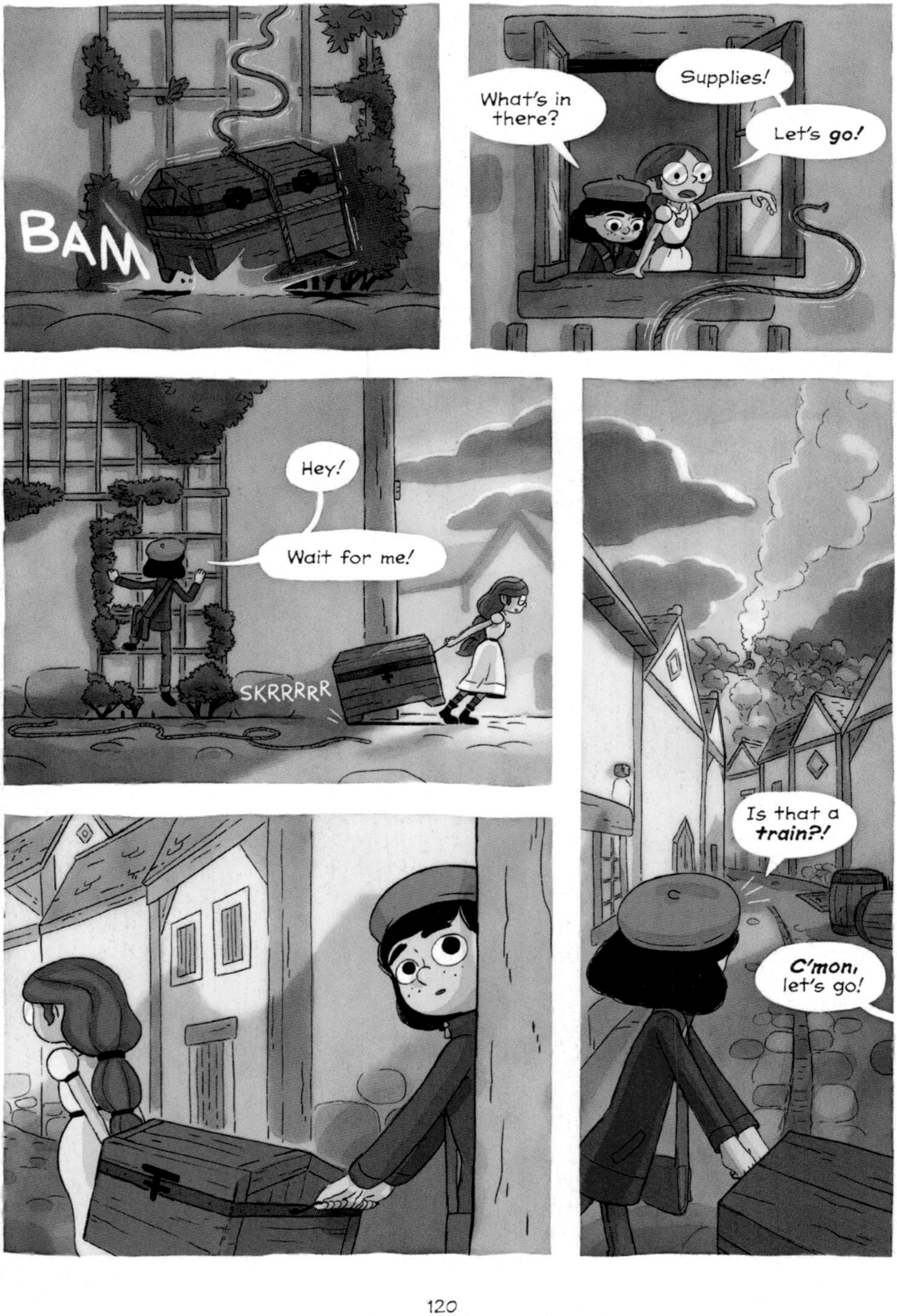
BAM
What's in there?
Supplies!
Let's go!
Hey!
Wait for me!
SKRRRRR
Is that a train?!
C'mon, let's go!

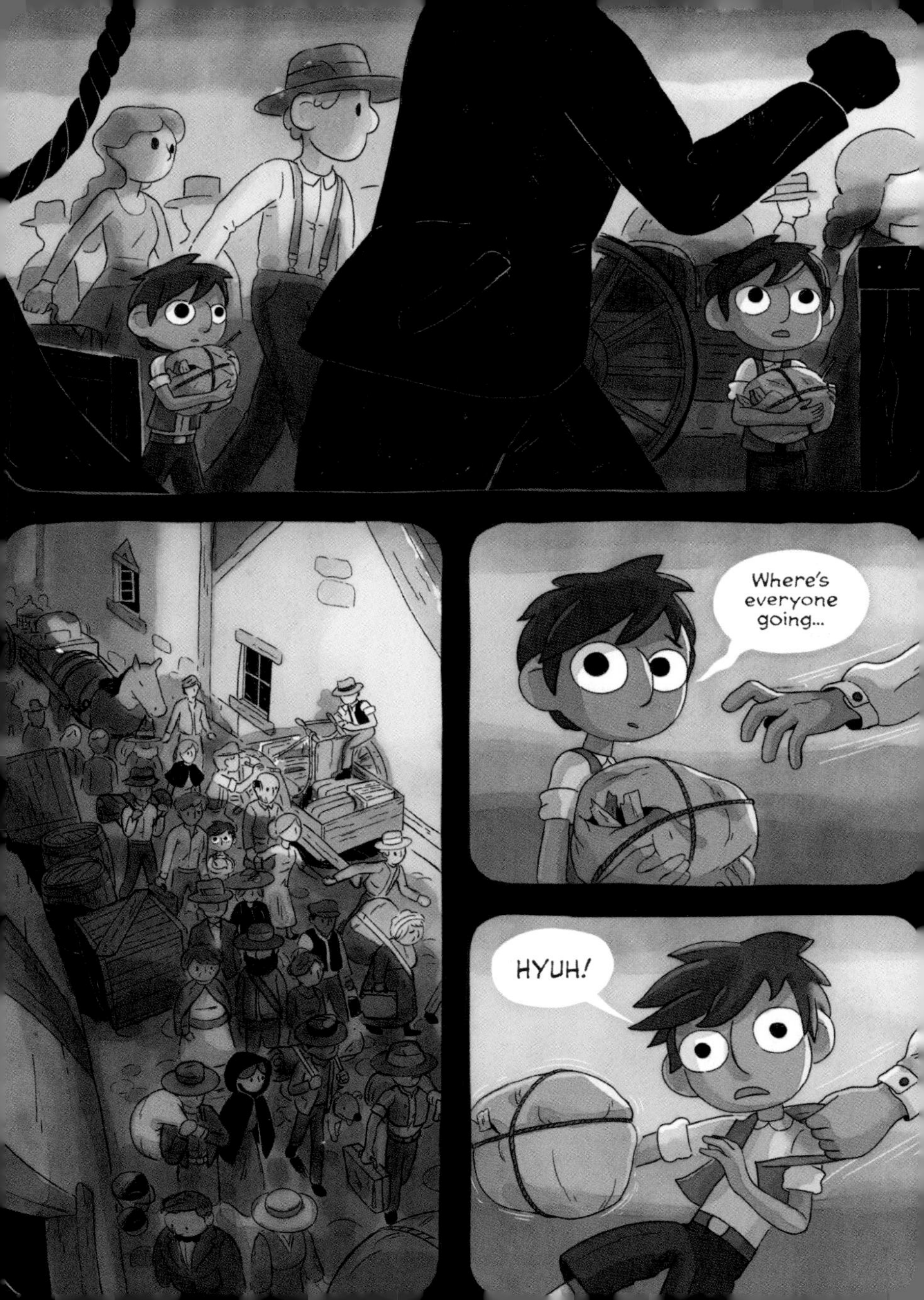
Where's everyone going...
HYUH!

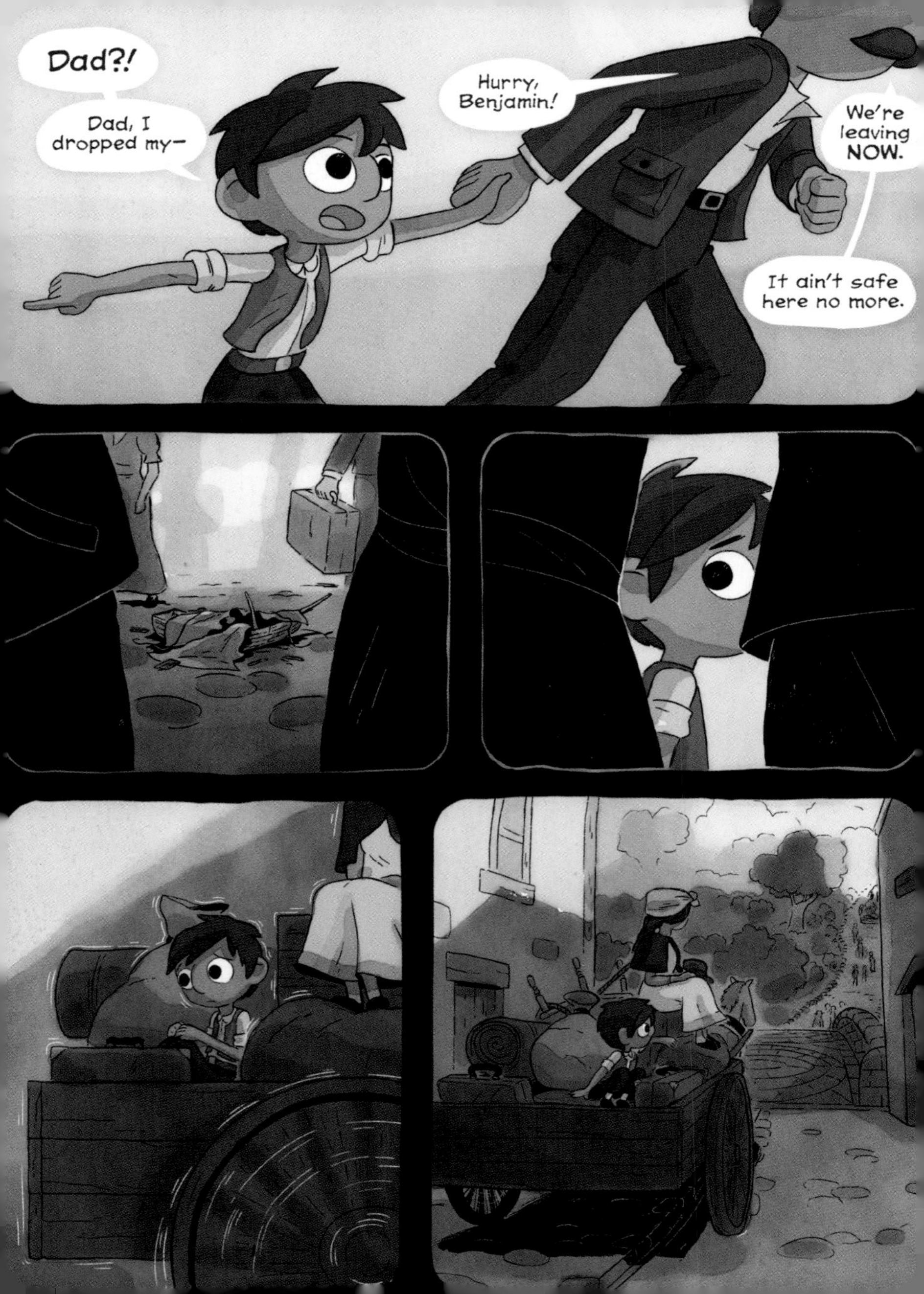
Dad?!
Dad, I dropped my—
Hurry, Benjamin!
We're leaving NOW.
It ain't safe here no more.

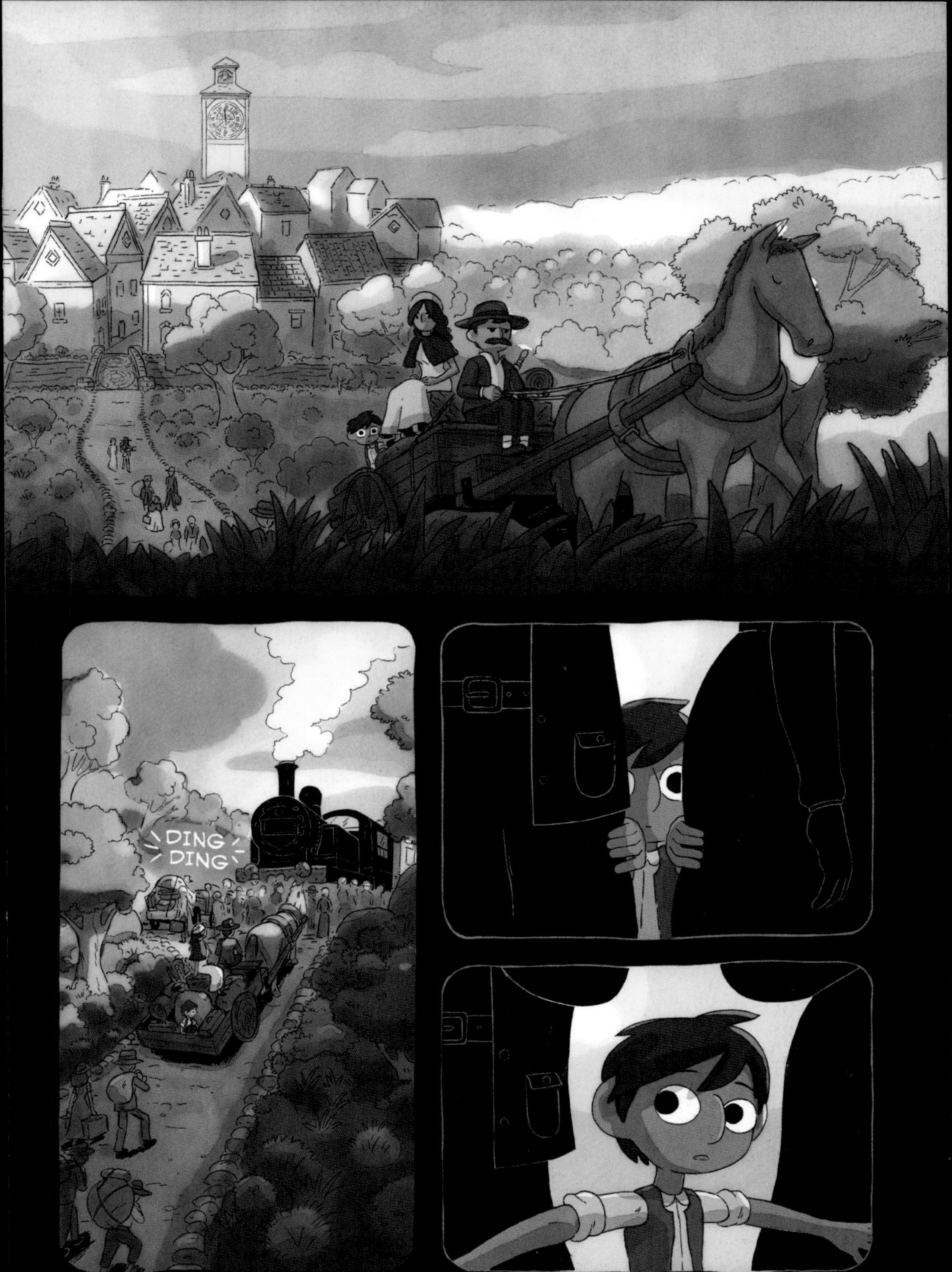
DING
DING

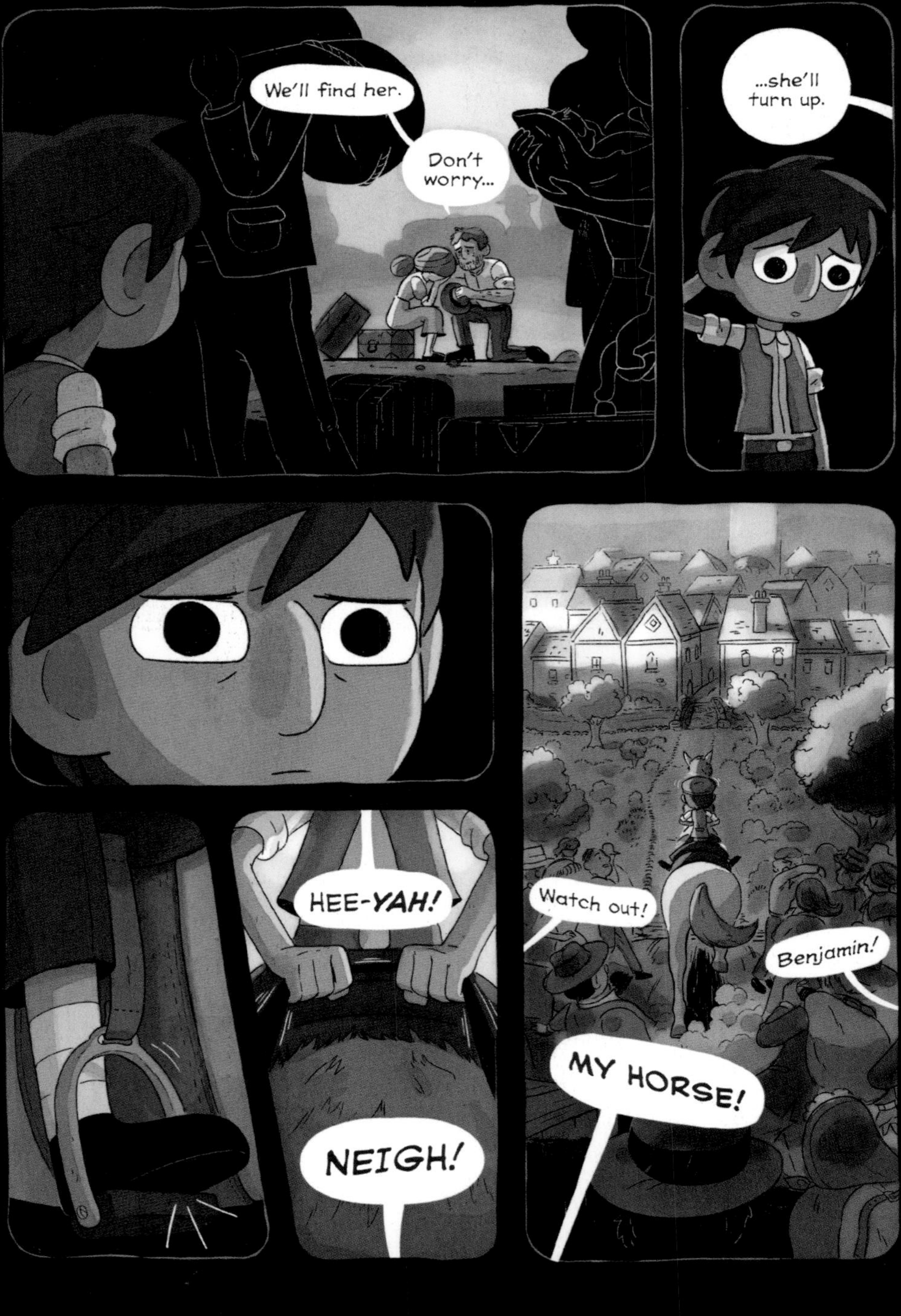
We'll find her.
Don't worry...
...she'll turn up.
HEE-YAH!
NEIGH!
Watch out!
Benjamin!
MY HORSE!

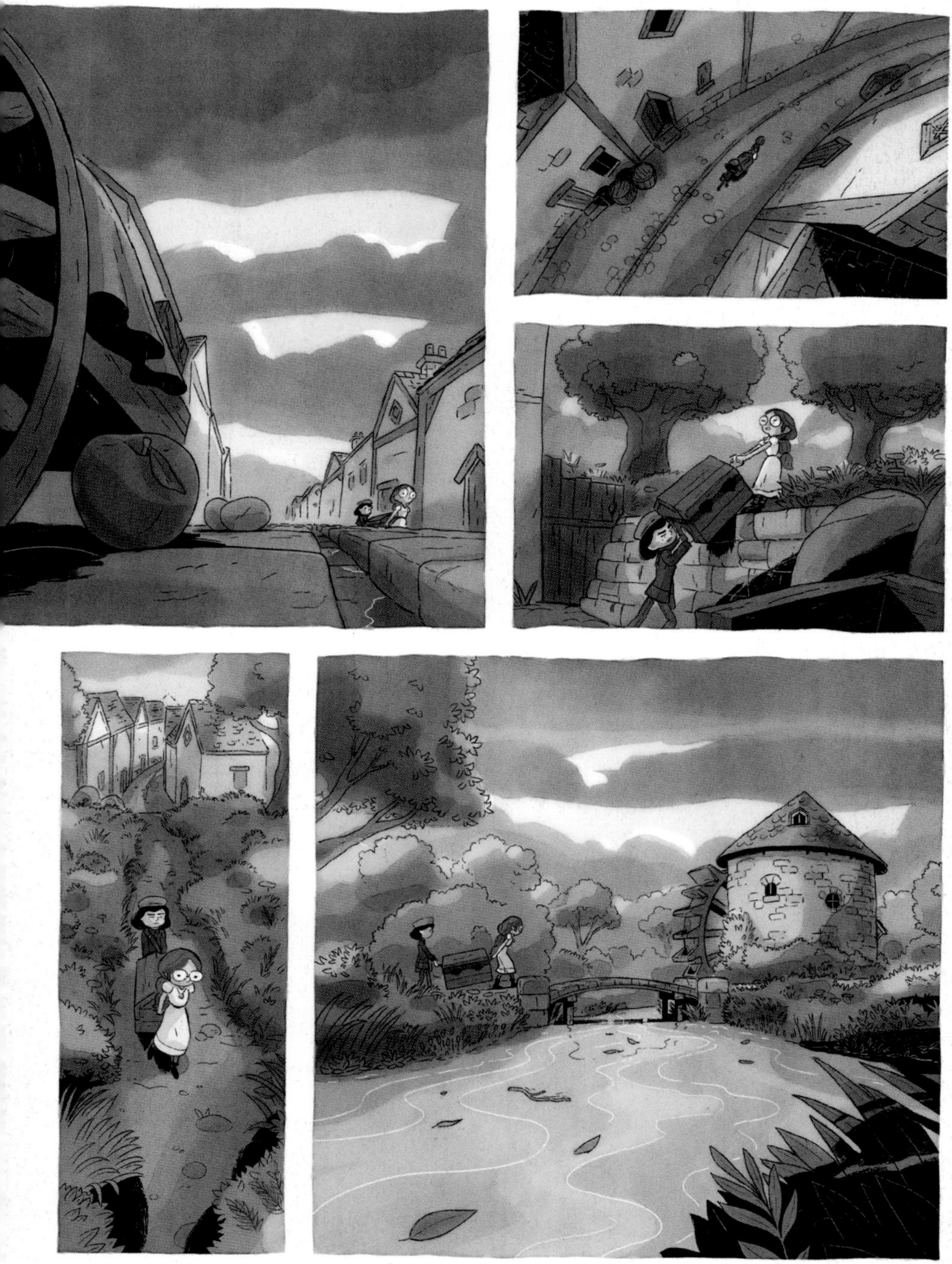

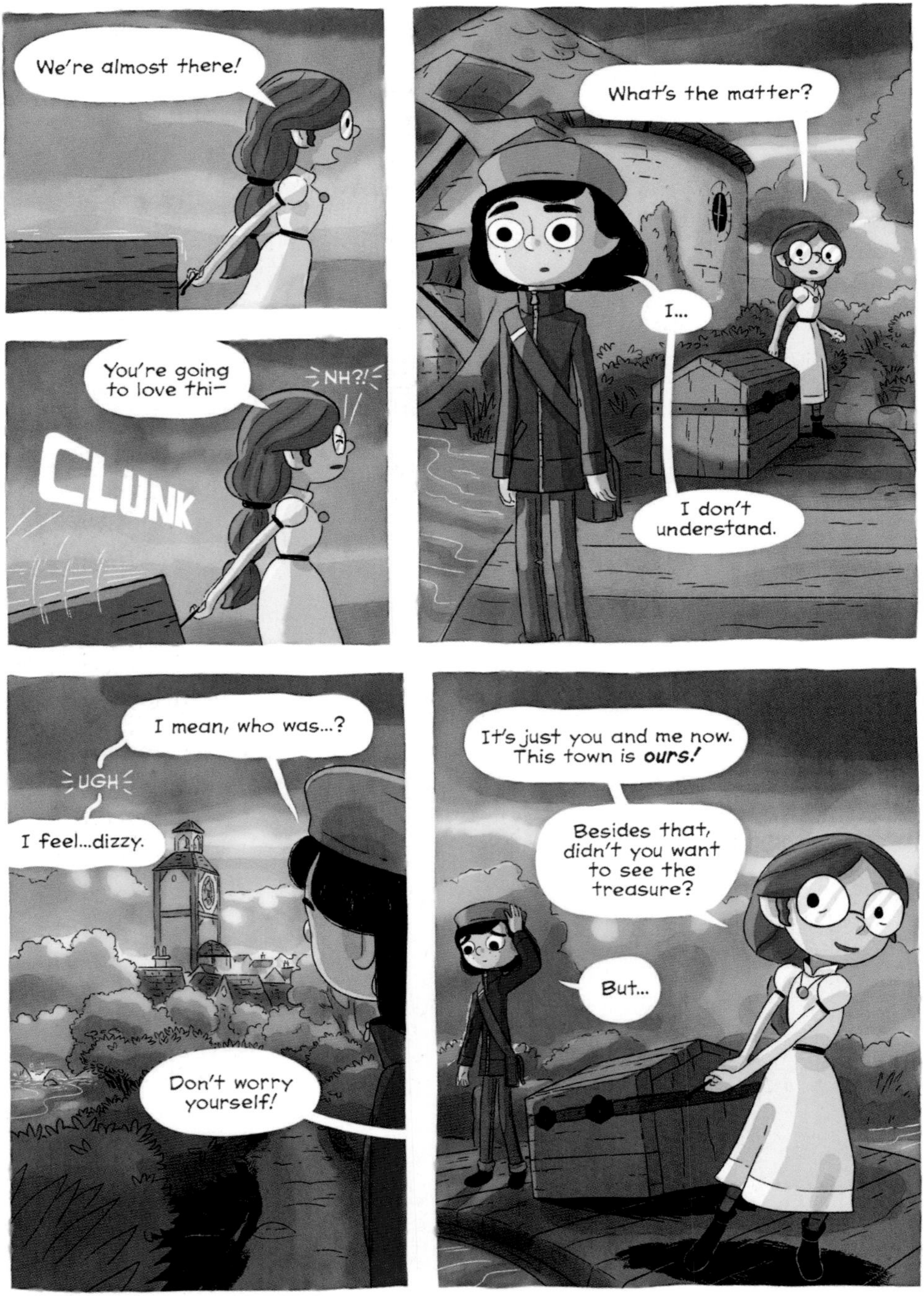
We're almost there!
You're going to love thi–
CLUNK
NH?!
What's the matter?
I...
I don't understand.
I mean, who was...?
UGH
I feel...dizzy.
Don't worry yourself!
It's just you and me now. This town is **ours!**
Besides that, didn't you want to see the treasure?
But...

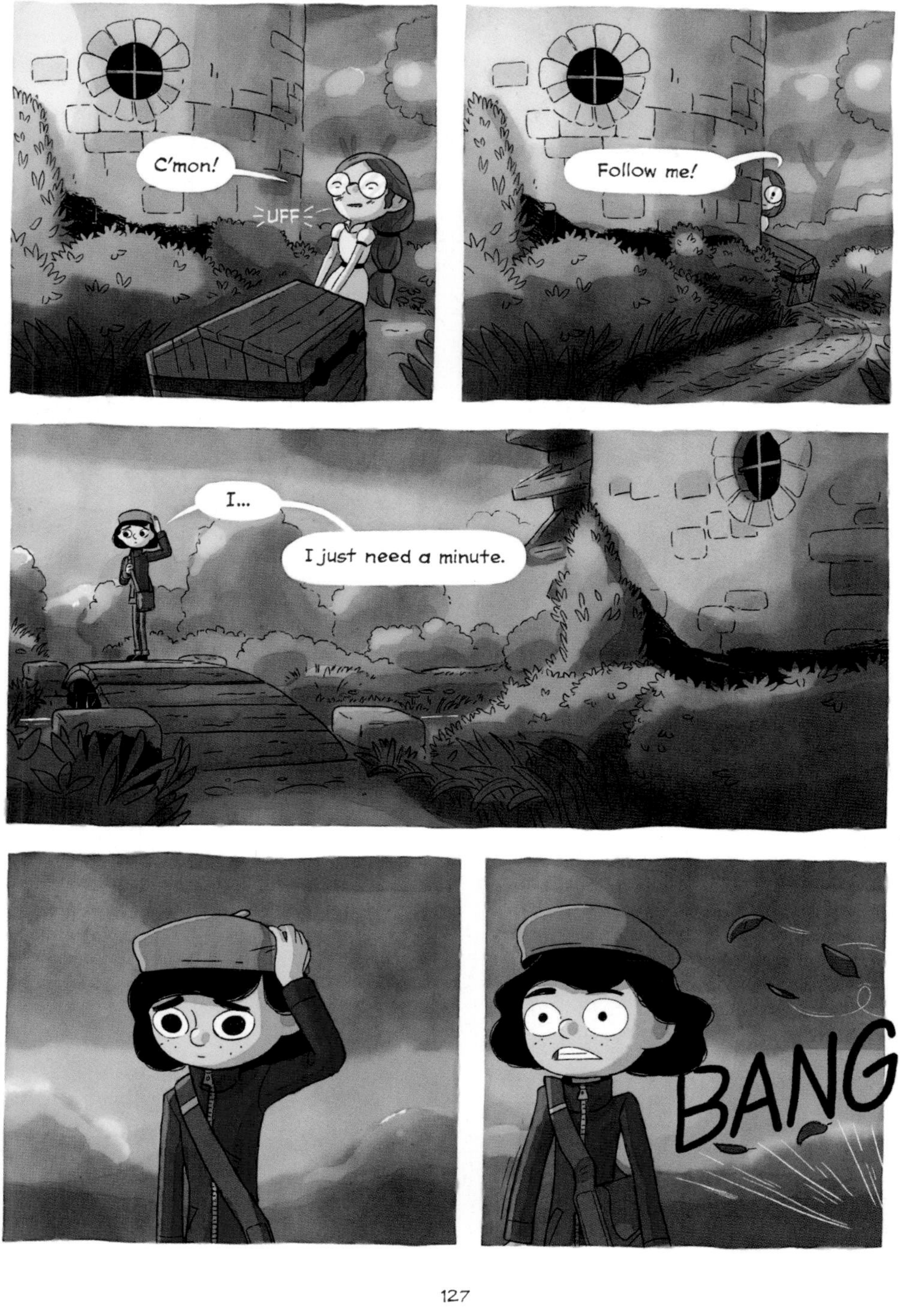
C'mon!
UFF
Follow me!
I...
I just need a minute.
BANG

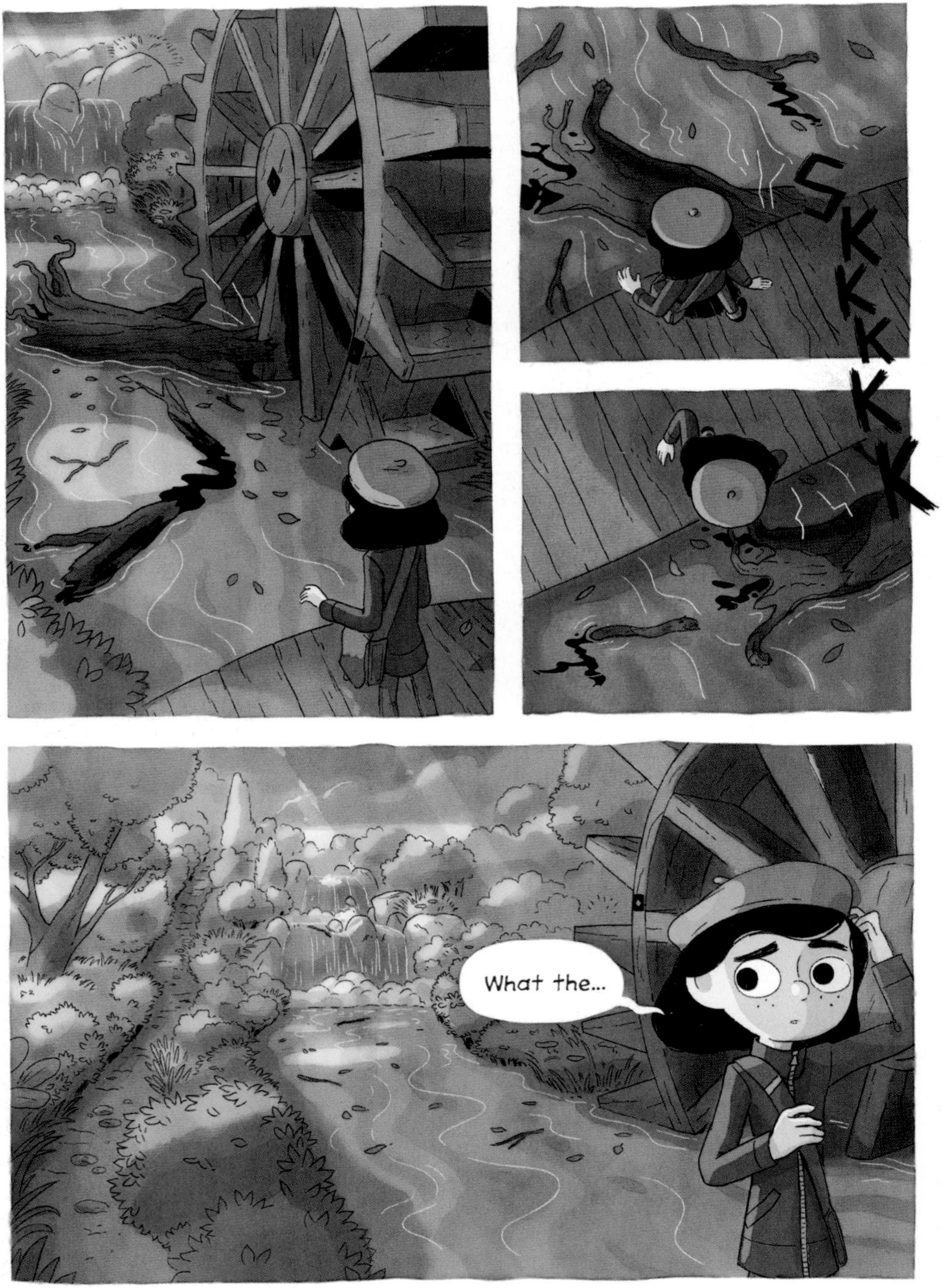
SKKKKK
What the...

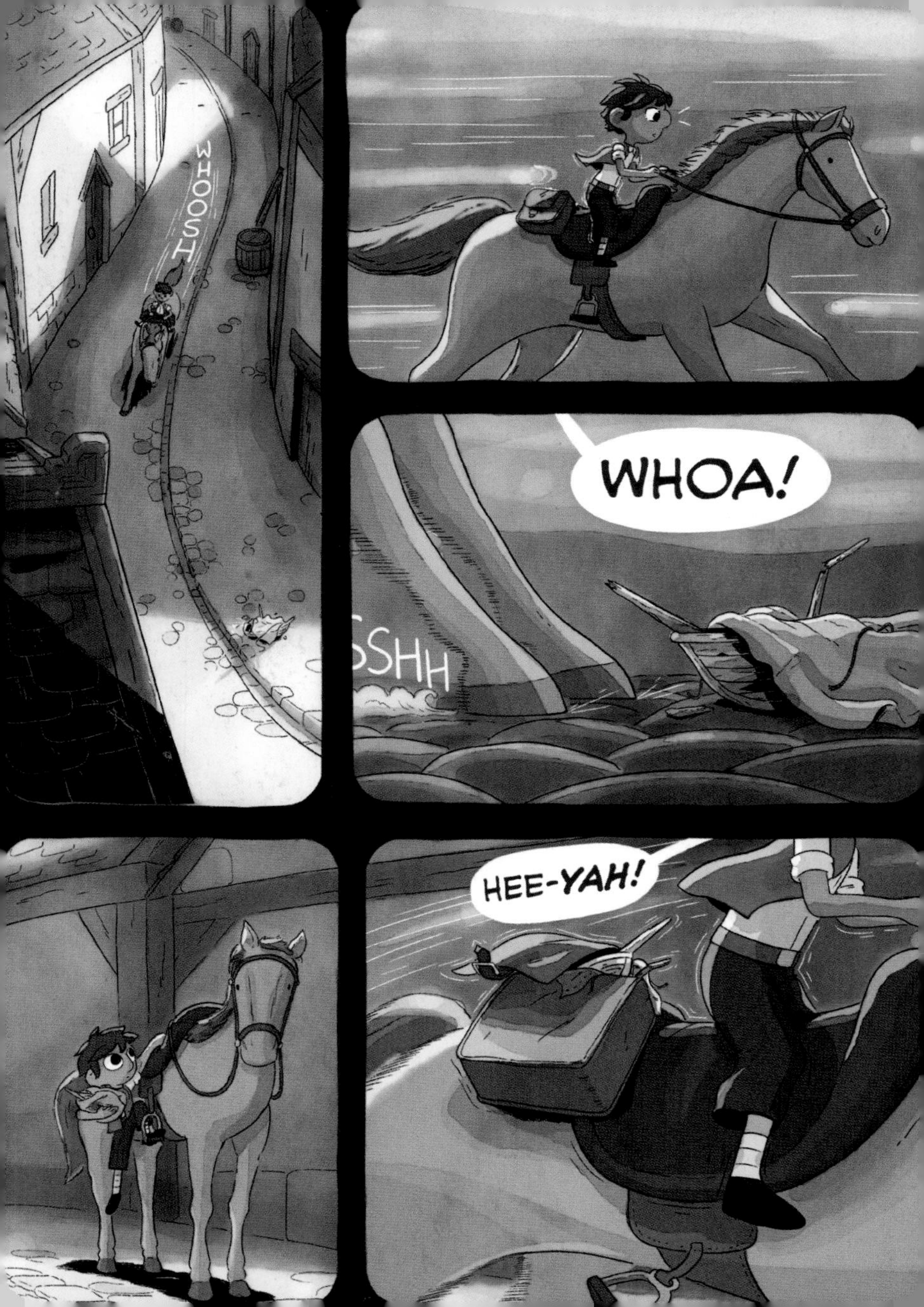
WHOOSH
WHOA!
SSHH
HEE-YAH!

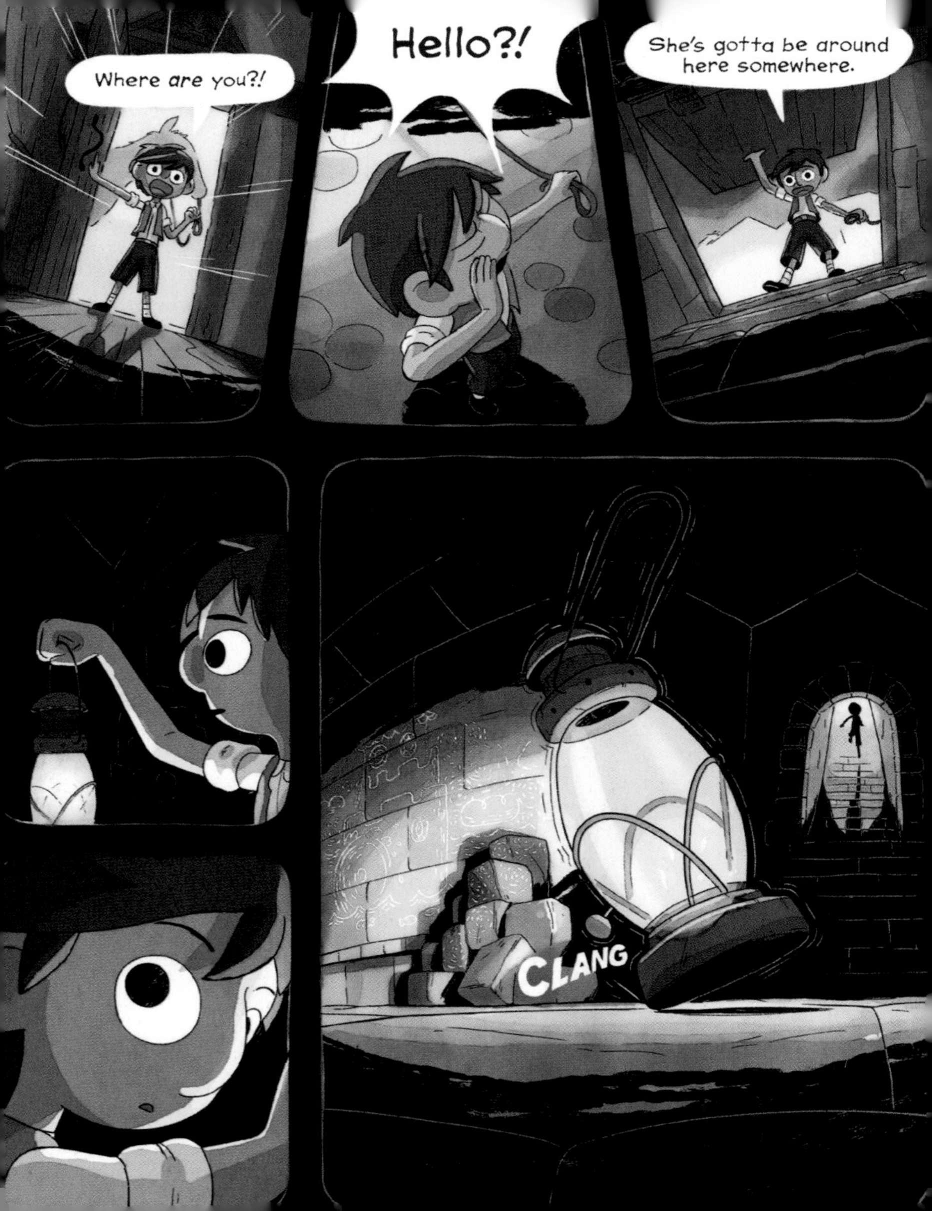
Where are you?!
Hello?!
She's gotta be around here somewhere.
CLANG

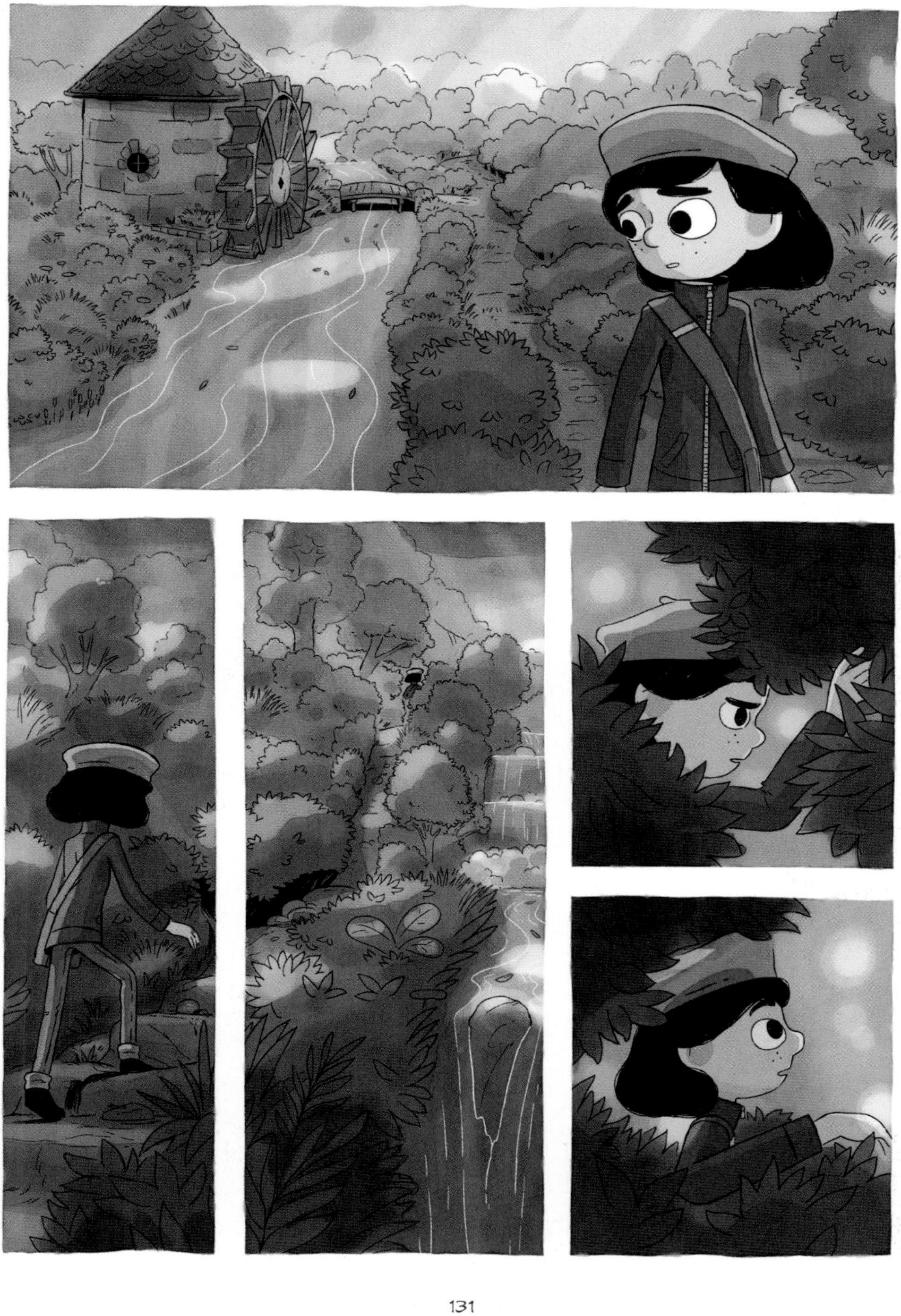

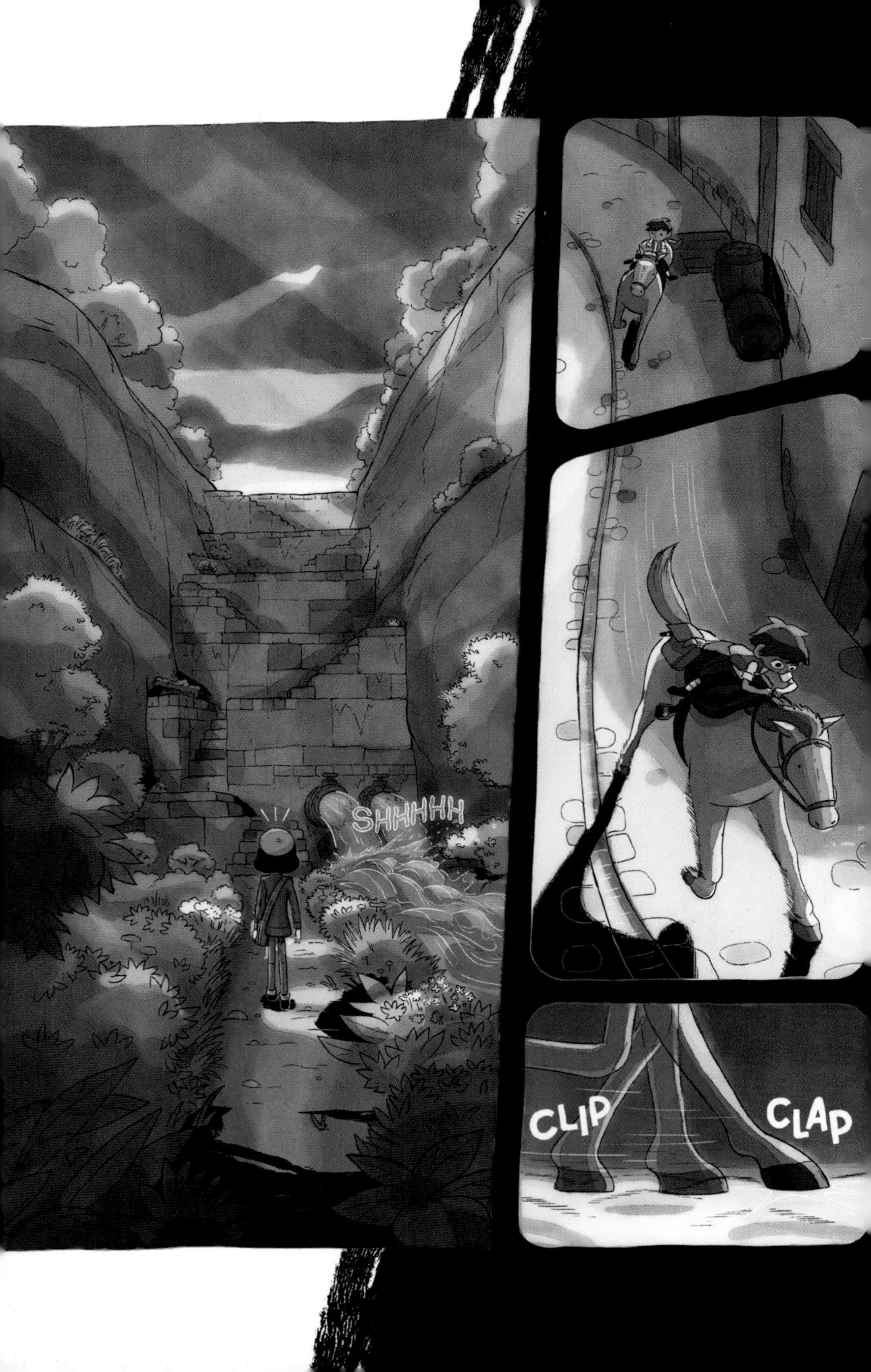
SHHHHH
CLIP
CLAP

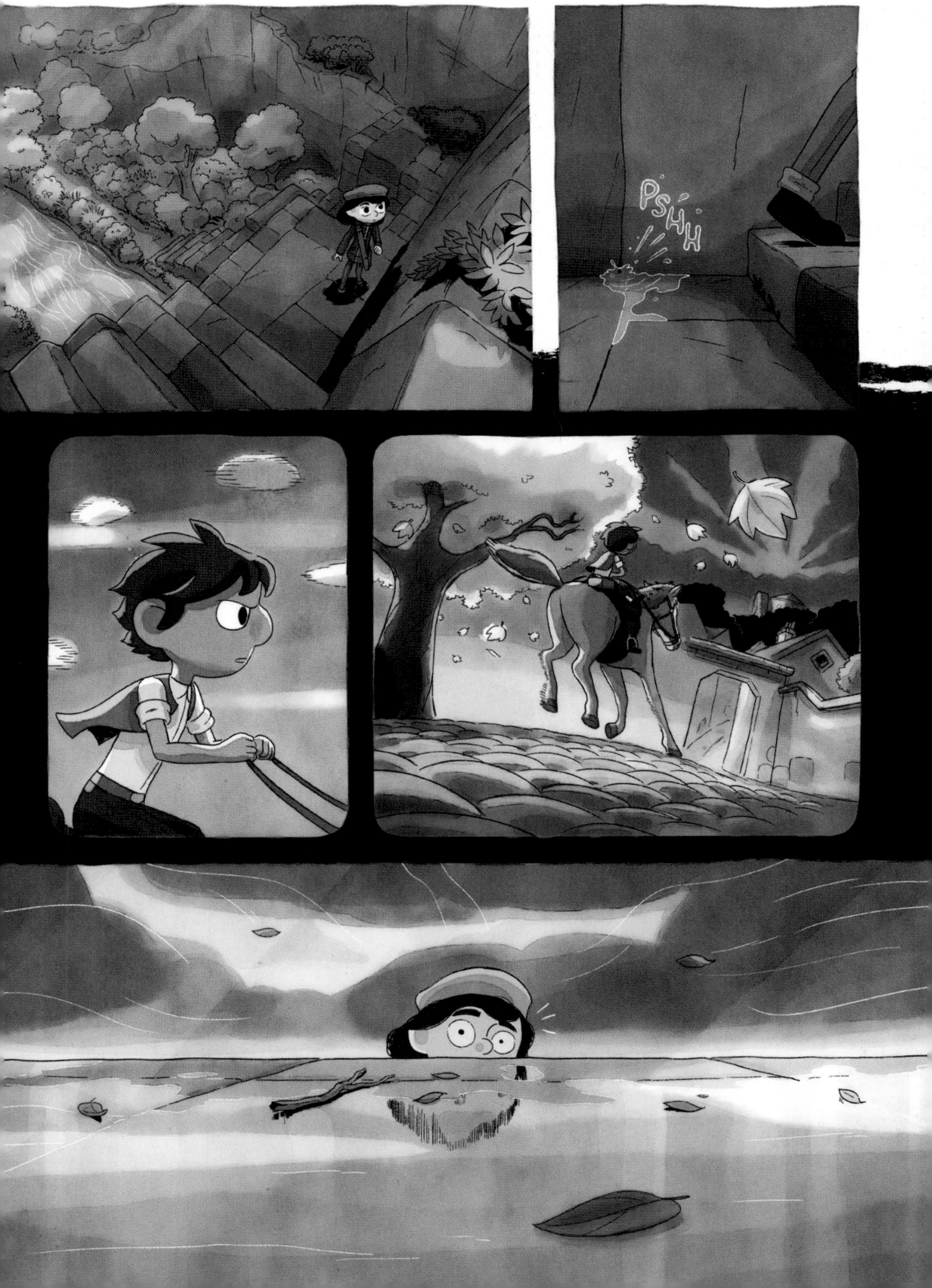
PSHH

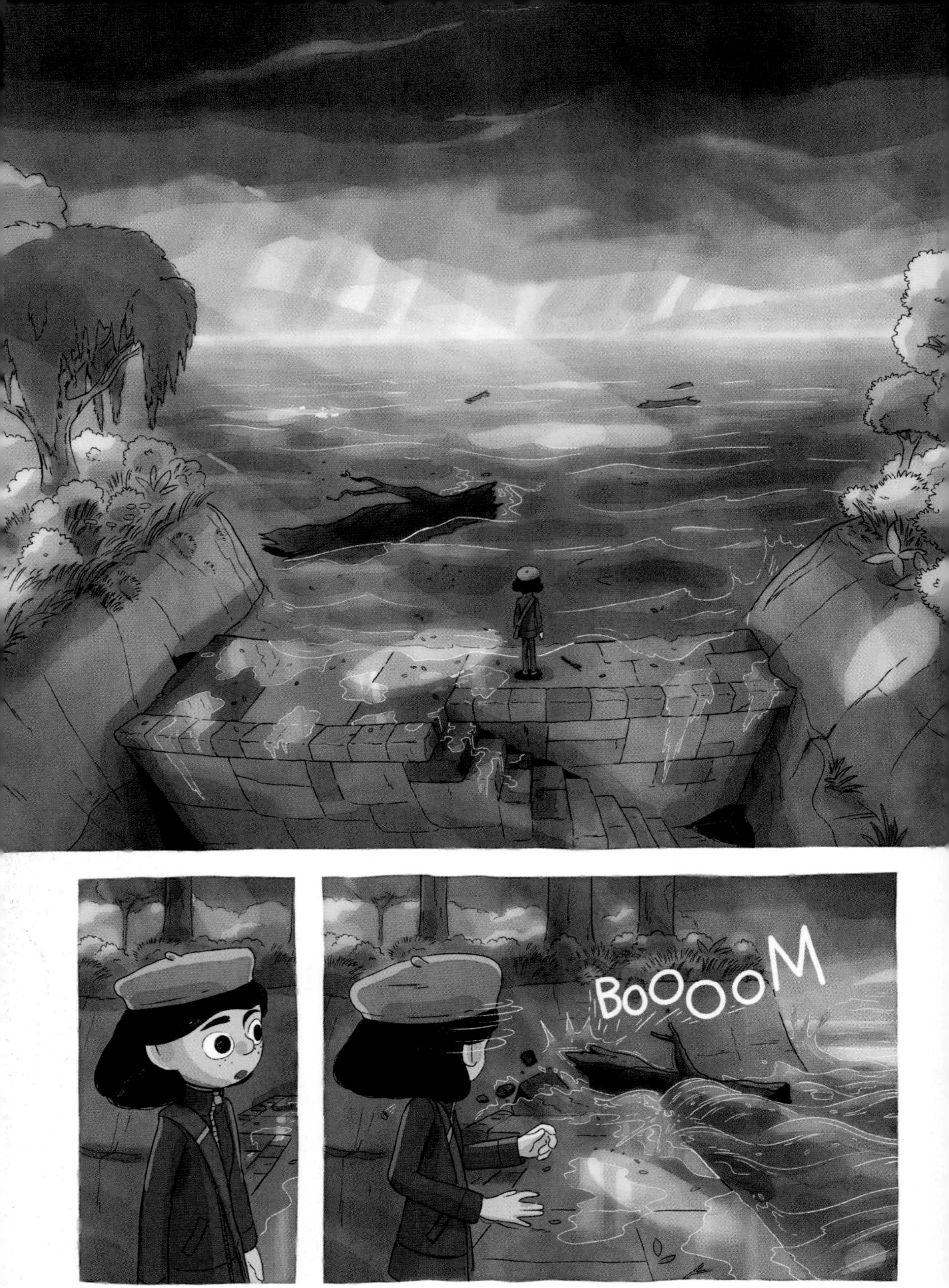
BOOOOM

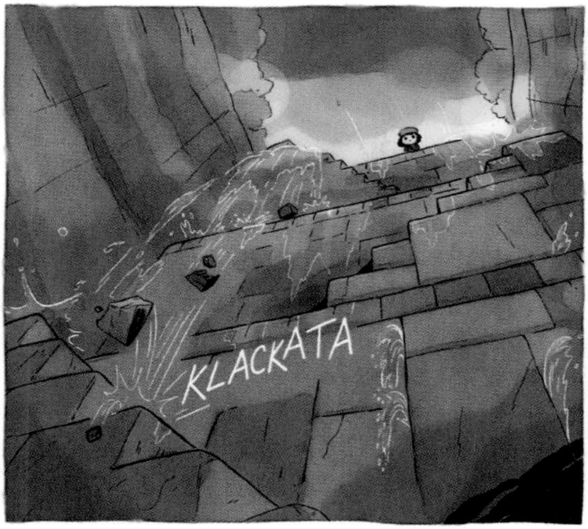
KLACKATA

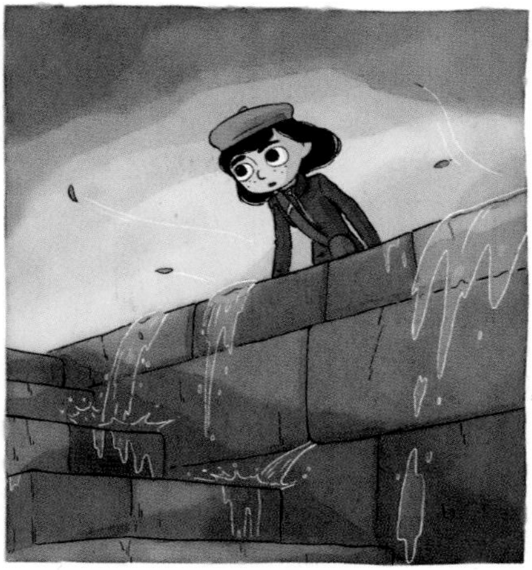

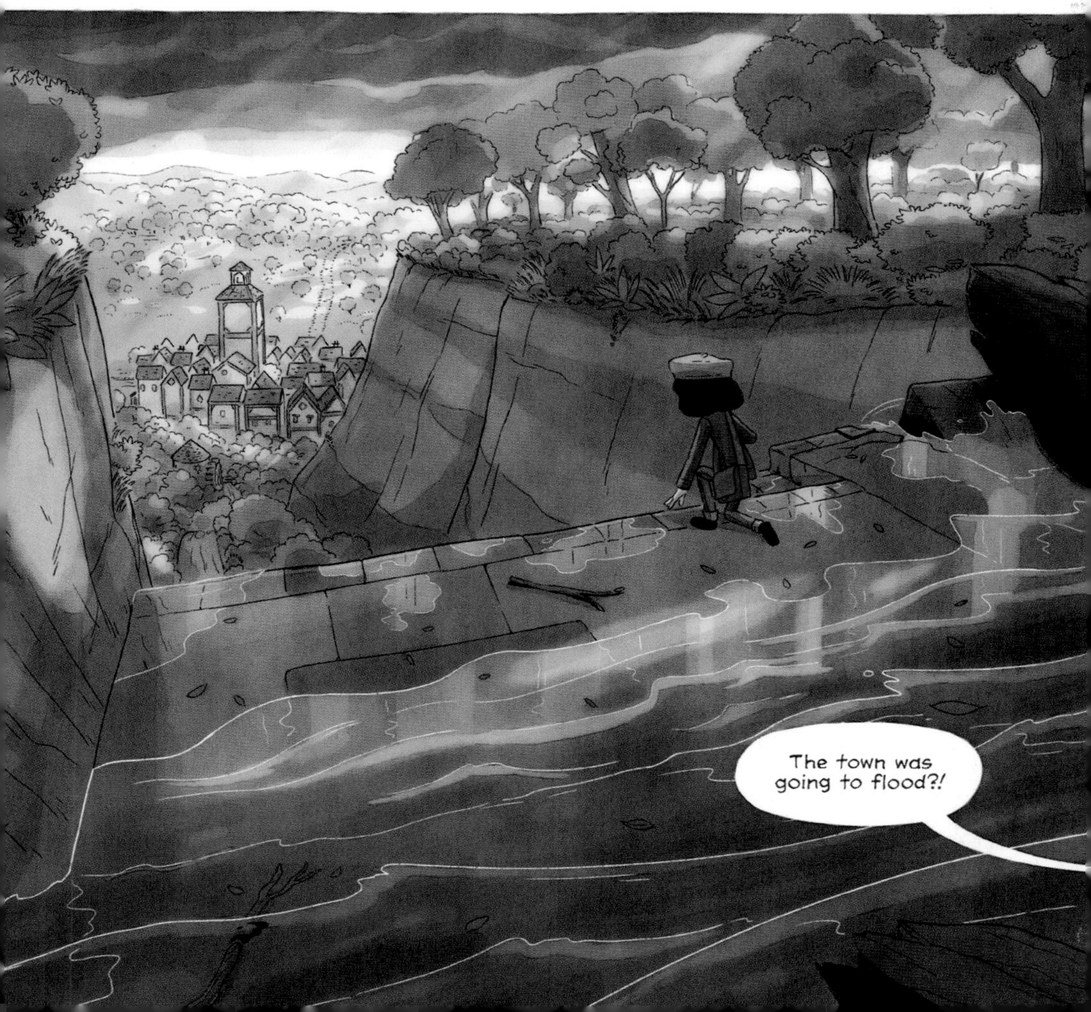
The town was going to flood?!

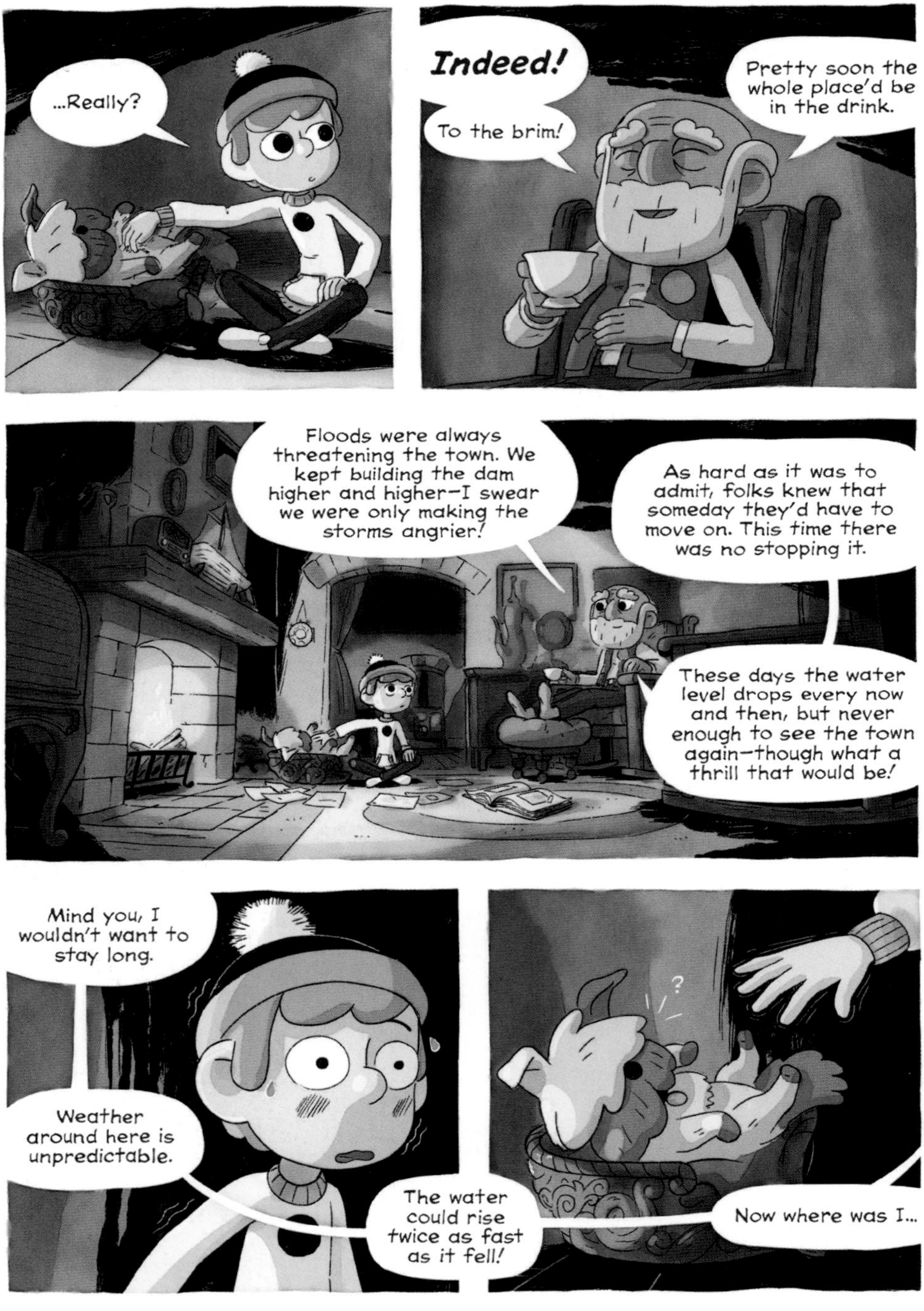
...Really?
Indeed!
To the brim!
Pretty soon the whole place'd be in the drink.
Floods were always threatening the town. We kept building the dam higher and higher—I swear we were only making the storms angrier!
As hard as it was to admit, folks knew that someday they'd have to move on. This time there was no stopping it.
These days the water level drops every now and then, but never enough to see the town again—though what a thrill that would be!
Mind you, I wouldn't want to stay long.
Weather around here is unpredictable.
The water could rise twice as fast as it fell!
Now where was I...

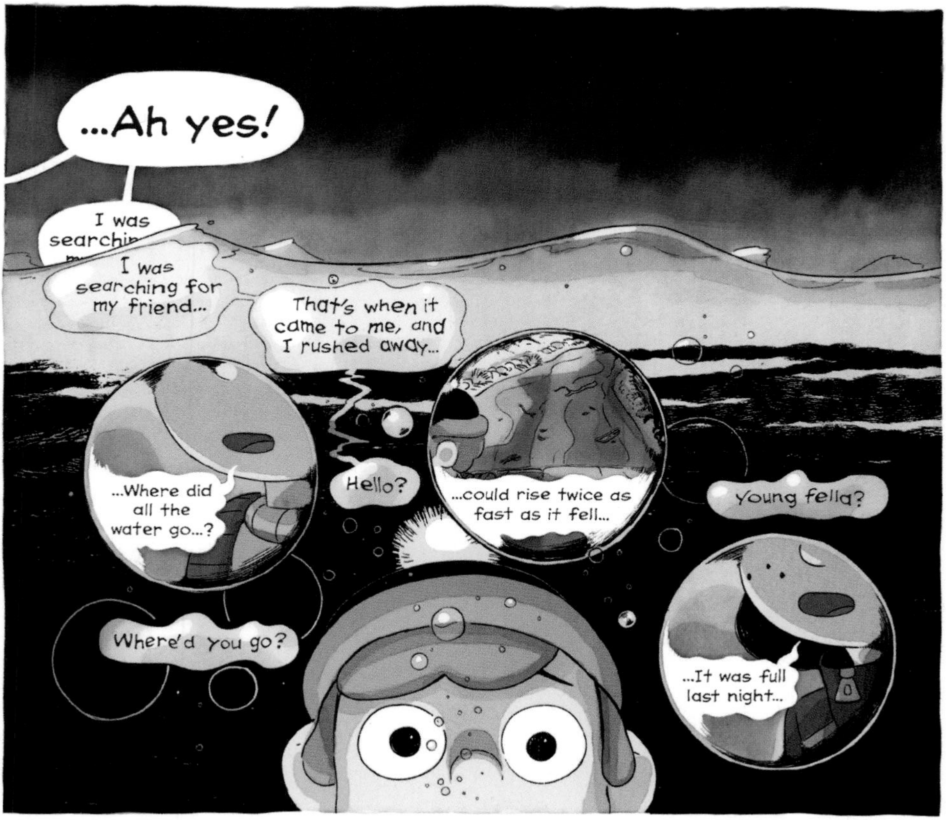
...Ah yes!
I was searching for my friend...
That's when it came to me, and I rushed away...
...Where did all the water go...?
Hello?
...could rise twice as fast as it fell...
Young fella?
Where'd you go?
...It was full last night...

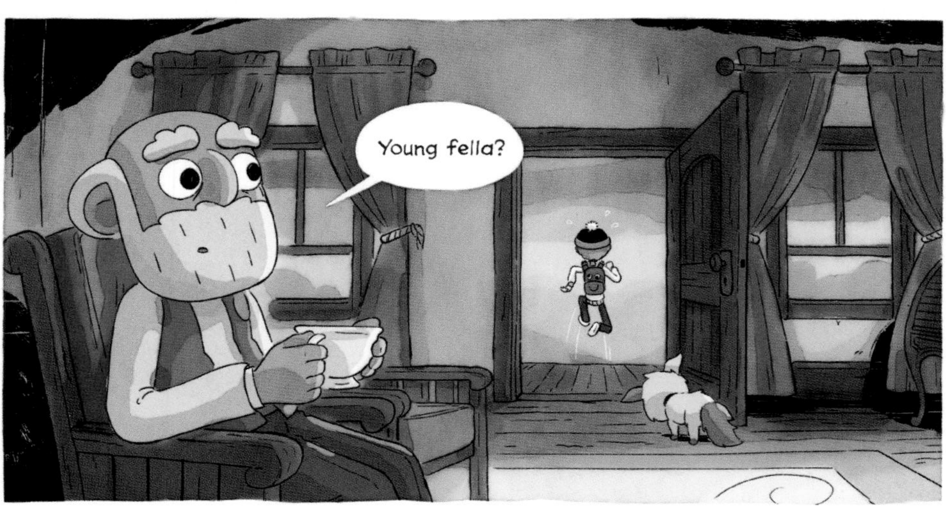
Young fella?

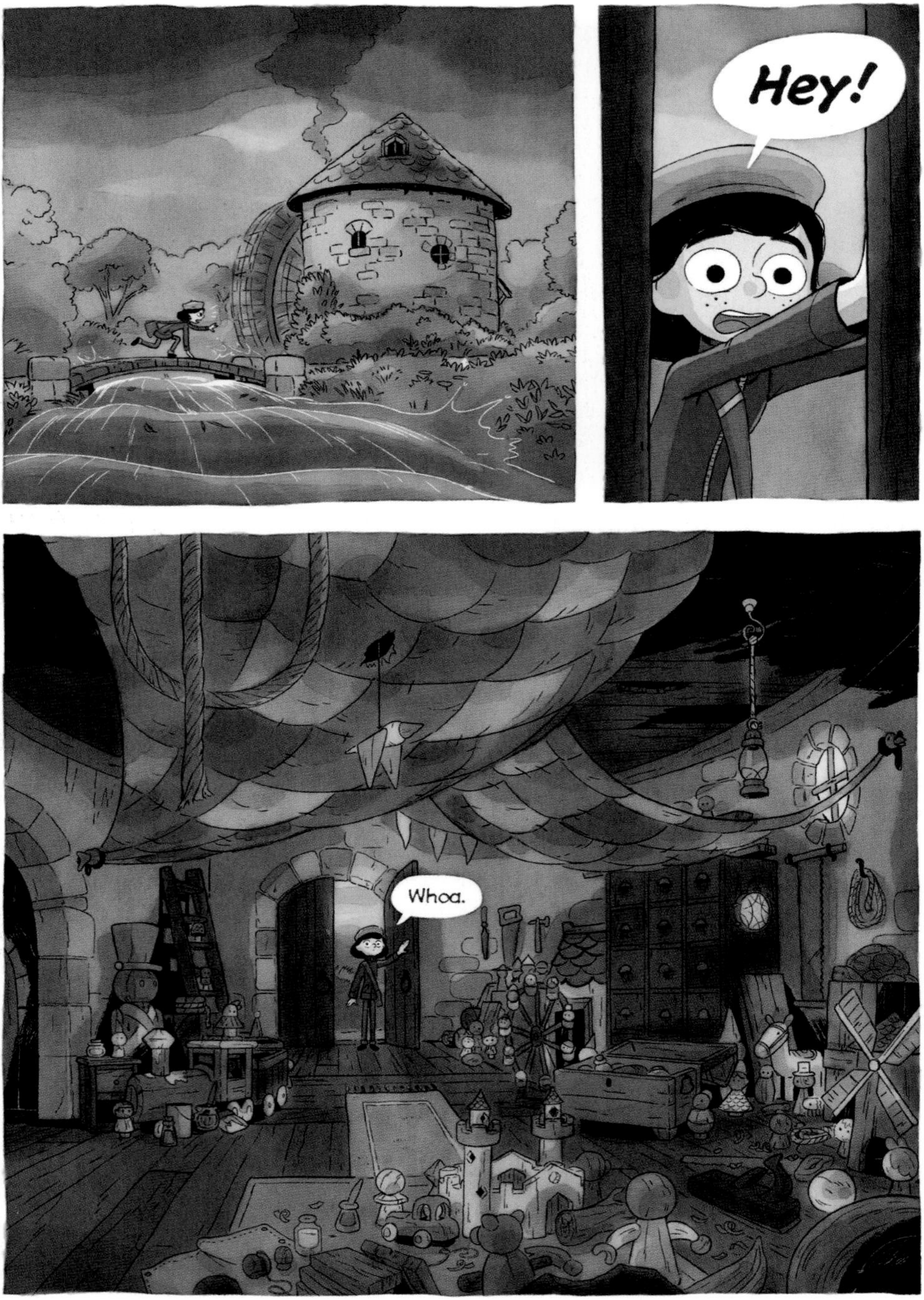
Hey!
Whoa.

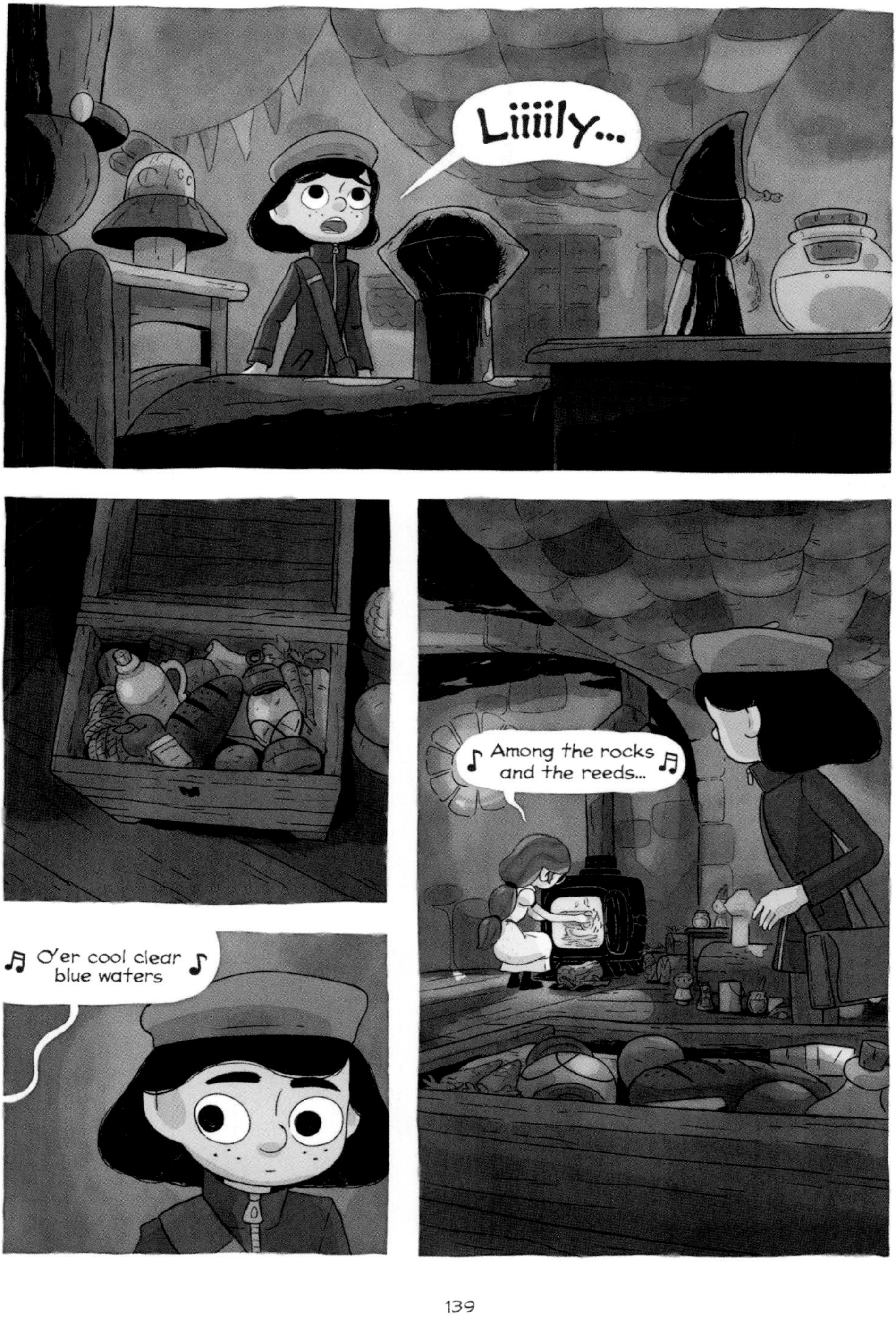
Liiiily...
Among the rocks and the reeds...
O'er cool clear blue waters

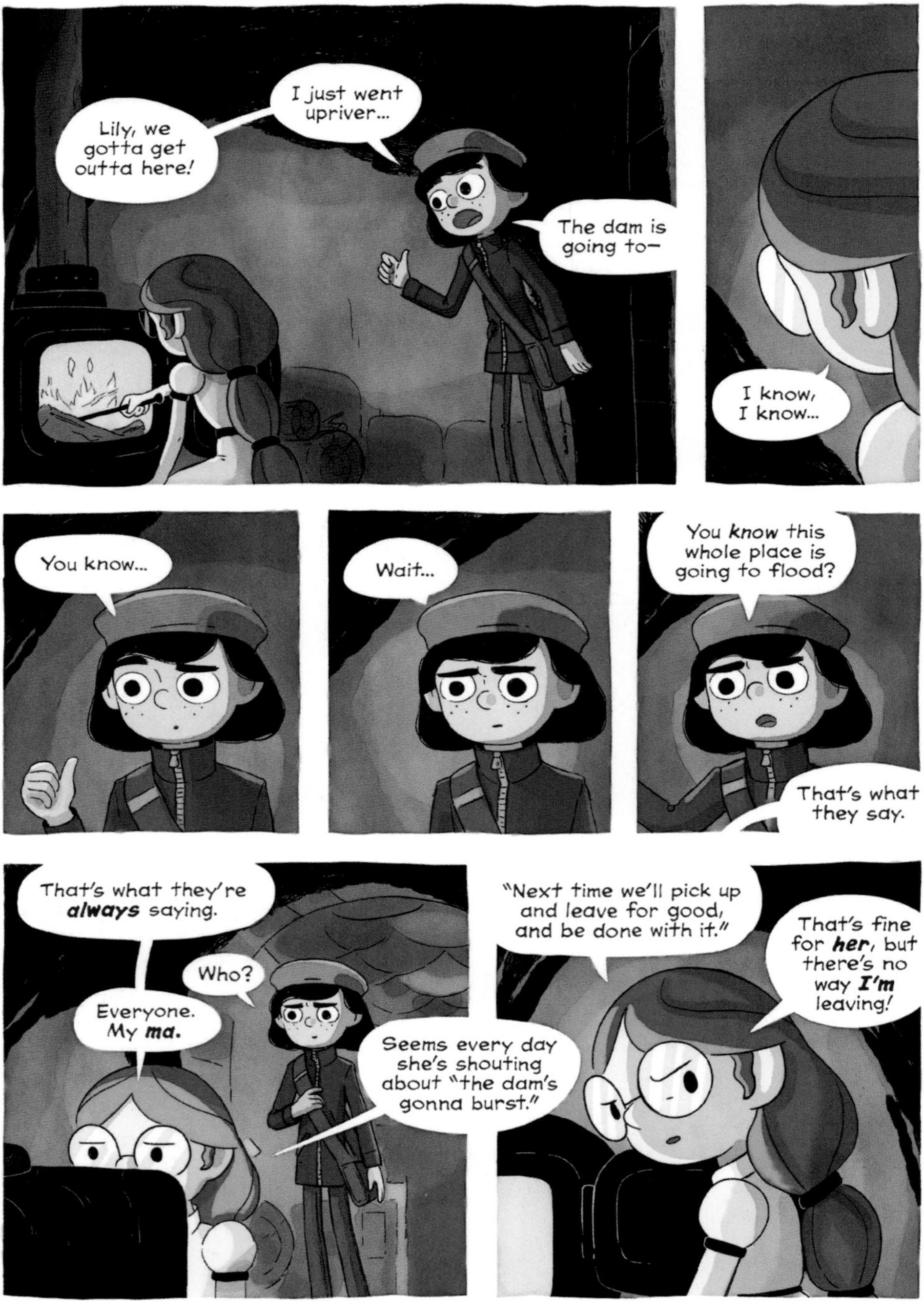
Lily, we gotta get outta here!
I just went upriver...
The dam is going to—
I know, I know...
You know...
Wait...
You know this whole place is going to flood?
That's what they say.
That's what they're always saying.
Who?
Everyone. My ma.
Seems every day she's shouting about "the dam's gonna burst."
"Next time we'll pick up and leave for good, and be done with it."
That's fine for her, but there's no way I'm leaving!

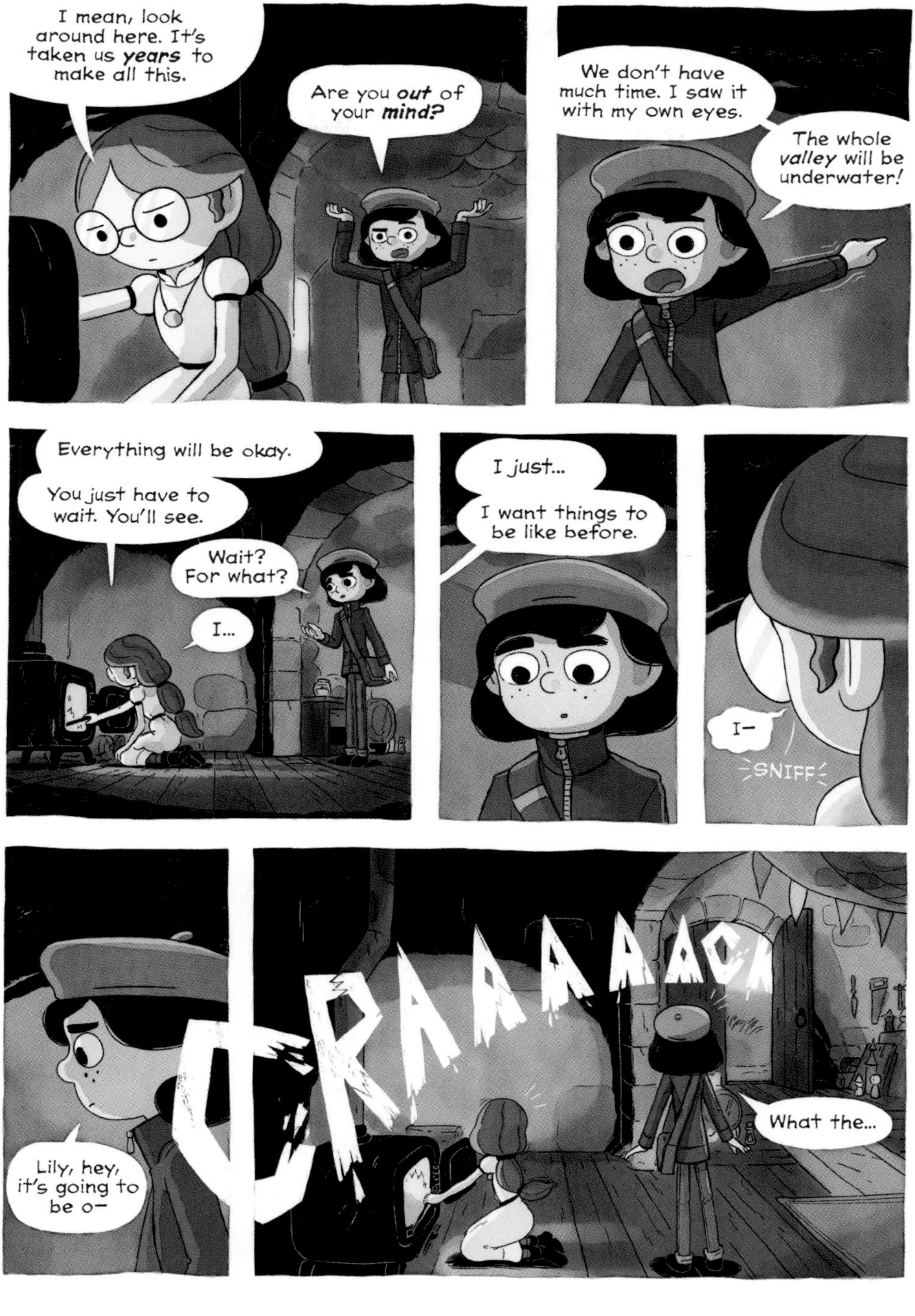
I mean, look around here. It's taken us *years* to make all this.
Are you *out* of your *mind?*
We don't have much time. I saw it with my own eyes.
The whole *valley* will be underwater!
Everything will be okay.
You just have to wait. You'll see.
Wait? For what?
I...
I just...
I want things to be like before.
I–
SNIFF
Lily, hey, it's going to be o–
CRAAAAACK
What the...

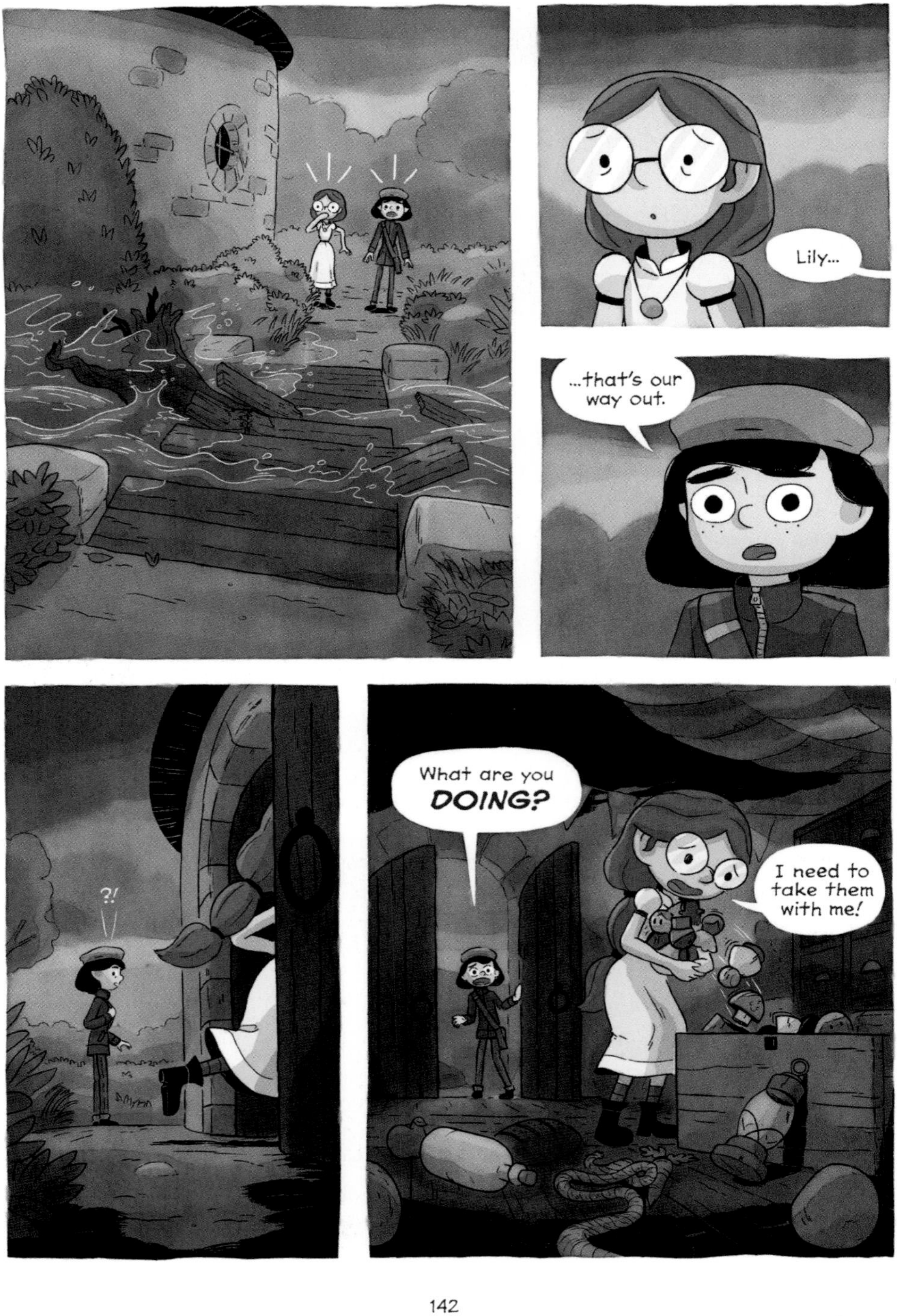
Lily...
...that's our way out.
?!
What are you DOING?
I need to take them with me!

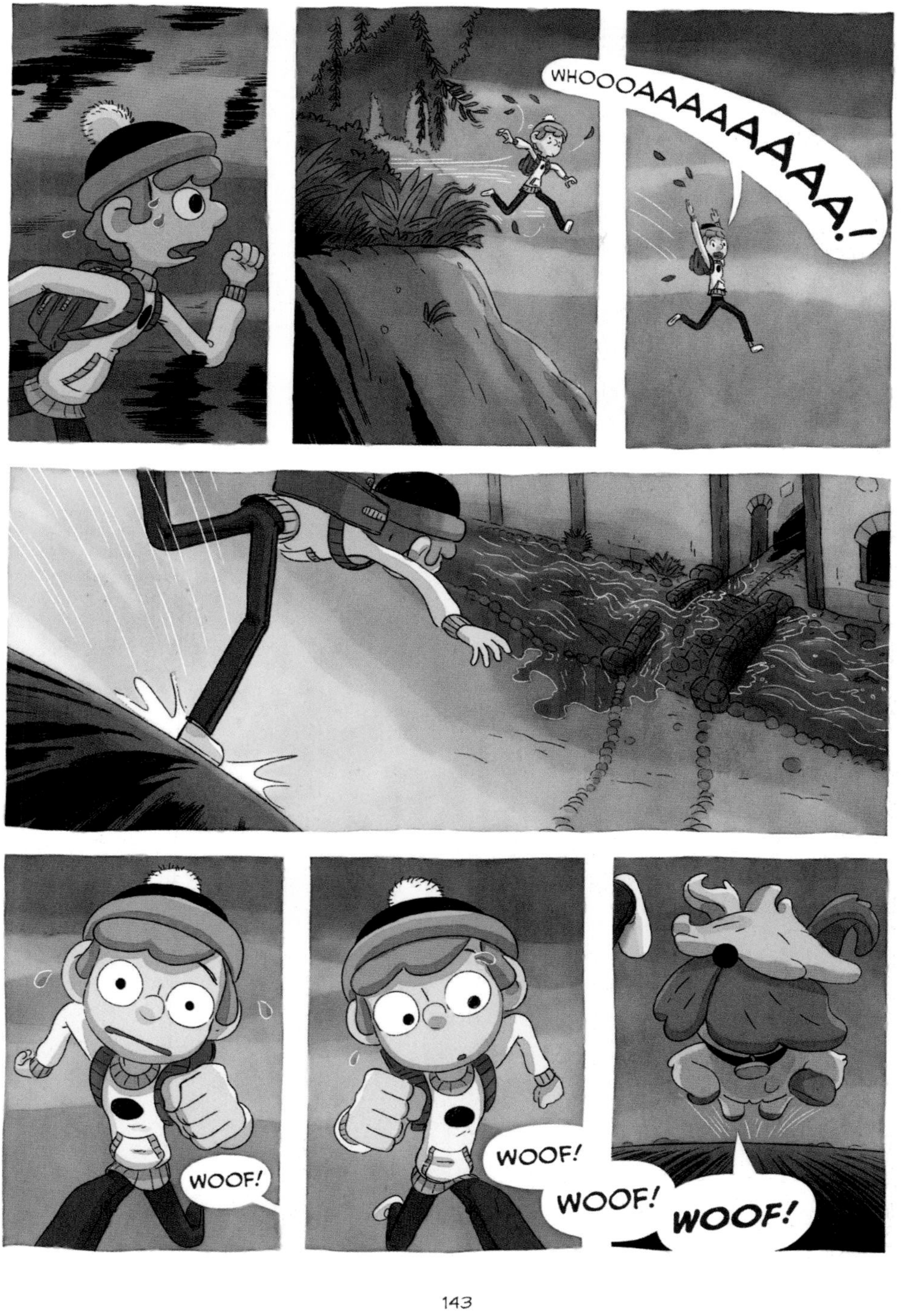
WHOOOAAAAAAAAAA!
WOOF!
WOOF!
WOOF!
WOOF!

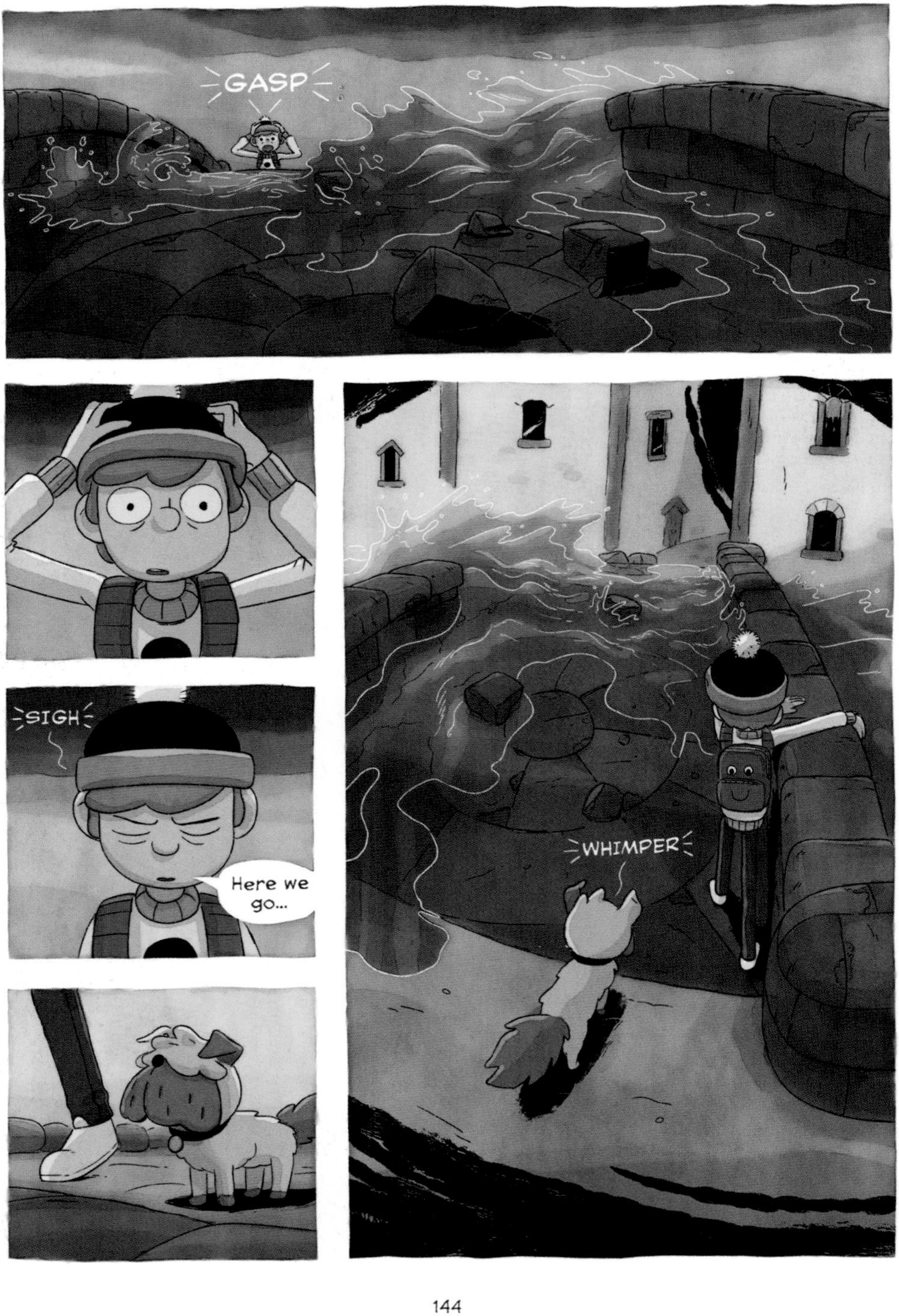
GASP
SIGH
Here we go...
WHIMPER

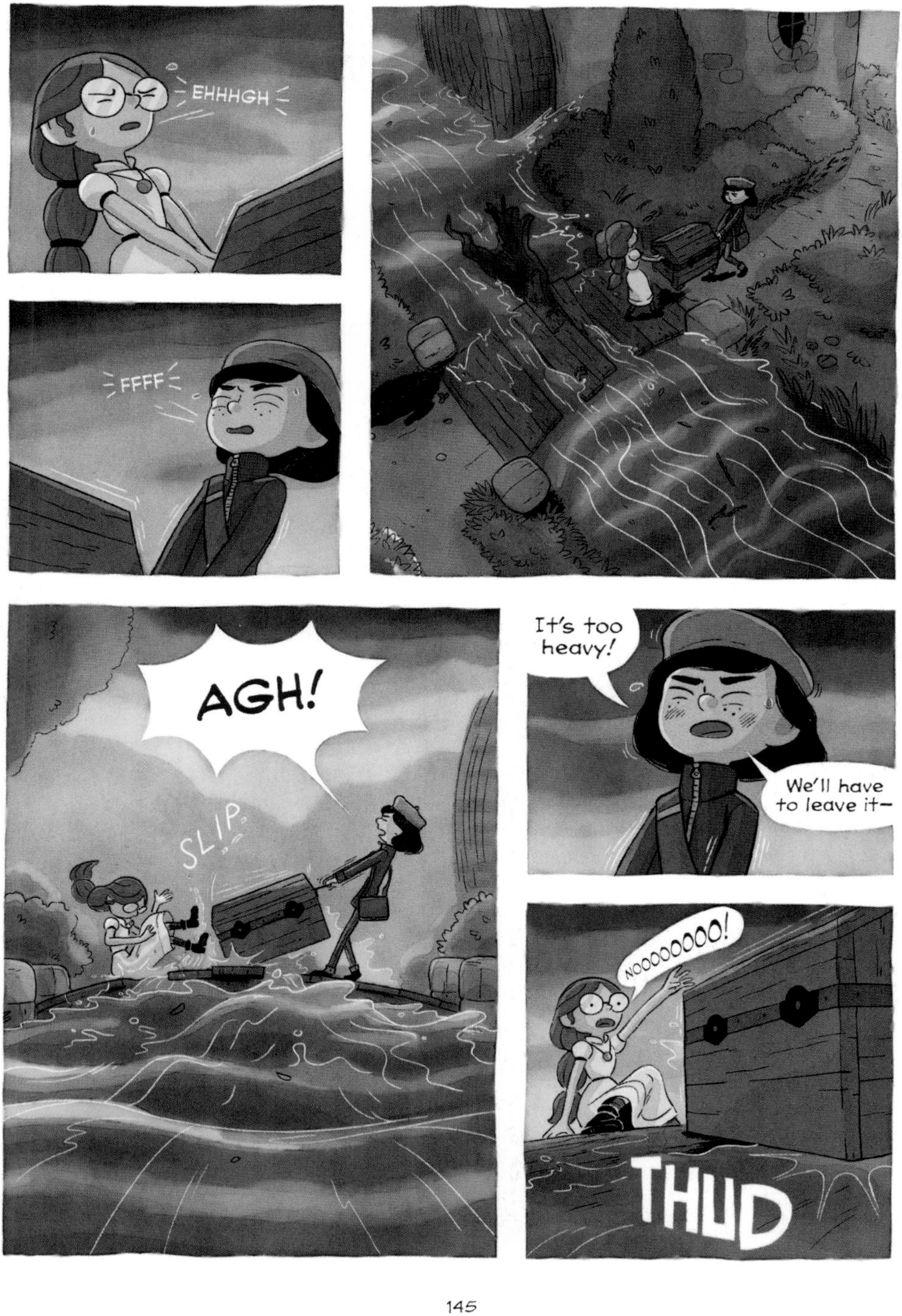
EHHHGH
FFFF
AGH!
SLIP
It's too heavy!
We'll have to leave it—
NOOOOOOOO!
THUD

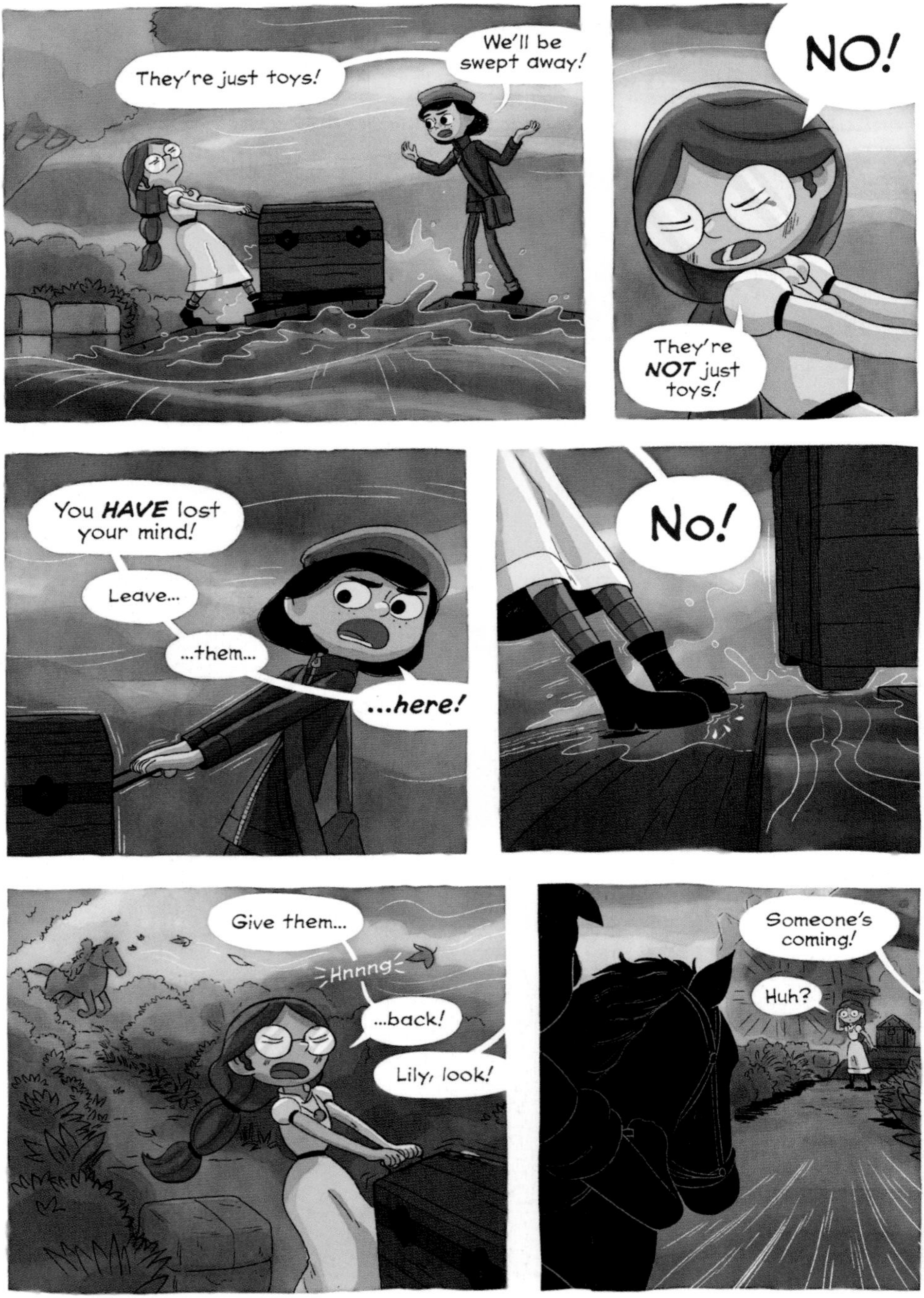

They're just toys!
We'll be swept away!
NO!
They're NOT just toys!
You HAVE lost your mind!
Leave...
...them...
...here!
No!
Give them...
Hnnng
...back!
Lily, look!
Someone's coming!
Huh?

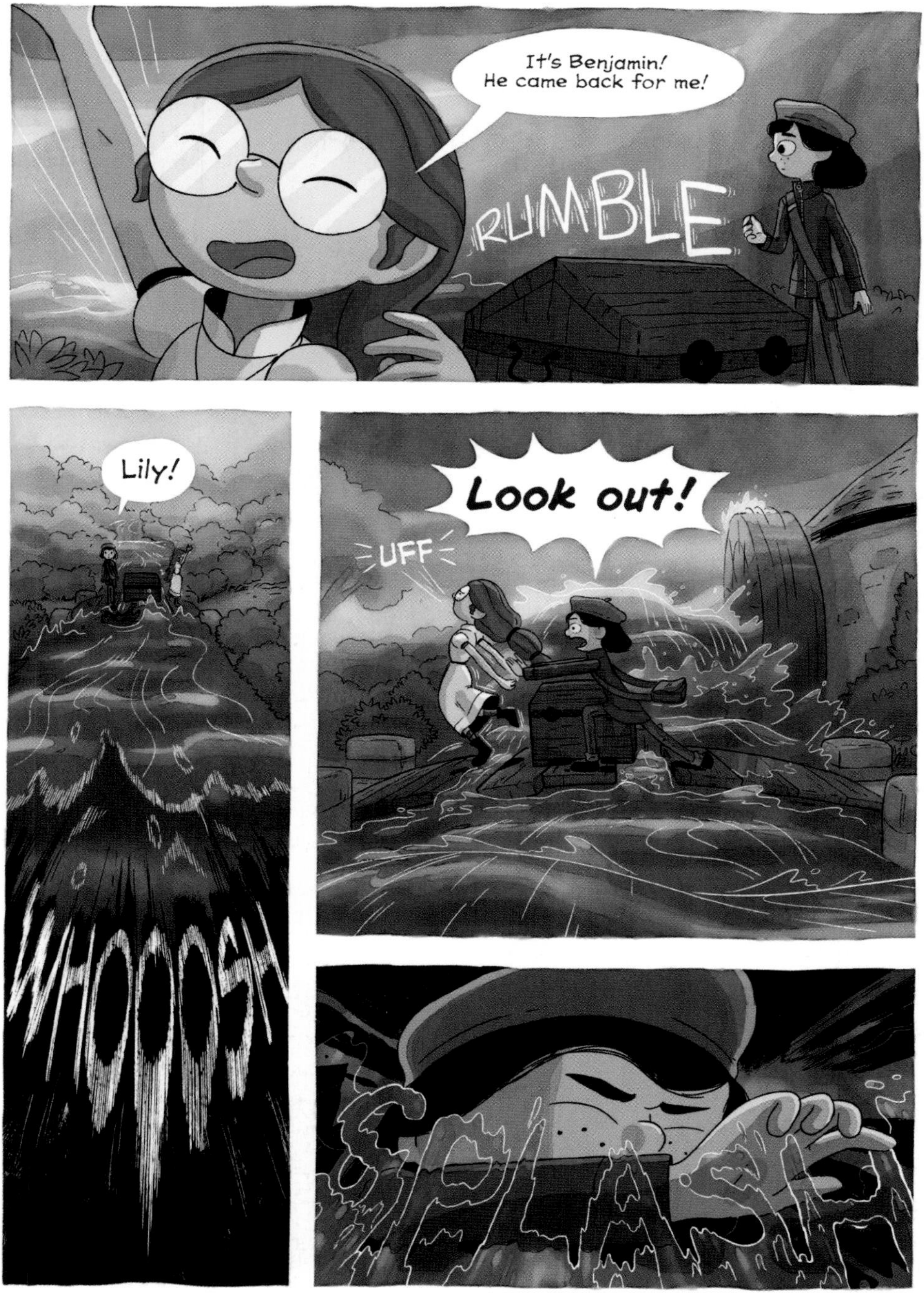
It's Benjamin! He came back for me!
RUMBLE
Lily!
WHOOSH
Look out!
UFF
SPLASH

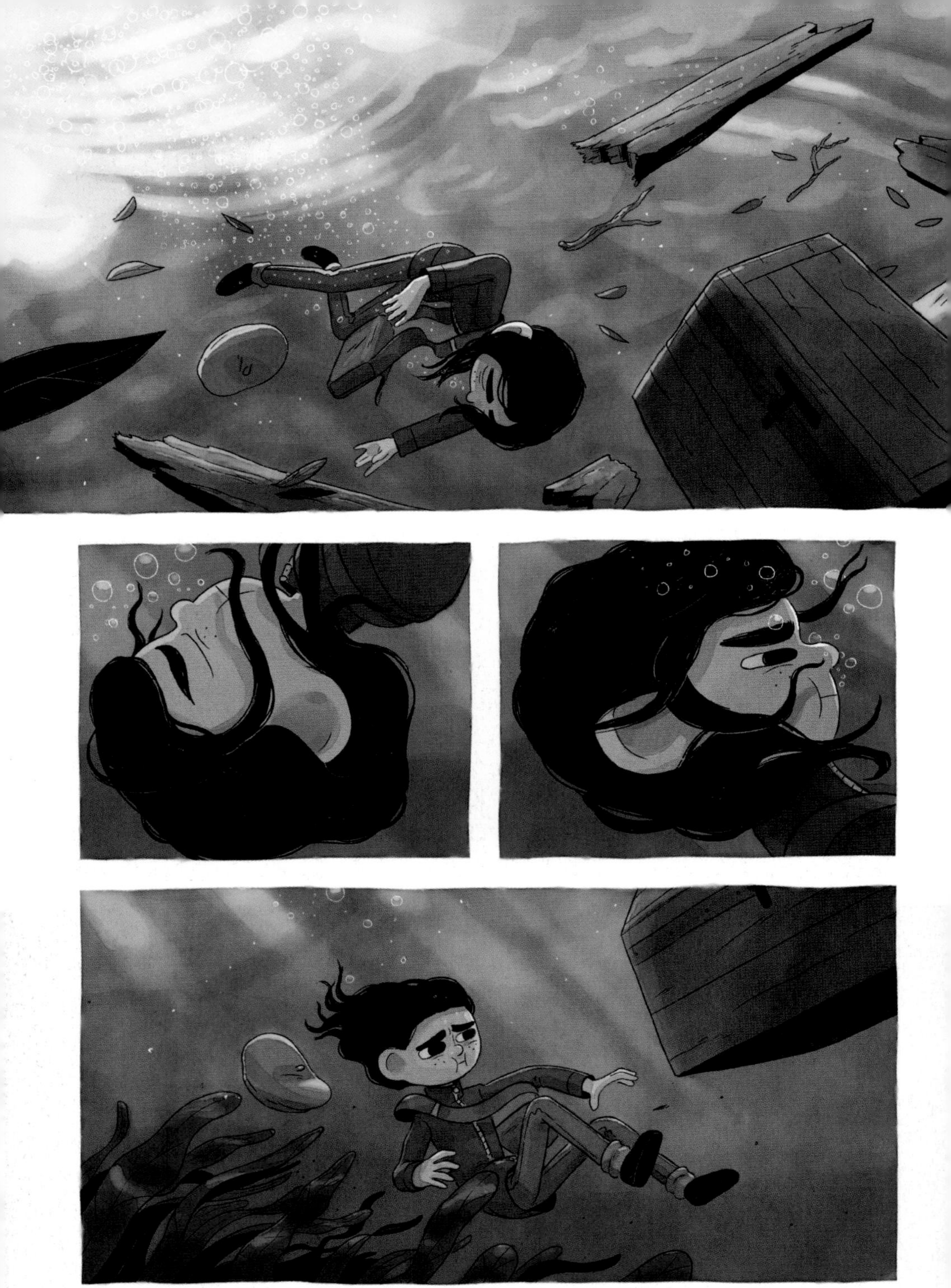

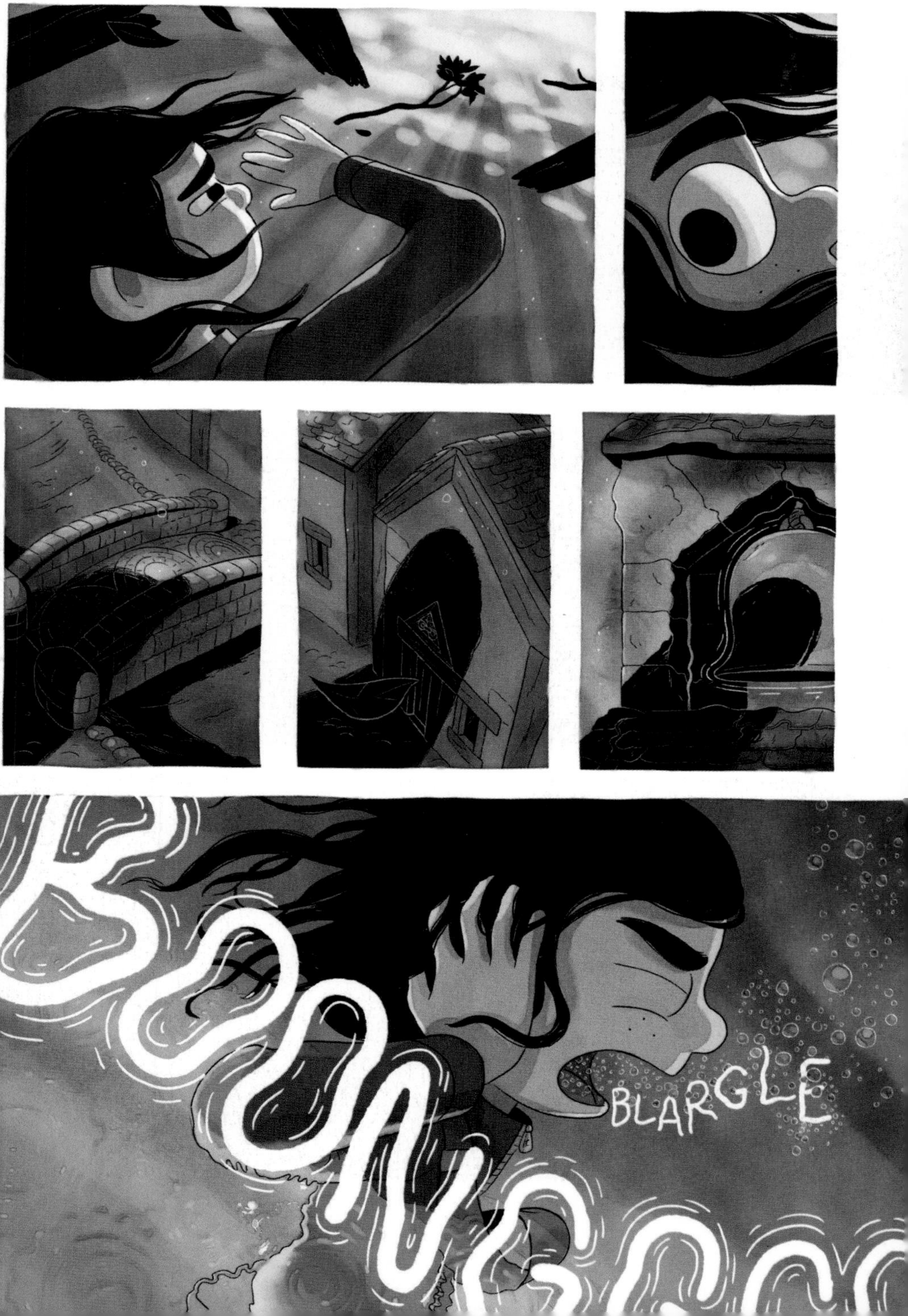
BLARGLE

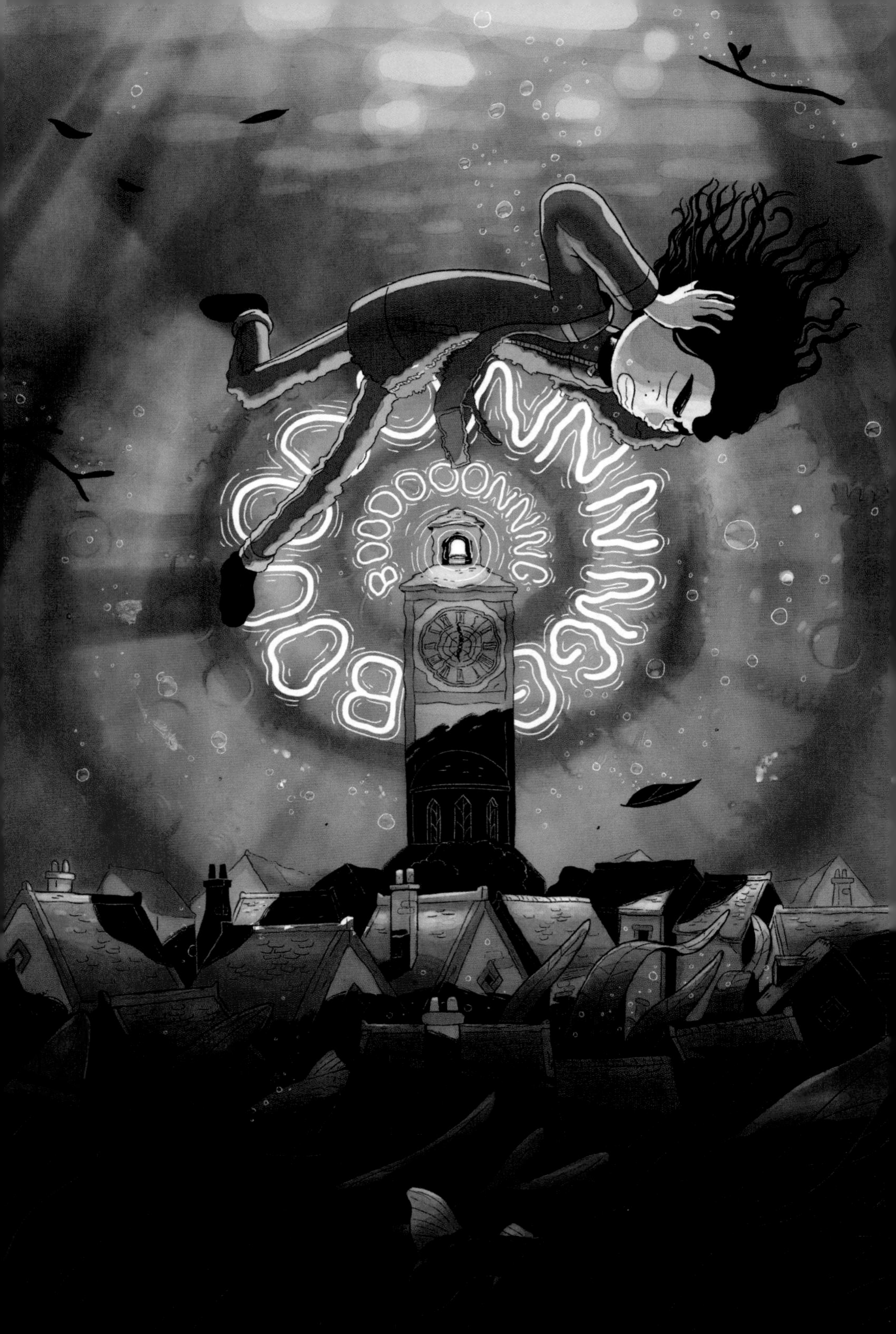
BOOOOONNNNG
BOOOOONNNG

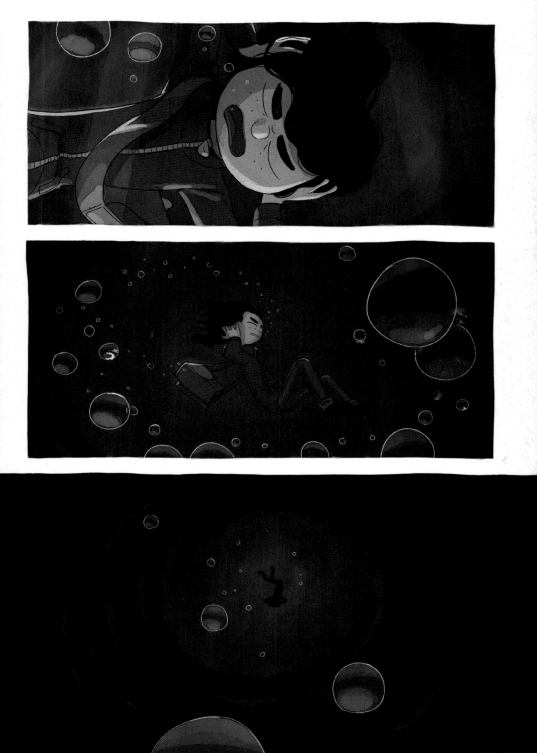

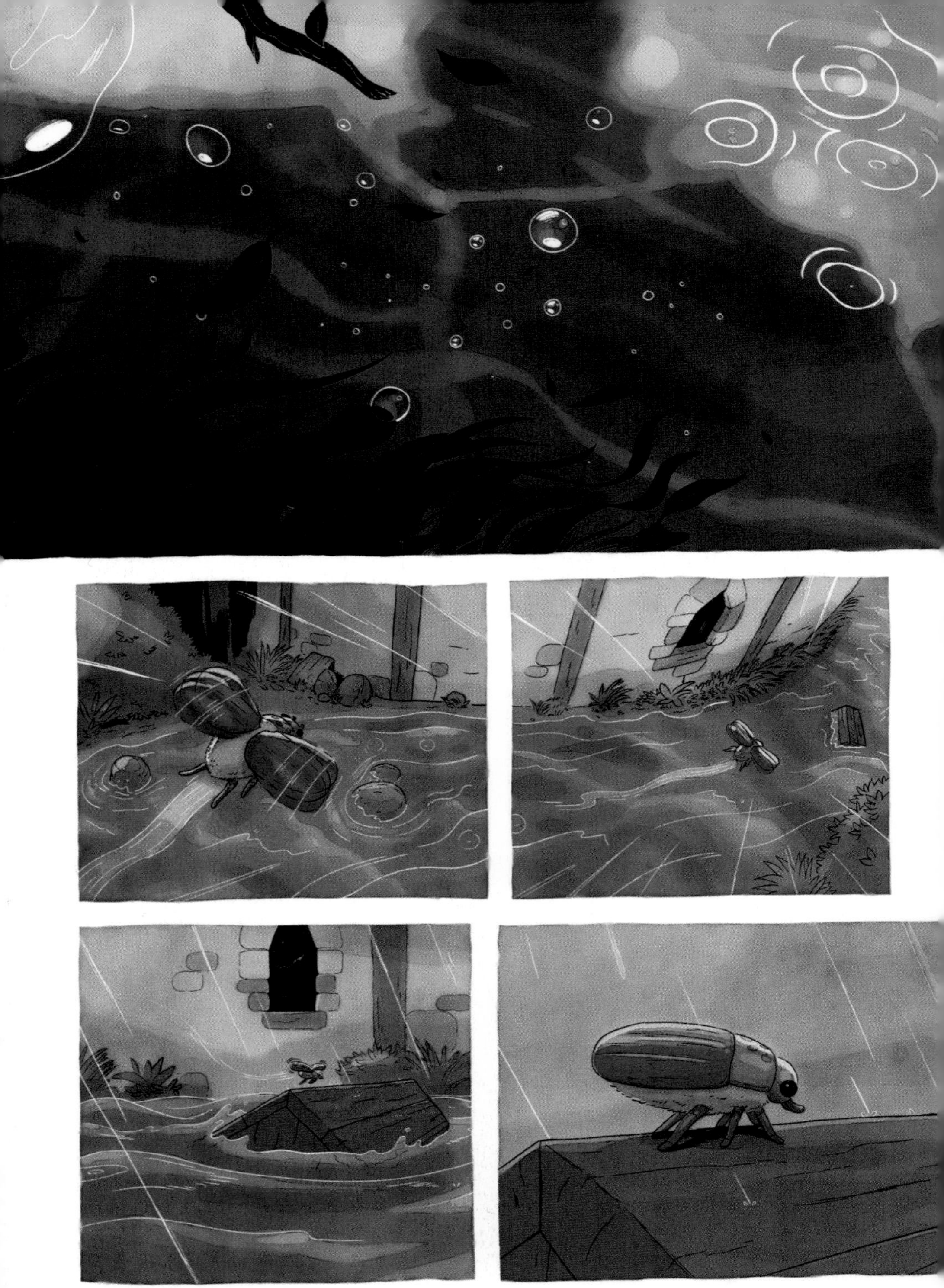

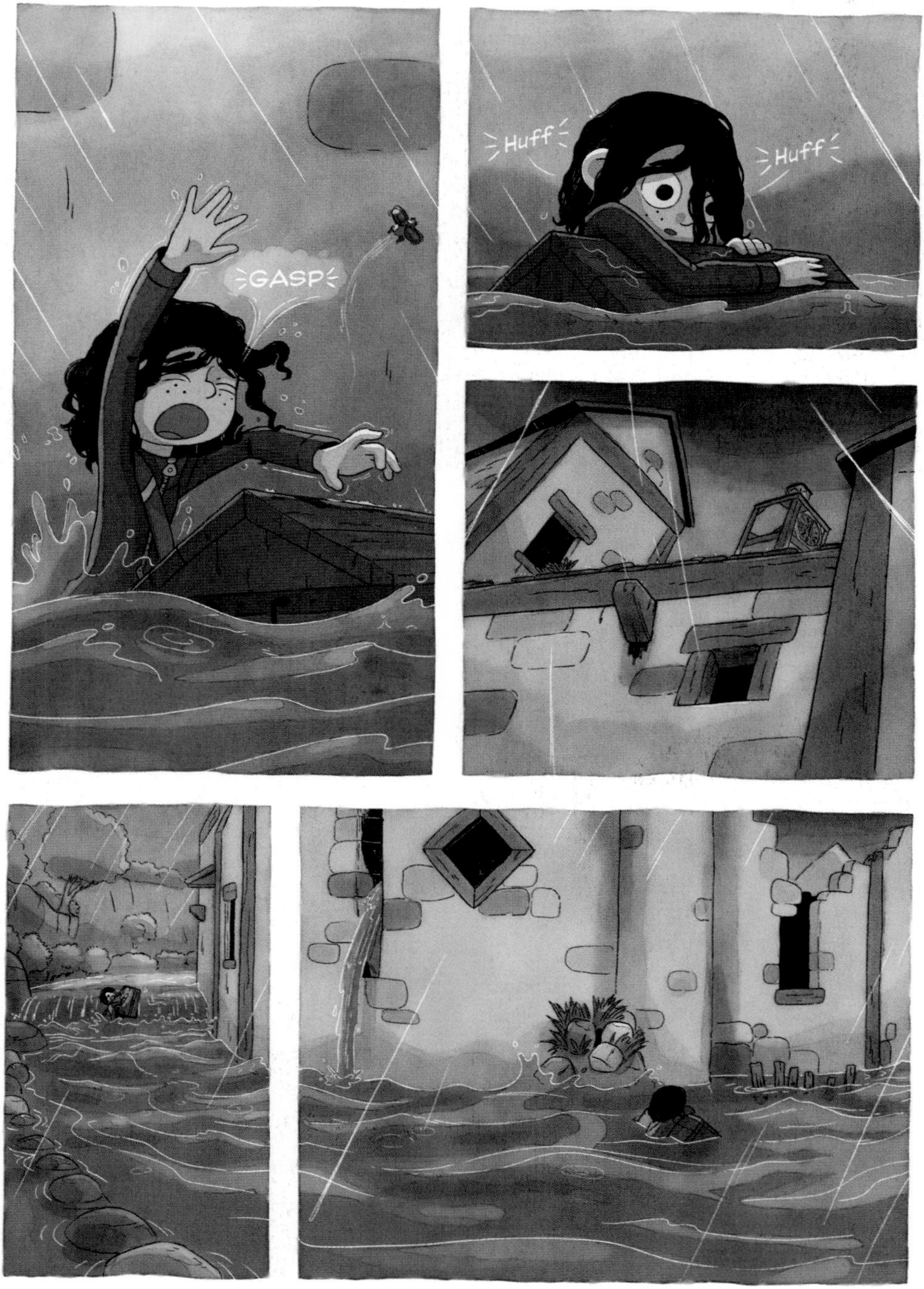
GASP
Huff
Huff

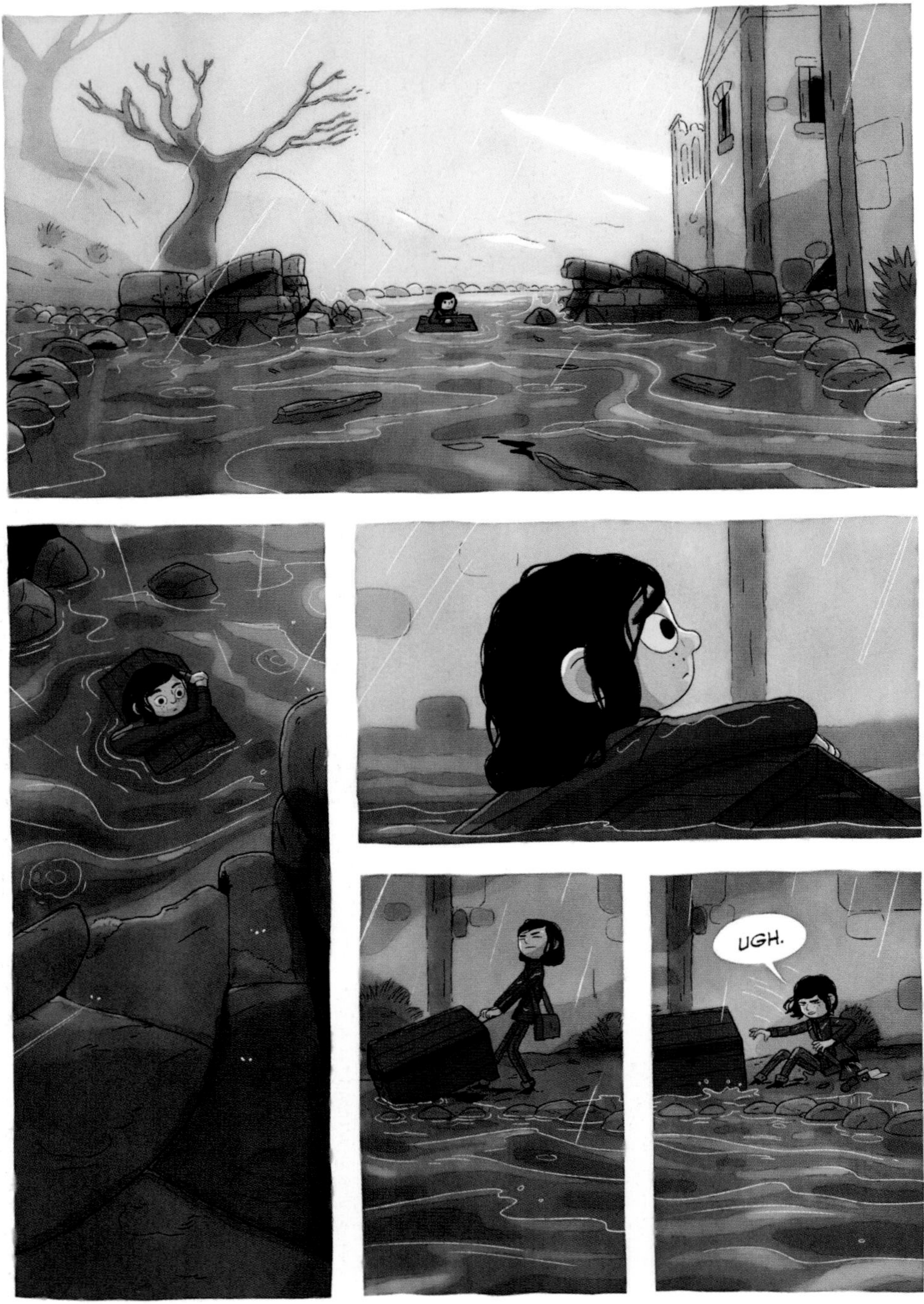
UGH.

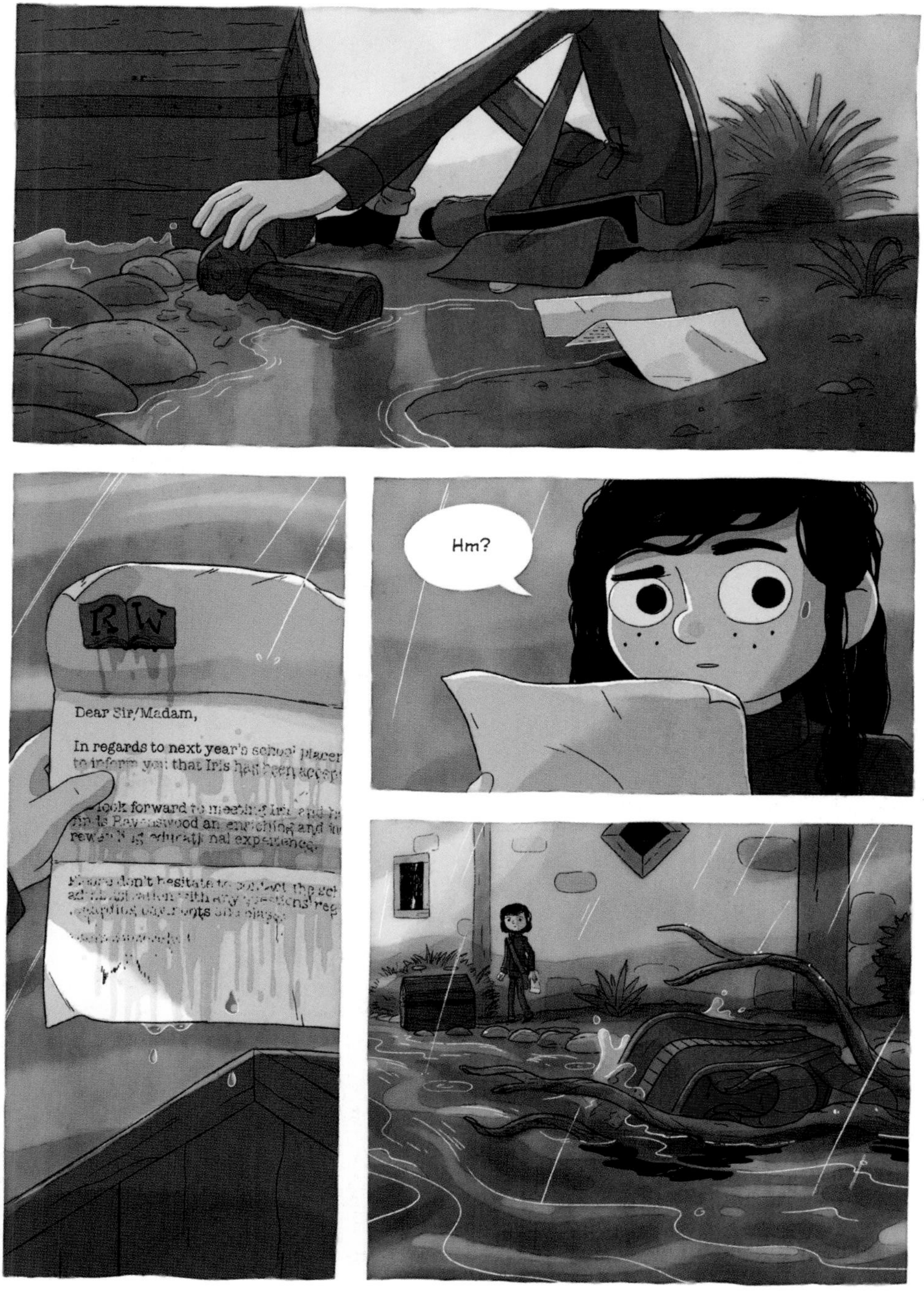

RW
Dear Sir/Madam,
In regards to next year's school
Hm?

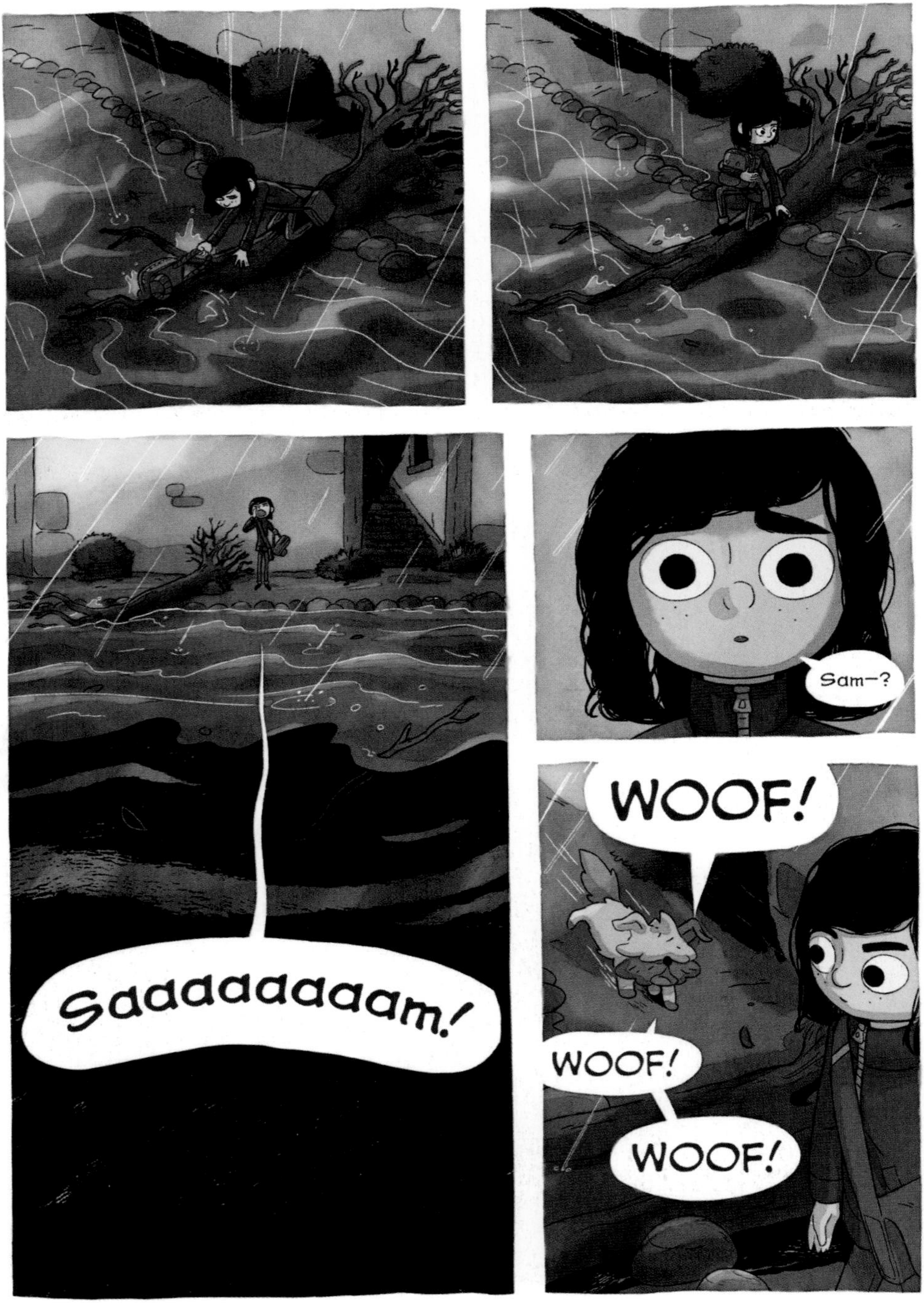
Saaaaaaaam!
Sam-?
WOOF!
WOOF!
WOOF!

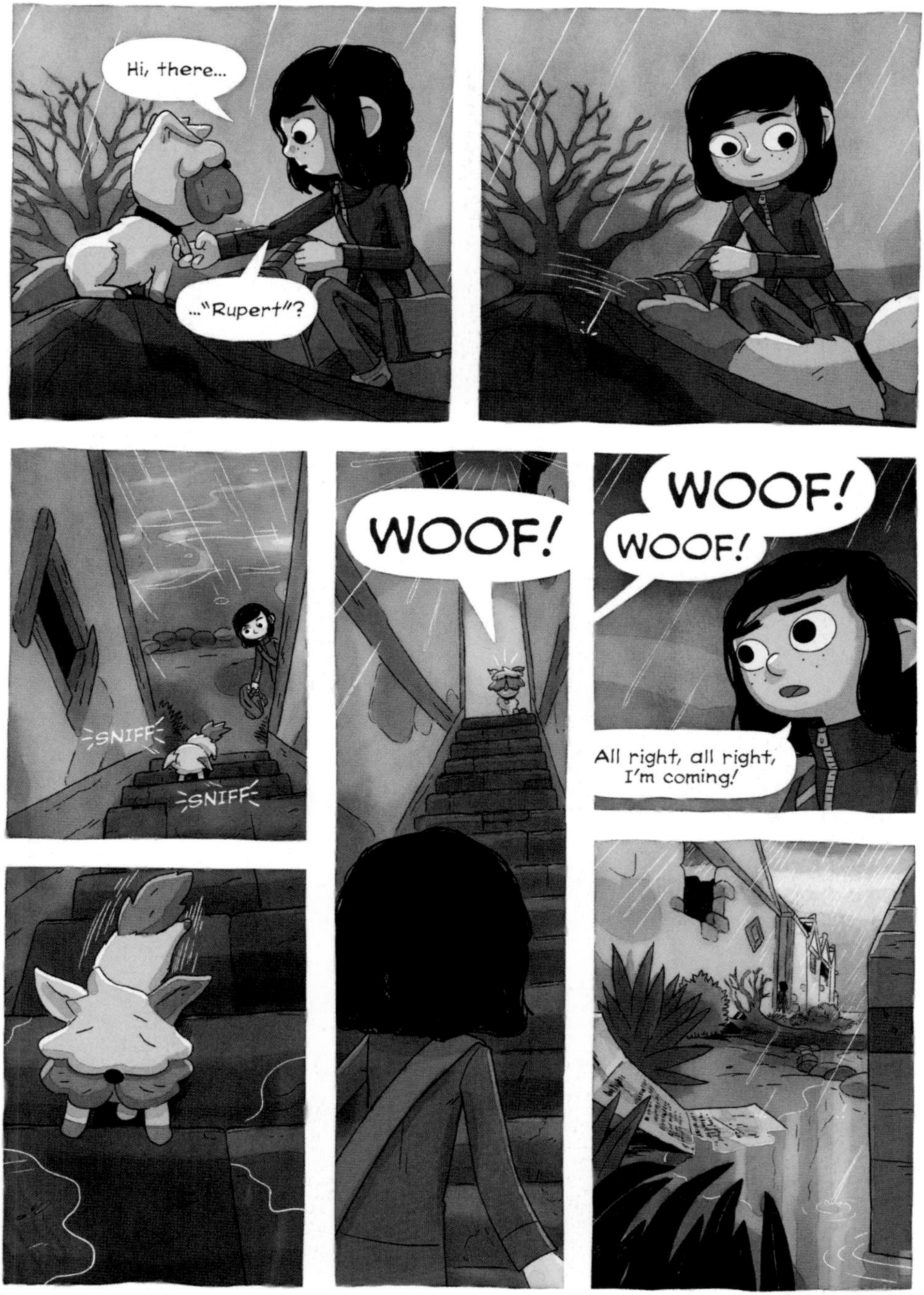
Hi, there...
..."Rupert"?
SNIFF
SNIFF
WOOF!
WOOF!
WOOF!
All right, all right, I'm coming!

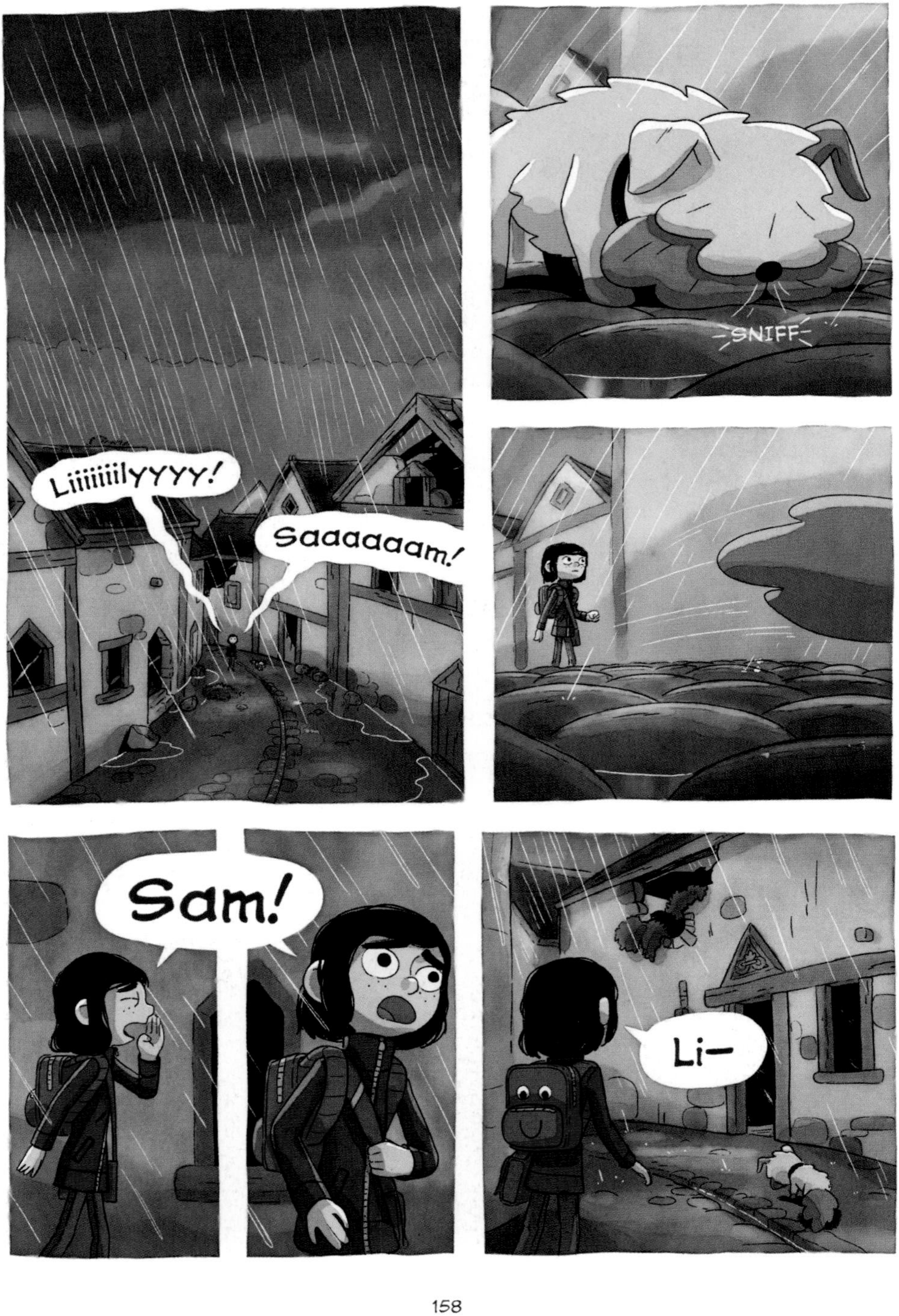
Liiiiiilyyyy!
Saaaaaam!
SNIFF
Sam!
Li—

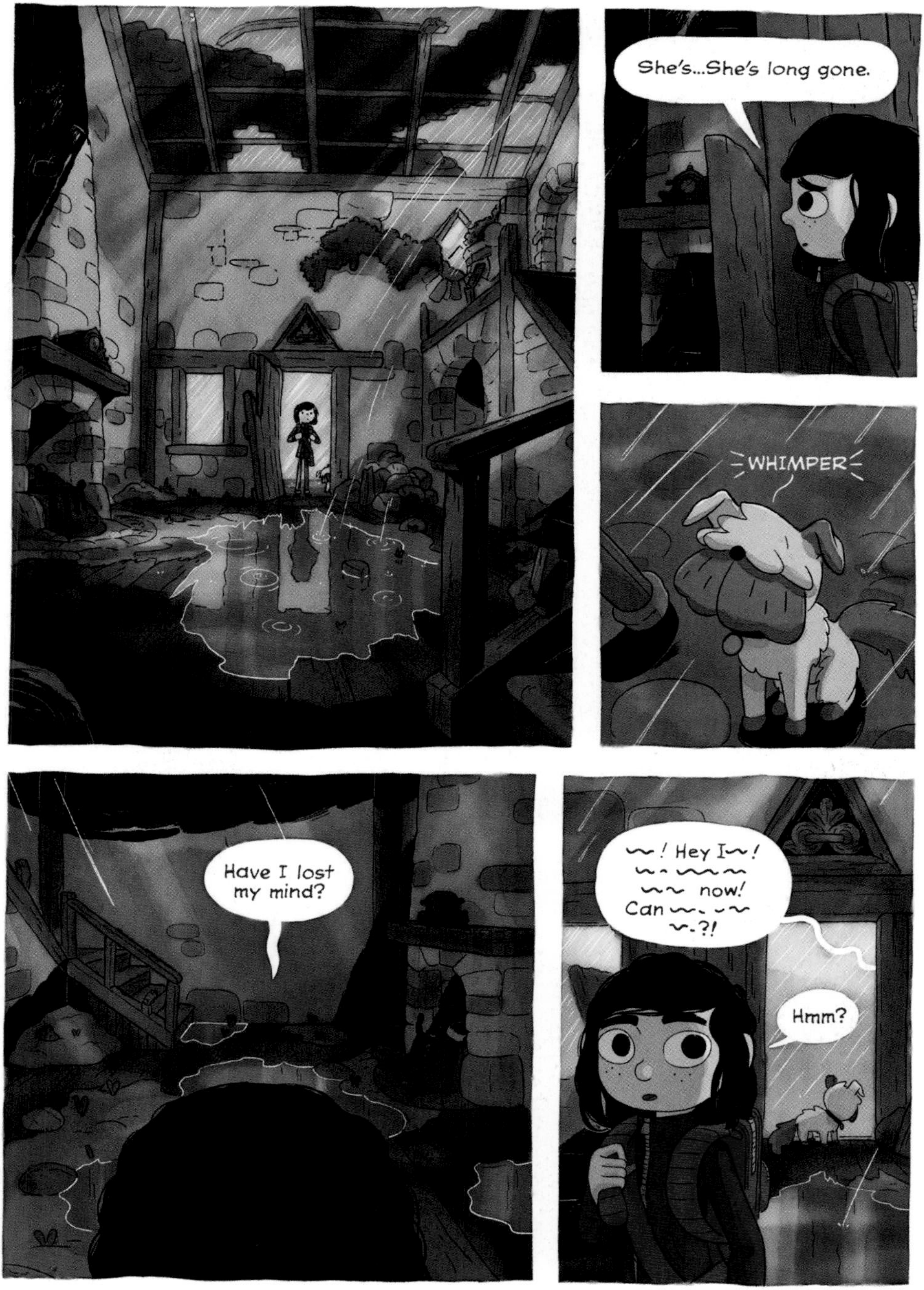

She's...She's long gone.
WHIMPER
Have I lost my mind?
! Hey I ! now! Can ?!
Hmm?

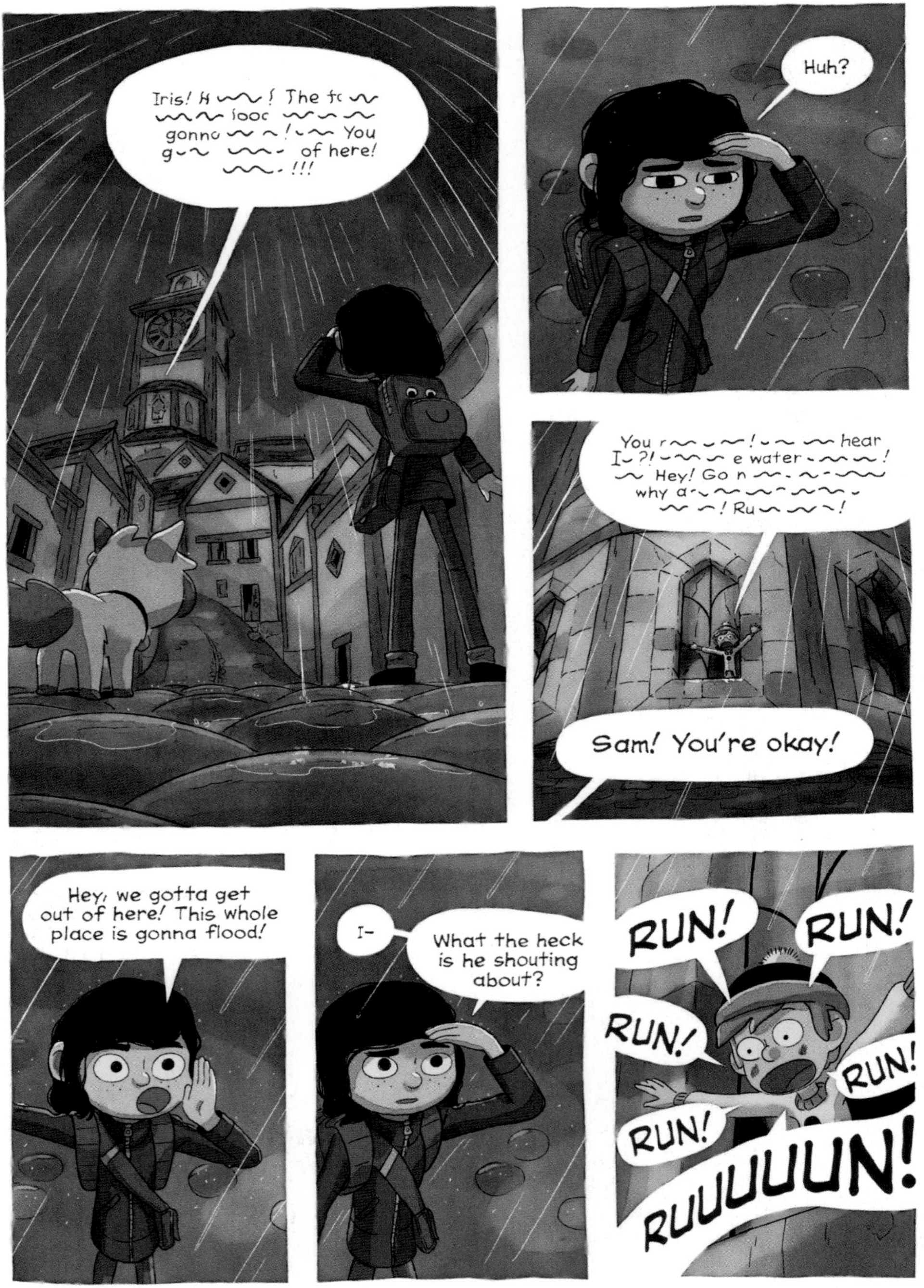

Iris! The of here! !!!
Huh?
You hear ?! e water ! Hey! Go why ! Ru !
Sam! You're okay!
Hey, we gotta get out of here! This whole place is gonna flood!
I–
What the heck is he shouting about?
RUN!
RUN!
RUN!
RUN!
RUN!
RUUUUUN!

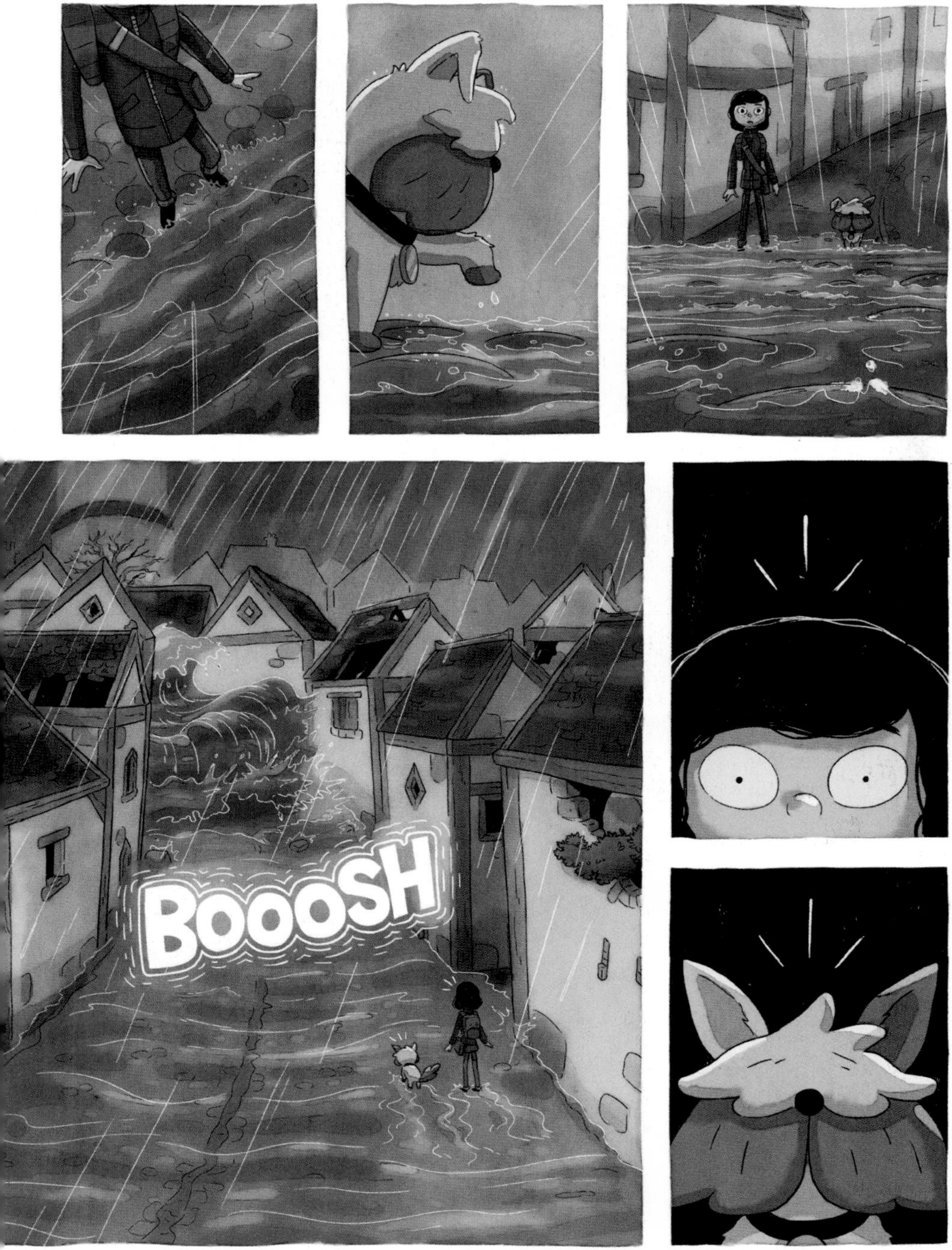
BOOOSH

SLAM

LOCK
CLOSE
LOCK!

WHIMPER

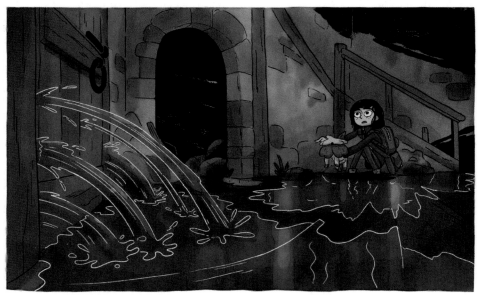

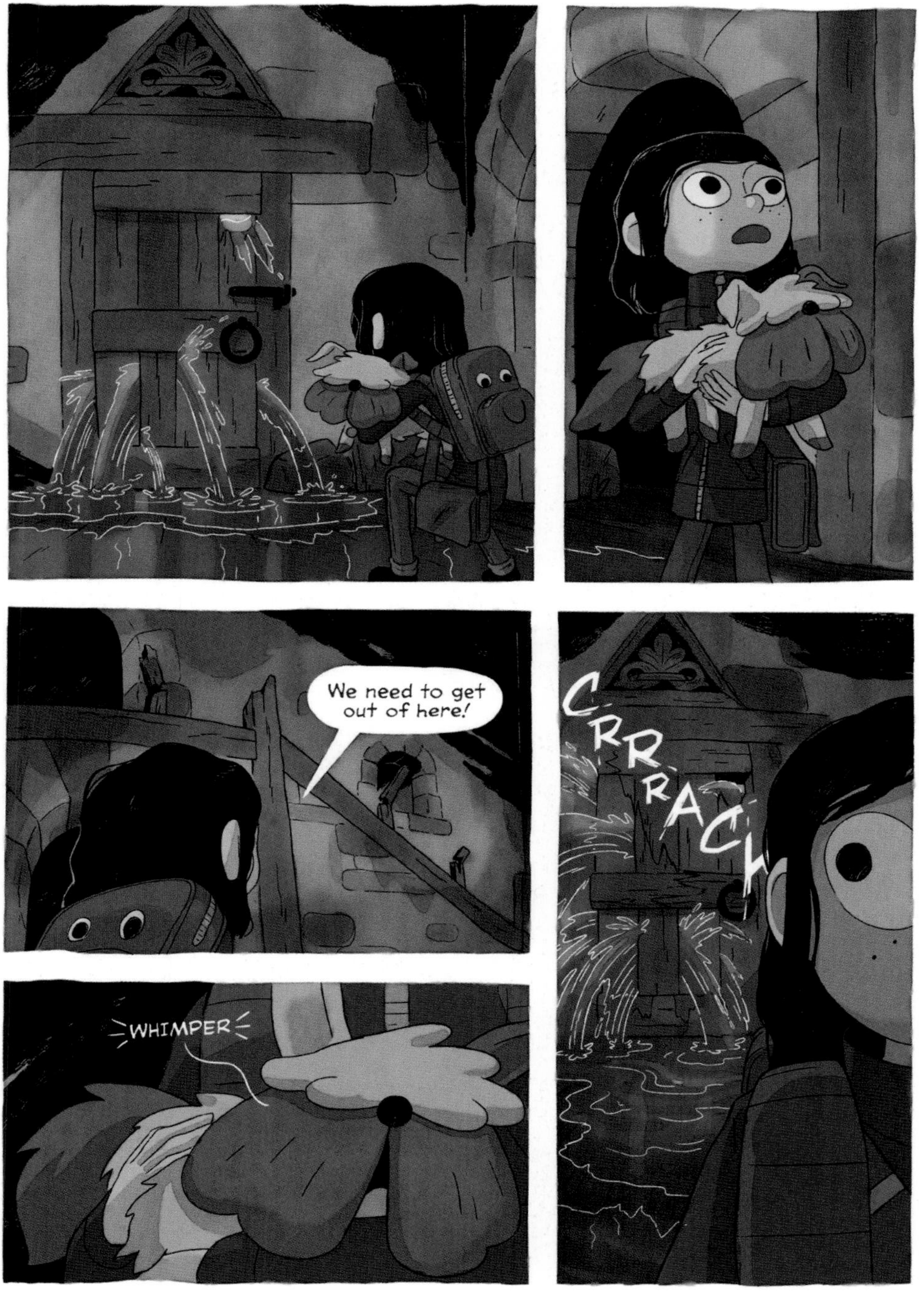

We need to get out of here!
WHIMPER
CRRRACK

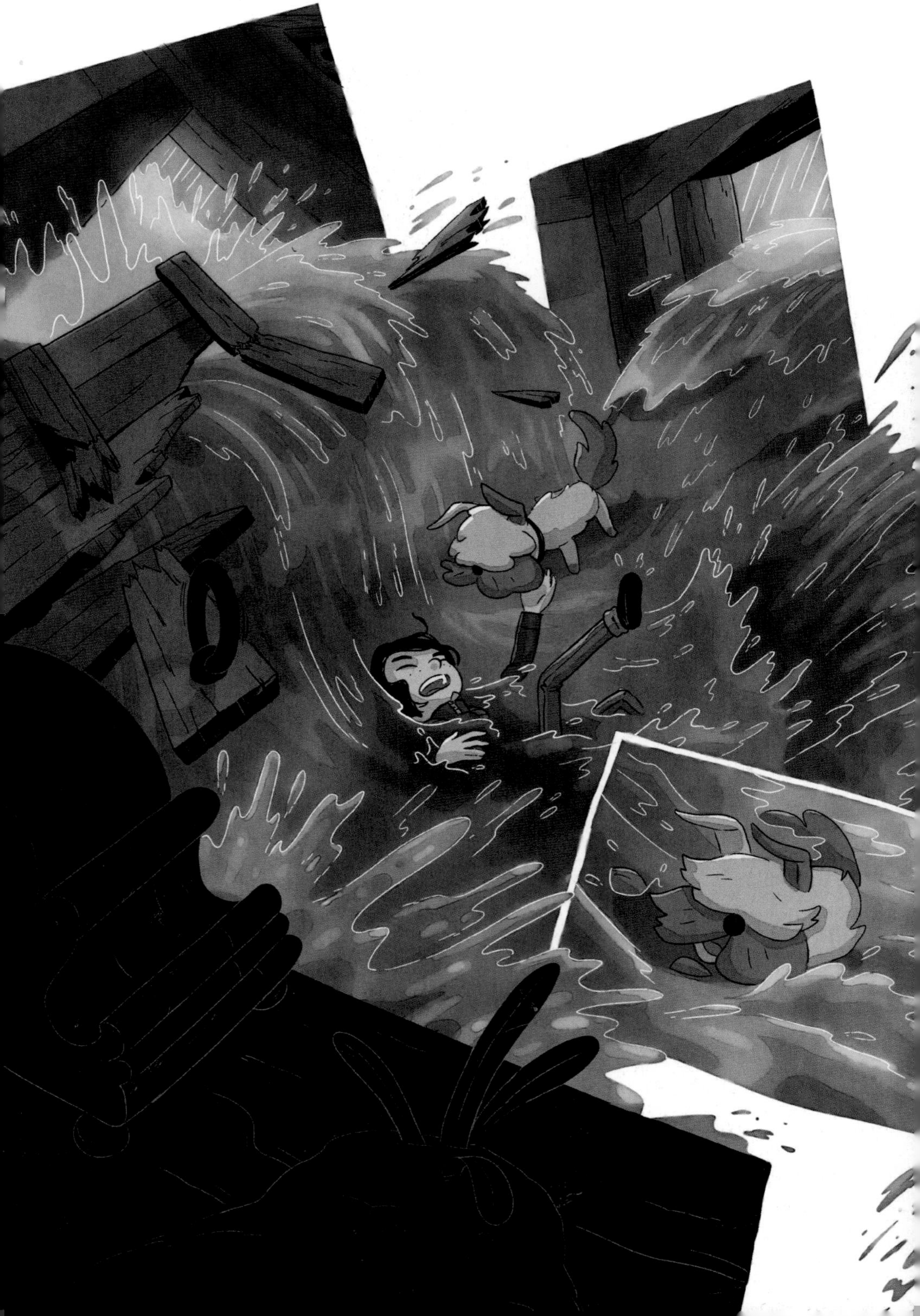

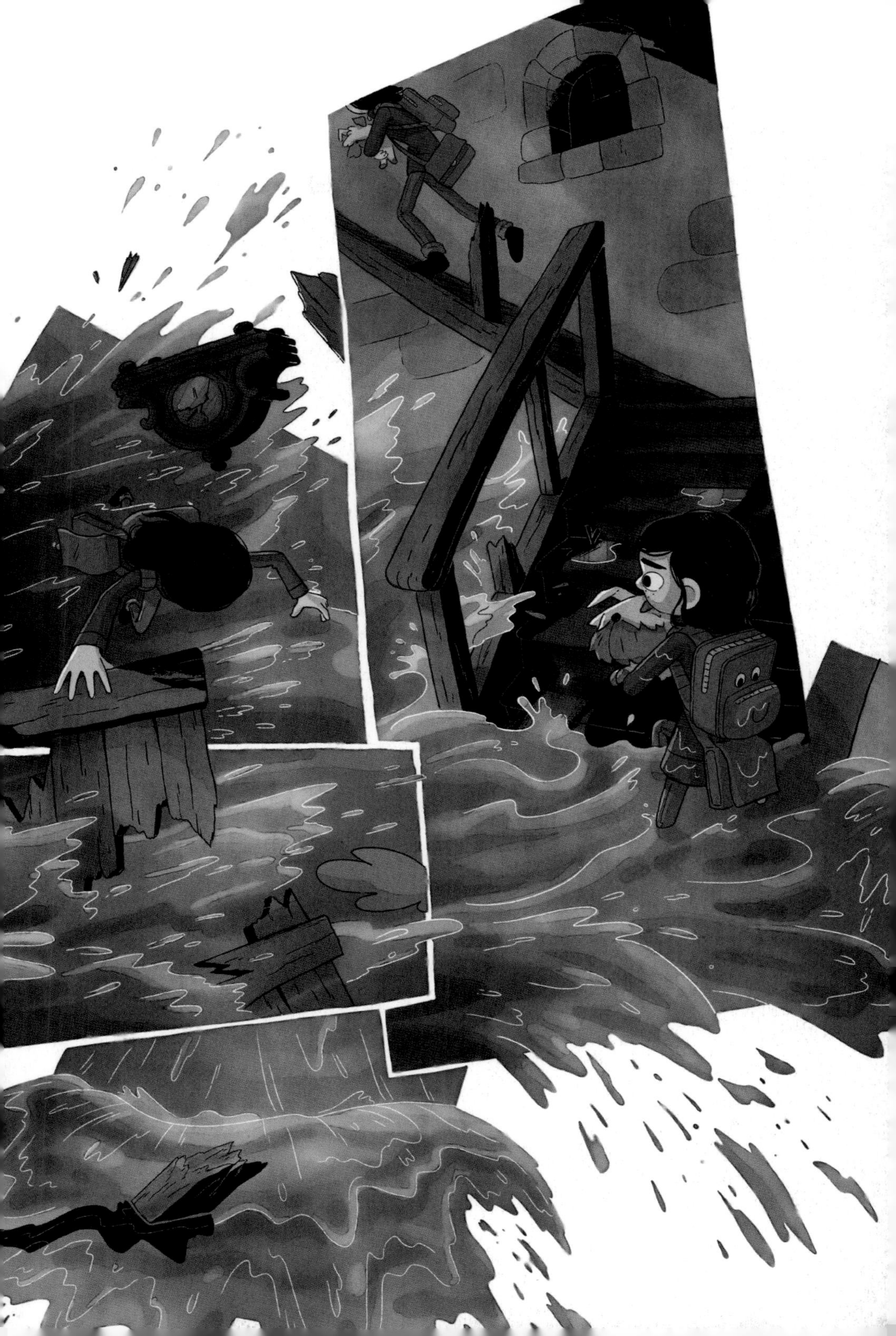

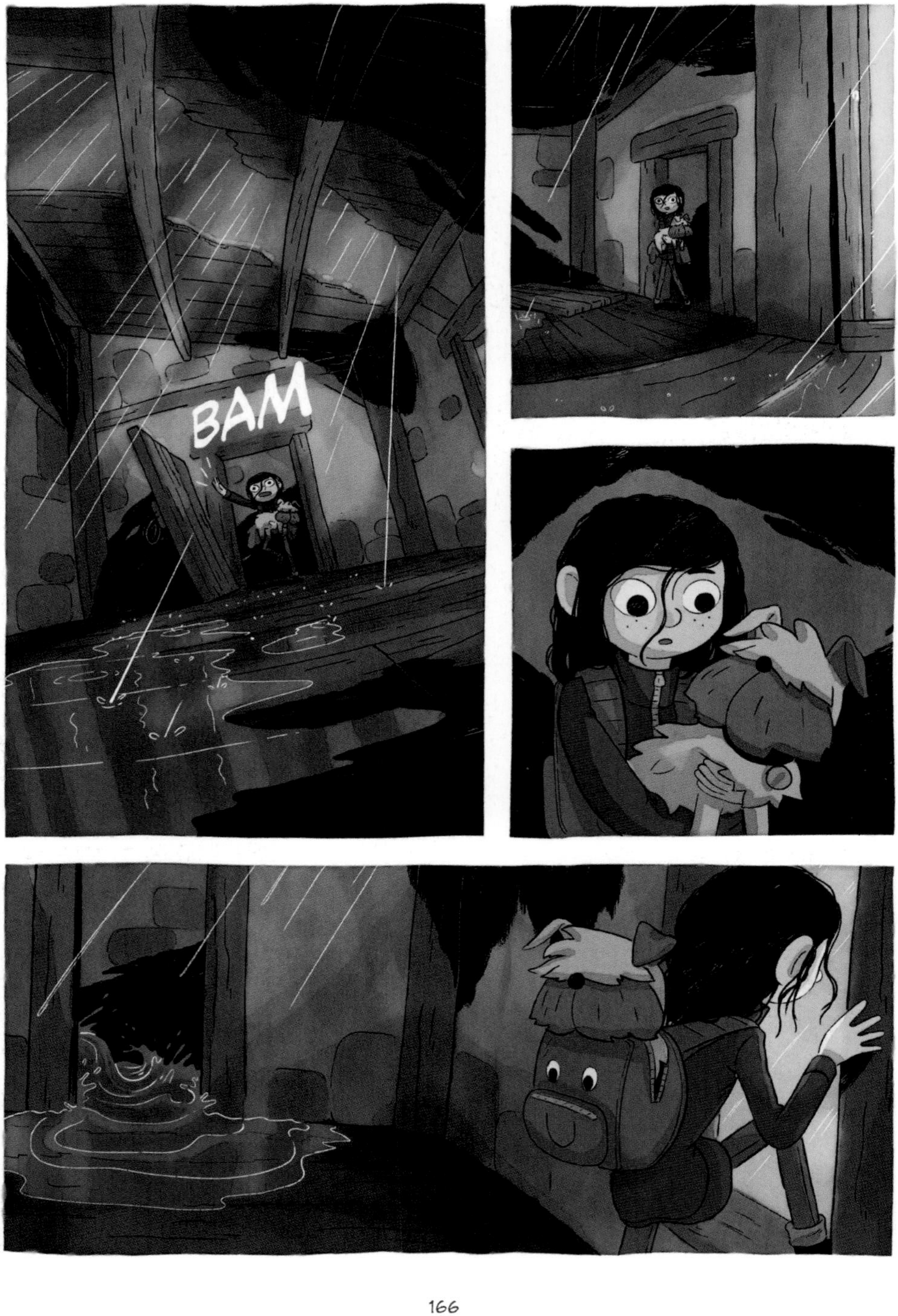
BAM

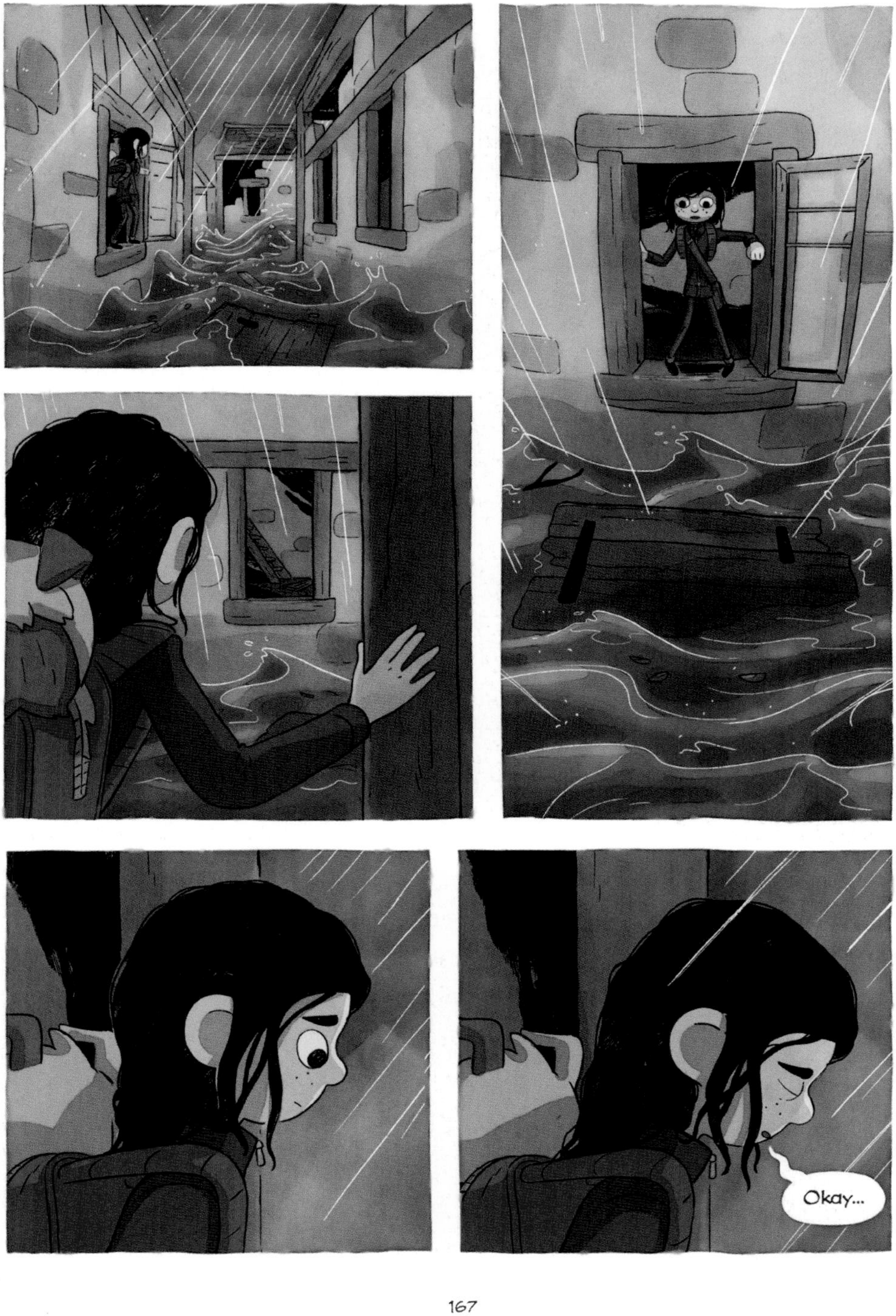
Okay...

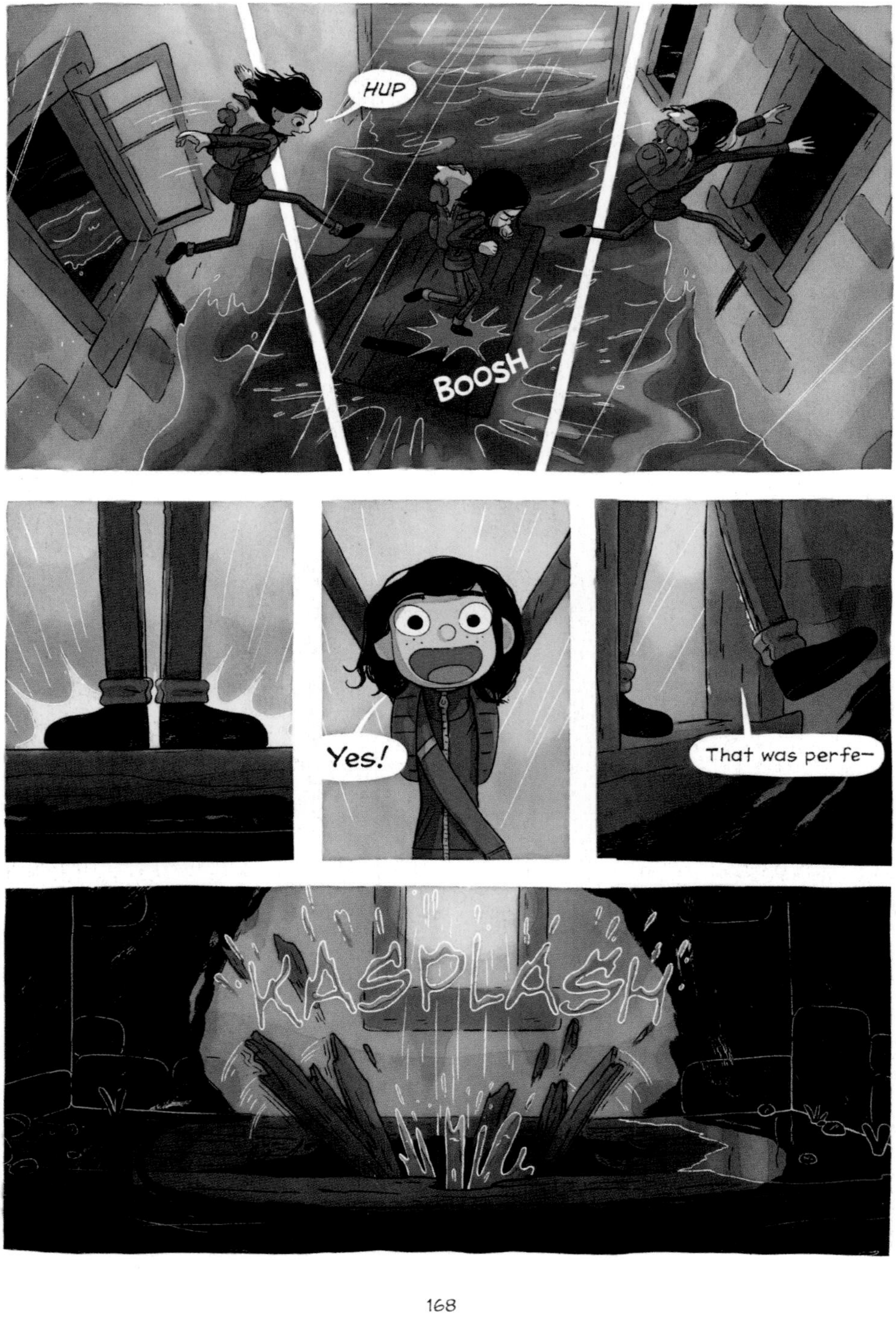
HUP
BOOSH
Yes!
That was perfe—
KASPLASH

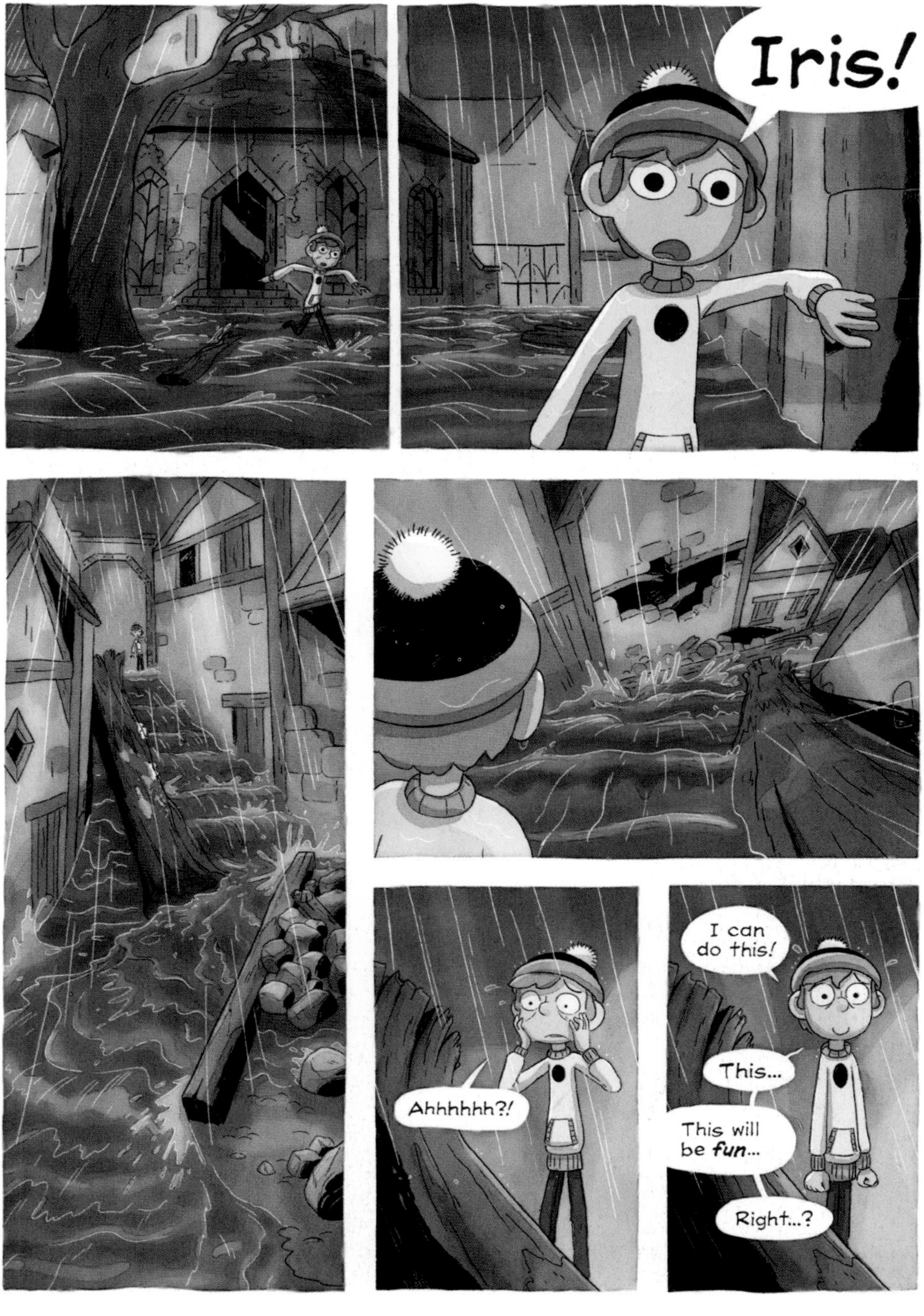
Iris!
Ahhhhhh?!
I can do this!
This...
This will be fun...
Right...?

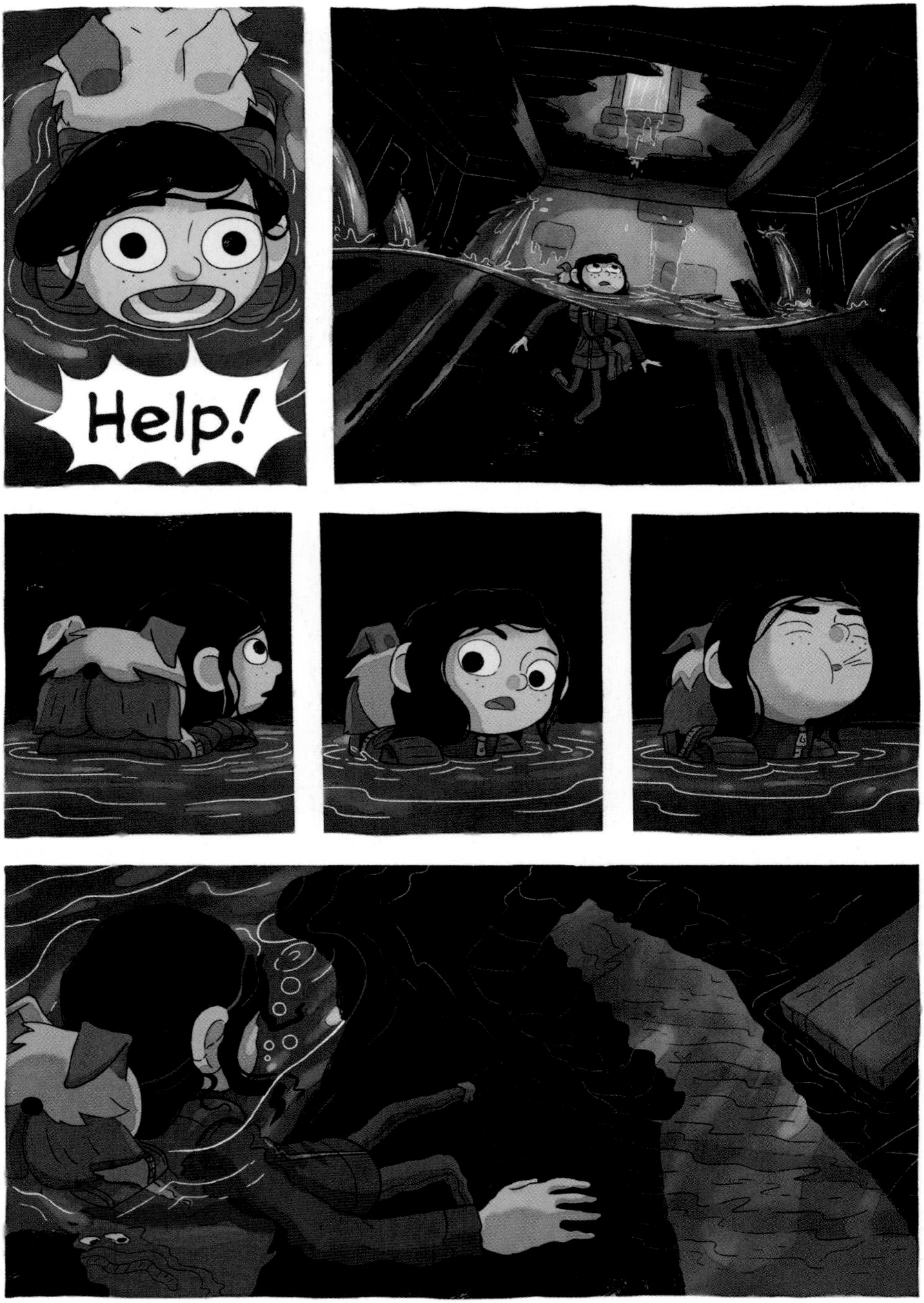
Help!

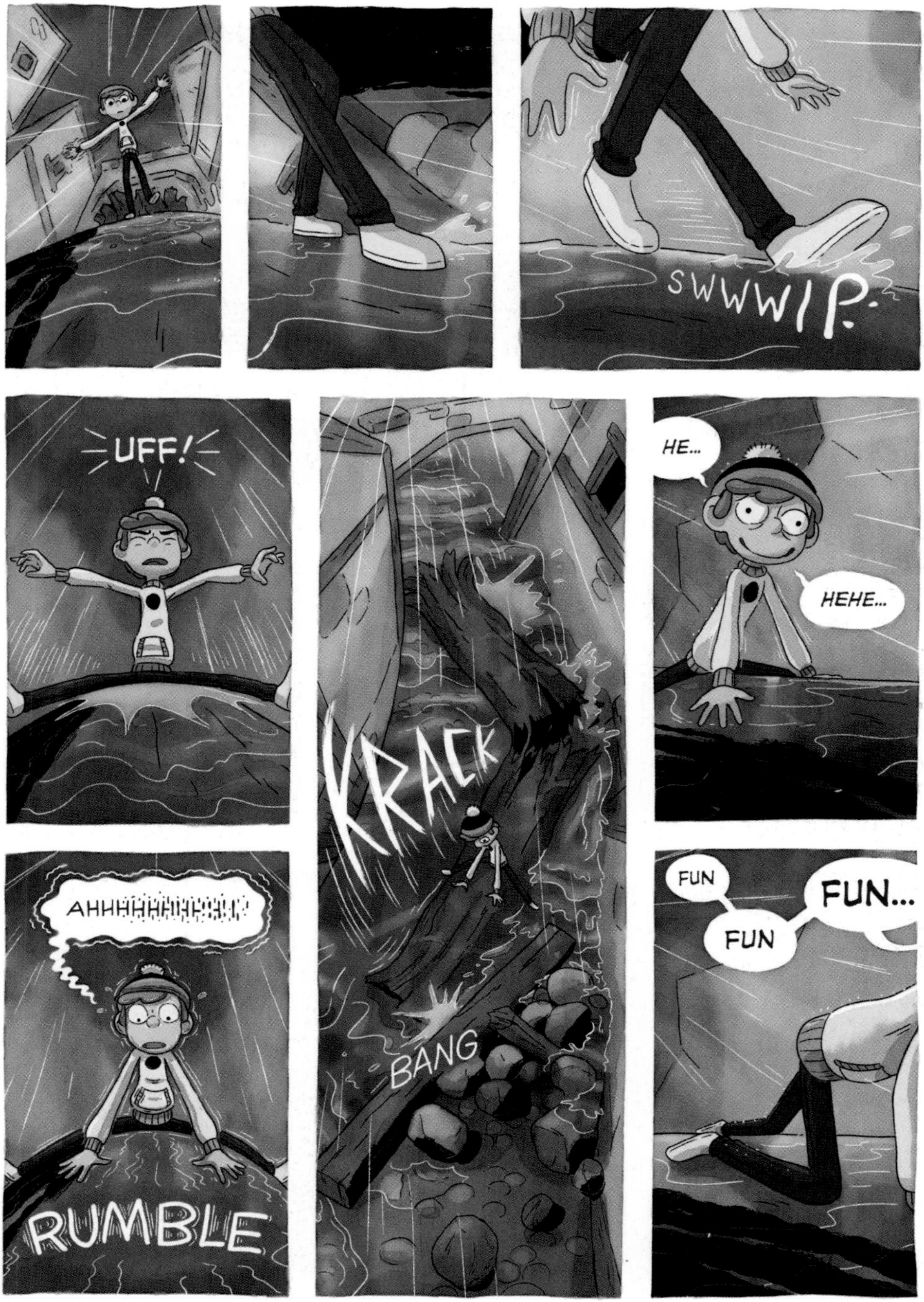
SWWWIP
UFF!
AHHHHHH
RUMBLE
KRACK
BANG
HE...
HEHE...
FUN
FUN
FUN...

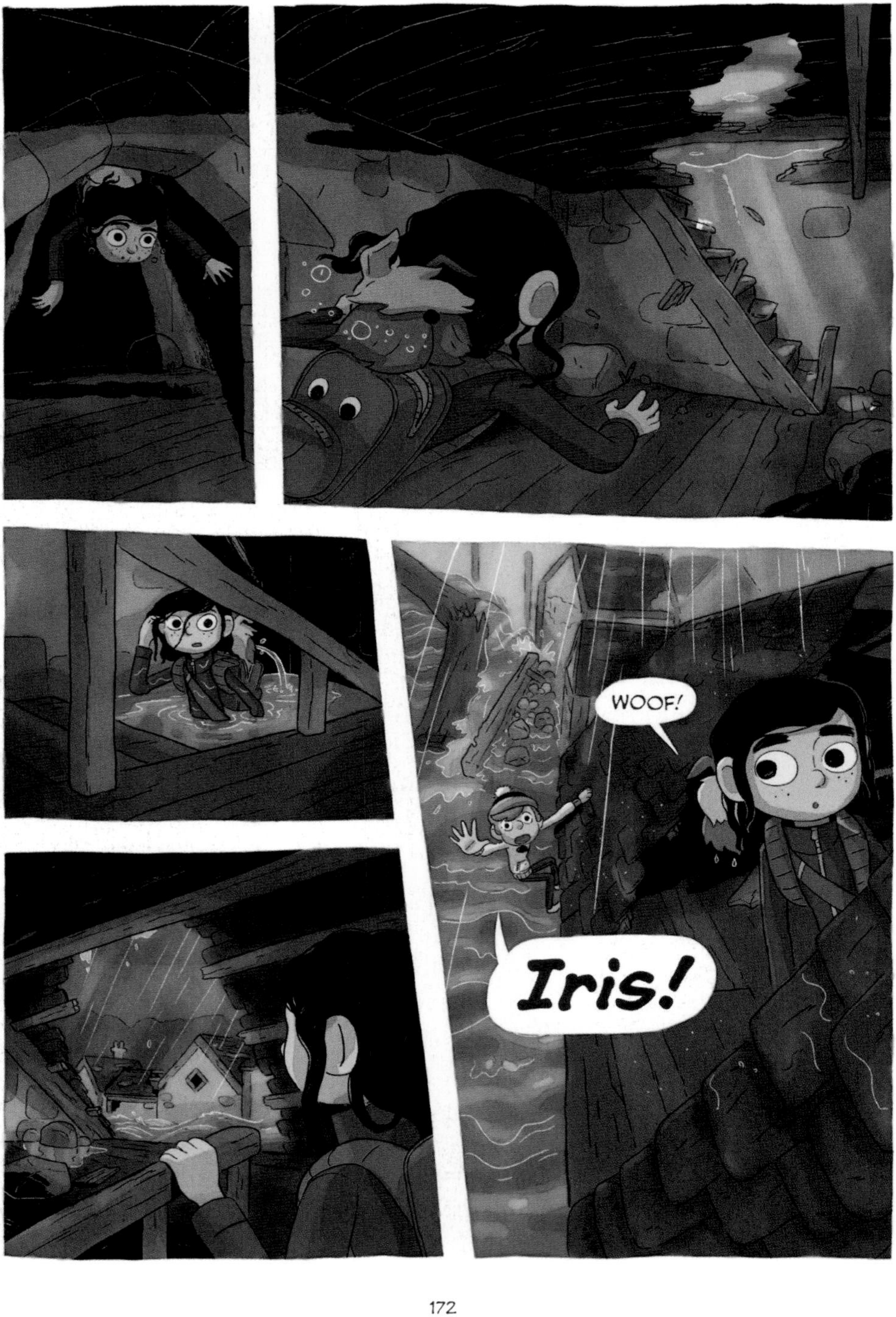
WOOF!
Iris!

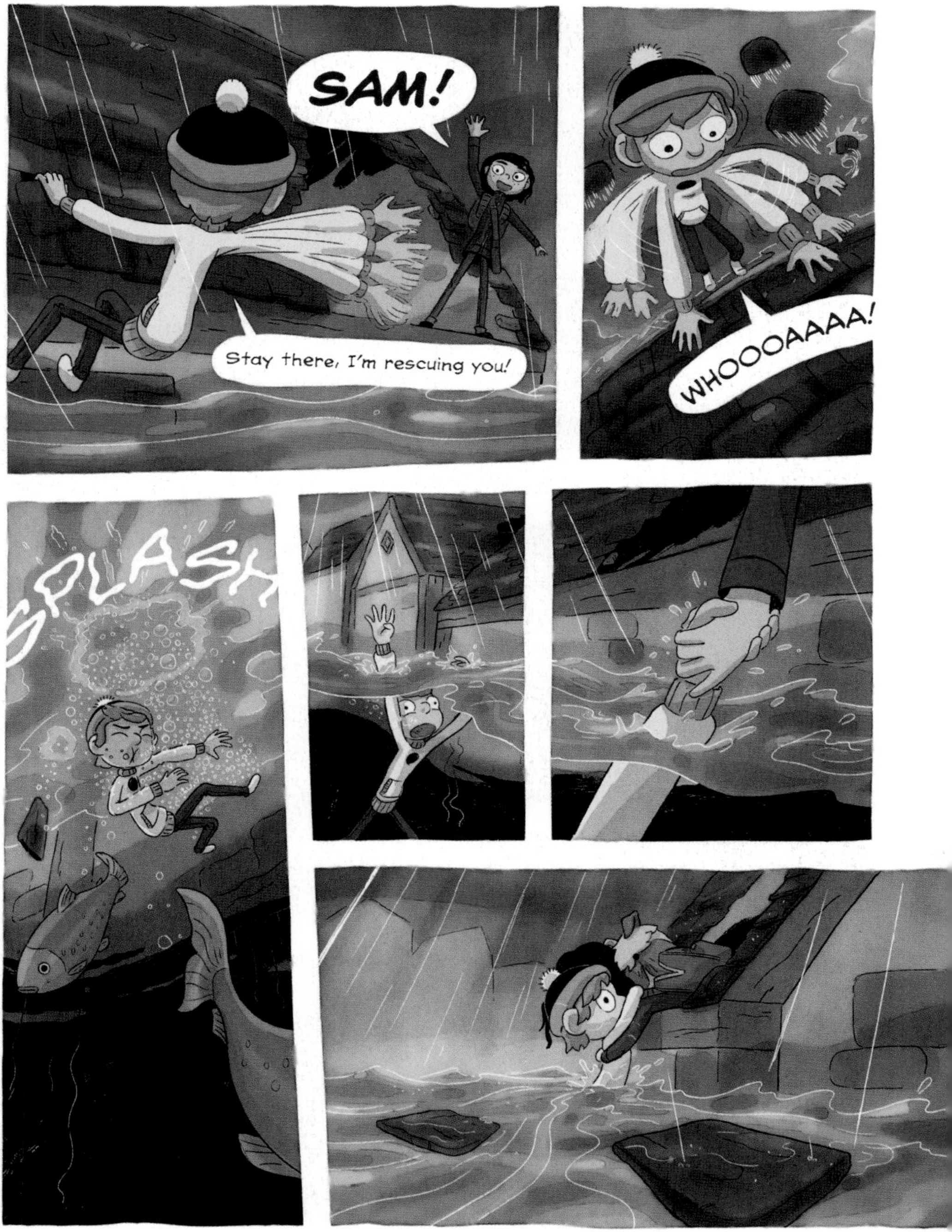
SAM!
Stay there, I'm rescuing you!
WHOOOAAAA!
SPLASH

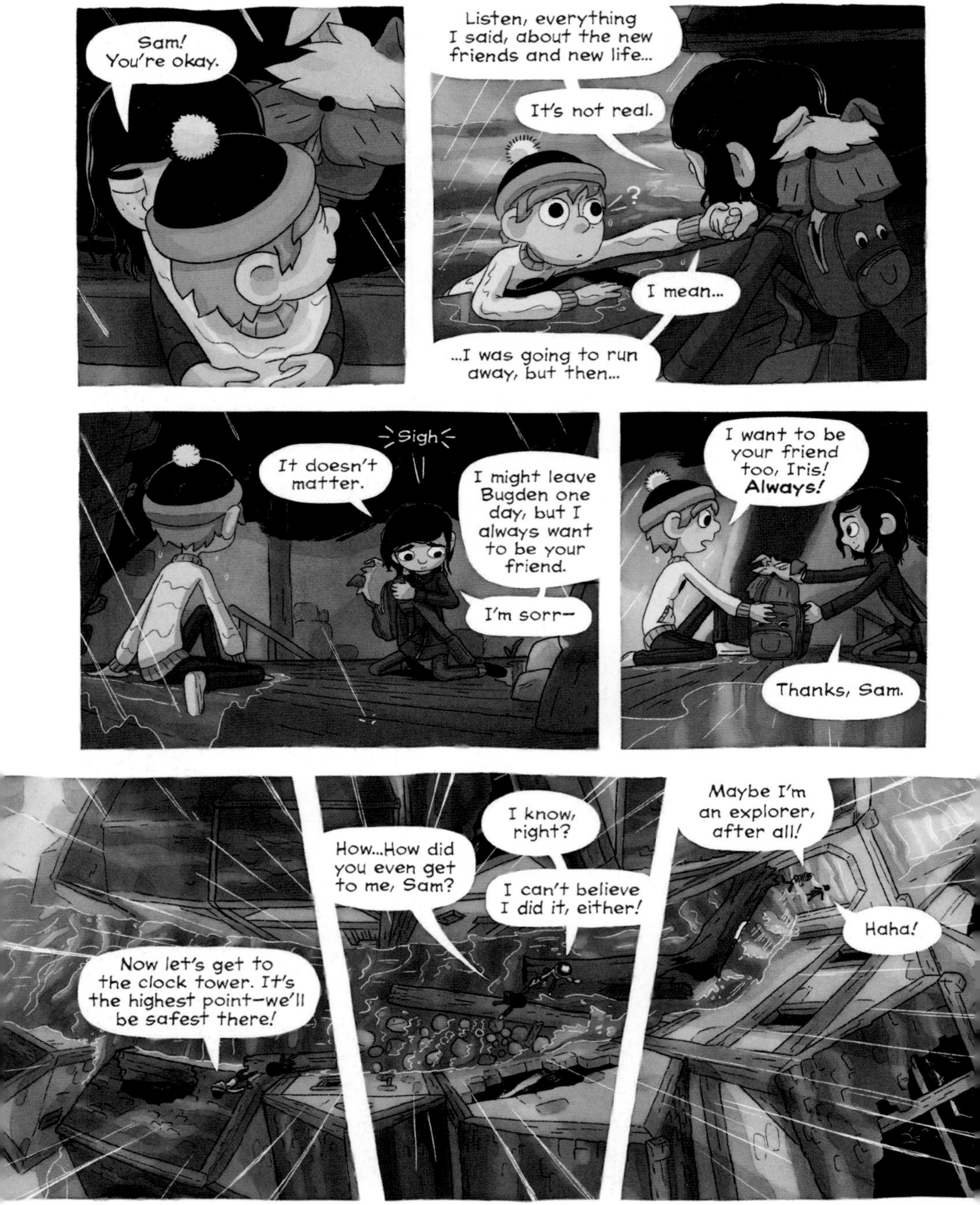
Sam! You're okay.
Listen, everything I said, about the new friends and new life...
It's not real.
I mean...
...I was going to run away, but then...
It doesn't matter.
Sigh
I might leave Bugden one day, but I always want to be your friend.
I'm sorr—
I want to be your friend too, Iris! **Always!**
Thanks, Sam.
Now let's get to the clock tower. It's the highest point—we'll be safest there!
How...How did you even get to me, Sam?
I know, right?
I can't believe I did it, either!
Maybe I'm an explorer, after all!
Haha!

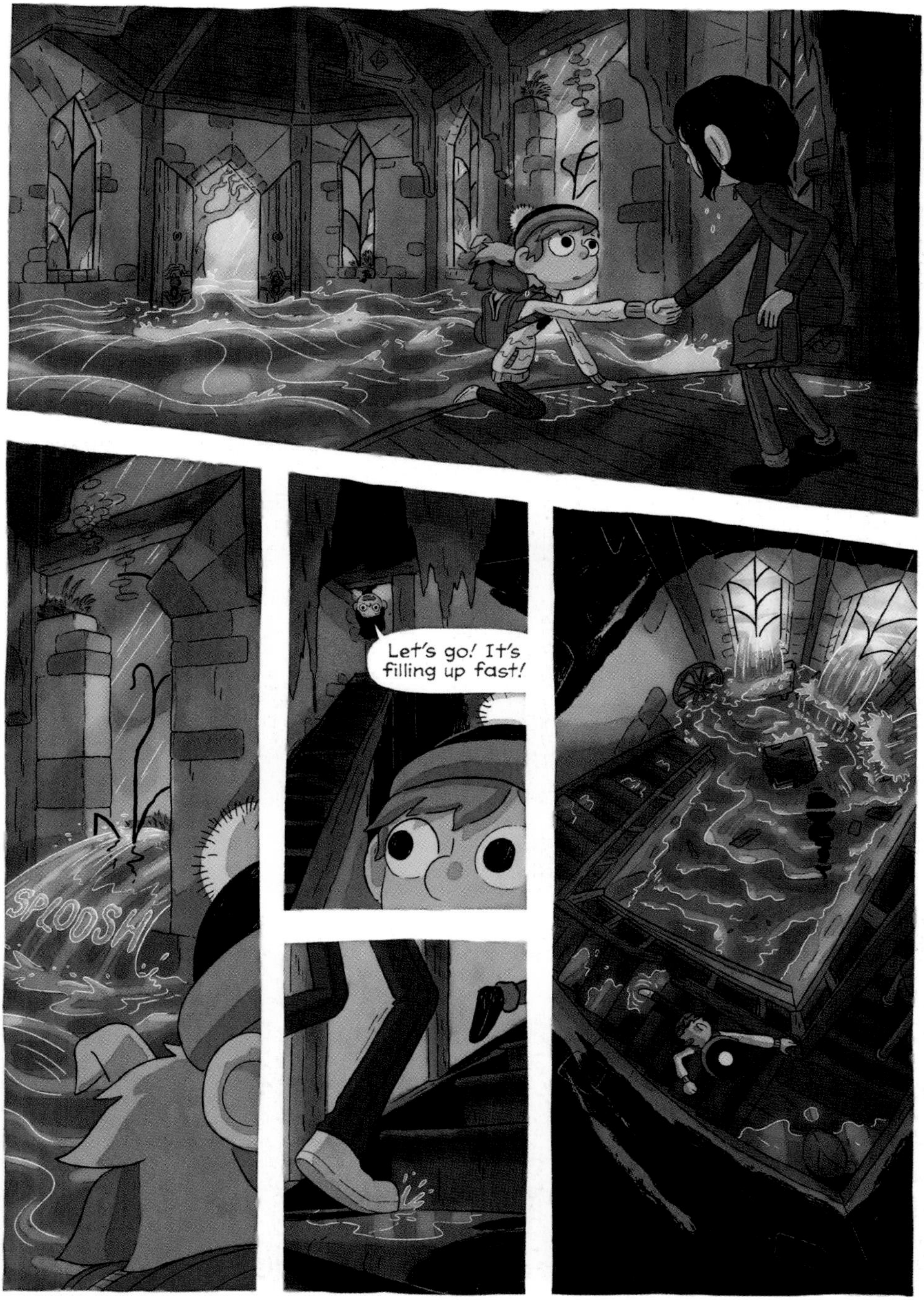
SPLOOSH
Let's go! It's filling up fast!

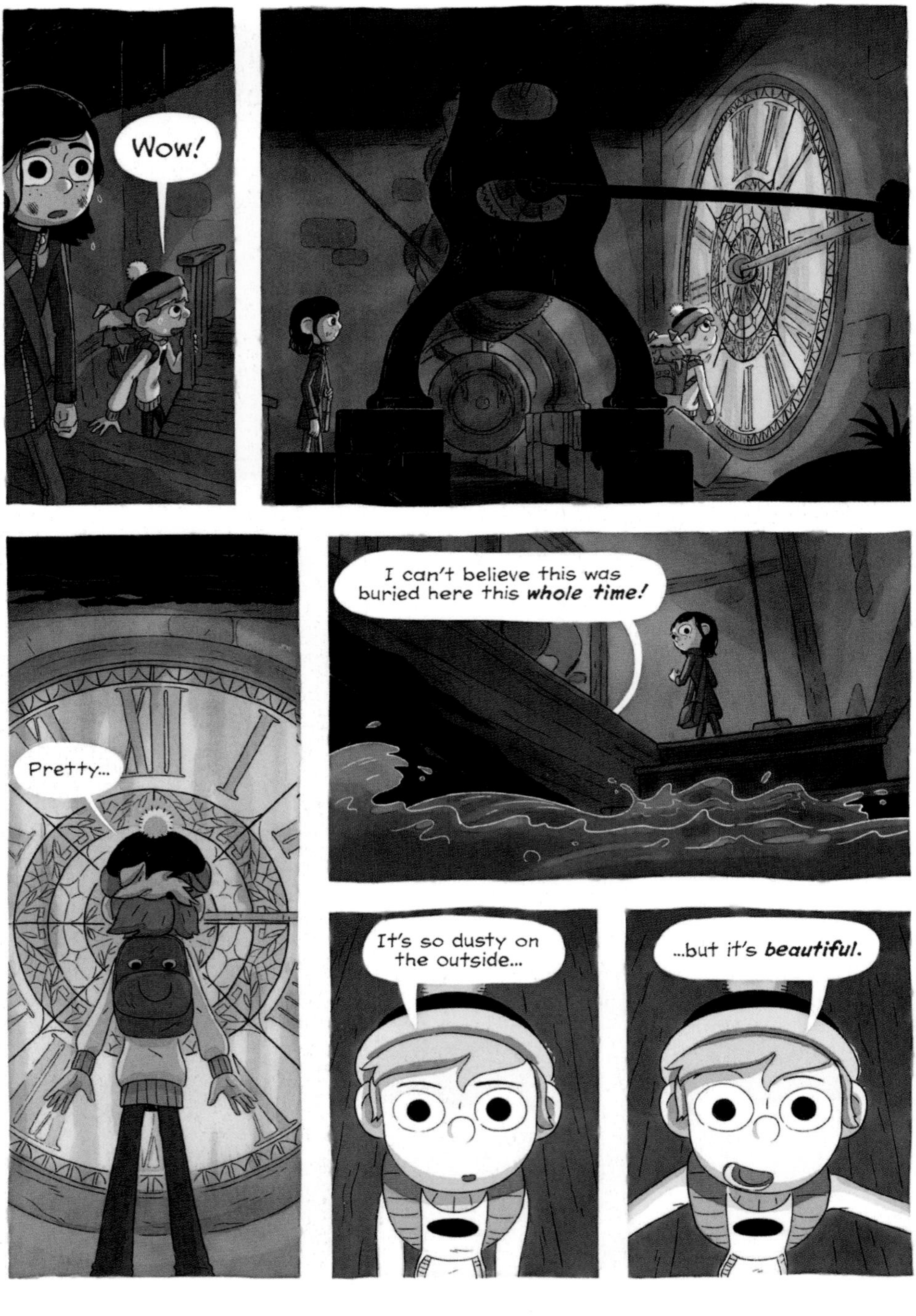

Wow!
Pretty...
I can't believe this was buried here this *whole time!*
It's so dusty on the outside...
...but it's *beautiful.*

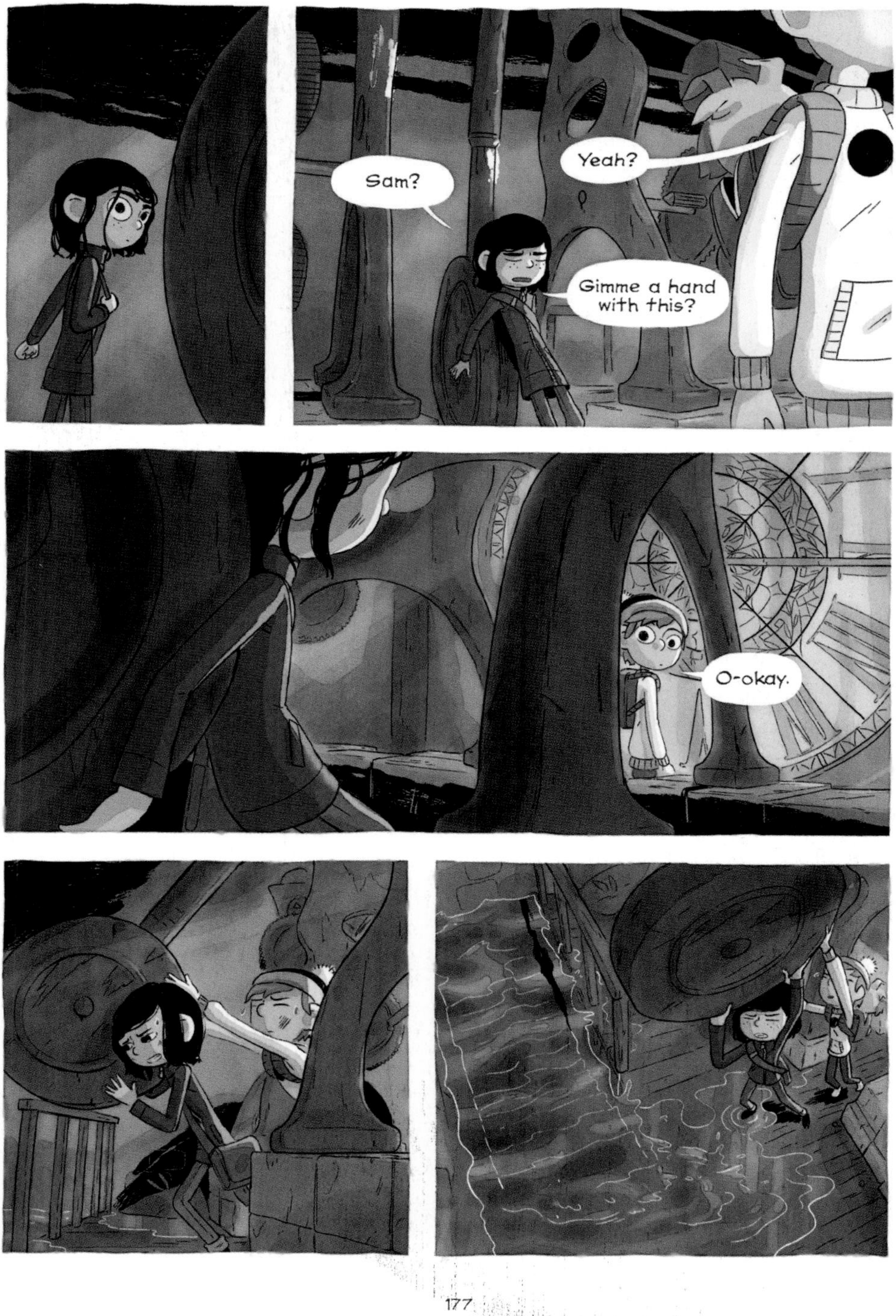
Sam?
Yeah?
Gimme a hand with this?
O-okay.

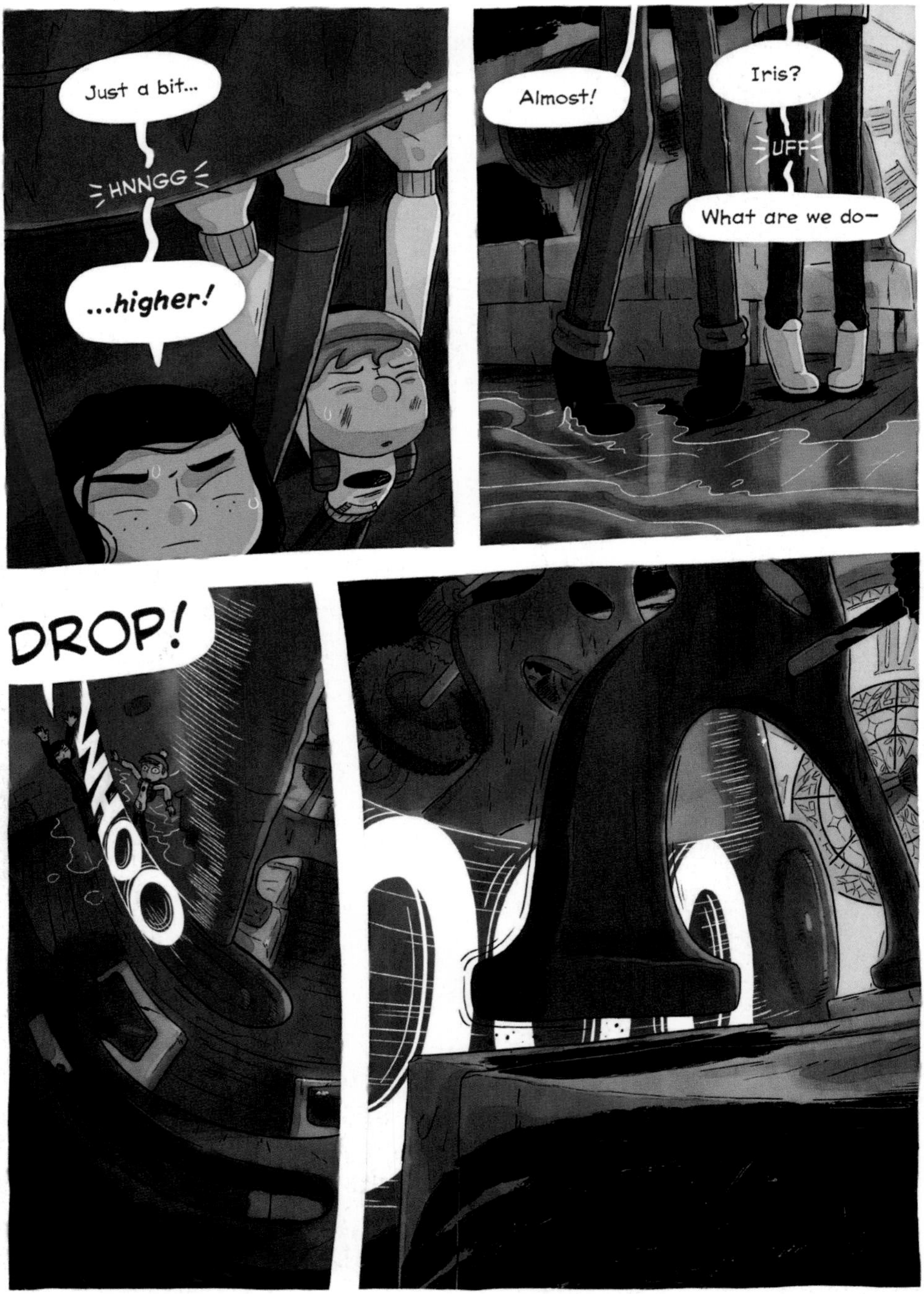
Just a bit...
HNNGG
...higher!
Almost!
Iris?
UFF
What are we do—
DROP!
WHOO

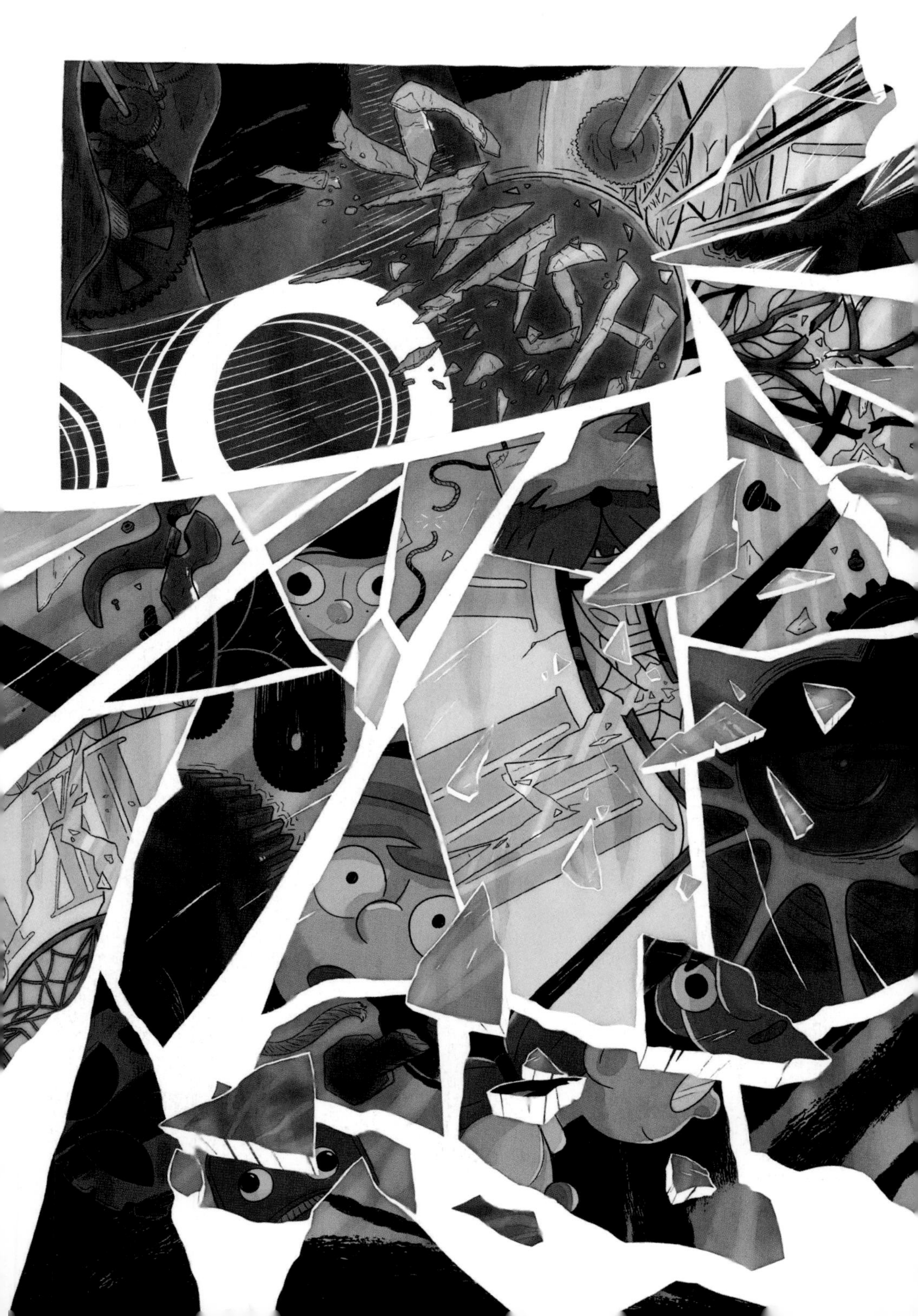

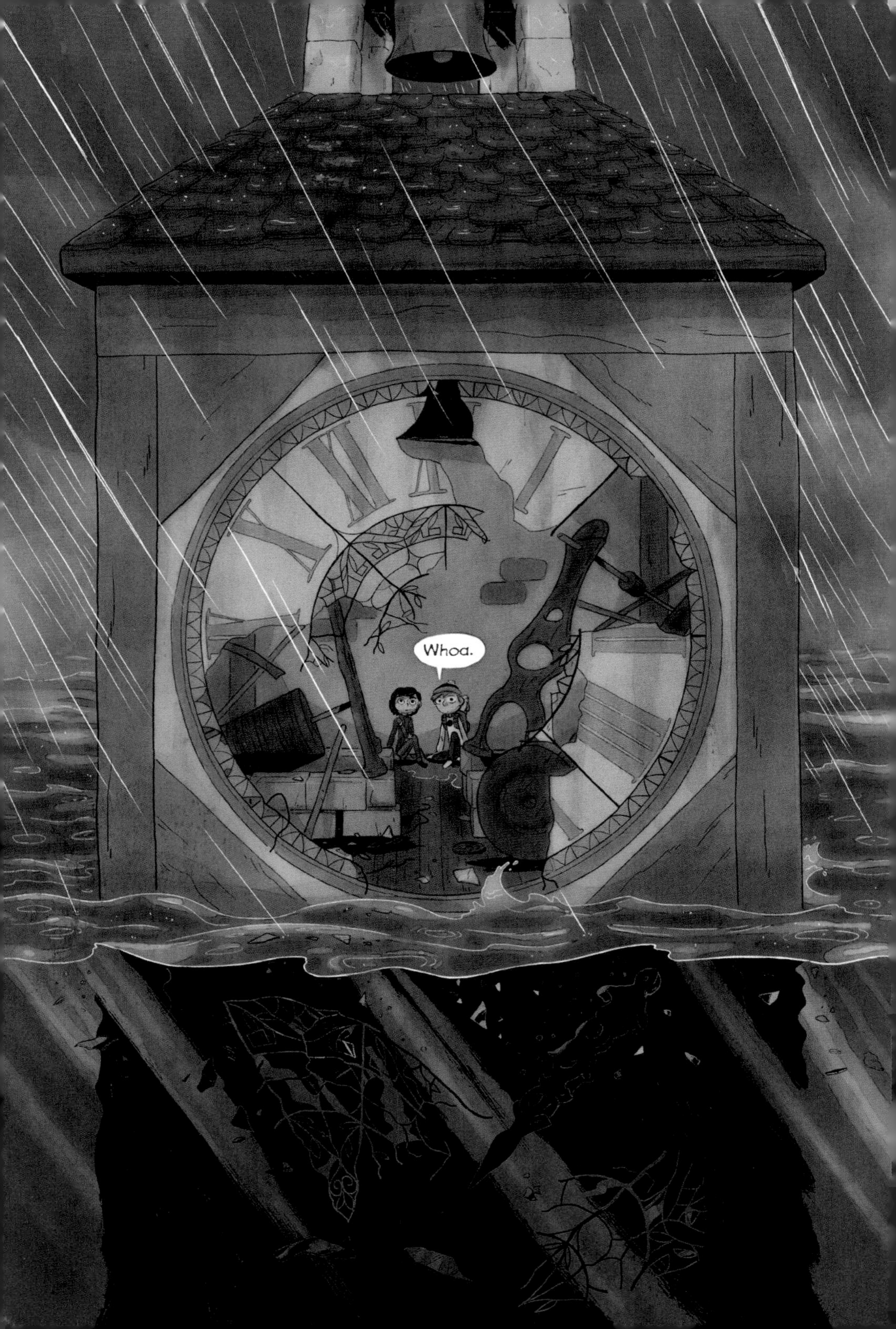
Whoa.

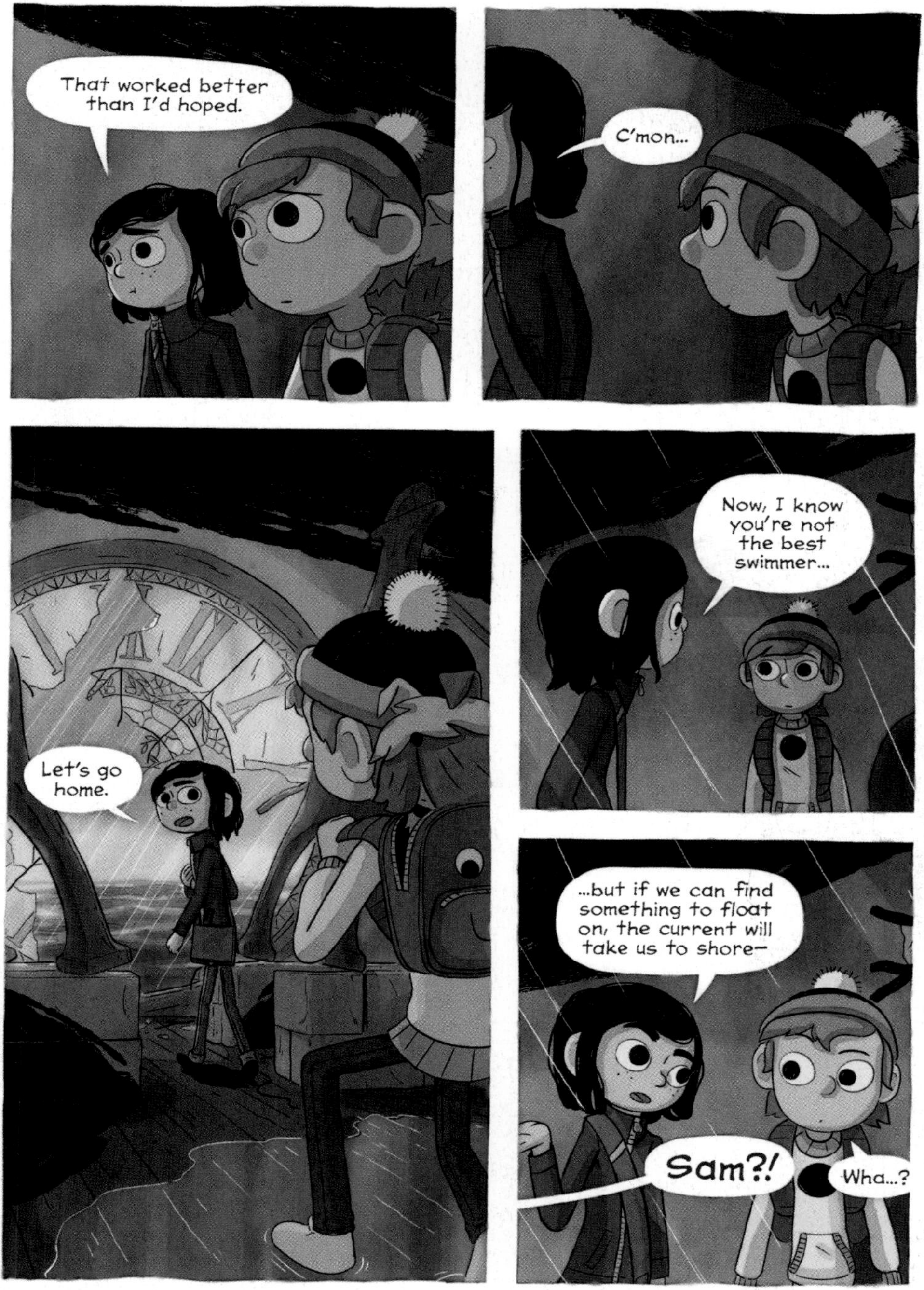
That worked better than I'd hoped.
C'mon...
Let's go home.
Now, I know you're not the best swimmer...
...but if we can find something to float on, the current will take us to shore—
Sam?!
Wha...?

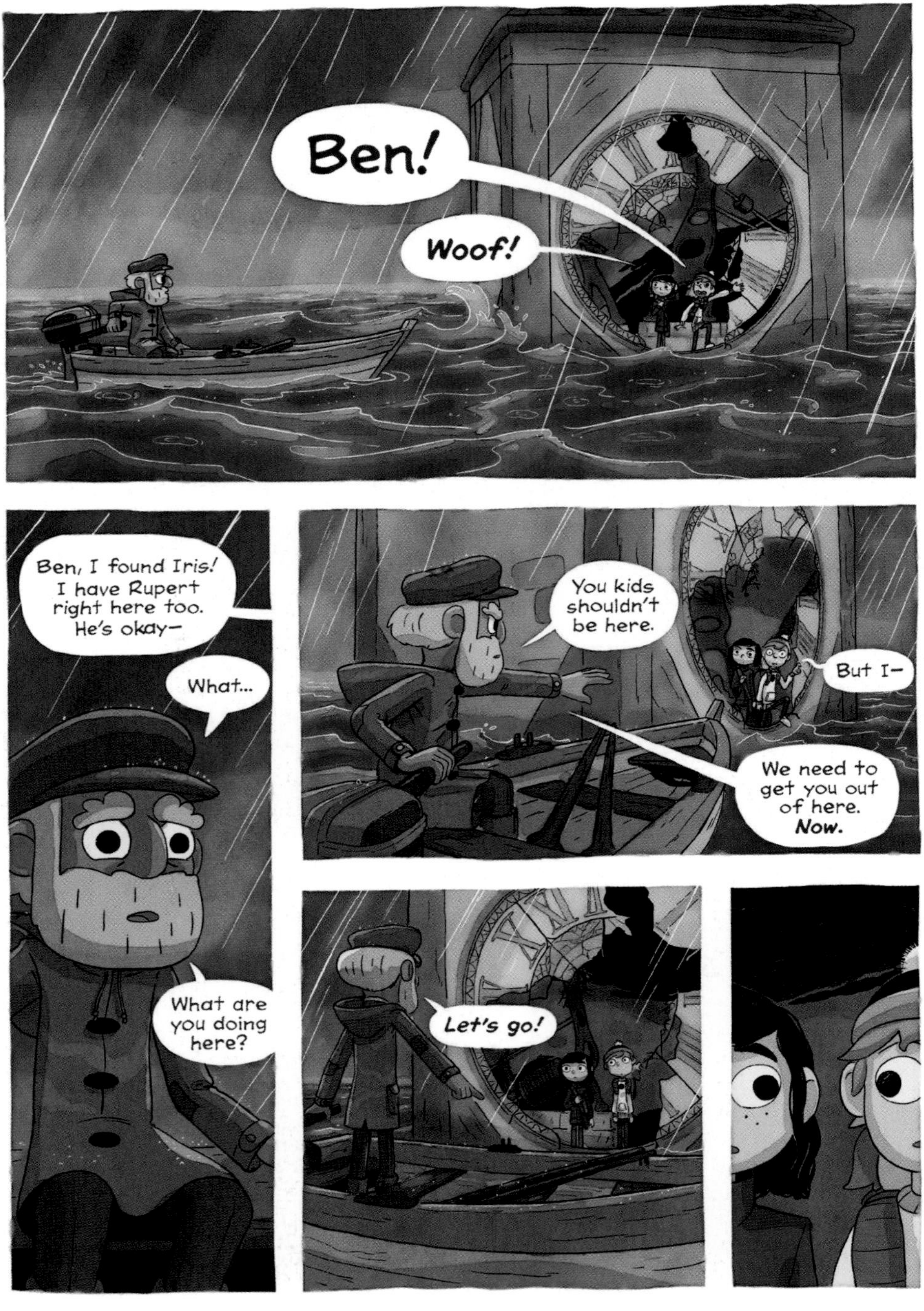
Ben!
Woof!
Ben, I found Iris! I have Rupert right here too. He's okay—
What...
What are you doing here?
You kids shouldn't be here.
But I—
We need to get you out of here. Now.
Let's go!

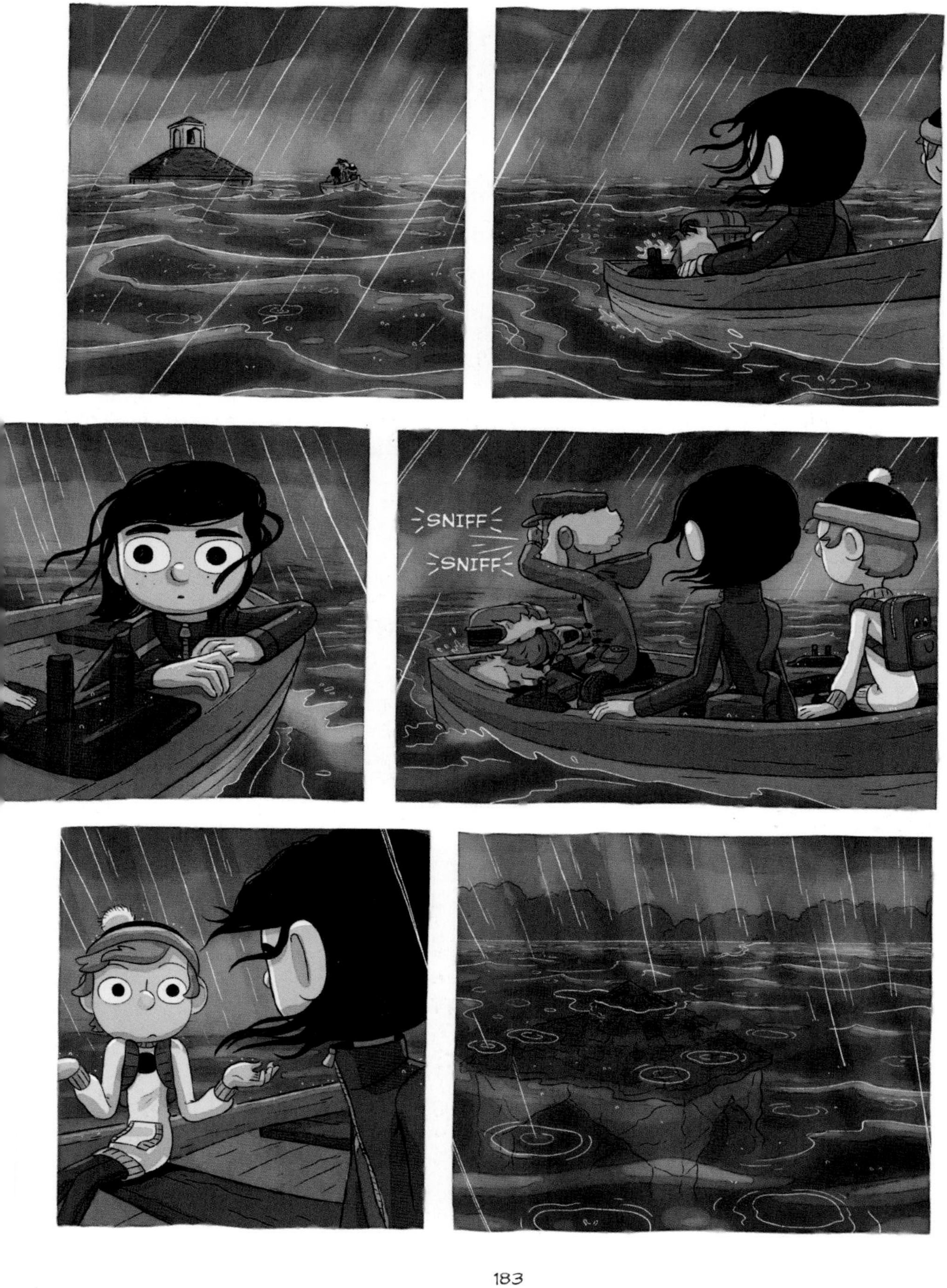
SNIFF
SNIFF

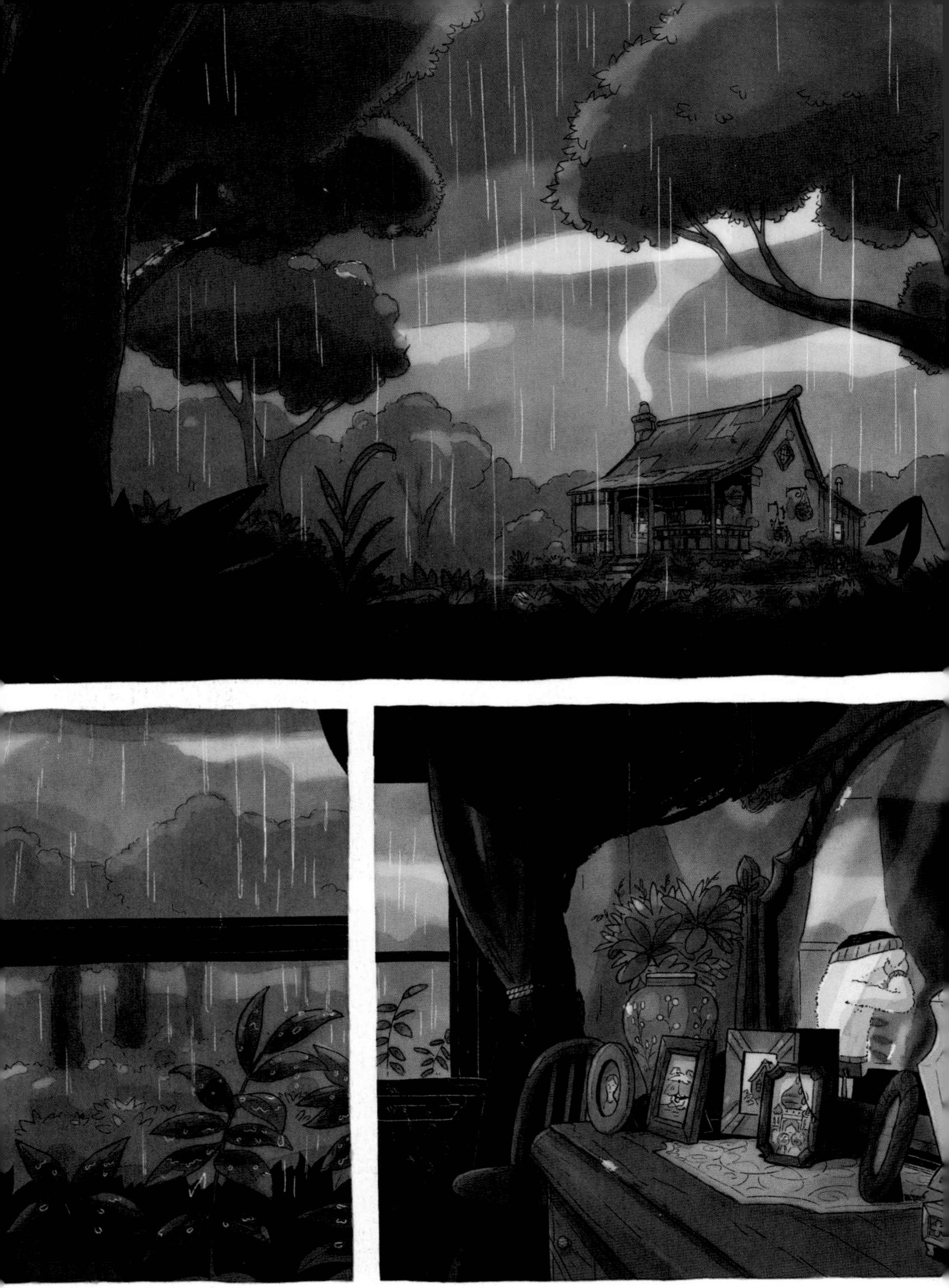

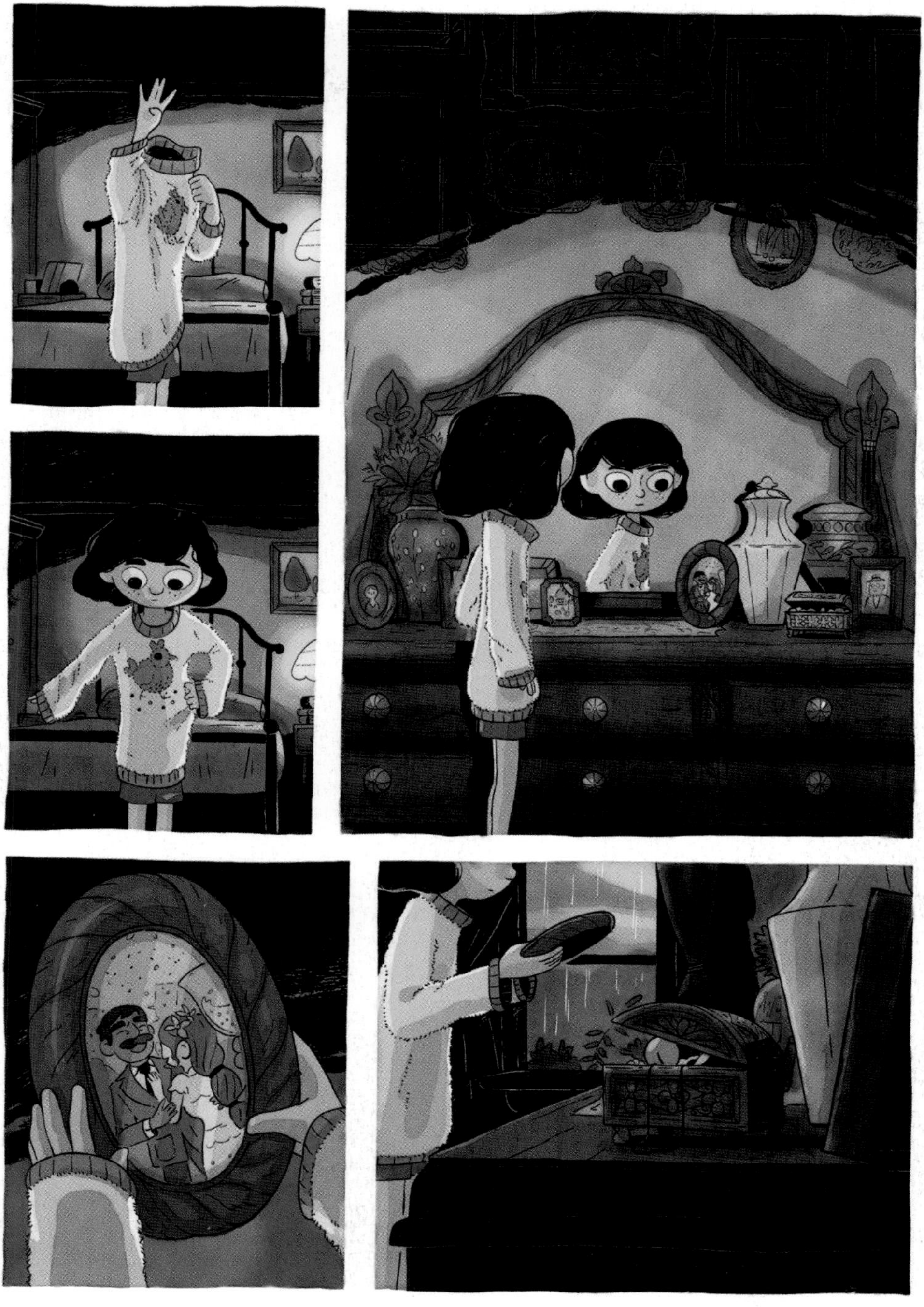

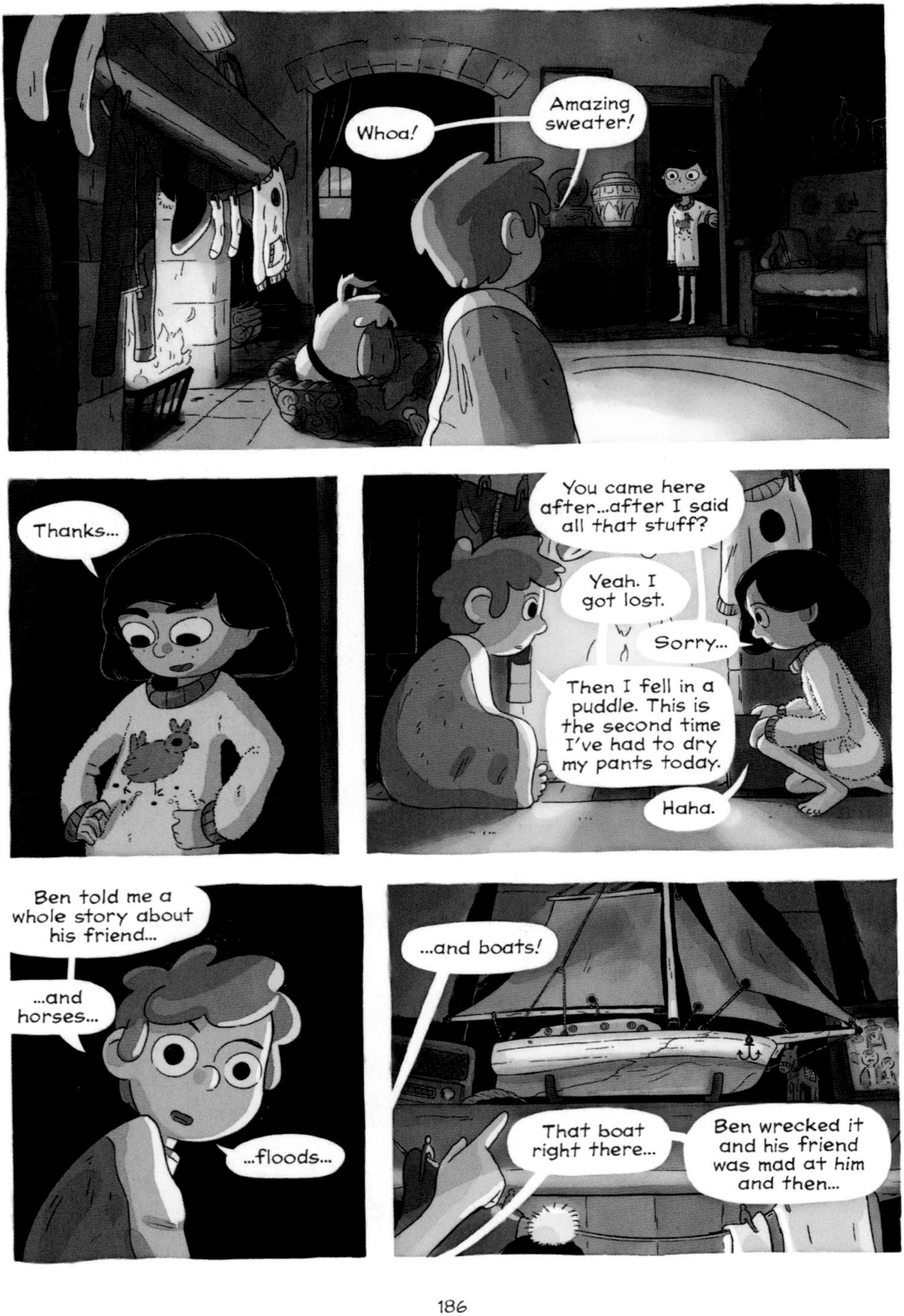
Whoa!
Amazing sweater!
Thanks...
You came here after...after I said all that stuff?
Yeah. I got lost.
Sorry...
Then I fell in a puddle. This is the second time I've had to dry my pants today.
Haha.
Ben told me a whole story about his friend...
...and horses...
...floods...
...and boats!
That boat right there...
Ben wrecked it and his friend was mad at *him* and then...

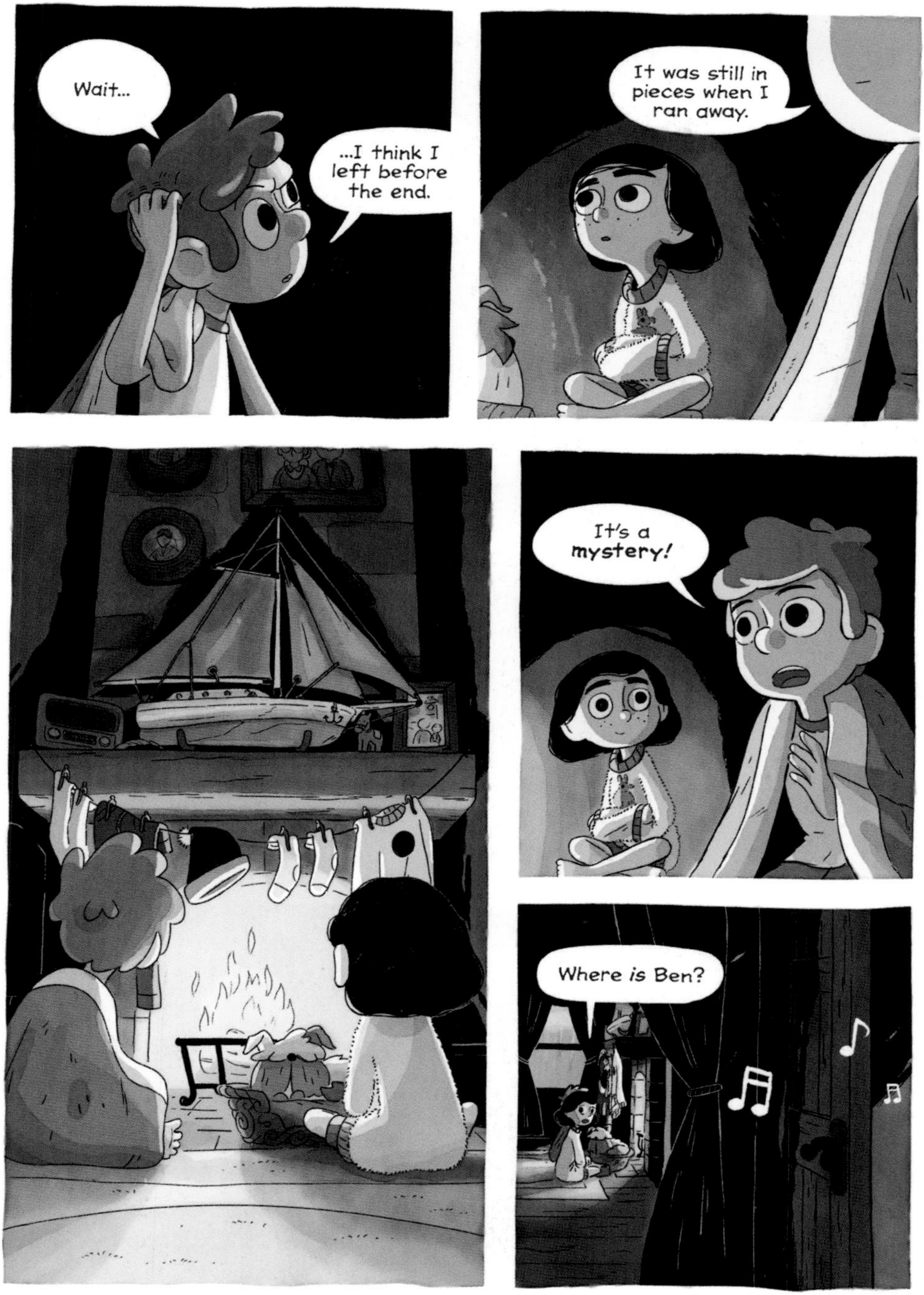
Wait...
...I think I left before the end.
It was still in pieces when I ran away.
It's a **mystery!**
Where *is* Ben?

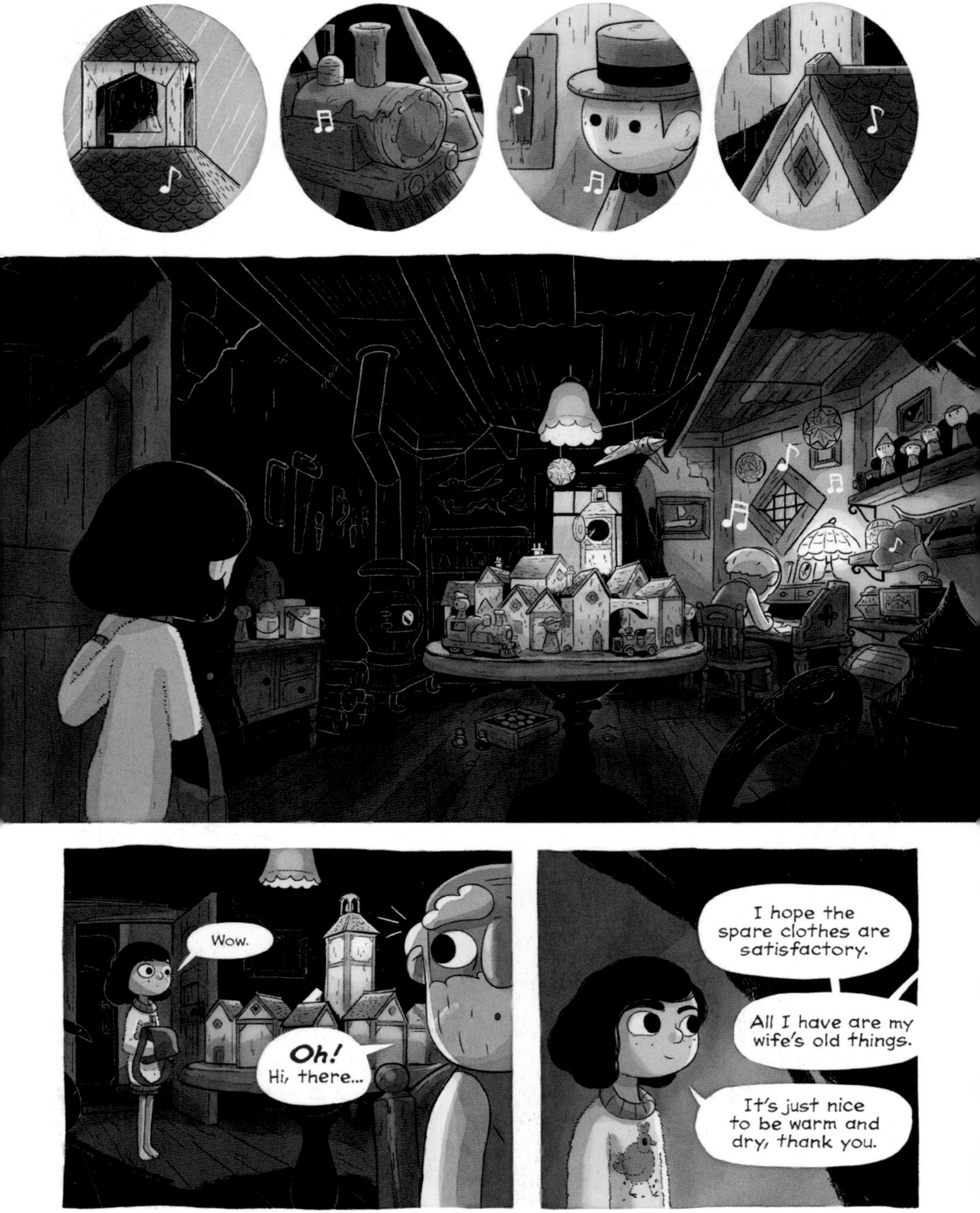

Wow.
Oh!
Hi, there...
I hope the spare clothes are satisfactory.
All I have are my wife's old things.
It's just nice to be warm and dry, thank you.

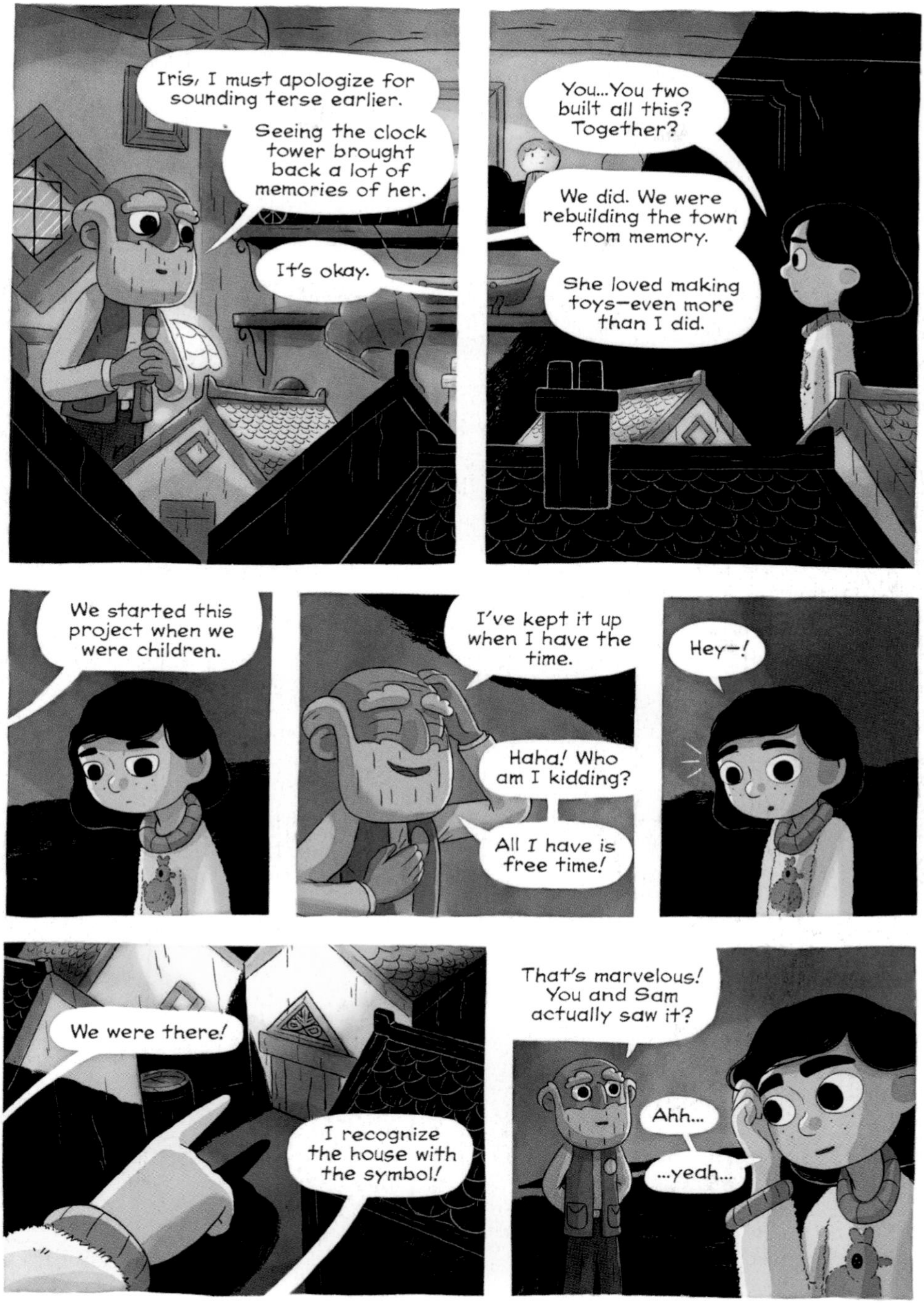

Iris, I must apologize for sounding terse earlier.
Seeing the clock tower brought back a lot of memories of her.
It's okay.
You...You two built all this? Together?
We did. We were rebuilding the town from memory.
She loved making toys—even more than I did.
We started this project when we were children.
I've kept it up when I have the time.
Haha! Who am I kidding?
All I have is free time!
Hey—!
We were there!
I recognize the house with the symbol!
That's marvelous! You and Sam actually saw it?
Ahh...
...yeah...

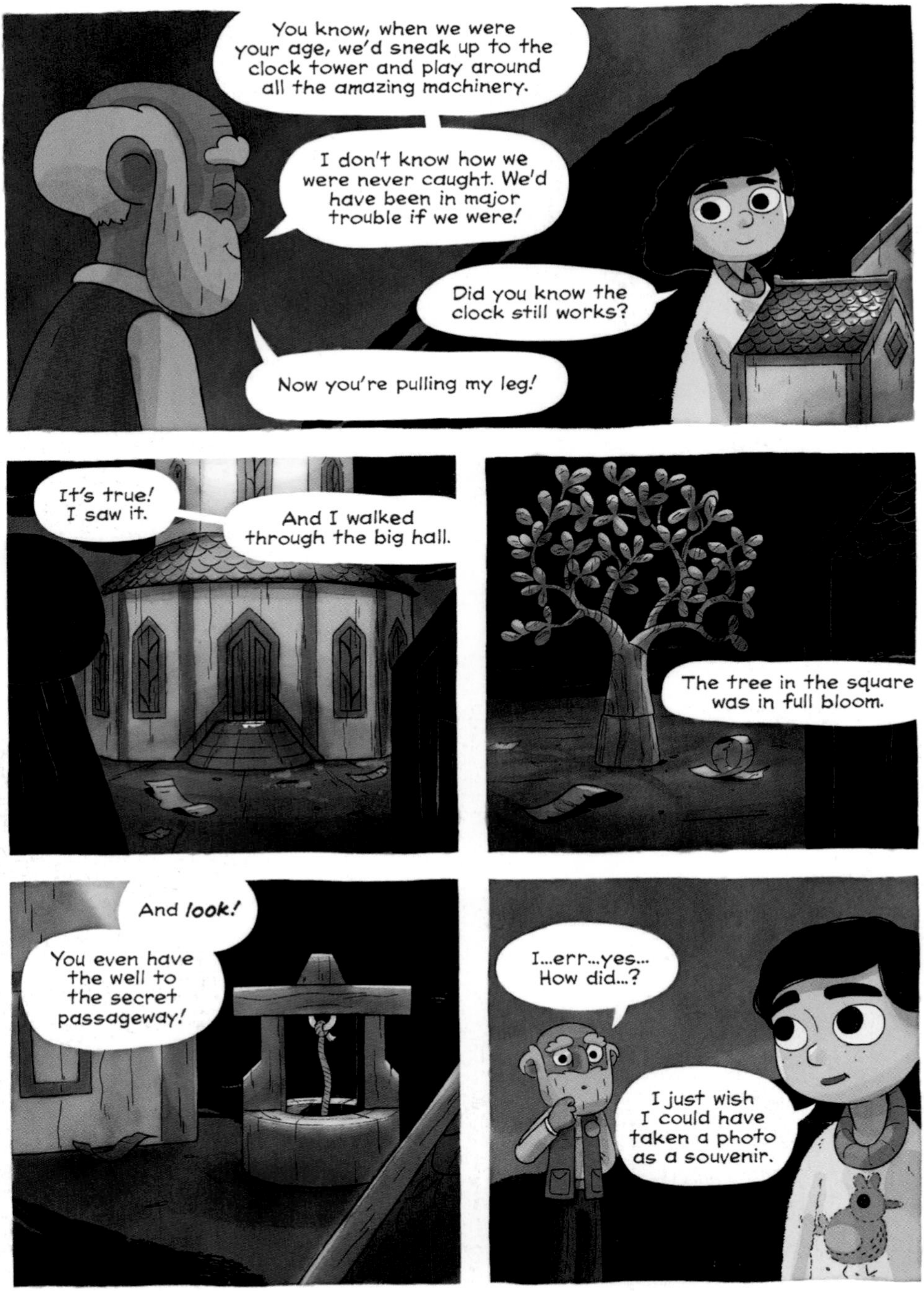

You know, when we were your age, we'd sneak up to the clock tower and play around all the *amazing* machinery.
I don't know how we were never caught. We'd have been in major trouble if we were!
Did you know the clock still works?
Now you're pulling my leg!
It's true! I saw it.
And I walked through the big hall.
The tree in the square was in full bloom.
And ***look!***
You even have the well to the secret passageway!
I...err...yes... How did...?
I just wish I could have taken a photo as a souvenir.

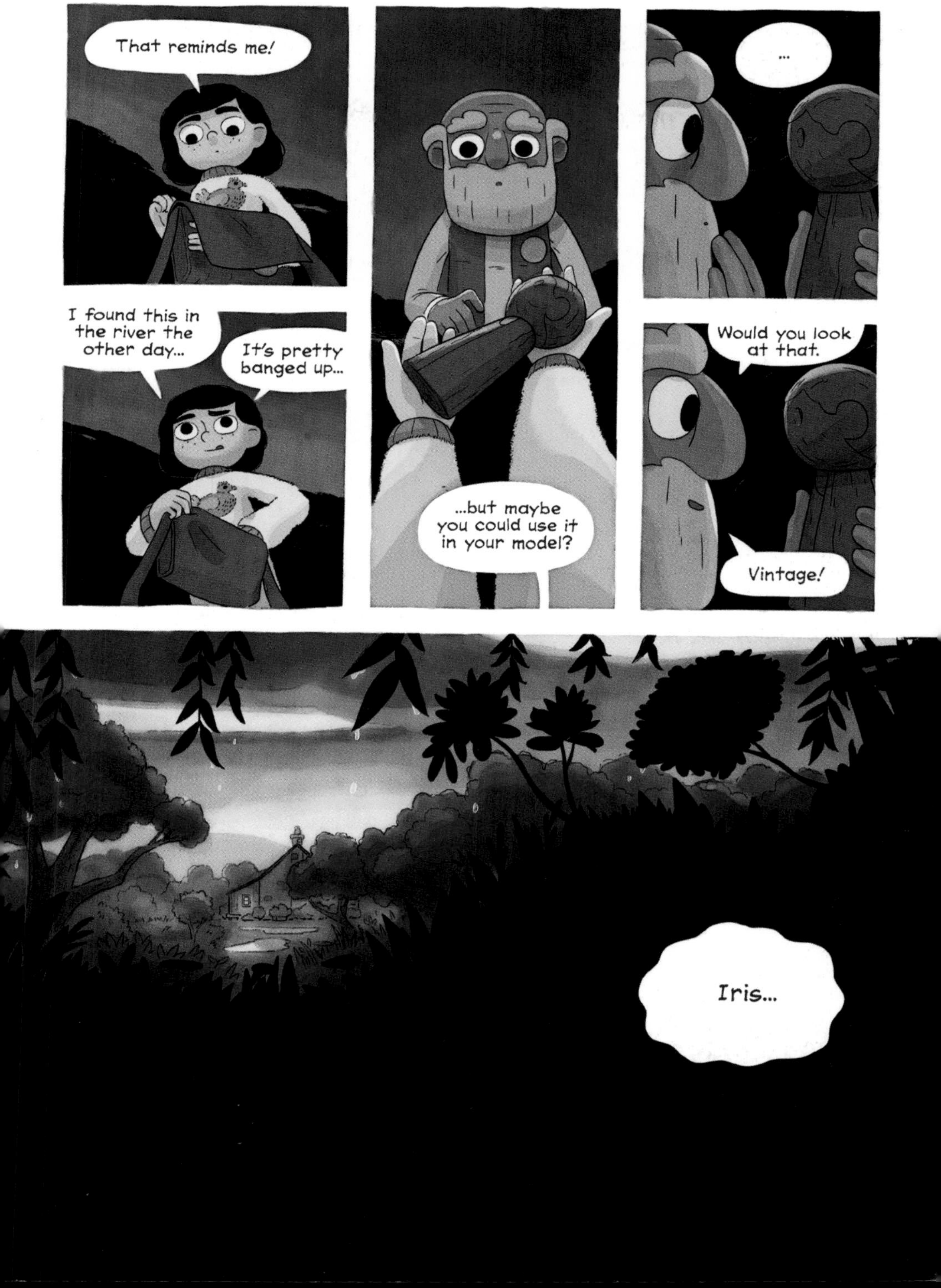
That reminds me!
I found this in the river the other day...
It's pretty banged up...
...but maybe you could use it in your model?
...
Would you look at that.
Vintage!
Iris...

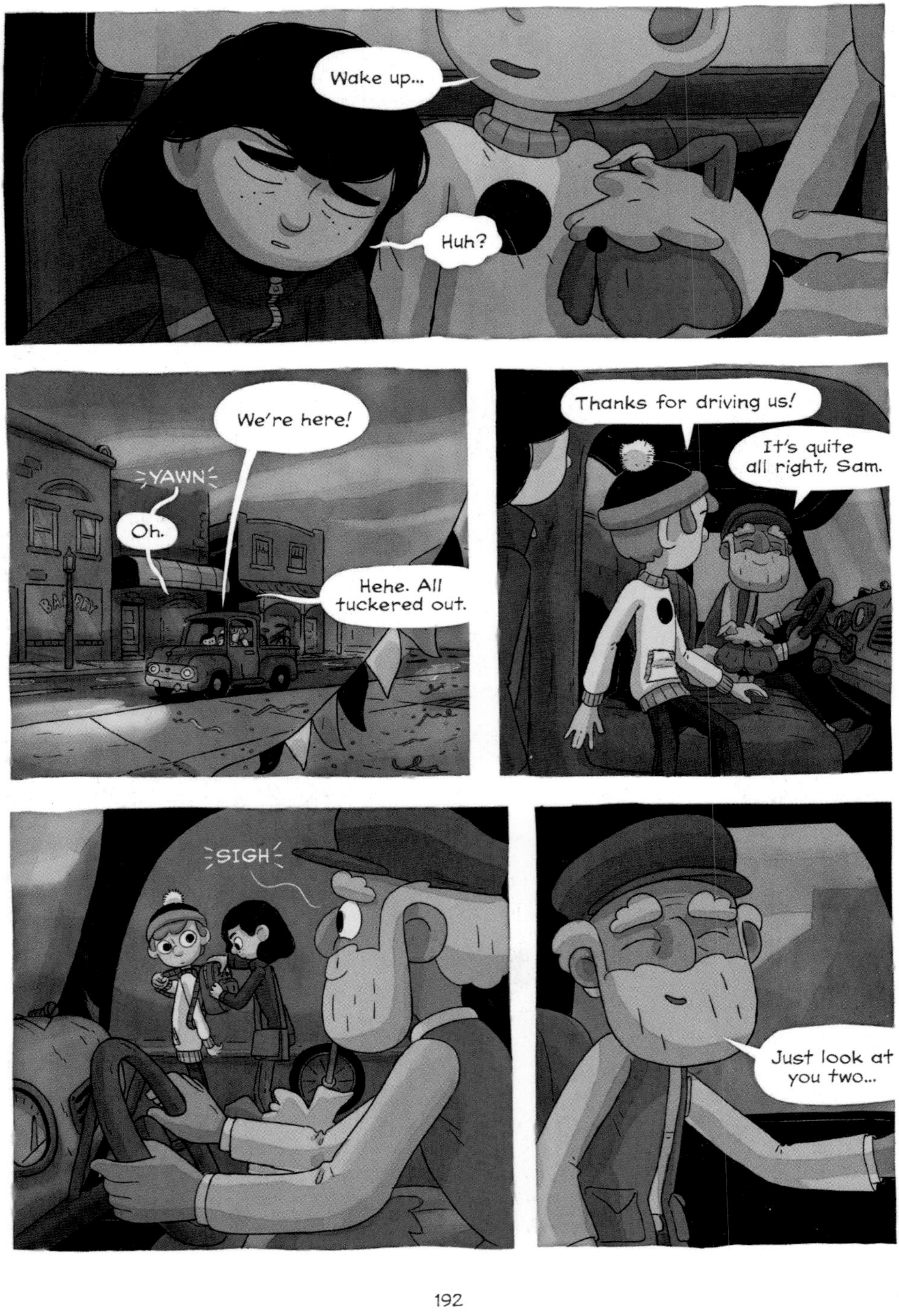

Wake up...
Huh?
We're here!
YAWN
Oh.
Hehe. All tuckered out.
BAKERY
Thanks for driving us!
It's quite all right, Sam.
SIGH
Just look at you two...

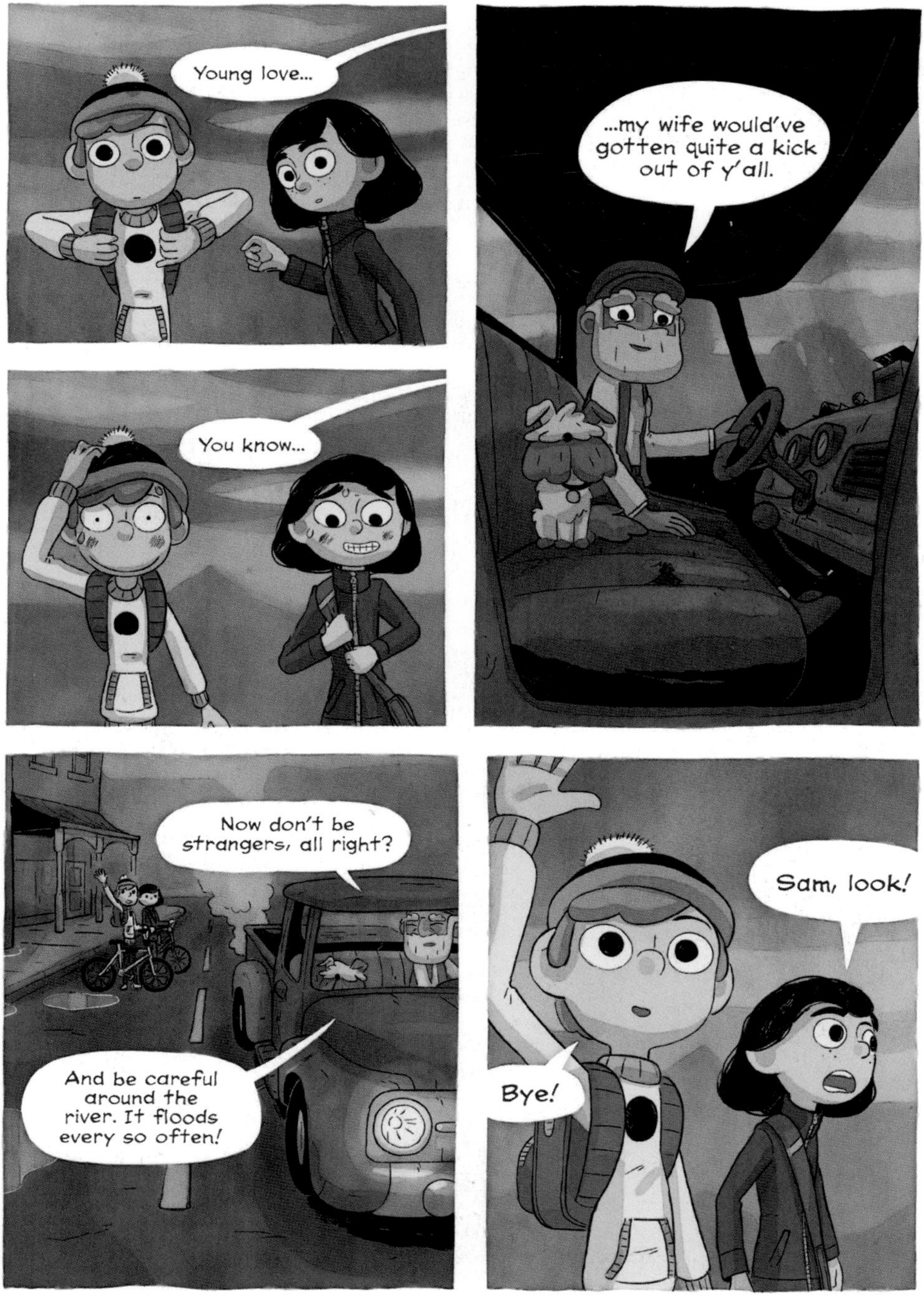
Young love...
You know...
...my wife would've gotten quite a kick out of y'all.
Now don't be strangers, all right?
And be careful around the river. It floods every so often!
Sam, look!
Bye!

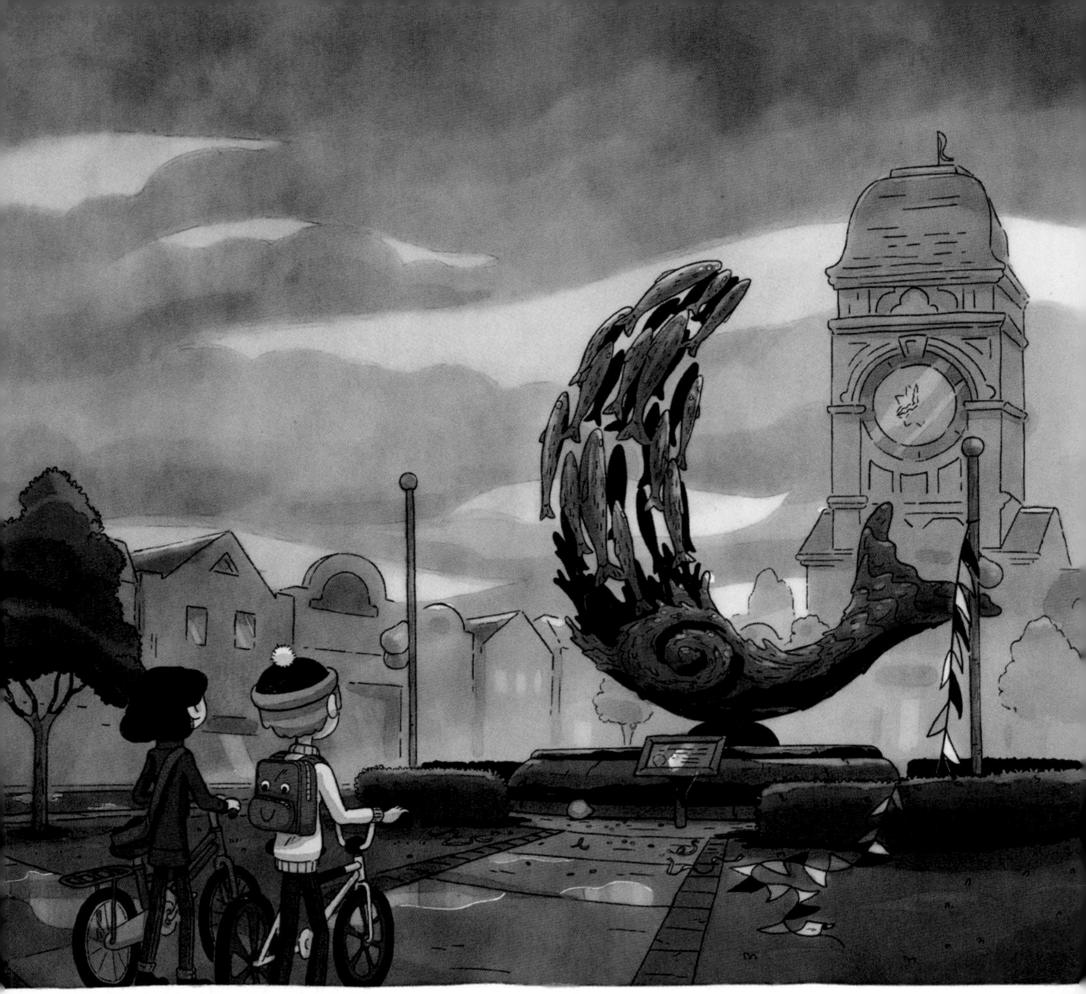

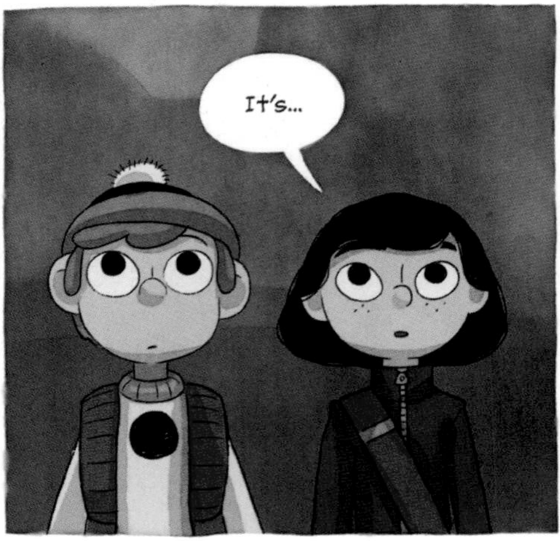
It's...

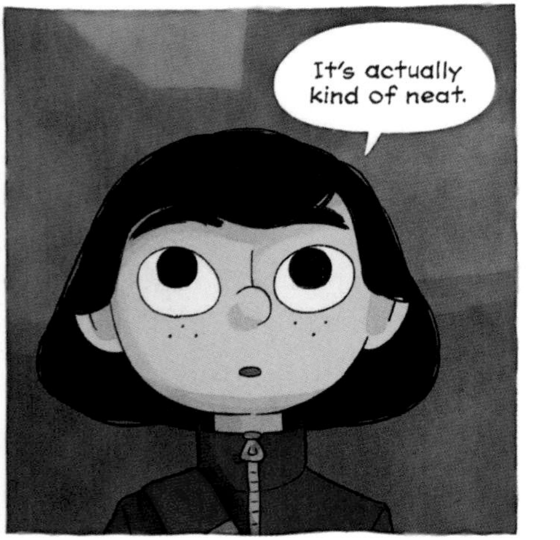
It's actually kind of neat.

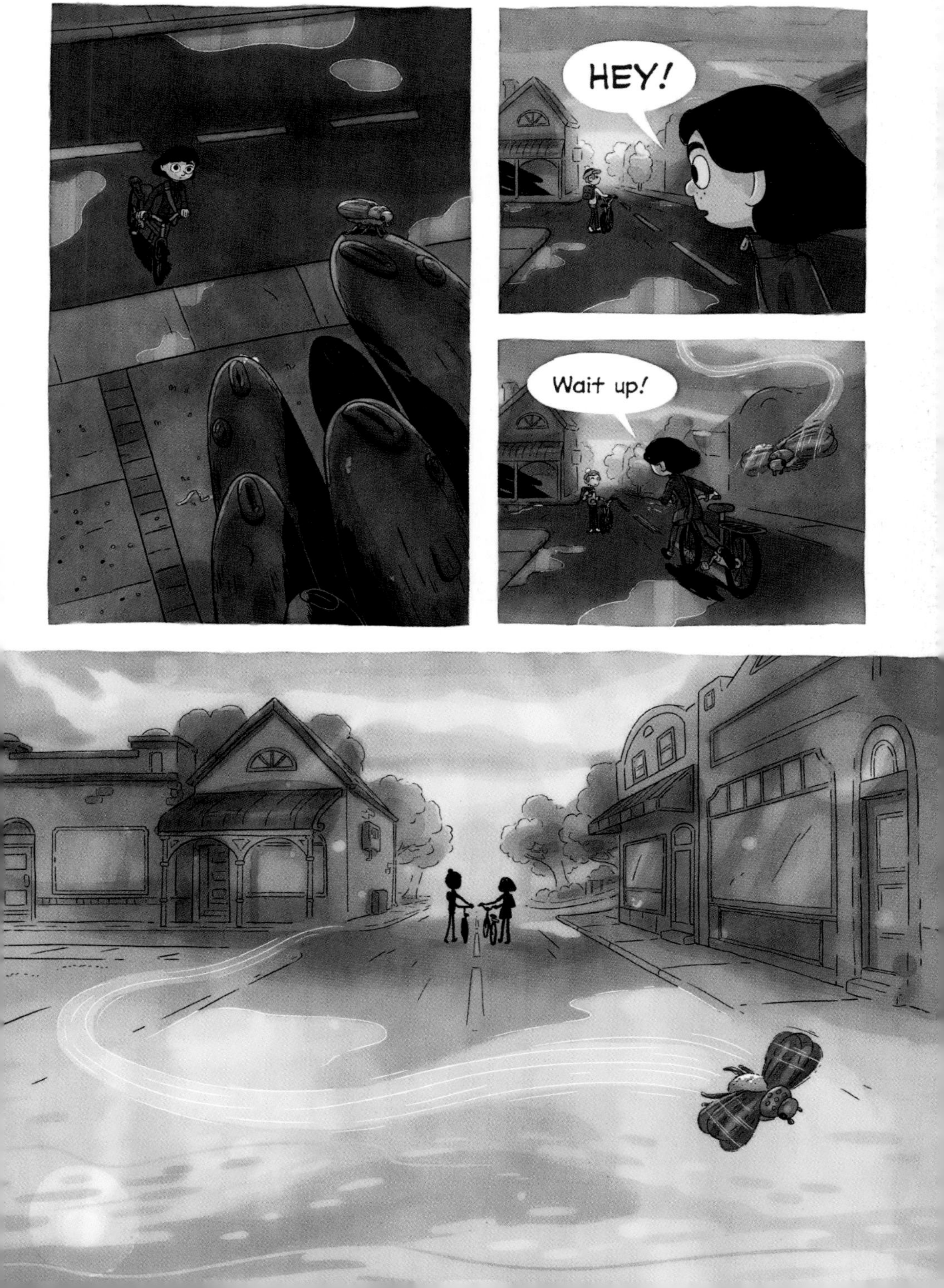
HEY!
Wait up!

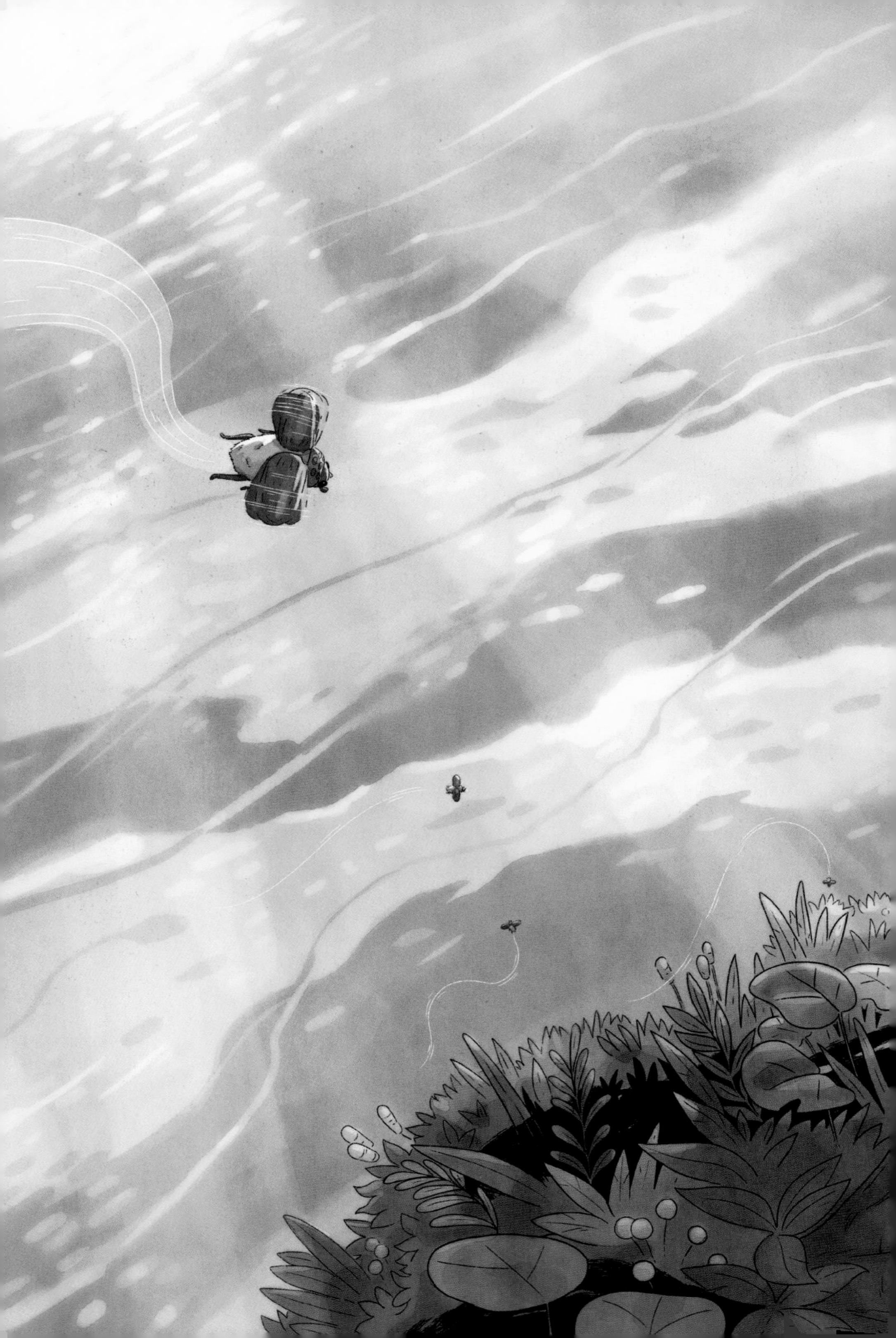

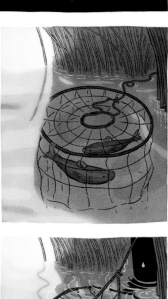

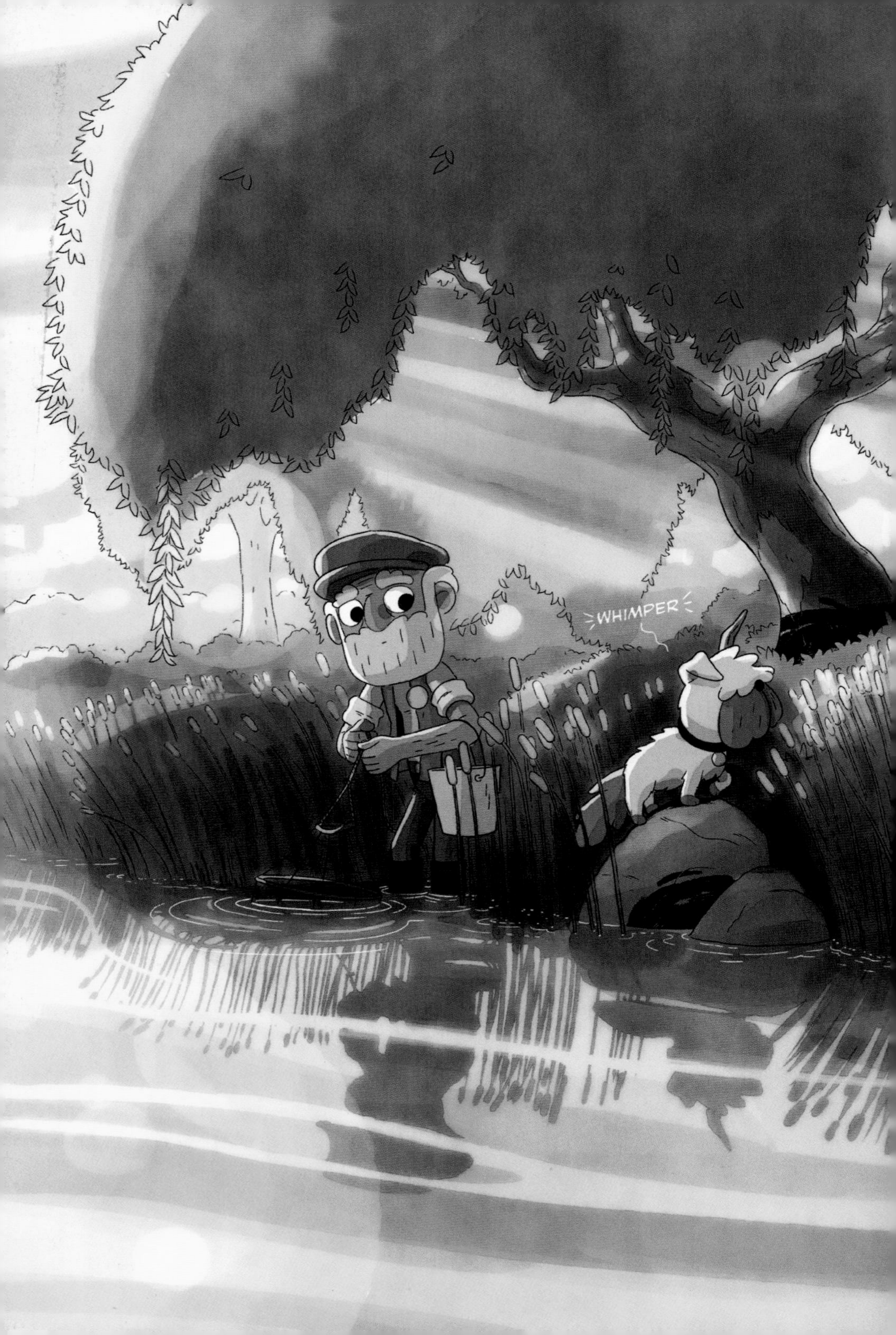
WHIMPER

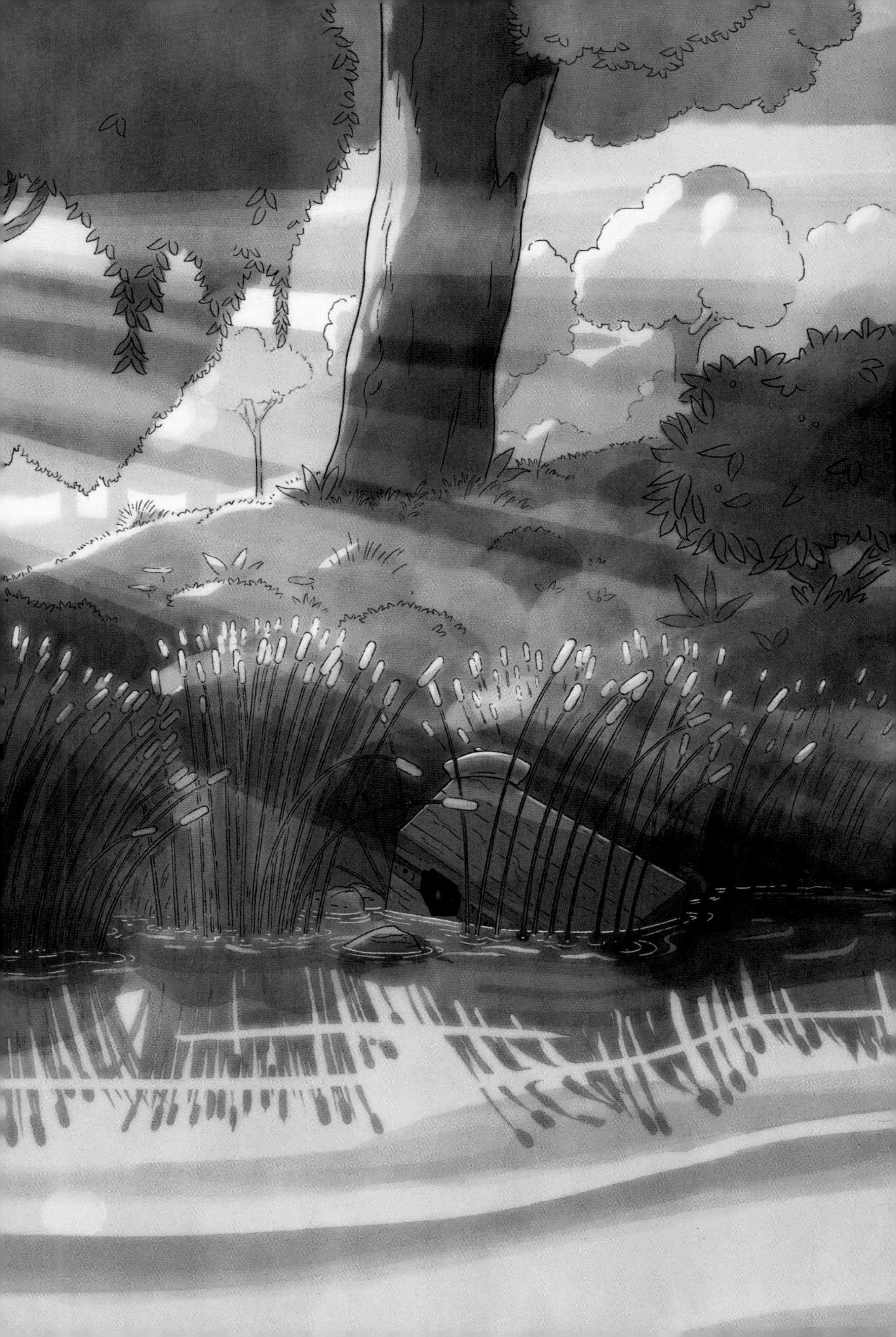

ACKNOWLEDGMENTS

Thank you to everyone who helped tell this story!

Thank you to Sara Crowe for your guidance and skill in finding the book a home. To my editors, Andrew Arnold and Rose Pleuler, for so thoughtfully and patiently helping me shape and refine the story. To Joe Merkel for your beautiful design, and everyone at HarperAlley for believing in this book. Thank you to Anna McFarlane for your valuable feedback and to the whole team at Allen & Unwin.

Thanks also to Chris Staros, Ari Gibson, Ryan Kirby, and Simon Westlake for your contributions over the journey.

Thank you to all my friends and family, especially my parents, for making me who I am.

Most of all, I'd like to acknowledge my incredible wife, Jessica, without whom this book would simply not exist. Thank you for supporting me and pushing me forward, the late night rewrites, the invaluable suggestions, and for your unwavering belief in me. ♡

DID YOU KNOW?

You may have heard of the lost city of Atlantis, but did you know there are submerged towns all over the world? It's true! Most were flooded on purpose to create reservoirs and waterways. Some were also the result of natural disasters and dams breaking—just like Ben and Lily's town.

Adaminaby

Between 1956-57, the Australian town of Adaminaby was moved to make way for a reservoir to power a hydroelectric system. Over one hundred buildings were lifted up and carried by truck. Two stone churches were even dismantled and reconstructed, brick by brick. Many buildings were sadly left behind, however. In 2007, severe drought caused the water level to drop so much that the old town reemerged! Surviving residents could walk the streets and reminisce about their childhood home.

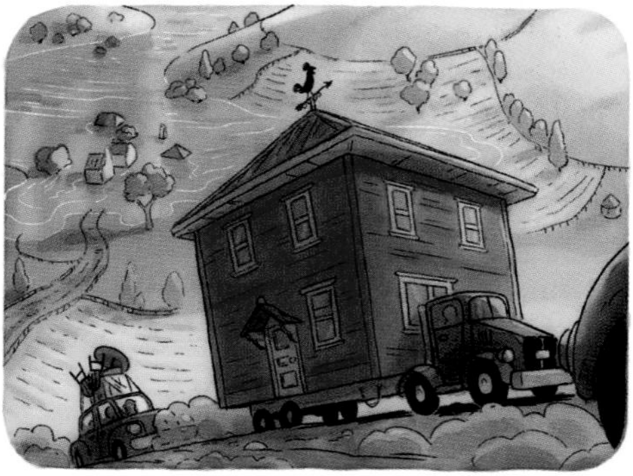

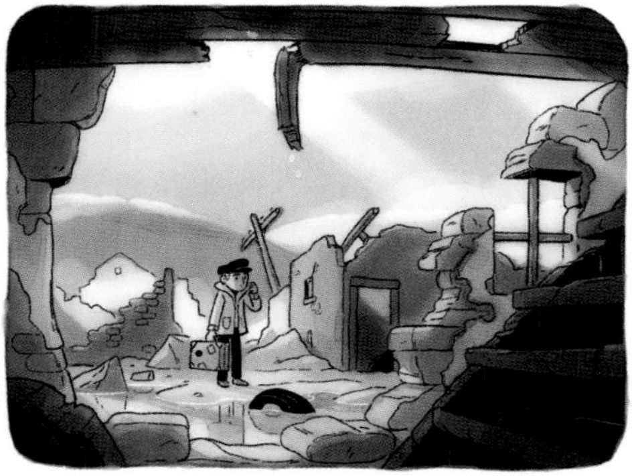

Villa Epecuén

The Argentinian village of Epecuén flooded in 1985 after a nearby dam broke. Once home to fifteen hundred people, the town was slowly consumed by salt water, reaching a peak of ten meters (thirty-three feet). In 2009, the water began to recede, revealing the town once again. One man by the name of Pablo Novak even returned to live there all by himself.

Lake Reschen

Lake Reschen in Italy is home to a fourteenth-century church tower that sticks up out of the water's surface. It belonged to a town called Graun, which in 1950 was flooded on purpose in the creation of a dam. When the lake freezes over in winter, you can even walk out to the tower. People say that on some nights you can still hear the bells ringing, despite them being removed over seventy years ago!

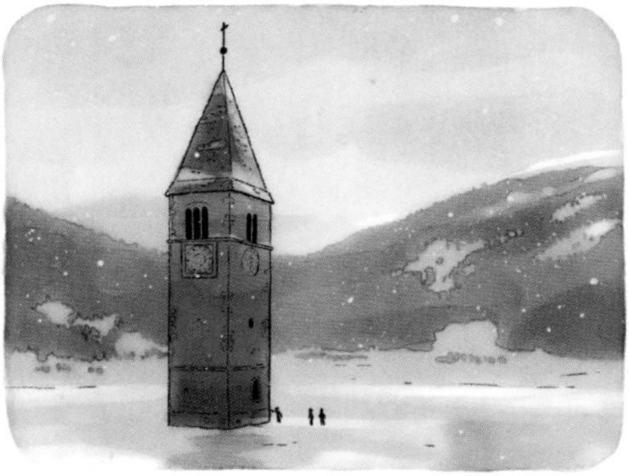

PROCESS

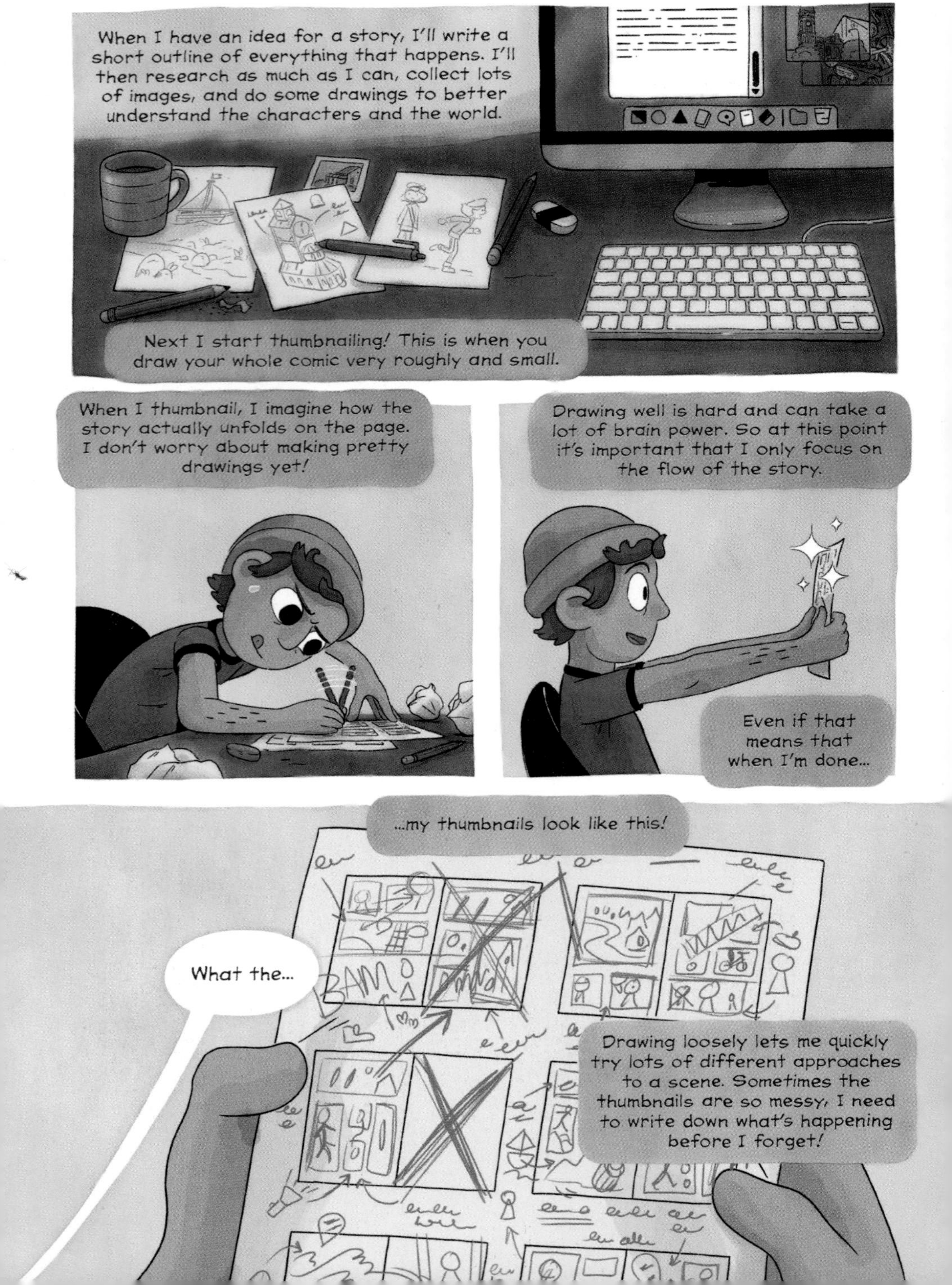
When I have an idea for a story, I'll write a short outline of everything that happens. I'll then research as much as I can, collect lots of images, and do some drawings to better understand the characters and the world.
Next I start thumbnailing! This is when you draw your whole comic very roughly and small.
When I thumbnail, I imagine how the story actually unfolds on the page. I don't worry about making pretty drawings yet!
Drawing well is hard and can take a lot of brain power. So at this point it's important that I only focus on the flow of the story.
Even if that means that when I'm done...
...my thumbnails look like this!
What the...
BAM
Drawing loosely lets me quickly try lots of different approaches to a scene. Sometimes the thumbnails are so messy, I need to write down what's happening before I forget!

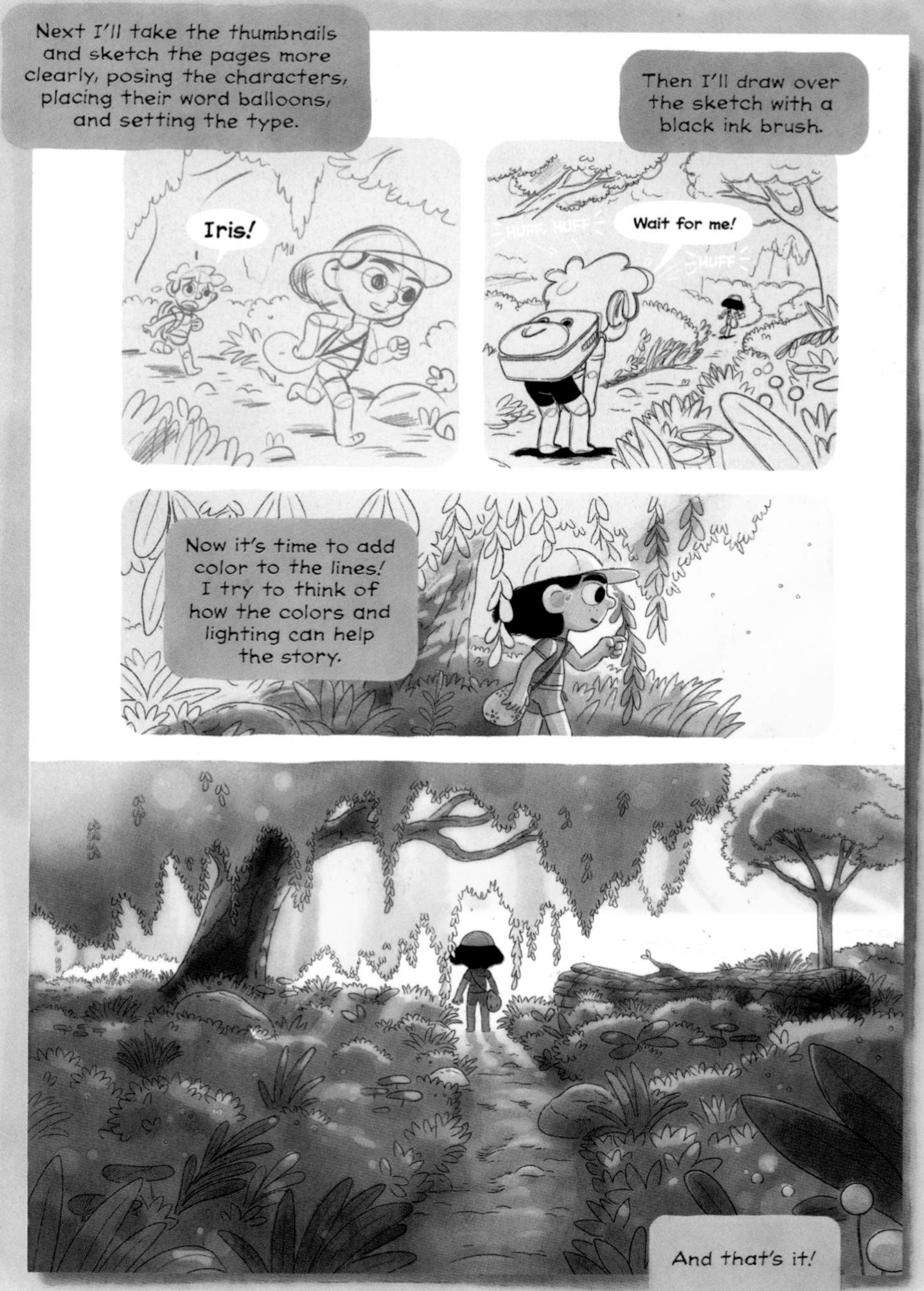
Next I'll take the thumbnails and sketch the pages more clearly, posing the characters, placing their word balloons, and setting the type.
Iris!
Then I'll draw over the sketch with a black ink brush.
HUFF, HUFF
Wait for me!
HUFF
Now it's time to add color to the lines! I try to think of how the colors and lighting can help the story.
And that's it!

EARLY SKETCHES

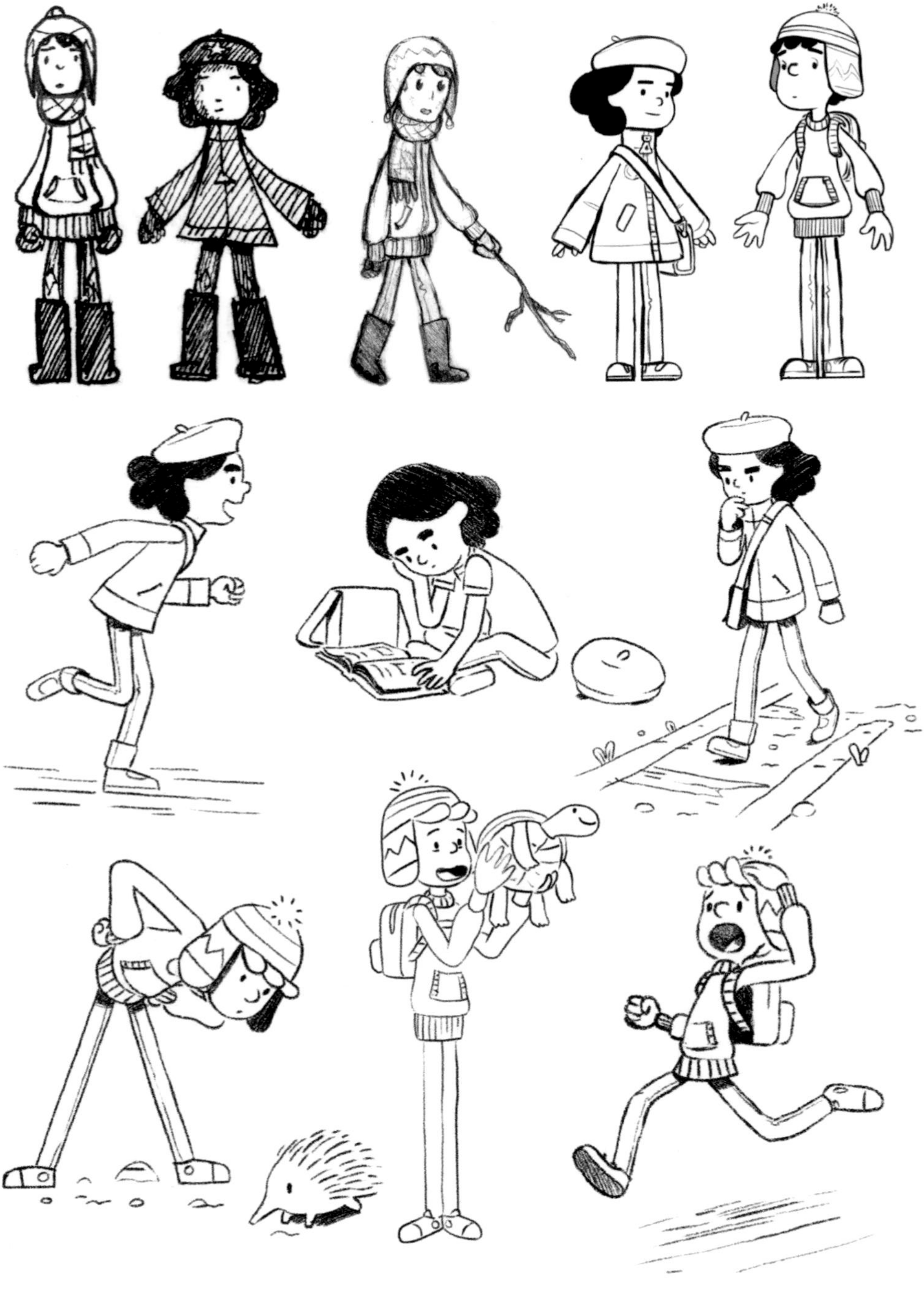

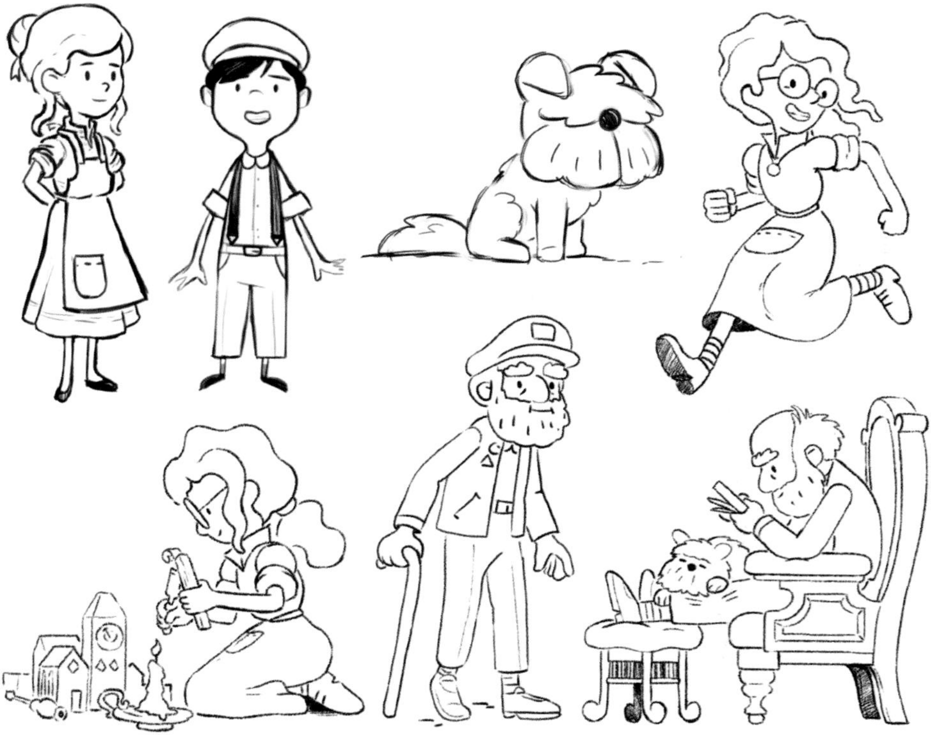

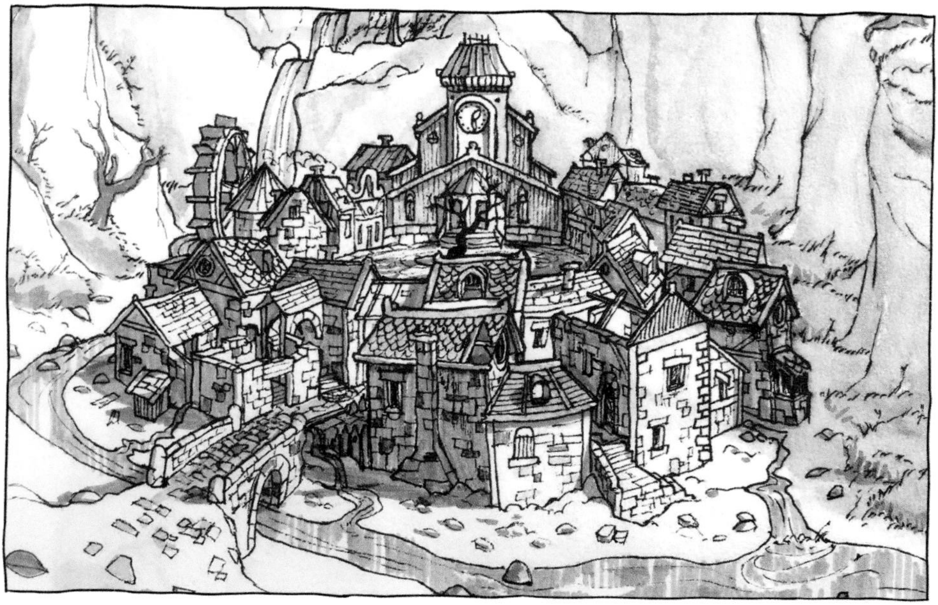

For Dad and Lilah.

HarperAlley is an imprint of HarperCollins Publishers.

Treasure in the Lake
Copyright © 2021 by Jason Pamment
All rights reserved. Printed in Spain.
No part of this book may be used or reproduced in any manner whatsoever without
written permission except in the case of brief quotations embodied in critical articles and reviews.
For information address HarperCollins Children's Books, a division of HarperCollins Publishers,
195 Broadway, New York, NY 10007.
www.harperalley.com

Library of Congress Control Number: 2021934291
ISBN 978-0-06-306518-5 — ISBN 978-0-06-306517-8 (pbk.)

Typography by Jason Pamment
21 22 23 24 25 EP 10 9 8 7 6 5 4 3 2 1
First Edition